WHAT A

TANGLED

WEB

Guy Hallowes

Published by OMNE Publishing in 2022

Text © Guy Hallowes 2022

 A catalogue record for this book is available from the National Library of Australia

Editing: Zena Shapter
Cover Design: Designerbility
Print Layout: Author Services
Kindle Formatting: Author Services

This book is available in print and ebook formats.

TABLE OF CONTENTS

Prologue. Jihad

As he rushed out of the suburban Milton Keynes house, Lieutenant David Phillips pulled on his respirator. David and his twelve-strong team were already wearing fire retardant overalls. He leapt onto a tailor-made running board mounted on the rear of the Land Rover Discovery, together with one other operator, then signalled for everyone to move in.

"Go! Now!"

The two assault vehicles accelerated. Fast. This rescue was for one of their own.

"Snipers in position?" David asked, then waited for a response through his earpiece. Back at the house – their hastily-commandeered 'forward headquarters' – a room full of MI5 spooks, SAS signallers, army intelligence officers, police, and senior home office bureaucrats were all listening in. This had to go to plan. Sergeant Jones's life depended on it.

"Snipers in position, we have visual. Ready to engage," a voice confirmed.

Curtains twitched as they plunged down the street, filling David with a surge of adrenalin. The video image of the jihadi holding an ornate sword to Sergeant Jones's throat, an ISIS flag as a backdrop behind them, only fuelled him more.

The Land Rover screamed into the cul de sac. A jihadi, dressed in jeans and an anorak, rushed around the side of the house, where he'd been sheltering from the light rain.

"One Tango, target reaching for weapon," a sniper said.

David could see the man, reaching behind his back.

The man drew a pistol.

"Clear to engage," David said, as they screeched to a halt.

There was the crack of a rifle.

The terrorist's head exploded.

"MOE team, go," David said, keeping his voice as calm as possible. He didn't feel it. He wasn't supposed to be here.

Two SAS men, his designated method-of-entry specialists, raced to the front door, and stuck a length of detonating cord along the hinges. One man played out the primer, a coiled tube filled with explosives, and hit the igniter. The door flew off its hinges.

David was already moving forward when a secondary explosion erupted, taking off half of the front of the house.

***

Earlier

4am. David Phillips was woken by a call from his mobile phone. It was his Commanding Officer Major Neville Powrie.

"Phillips, we're on."

"On with what?" David asked. It was early and he was half asleep. He left Melinda in bed and walked through the lounge to take his squadron commander's call in private. "Is this about Sergeant Jones?"

"Of course it's bloody Jones. He's still missing. The police, the spooks and the SAS have all been looking for him, following up false leads, and getting ready to mount a rescue half a dozen times. But the rest of the regiment's either overseas in Afghanistan or tied up in training. We have no choice but to call in you bloody reservists."

"Crikey – you mean, we're *all* you've got?" David said.

"Pretty much."

"But we don't have the experience for this."

"Trust me, it's not my first choice. But if it's any consolation, the CO said he was relieved it was at least you on the first rotation of part-timers. Also, he knows you're close to Jones, what with him training you and all that. You have any idea what he was doing?"

"Yes, sir," David said. "Obviously, sir, I'm in. Jones is my absolute priority, no questions asked. Although, I do have one slight problem."

"Spit it out, man."

"I have my university finals tomorrow. Last exam. If I miss it, I'll fail the year, if not the whole degree."

There was a disbelieving grunt on the line.

"Of course it's nothing compared to a man's life," David added quickly. "But if you could just make one phone call?"

"If I could what?"

"Phone the rector. If you explain the situation to him, they might let me re-sit the exam *after* the mission? Please, sir, it would really help me out."

There was a pause on the line.

"Fine," Powrie muttered. "Give me the number. I hope you know that I wouldn't do this for anyone else. We both know who'd have my guts if I didn't. And the bloody rector, no less. I almost forgot you're part of the privileged fucking few." He laughed mirthlessly.

David gave him the number. "Sir, it would also be best if phone him early – to ensure he gets the message and understands how important this is. If you wouldn't mind?"

Powrie laughed again. "Okay, Phillips, but get your arse over here double quick."

"Yes, sir; of course, sir." David ended the call, only to hear Melinda stirring in the bedroom.

"What was that all about?" she asked as he walked in.

"Special Air Service. Sorry to wake you, darling, but… they need me. Now." He started getting ready.

"What for? Anything dangerous?"

"You know I can't tell you. I wish I could, but I can't."

She groaned and rolled over in bed. She looked so beautiful in this light, her skin soft and warm. He stopped fastening the buttons on his shirt, instinctively drawn to her. As always. But Jones wasn't only a friend. He had been hunting down violent jihadis intent on causing as much damage as they could, wherever they could. He needed to go.

Once he was dressed in the suit he'd bought with his army allowance, he leant over and kissed her. A long lingering kiss that would see him through the hours to follow. After a quick breakfast of fruit and a bowl of cornflakes, he left her sleeping and started the two-hour journey from Oxford to SAS headquarters in Hereford.

He found Powrie in the canteen around seven thirty. David saluted.

"Good, you're early. Sit down, sit down," said the major. "I phoned your rector – he was not pleased to be woken just after six, but I'm sure he's now on side."

"Thank you, sir. I appreciate it."

Powrie grumbled. "Yes, well, the briefing will be at eight on the dot. We're just waiting for the final intel. Coffee's fresh." Powrie gestured to a nearby urn.

David followed his suggestion and poured himself a cup.

The major continued, "As you know, Jones was volunteering to do some surveillance on a group of jihadis in the Birmingham area, because he knows the area well; but he's been missing now for three days. Apparently, something's come in."

"How did the SAS even become involved in this?" David had wondered ever since Jones told him what he was doing. "Isn't it a domestic issue?"

"It's more than that. The people we're dealing with have been assessed as a threat to national security. This is serious, David, very serious. We need him back."

"Of course, sir; I'll do everything I can."

"Good, because this is your chance, Phillips – your chance to prove everyone wrong about you."

***

The briefing was conducted by a young, tall female SAS sergeant, Catherine Roberts, who asked everyone to introduce themselves quickly and succinctly.

Everyone already knew Major Neville Powrie. A middle-aged MI5 man introduced himself with the codename John Smith. Then there was a Corporal John from the SAS, a Detective Inspector Medhurst from the Metropolitan police, and of course David.

Sergeant Roberts turned on a screen. "We received this yesterday." She pressed a button and a video played of a scarfed jihadi brandishing a sword in front of an ISIS flag. Sergeant Jones was tied to a chair, bruised and bleeding. While the jihadi made a series of threats to the British people and demands to the government, Jones mouthed something incomprehensible. He didn't look good, his body slumped, head limp and eyes rolling without focus. "Jones is clearly trying to tell us something here, but we're not sure what. Then he..."

The jihadi stepped forward to slowly move his sword across Jones's throat, nicking his skin but not slicing. Jones's eyes widened, as if fearing the end. But instead the jihadi made another threat and pointed his sword at the camera. Then the video finished.

Roberts displayed a map of a Birmingham suburb. "They've promised to kill Jones before tomorrow if we don't meet their requests. We believe this is a stalling tactic while they get into position to launch a more serious attack. We thought the group was here." She pointed to two houses. "Any update on that Mr Smith?"

"For the last eighteen months, we've had an undercover operative posing as the leader's girlfriend. Communication has been via confidential letterbox drop every two days. According to our contact, the group are committed to violent acts in support of an Islamist insurgency, under instruction from a group in Syria. They are well-armed with submachine guns and pistols, and they've started making bombs. There are seven men and three women."

David made a mental note of the numbers.

"But", the MI5 man continued, "we lost contact with her a week ago. Jones increased surveillance and we realised the houses have been evacuated. Then he disappeared too."

The Detective Inspector stepped forward. "A few days ago, we moved in. Both houses were scrubbed clean – we did not find a single fingerprint but did find plenty traces of explosives. So the threat is real and imminent."

The MI5 man added, "One of the jihadis owns a property in Milton Keynes in Buckinghamshire, so they may have retreated there. Ah, just a moment." He left the room to answer his phone. On his return he said, calmly, "Yes, we have just had confirmation that we have had sight of Jones in Milton Keynes."

"That's what he's saying!" David mumbled, then spoke up. "Replay the video! He's saying 'Milton Keynes' – watch his mouth."

Roberts replayed the video, and yes – Jones was mouthing 'Milton Keynes'.

The briefing wrapped up quickly after that, with Sergeant Roberts providing all the details they had of the seven jihadi men and three female accomplices, all of whom were confirmed as British citizens. Most had middle eastern origins, although three of the men had English names and were born in England.

"David," Powrie beckoned him over, "I need you to come up with a list of what we need. Don't leave anything out."

"Yes, sir. I'm on it."

***

It was almost midnight before David and his team were choppered from SAS HQ to an unseen corner of Cranfield Airport near Bedford.

They were quickly transported to the SAS forward headquarters, but none of it was quick enough for David. 'Tomorrow' started at midnight.

"We'll be lucky if Jones is still alive," he told one of the MI5 spooks on arrival.

"Then luck is with us, Phillips," he said. "We've had another sighting – Sergeant Jones is still in the target house."

"We have all the exit roads blocked," reported the senior police officer, a tall and athletic Superintendent McConnell. "But that's about all we can do. We don't have the resources to take on a well-armed terrorist group, like the one present in the target house."

"Understood, superintendent. It's not your fault you don't have the resources. We do, so that's why we're here."

"Very good, Phillips. I formally authorise you, Lieutenant Phillips, to assume this responsibility and apprehend those who have illegally imprisoned Sergeant Jones and are a threat to his life."

"In that case, if everyone's ready?" David picked up his respirator and rushed out of the house.

***

David flew through the air, the explosion at the front of the target house shunting him violently backwards. He dragged himself to his feet, then realised, with a sense of dread, that the method-of-entry men had set off a secondary explosion with their breeching charge. There would be casualties. Was it his fault?

He staggered forward, counting the men from his team covered in blood and too disorientated to continue. David had a helicopter hovering overhead with a further team of four ready to provide reinforcements if needed, under a Sergeant Davis; but he'd have to leave these men behind – the jihadis knew they were coming now.

A powerful vehicle screeched out of the target driveway and up the street.

"Vehicle just left the property, driving north," David yelled into his radio.

"Roger. We will apprehend," was the immediate response.

"There was a booby trap!" David told everyone listening. "I'm going in. Head shots only." He dived through the door, firing his MP5 into the two jihadi who suddenly appeared in front of him.

Sergeant Roberts, following right behind him, took down another jihadi who tried to get away.

Gunfire ratcheted around the walls.

"Two MOE operatives down," reported Sergeant Roberts.

David's stomach twisted at the thought: two more of his men already down. But they'd all been trained for this. He had to focus on getting the job done. "Sergeant Davis," he said into his mic. "Send reinforcements, immediately."

Within minutes, the four extra SAS personnel fast-roped down from the helicopter into the garden. They ran around the house, blocking any potential exits.

"One vehicle apprehended. One male and two female occupants."

David registered the report but didn't stop moving. "Sergeant, watch my back, two males and a female unaccounted for." He dived into the next room, narrowly avoiding a burst of fire from a submachine gun. He shot a man in the head, who went down in a crumpled heap. "One male and one female still at large," David reported before entering the next room. There was a figure on a chair.

It was him – Sergeant Jones – tied in place, unconscious, both knees shot out.

"I have Jones!" David stepped forward, keeping his back to the wall. He checked Jones's pulse. "He's wounded but alive. Dispatch ambulances immediately," David reported.

"Roger," was the response.

He used his knife to cut Jones free, then crept on to explore the rest of the now badly damaged house.

Sergeant Roberts was with him all the way, searching. "It's quiet," she whispered, "too quiet…"

David held up his hand, looked down. "I just heard a click – below us – like someone cocking a weapon. They're in the root cellar."

"What root cellar?" Roberts muttered.

He signalled for her to move around him. "These houses were built in medieval times, they always had a root cellar; no refrigeration. We have to find its entrance." He checked the next room, while Roberts checked the kitchen.

David's room was clear.

"Found it," said Roberts.

David hurried past Jones to join her, signalling for the arriving paramedics to take Jones on their stretcher, as well as the two MOE operatives groaning in pain nearby. In the kitchen, Roberts had shunted a floor mat aside to reveal a trap door near a breakfast table. "Stand back," instructed David as he ripped open the trap door.

A burst of submachine gun fire sent bullets flying through the opening, causing David and Roberts to dive out of the way.

Without hesitation, David dropped a stun grenade into the cellar, then dived down the stairs to find a dazed man and woman. He tore the submachine gun out of the man's hands, then handcuffed his hands behind his back. Sergeant Roberts bound the woman in the same way.

Bomb-making equipment filled the cellar. Clearly, they hadn't just found Jones in time...

"One male and one female in custody," David reported as they escorted the two captives upstairs. "All jihadis are now accounted for, what with the one male and two females you apprehended, so we can..." He was about to declare 'all clear' when the door of a built-in cupboard in the main room eased open. Without hesitation David took steps to close the distance, drawing his Glock 17 pistol at the same time as flinging the door open. He fired two shots into the face of the man in front of him.

They dragged the now dead jihadi out from his hiding place. His body was layered with explosives.

"Clear the room!" yelled David. "He has a bomb! Send the bomb disposal crew – now!"

He and Roberts dragged their prisoners out of the house, slamming what was left of the front door shut.

After a few seconds, the SAS forward headquarters responded simply, "Bomb disposal crew dispatched."

David and his team stood warily in the front garden of the target house, until three members of the bomb disposal crew arrived. Two members of David's team were then directed to keep an eye on the captives, while he briefed the bomb disposal crew quickly about the hidden jihadi.

The head of the bomb disposal crew listened to David's directions, then instructed them to exit the garden. "It's best if you evacuate the premises entirely, sir."

"Very well." David led his team into the next-door garden, where a local man nervously peered out through a chink in the curtains. "Everything's under control now, sir," David told him gently, gesturing for him to stay calm.

Thirty minutes later, the head of the bomb disposal squad reported. "Suicide vest on the deceased jihadi has been disabled and removed. We have also scoured the house, which is now clear of any immediate danger from unexploded ordinance."

Relieved, David and his team returned to the target house, taking their prisoners with them. "All clear," he reported to the SAS forward headquarters.

The target house was then flooded with MI5 personnel and police. Two Black Mariah police vans and two further ambulances appeared, just as dawn nudged its first light over the horizon.

Superintendent McConnell approached David, rested a grateful hand on his shoulder. "You did well, Phillips. Sorry about your two men. We can take over from here. We'll just need fingerprints of all your personnel."

"Thank you, superintendent." David felt a wave of exhaustion and relief surge over him. "I'll have SAS HQ send them over."

"Very good, Phillips."

Was it 'good', though? Jones was safe, but only just. The explosives had been found, but only just. His men lay in hospital, injured. Was this really how the SAS worked, relying on its reserves at the last minute? Was this really the best David could do?

As the prisoners were loaded into the vans, David and his team made their weary way back to the SAS forward HQ. In the kitchen, a team of two were cooking breakfast for everyone. David made certain his team were fed, their injuries attended to by a medic, then overheard Roberts requesting transport to the hospital.

"I just need to know he's okay," she was telling an officer holding car keys.

"That who's okay?" David asked.

Her lips quivered. "James Templeton. We're... together."

"I'll come with you. I need to check on everyone who was... injured." He cleared his throat to hide his building sense of guilt, then signalled for the officer to lead the way.

But as they rushed through the streets, then through the hospital corridors, past nurses who looked away as they passed, David's stomach started to sink. By the time they reached the empty room where Templeton was supposed to be, a doctor with a clipboard was waiting. As he started to tell Roberts the news, she broke down into tears. It was worse than he'd thought.

"Templeton died just after he was brought in," the doctor explained. "We tried our best, but there was nothing we could do. He had the most terrible injuries, I'm sorry."

"And Jones?" David asked, his throat tight. "And the other men who were hurt in the same incident?"

"Badly injured, but they will recover. It will take months though. Especially Jones. We're sending him to London for specialist surgery."

"Thank you, doctor."

The doctor left them, and David ushered Roberts to a seat.

"We were only together a few months," she sobbed, "but I really loved him. He understood the risks of course," she whispered, continuing to cry. "His parents were so proud of him, they'll be devastated. I have to be the one to tell them – it's my duty."

David nodded. He wasn't sure what the protocols were.

She wiped away her tears. "I need to see him. Can you arrange it?"

"Of course. I'll be back." David spoke to some nurses, then beckoned to Roberts and escorted her to the hospital morgue. He waited outside while the doctor showed her into the facility.

She returned a few minutes later, finally dry-eyed. "We'd better get back," she said quietly.

"Are you okay, Roberts?"

"Catherine," she murmured. "You can call me Catherine."

On the way back to the SAS forward HQ, she told him, "They only showed me his face. It was almost unrecognisable. If he had lived, he would have been a cripple. He would've hated that."

***

A chopper soon returned David and his team to Hereford, where they cleaned and returned their weapons and unused ammunition to the armoury, then dispersed.

David thought he might fall asleep on his feet but organised for all their fingerprints to be sent to the superintendent, then went looking for Powrie.

He was at his desk. "Good work, Phillips." He gave David an impressed look, as if all past wrongs were now forgiven. "I admit, I may have been wrong about you from the beginning."

David wasn't sure which 'beginning' he meant.

"How did you know about the cellar?" Powrie asked.

"I had a good history teacher," David said simply.

"Well, it seems your upbringing might have finally had some use for us." Powrie smirked.

"I didn't know about the booby trap though," David admitted.

"Yes, well, it's not always possible to know these things – that's why they're called traps. There will be an enquiry of course, because of the death of Templeton, and because the terrorists seemed to know you were coming."

"Yes, sir, the trap and hidden jihadis would suggest that."

"Be sure to include all your observations in your report." He hesitated. "The enquiry will throw all sorts of shit at you of course; you need to be prepared for that."

"Yes, sir."

"Good. I have arranged a car and a driver for you to Oxford. Your car has already been sent back – I presumed you'd be too tired to drive. Oh, and your rector has arranged for you to sit your last exam privately, given you haven't had any access to the papers." Then he added, "You are obviously a very good soldier, Phillips. If you ever want a full-time position, talk to me."

David saluted as he left, straightening his back with hope. Was he finally becoming an accepted part of the outfit? Any previous hostility now forgotten?

Only time would tell.

PART 1: OXFORD

Chapter 1. David at Oxford

David was playing his second game for the university rugby side. Twice the ball came to him, twenty yards short of the opposing try-line. The first time he dummied right, then went left to score under the posts. The second time he dummied left and went right to again score under the posts. He converted both tries. The third time he attempted a similar move, the opposition had got wise to him and he was flattened in a devastating tackle. If only he'd passed to ball to one of his team's flank forwards, who was following up next to him, they would have scored and won the game. Oxford lost by a point.

He should have known.

At the match 'after party', a pretty girl calling herself Gwyneth attached herself to him, cheering him up when no one else would. Somehow, she accompanied him home.

As he woke the next morning, David was conscious of the overwhelming stench of puke. He was cold, and his bedclothes were mostly on the floor. The only visible sign of clothing was a sock on his left foot. He had a thumping headache. He was also not alone. Someone was heaving their guts out in the direction of the lavatory.

"Who's there?" he asked in a weak voice.

No answer.

He slowly raised himself off the bed and crawled on all fours towards the offending noise.

A naked female form was crouched over the lavatory bowl. There were large globs of sick across the floor, which he unsuccessfully tried to avoid.

He cleared his throat and wondered what to say. He rejected 'Who the fuck are you?' as being too harsh; 'Can I help you?' as being too soft. Eventually he said, "I need to go to the loo."

The apparition sat down heavily next to the toilet bowl. "Be my guest," she said.

He blinked and managed to stand up holding tightly onto the nearby towel rail. Most of the contents of his bladder went into the loo.

"Don't mind me," said the apparition, trying to wipe away droplets of pee from her arm and back. "Ah, I see that thing that dangles between your legs does function after all."

"If you don't mind me asking, who the fuck are you and why are you here?"

"I'm Gwyneth," said the apparition. "We were together at the after-match party."

"Mm, I see. Is this all your puke, or did I contribute to the mess?"

Gwyneth shrugged. "I was expecting a good solid common or garden fuck from the star of the side. You just went to sleep. Occasionally you put your finger on the floor, saying something like 'it helps to stop the bed spin'. I undressed you."

David lifted his left foot, still enclosed in the sock.

"Yes, sorry I seem to have missed something. Anyway, you didn't stir. I even sucked your dick, couldn't raise even a flicker of interest. So I went exploring and found some rather nice wine. I drank several bottles of it, hoping you might wake up..."

David looked desperately around. "I was keeping them for a special occasion."

"Well, I tried to make it a special occasion. It seemed that, along with everything else, it was rather a disappointment. Even now, looking at your member of parliament, there still doesn't seem to be the slightest interest."

"I've never fucked a woman covered in puke before. It's not very appealing."

"I could have a shower."

"Good idea. Then you can help me clean this place up." As Gwyneth moved unsteadily towards the shower he asked, "How did we get here?"

"Taxi, he charged double. Always double for drunks the driver said. You paid."

David took a lengthy turn in the shower, then heard the door of his flat open and slam. When he emerged, there was no sign of Gwyneth.

He sat on the bed, holding his head in his hands. He looked in the fridge, where he found a half empty carton of milk. It smelt worse than the puke. "Thank god, it's Sunday," he muttered, grabbing his keys and leaving the chaos behind.

A few hours later, after a desultory breakfast in a local cafe and a walk along the River Isis, he returned to his flat. The stench was even more overpowering than he remembered.

Well, that's not going to happen again, he said to himself, feeling totally disgusted. He spent the rest of the day cleaning up. But even after he poured disinfectant over the floor, the smell of puke still permeated through the pong. His precious flat: its small lounge with an elegant-looking bookshelf on one side, all his study books and a couple of novels all neatly arranged on the shelves; the Persian carpet given to him by his indulgent mother, the river view out of the window. The small spare bedroom, mostly used as a storeroom. There was a small but well-appointed kitchen, which he had now tidied up, having made the bed. He dropped the unused condom into the drawer in his bedside table. He tried cleaning his teeth for the fifth time that day in the now clean, neat, but old-fashioned bathroom.

As he brushed, he saw the post-it note he'd left for himself, reminding him about the meeting scheduled for the next day with one of his tutors. He quickly put it out of his mind, knowing it would not be good news. On the table, a stack of his marked essays carried a term's worth of bad grades.

At about six there was a knock on the door, "Christ," exclaimed Alexander as he entered the flat, "what have you been doing? This place stinks like a fucking whorehouse."

"Yeah. Let's go out, I'll tell you all about it, starting with a girl called Gwyneth."

"Who the hell is Gwyneth?" Alexander asked.

"Exactly."

Alexander shrugged and led David to the local pub.

***

The next day, David dragged himself to his tutor meeting, who said, "Mr Phillips, I can tell you that, unless your results improve substantially, you will be sent down at the end of the year. We can't waste a precious place at this university on someone who has no apparent interest or talent."

"I will try harder, sir," David said, and meant it. If he was sent down, he didn't know what he would do, or how his parents would react. As soon as he got back to his flat, he would sit down and make plans to rebuild his life. Cut down on the student drinking. Cut down on the sports ego. Increase the study.

He stopped in the doorway and his heart skipped a beat. "What the hell?"

The place had been completely trashed. His books were all over the floor, his bedclothes had been shredded. Someone had even crapped in the middle of his Persian carpet. He stood still for a few moments staring at the disaster. When he could move, he found his best clothes had been stolen, as well as his valuable record player and most of his records and tapes.

He called the police, who eventually appeared and took all the details, but were less than sympathetic. "The door isn't broken, which means they had a key."

"But there aren't any spare keys. I have the only one."

"Have you had any visitors lately, anyone who could have stolen your keys for a time, then returned them?"

David instantly thought of Gwyneth and cringed.

One of the officers noticed his expression. "There is a gang of women operating locally who, with the promise of sex, get into the flats of idiots like you. They steal the keys, and this is the result. Whoever you're thinking about, you won't see her for dust. They'll have moved on by now. Any discussion involving sex was just that – you were had, mate, big time and," he muttered, "you deserve everything that came your way."

"A gang of women, you say? She drank half my wine, then spent the night puking all over the flat. She could have just picked up her stuff and left, having nicked the keys."

"She may have lost the plot for a bit – these women are not geniuses you know. But if she had just nicked your keys, you may have reported the incident to the police earlier and ruined any chance of raiding your place."

I'll get the locks changed, he thought to himself. *I'm just a bloody fool – what am I even doing at Oxford? If I can let this happen to me, I hardly deserve the opportunity it affords.*

When he reflected further on the situation further, all he felt was an acute sense of shame.

***

David decided to try harder. As the term progressed, he gradually started to make progress with his studies. His tutor meetings even took on a more positive note.

"Mr Phillips, if you keep this up, I expect you will pass the year. You obviously changed your ways after our earlier discussion."

David nodded and cringed inwardly about the disastrous episode with Gwyneth and how it had motivated him to do better. "I've also decided to stay on in Oxford during the holiday period," David informed him. "I have secured a job on an assembly line at a car manufacturing plant for three months until the start of the new term. I will study in my spare time." He could have gone home to enjoy another unproductive holiday with late nights and idle days, but he was determined to make a change.

"Hm," reflected the tutor, "perhaps something more than just a lecture from me has helped to change your attitude?"

"Perhaps," David mumbled.

That evening at the pub, he told Alexander his plans. "...so I'll be here all summer."

"As will I," Alexander said with a 'cheers'. "For what it's worth."

There was something in his friend's tone that gave David reason to pause. "It *does* all seem so fucking inconsequential, doesn't it?" he mused, then hesitated. "This place I mean…" He waved his arms around as if to encompass the whole university. "I'm doing better this term, and I'm not ungrateful; but is it really preparing me for life, or sheltering me from it? Is it making me wiser, or more naïve? After that whole Gwyneth thing… sometimes I really don't know."

"Yeah, I get it." Alexander stood, then flinched into a hobble towards the toilets. He rubbed his thigh. "The only real-life experiences I get these days are in the TA. You should have been at training the other day; they really ran us into the ground. If you want more of that, they're asking for volunteers for the SAS Reserves. Maybe we should join?" he said with a chuckle before pushing open the toilet door.

David sipped his drink and glanced at a scratch on his hand, from where he rounded a gorse bush too close while jogging over the local heathland last week. Maybe Alexander was right – being members of the part time Territorial Army was about the only place where things felt real. When Alexander returned, he asked. "What exactly would we need to do, to join the SAS?"

"You're seriously thinking about it?"

"Well, why not? Nothing I have experienced at uni so far prepares me for anything except a smooth ride into a prosperous entitled future. I was such a fool with the Gwyneth episode, what the hell would I do if anything more serious came along? I need something to challenge me, to push me to my limits, to be prepared for anything... and anyone."

Alexander studied him a moment, then cleared his throat. "We'd have to get fit."

"I think I'm quite fit, with rugby and rowing..."

"You wouldn't even get past first base if you think that's fit. Also, once one gets accepted you really get tested, mentally as well as physically."

"After Oxford, I'm hoping to go into the merchant banking business..."

"Merchant fucking wankers – if you really want to make it in that jungle be prepared to take well thought through calculated risks. With the SAS you will be asked to put your life on the line from time to time. That will tell you how tough you really are. If you make it, you will know how far you can go, mentally I mean. Again if you make it, it will give you confidence few others have. I'll tell you what; I have a pal in the SAS itself. I'll ask him to set-up a basic fitness test for both of us. We can go from there."

"Great!" David smiled, and for the first time in a long time he felt excitement.

***

Two weekends after their conversation, David and Alexander met with Alexander's friend, Hogarth, early one morning at a local running track. He had advised them to keep both days of the weekend free. Hogarth turned out to be a sergeant in one of the regular SAS regiments, on a two-week leave break. He was a muscular six-foot-six and weighed something like one hundred and ten kilos, he had a brush cut and was wearing a track suit. He looked David up and down, a mere six foot and weighing a slim ninety-five kilos, almost as if to say, *What the hell am I getting myself into here? Public school git, by the looks of things.*

After David and Alexander had given Hogarth an idea of their regular exercise programme, Hogarth pointed at the track. "Okay, a few stretches to start, then I want eight laps, just to get a feel of your levels of fitness."

David finished in a little over nine minutes, with Alexander finishing half a lap behind. David was stunned. Sandy-haired Alexander, tall and athletic – David had always thought of him as being one of the best athletes in the university.

Hogarth looked pleasantly surprised, as if thinking: *Maybe there is something I can work with here. Don't suppose he has any balls though.*

At the nearby pool an hour later he told them, "Forty laps, flat out."

David finished in less than thirty-five minutes, with Alexander finishing just ahead of him.

Hogarth was again surprised. "Bit more of a test this afternoon," he announced over lunch. "Anyway, why are you doing this? What do you want with the SAS?" he asked David quietly over a light lunch. "I mean Oxford and some sort of job in the city?" He waved his enormous hand around dismissively. "The SAS seems out of place with all that."

David shrugged. "That's exactly the point," he said. "I could go on my current trajectory, public school, this place, Oxford, and as you say a job in the city. But I'm an idiot! And I need to not be. So maybe, just maybe, the SAS reserve will teach me what I need." He smiled at Hogarth, sensing that the man was contemptuous of his background and privileged upbringing. "Also," he went on, "and this may sound like patronising bullshit, but I do love my country." As he said it, the thought lifted him with pride. He didn't know until that moment how much it was true. "How lucky am I to have had the life I have? If I want to preserve that for future generations, and share it with others, it needs protecting." He stole a questioning glance at Hogarth.

"The SAS reserve is a very big commitment – three days every other weekend. What'll that do to your rugby and everything?"

"I know. If I can't cope with that then fuckit, I don't know..."

Hogarth pursed his lips in thought and left it at that.

The afternoon consisted of a ten-kilometre run through the streets of Oxford. David finished comfortably in thirty-five minutes, with Alexander a few minutes behind.

"You are both much fitter than I expected," said Hogarth. He gave Alexander a card, "this fellow will get you up to scratch in about nine months; he lives nearby." He offhandedly declined their offer of an evening meal. Before he left, he spoke privately to Alexander when they were out of earshot, both of them staring at him.

"Was that about me?" David asked once Hogarth had gone.

"He doesn't think you'll follow-up," Alexander told him. "He thinks bastards like you have always had it too easy, so you won't cope; and if you do get in, by some fluke, you'll get such a hard time that you'll bale out in a few months. I'll be well accepted, though, with my working-class background."

"He actually said that?"

"He did. I told him it's possible he underestimated you; if asked, most would say that I was the better athlete; but I think you surprised even yourself today."

David smiled and thought to himself, *a few months ago, maybe he would have been right. Not anymore.*

David tried to engage a few different people in what he thought of as his dilemma. His tutor wondered if he would be able to cope with the commitment to the SAS as well getting a decent result at the university. "David, it may be the difference between a first and something less." The tutor didn't seem to understand that David was trying to see if there was something more than just a good university degree and the resulting well-paid job, and what that all meant in the wider context of the community at large.

There was an angry call from his father once he had got wind of the fact that David had been in danger of being sent down due to his results:

"You are just wasting the opportunity Oxford University provides, David. You have no idea how much your mother and I sacrificed to get you that place at Oxford. The expensive school, and you seem to be less than committed to the university rugby side. Your brother is a good example to follow – he got a first and is now going to captain the English rugby side."

David was shocked at the tirade but said nothing.

"Don't you have anything to say to that?"

"No, Dad, I don't."

He put the phone down. He reflected for a few minutes. He almost cried.

None of that was fair, he thought. *But I will prove him wrong. I hope that if I am ever in a position such as his I will be more supportive.*

***

David and Alexander followed up with Hogarth's contact and, nine months later, as promised, they presented themselves for selection for the Reserves at the Hereford SAS headquarters, where they easily passed the fitness tests and were accepted as trainees.

David could see Alexander's enthusiasm for the programme fading even after the first two weekends. After four of the prescribed nine weekends, Alexander said to David, "It's much tougher than I thought, with the athletics season coming up and my academic results so important this year, and I've just met a new bird..." Alexander withdrew from the programme shortly after.

Alone, David stood out more now from the other trainees, separated by the hostility they clearly aimed at him. Sergeant Jones noticed him standing alone one day between sessions. "Phillips, isn't it?" he asked, already knowing. "Hogarth mentioned your name. I don't know what you did to upset him. You won't get any special treatment from me. We don't take kindly to wimps here."

David said nothing.

"Have you nothing to say to that?" Jones looked at David.

When there was no response, David merely looked at him and said, "No, sergeant."

Chapter 2. SAS

For reasons David did not understand, the SAS training staff appeared to want him to fail and eliminate him from the programme altogether. He was therefore determined to show Sergeant Jones that he was no quitter, not like Alexander. So he used any hostility issued against him to drive him forward over the nine weekends of training and even, sometimes, do better than his fellow trainees.

The final endurance test over the Brecon Beacons in Wales was an opportunity to do just that. Despite his much better-than-average performances during the previous nine weeks, he got the feeling from the training group that they all expected him to fail. He and the twenty-five other volunteers for the SAS Reserve started off three hours before dawn, each carrying a sixty-pound Bergen rucksack, a rifle and a full water bottle, over a distance of forty miles. The trainers refused to tell anyone what the time limit was.

Rumour has it, it's about twenty hours, David thought, *I'd better see if I can do it in eighteen.*

There was no memory of the pain David endured over the trail; his total focus was on completing the course within the time frame he had set. He passed all his colleagues. "This is an individual test," he'd been told, "if you are tempted to help anyone you will be removed from the programme."

During the last few miles, he came across a man who appeared to be struggling. He took one look. It was not one of his fellow trainees. It was not one of the trainers. He then realised it was a trap, so ran on without stopping.

On arrival at the finish, there was Sergeant Jones looking at his watch. "Eighteen hours, Phillips, you must have taken a short cut somewhere, nobody does it in eighteen hours."

"Sergeant, you know that's untrue. Also, you know me well enough by now that I do not cheat, even if you do."

"Meaning what?"

"Well, there's a fellow a mile or two back there," David pointed, "who tried to con me into helping him. You must think we're all really dumb."

"What fellow?"

"A couple of miles back there, asking for help."

"There is nobody back there doing anything of the sort."

"Sergeant, I'll take you there, if you don't believe me."

They did indeed go back, with David still carrying his rifle and pack, finding the man in a very bad way.

They got some water down the man's throat and, together, half-carried him the two miles back to the finish, where they called an ambulance.

"He's from another unit," Jones informed David, "must have got lost somewhere."

David then had three very unpleasant days. He was told he was out of the programme having failed the endurance test. Eventually, after many protests, he was allowed to see his Commanding Officer, Major Neville Powrie.

"The records here say that you finished two hours over time," he was told.

"No, sir. I finished in eighteen hours, then with Sergeant Jones I spent several hours rescuing a man who would have died otherwise. There are at least a dozen witnesses. For some reason I was logged in after I had rescued the man with Sergeant Jones and not when I first finished the course."

"Jones is on leave and uncontactable."

David, saying nothing, merely looked at the CO, who started to look uncomfortable.

"I will investigate," he eventually offered.

After three agonising days, he was told that they had been unable to verify his account of what had occurred and he was told he was out of the programme. He asked to see the commanding officer again. Permission was eventually granted.

David pleaded his case.

"You have one other option," he was told.

"What's that?"

"Repeat the programme."

"The whole nine-week programme?" said a disbelieving David.

The OC looked at him balefully. "I will arrange for you just to do the final endurance test over the Brecon Beacons. The next intake is doing that in two weeks from now.

"Thank you, sir."

"Okay, Phillips, don't let me down."

"I won't, sir."

David made sure that in the following two weeks he maintained his fitness programme, although he did taper his training in the last few days.

The sergeant responsible for the programme told him before the test began, "We don't want any mishaps like the last time, so I have detailed someone to be with you all the way."

"Sergeant. Last time I completed the course in eighteen hours. I intend to do that again. Could I respectfully suggest that someone you trust also be placed somewhere about halfway in case he is needed?"

The sergeant had some sympathy with David but said nothing, just nodded.

As before, David set off with the twenty-five hopefuls. An experienced corporal had been told to keep up with David all the way. David pushed it really hard, being motivated 'to show the bastards up'. The pain was the same, the corporal had difficulty in keeping up and was almost out on his feet and seemed glad to hand David's surveillance to another corporal at the half-way mark.

"Phillips is really on the money," he told the 'fresh' corporal, "hope you'll be able to keep up."

David took no notice, just ploughed on. He finished in seventeen and a half hours. There was another sergeant on duty at the finish line who dutifully recorded David's time, having checked with the 'surveillance corporal' when he arrived some fifteen minutes after David. He was eventually told he had passed the test and could continue with the programme.

He asked to see the commanding officer again. Permission was refused. One of the other trainers later said to him, "All part of the test, Phillips. You have bigger balls than we thought."

"Why weren't any of the other trainees dealt with in the same way?" David asked.

"Don't push it," was the answer, "you were lucky to survive this one, may not be so lucky next time."

Don't always trust everybody, and persist if you think you are right, David decided. *Finally I'm learning something.*

Chapter 3. Lizzie

Soon after David had been accepted as a member of the SAS Reserve, he was obliged to spend ten days engaged in training exercises at the SAS base in Hereford. All those involved were given the first Saturday of their sojourn off. David found himself in the car park of an upmarket shopping centre in the town. He noticed a pretty woman in the car park, carrying a few shopping bags to an ancient and decrepit-looking car, in vast contrast to most of the other fancy looking vehicles around; he then realised the woman was his commanding officer's wife. Taking little notice, he was about to go about his own business, then quickly realised she was having difficulty starting the vehicle, so he walked over to help – it was the right thing to do.

His SAS uniform made his status obvious, so he smiled at the scowling woman, "Ma'am, is there anything I can do to help?"

She looked at him, noticing his uniform, and was about to dismiss his offer out of hand when something made her change her mind. "Mnn, yes, soldier, thank you. I'm having trouble starting this thing." She waved at the car in a dismissive way. "You boys are supposed to be able to get vehicles going, even in the most extreme situations, aren't you?"

"Yes, ma'am, though these are hardly extreme circumstances." He opened the bonnet. "Do you have any tools, a screwdriver or some spanners perhaps?" he asked after a few minutes.

She was standing disconsolately nearby. "Spanners?" She laughed easily. "What the hell would I do with spanners? No, I don't have anything like that either here or at home."

David smiled again, intent on persisting, like he had in Wales. "I'm sure I can get this thing going. If you need to do some more shopping, I need half an hour."

She looked at him, probably wondering if she could trust him; but then an expression of relief came over her face, "Yes, that would be useful. Please look after the groceries."

"I won't be far away," said David. "I just need to go to the hardware store over there," he pointed, "for the screwdriver and a few spanners I mentioned, but give me the car keys and I'll keep it locked."

She handed over a bunch of keys. "I don't normally give all my house keys to complete strangers," she said, smiling in a more relaxed way.

"Even if I wanted to steal your car, I doubt it would get much further than the next village, and I don't know where you live, so you're not in much danger. Anyway, the gaffer would skin me alive if I did anything wrong."

There was a peal of laughter from the woman. "The gaffer? You mean, my husband; is that what you all call him? I'll remind him of that when he returns."

David watched her wander back into the shopping centre; he couldn't help noticing her slim trim figure, dressed in a fashionable fawn skirt and a green polo necked jersey, which showed her figure off to its best; she was tall, at about five-feet-ten he judged. She had short blond hair. He placed her grocery bags on the back seat of the car, idly noticing they were all from the local Waitrose.

Forty minutes later, David had the car going and was wondering how long he would have to wait when the woman reappeared. She put her few additional purchases into the rear seat and made as if to climb into the driver's seat.

"Ma'am, this vehicle urgently needs a service; there was almost no oil in the engine, although I've remedied that now, and it can't have been to a garage for years, frankly it's dangerous to drive. Maybe I could drive you home and spend an hour attending to some of the basics. You should then get the gaffer to take it to the local garage."

"Service," she laughed, "it's not the only thing that needs a service," she said flirtatiously. "Okay, soldier, do you want me to get into the back seat? Sorry, I don't have a chauffeur's cap for you."

David firmly opened the front passenger door and briefly glimpsed the woman's shapely legs and soft looking thighs as she settled herself. *What the hell am I getting myself into?* he thought. *Taking the Commanding Officer's wife home – my friend you are really getting yourself into big trouble.* He hoped he wasn't making another Gwyneth-mistake.

She directed him to an old well-established village outside Hereford.

This place smells of money, he thought to himself as they drove in through some wrought iron gates onto a gravel driveway. *I didn't realise they paid the gaffer enough to afford such a place.* David briefly admired the large beautifully proportioned ivy-clad mansion in front of him; he could see a substantial well-kept garden to the side of the mansion, which extended to the rear. There appeared to be two entrances to the establishment. "If I may, I will help you with your purchases, then I'll get to your car? It really needs attention," he said.

The woman nodded.

An hour and a half later, David was still buried under the vehicle in the driveway, when he heard an anxious voice, "Soldier, what the hell are you doing? I'll offer you a cup of tea if you emerge from wherever you are." David crawled out from under the vehicle and his hostess burst out laughing, "What's that get-up all about?" she said referring to the disposable overalls and hair net David was wearing.

"Didn't want to get oil all over my uniform, ma'am. Grease on the uniform usually results in a good hour running round the parade ground or some other useless unproductive activity, so I bought them in the hardware store. Anyway, I've done some of the basics, but with respect this," he waved his hand at the unfortunate vehicle, "I was going to say is a heap of shit, but I won't. You see what I mean I hope. You need to get the gaffer to get you something better; this thing is a death trap."

"Mnn, the gaffer, as you call him, buys nothing round here, but I suppose I can trade this in for something better."

"Trade it in?" laughed David. "You'll probably have to pay someone to take it away. Anyway, get the gaffer to at least help you with what to buy next."

"Forget that; he has about as much interest in cars as I do. Talk about the blind leading the blind."

"Well, I could help you, but I live in Oxford, so the logistics could be a bit tricky."

"Okay, we'll think about that."

"Changing the subject, could I just use the bathroom to clean myself up a bit, then I'll be on my way?" asked David.

"On your way? How are you going to get back to the base?"

"Shank's pony, bus, or I may be able to hitch a ride; people in the town are very supportive of anyone in uniform."

"I could of course offer to drive you back to base."

"No, ma'am. My earnest advice is never to go anywhere near that car again. The brakes are unreliable, the car over steers, and the engine is about to give up the ghost judging from the amount of smoke coming out of the exhaust. It's dangerous."

She led the way upstairs and into a very well-equipped kitchen. "I'll just make that pot of tea," she announced as she filled the kettle, "milk, sugar?"

"Just black thanks."

"In that case I'll be back in a minute," she said. "I expect a competent man like you will manage to pour boiling water into the teapot. Neville even has trouble with that."

"Neville?"

"Your gaffer? I don't exactly call him Officer-Major Powrie."

David nodded, smiling as he washed his hands in the kitchen sink. Looking around he could see no sign of his Commanding Officer, or indeed any male presence at all.

As the kettle boiled a few minutes later, David heard light footsteps coming down the passage and his hostess emerged into the kitchen wearing a brief blue bikini, which set her figure off to its very best. She was carrying a large white towel over her shoulder.

"Fancy a swim, before you go?" she asked, as David admired her slim legs, flat stomach and very shapely breasts straining to be released from the restraints of a small bikini top.

Despite her humorous disposition, David also noticed a slight but well-hidden air of vulnerability, perhaps of something missing in her life? Something he could fulfill? "Ma'am, has anyone told you recently, you really are stunningly beautiful." He brushed away any thoughts of Gwyneth. *This is completely different*, he thought.

She blushed under his gaze. "Thank you, but please call me Daphne, you can't keep calling me ma'am. Now, how about that swim?"

A large pool sparkled outside through a set of French doors.

"Daphne, there is no possibility that a beautiful woman like you should be saddled with a name like that." He laughed. "It's a suitable name for your car perhaps. You must have a middle name or a nickname I could use instead? What do your friends call you?"

"You're very rude," said Daphne with an amused smile on her face. "Firstly you tell me that my car is a heap of shit, and now you are telling me you don't like my name..."

"Okay, Daphne," laughed David. "I suppose it could be worse – they might have called you Jolene, or Benedykta, or Ichabod; and yes if we could find a swimming costume I would love a swim. Are you sure you don't have another name?"

Daphne laughed and laughed. "You really are silly. Fine, my friends call me Elizabeth. My surname is Hall, on my father's advice I kept my maiden name and didn't take my husband's. What about you? I can't keep calling you 'soldier'."

"David Phillips," he answered.

"Oh, yes, Neville has mentioned you on several occasions..."

"Something good?"

"Yes, I suppose so, he said his staff expected you to fall at the first hurdle, but in the end you passed everything with flying colours."

David nodded. "It's irritating, but I've come to realise that one of my strengths is that people often underestimate me. Including you probably... Lizzie."

"Lizzie? Oh I see, short for 'Elizabeth'. Okay, I like it. You know, David, the pool is completely private." Then she added coyly, "I wonder if we could altogether dispense with the idea of swimming costumes?"

Jesus, David thought happily, *I really am in the shit now.*

"What about your husband?"

"Don't worry about him, we lead completely separate lives these days."

"Are you sure, because I wouldn't want him setting the SAS mafia onto me."

"SAS mafia, what the hell are you talking about?"

"Many in the SAS retire after, say, twenty years on what they consider to be an insufficient pension. So they use their somewhat unusual skills in legitimate or perhaps not so legitimate activities. Much of the time they get paid handsomely for their services."

"Pff, Neville has never mentioned anything like that. What do you mean most of the time?"

"Certain favoured people, mostly ex-members of the chosen few, if they get into trouble or need help, can call on what I have described as the mafia, although they would not appreciate the label, and whatever needs to be done will be done and will cost nothing."

"How do you know all that?"

"It's extraordinary what one can learn by keeping one's mouth shut and ears open."

"So could Neville call on these people to deal with you, for example…?"

"I doubt if they would take it on. If they became embroiled in a current or ex-member's domestic affairs, they wouldn't have time for anything else."

Without a word David reached out and they found themselves kissing passionately. The tea was forgotten. Memories of Gwyneth were forgotten. David found himself being skilfully stripped of his overall and then his socks. He undid Lizzie's bikini top and her ample breasts popped out standing attractively erect. He undid the bows on her bikini bottom and it fell to the floor as his underpants were removed. He picked Lizzie up and almost ran through the wide-open French doors and jumped into the pool, with her in his arms. David was aware of an excited but mild protest from his hostess as they sank below the surface. They came up sputtering with Lizzie's legs wrapped around David's waist. He entered her and, with her legs still in place, he walked out of the pool and laid Lizzie down on the soft grass. She climaxed, once, twice, three times…

After a few minutes Lizzie mumbled, "As I said earlier, the car isn't the only thing that needed servicing. That was wonderful."

David, stirring, said, "I'll just get a towel." He raced inside, picked up the towel that Lizzie had discarded and returned to the poolside. He spent ten minutes carefully drying every inch of her.

"That was almost as good," said Lizzie. "Soon, I could do all that again."

"Yes, but this time in bed, much more comfortable there; come," he led her towards where he assumed were the bedrooms.

"Ouch, look at my hair," mumbled Lizzie as she caught a glimpse of herself in the mirror.

"I'll fix that for you. We can do it now, or after a bit more bed. You choose."

To his surprise she said, "Let's do the hair first. I've never had my hair washed by a rampant naked man before. I'll be ready for anything after that."

David found some suitable shampoo and a hair dryer. When he finished she said, "You can do that anytime you like, I really am ready for whatever you can manage in bed."

"There are a few little wispy bits of hair that I need to snip off, so just sit still for a moment please." He spent five minutes tidying up her substantial head of hair. "Now look at yourself in the mirror."

"Wonderful, wonderful," said Lizzie enthusiastically, "Makes me feel a whole lot better. Now come on, time for bed." They dashed into the bedroom where David had carefully turned down the bedclothes.

Afterwards, David briefly wondered where all this was going. *The SAS was supposed to create more purpose in my life,* he thought, *what will happen when the gaffer finds out? She said something about them leading completely separate lives, I need to find out more about that.*

He relaxed when Lizzie opened her eyes and smiled at him.

Chapter 4. Investments

An hour later, David was still in Lizzie's bed, lying on his back with Lizzie resting beside him. He gazed around the room. What was he doing here? The SAS was supposed to give him what he needed to become a more competent and self-assured young man. He felt he had achieved this in many respects, but he still clearly couldn't help himself around women. This was the gaffer's wife! Outside, the sky was getting dark. "It's getting a bit late to return to the base," he told Lizzie. "Can I stay here? I suppose that depends on what the gaffer's plans are."

"Don't worry about him. He won't be back until early next week."

"Okay, I'm supposed to inform the base of my whereabouts after a certain time, so I need to phone them and give them an address and phone number, if that's alright with you."

She gave him the address. "But don't forget this is (a) where Neville lives is (b) you need to make sure there's no confusion, you probably noticed the downstairs entrance. The phone number is just for here. He has his own line."

"Something to eat?" asked Lizzie, a moment later, "after all that exertion I'm starving, and we had no lunch. Steak, baked potato and vegetables, okay?"

David nodded. "I'll help with the vegetables."

They crawled out of bed.

Lizzie scouted around looking for something to wear.

"Please," said David laughing, "wear as little as possible, as far as I am concerned any clothes will spoil the view." She rummaged in a cupboard and tossed him a light silk dressing gown, while she scrambled into a similar one herself.

While they were sitting at the breakfast bar in the kitchen enjoying their simple meal David asked, "Tell me about the gaffer, you said you lead different lives? He's obviously a bit older than you."

"Neville just turned fifty; I'm thirty-two," said Lizzie, pausing as if wondering how much to tell David, then she continued, saying, "My father left me quite a large sum of money when he died. The marriage went pear-shaped when Neville realised I, and not him, would always remain in control of the money. It all came to a head when I caught him in bed with one of the barmaids from the local pub. That's when he moved into (b). We do indeed lead very separate lives."

Lizzie continued after a further silence, "Dad was a very keen observer of human behaviour. So, after our marriage and during the periods when Neville was away, Dad took me through all his various investments; I spent several weeks, over a period of years, with him and his investment advisors in London and got to understand the situation very well. On many occasions Dad said to me, "You must stay in control of the money, girl. All this is coming to you and if you want my advice don't let Powrie anywhere near it, he'll just waste it; he's never had money and with respect to all his other fine qualities it will just go to his head."

David nodded. He thought there would be a bit more to the story if he got to know Lizzie better. She was so intriguing. He wondered if this was a mere fling as far as she was concerned, or if indeed there was any possibility of getting to know her better.

Maybe I could use her car as an excuse to see her again? he thought. "Can I change the subject for a moment," said David. "I was wondering how I could help you with your car, the bloody thing is a death trap, and sooner or later you'll have an accident and be badly hurt."

"Any suggestions?"

"I have to return to Oxford next week, after the training exercises. I thought I could take the car."

"If it's dangerous for me, then the same applies to you."

David smiled. "Yes, but that way I can do a bit of research and, if you come down to Oxford next Friday, that's in ten days, for the weekend, we can make a decision and buy you a new car."

"You'll trade in the old one then."

"Maybe, but frankly if you left it in the local car park with a sign on it saying: 'steal me please' you wouldn't get any takers. It's a wreck. Part of the arrangement would be that the dealer would get rid of it though. We'll make that part of the negotiation. What sort of car would you like, do you think?"

She shrugged. "Haven't a clue, but the idea of a weekend away with you is very appealing. It'll certainly give me something to look forward to over the next few days." She looked at him with a smile on her face, "Won't my being there upset your girlfriend?"

"No, I don't have a girlfriend right now. My commitment to the SAS tends to restrict my social life a bit. So, no there is no danger of upsetting anyone. You'll have to watch me playing rugby on the Saturday afternoon though. I'll make sure you have a decent ticket."

"Mmm, rugby. You mention a ticket. So it's not the thirsty thirds then."

David laughed. "No, it's the university side. Should be a good game."

"You're not one of the ones at the front who grunt all the time, I hope?"

"No, I play in the backs, fly half actually. The backs hardly ever grunt." He laughed.

After a brief silence Lizzie looked at him, "I only met you, by accident, this morning and now you are in the process of taking over my life. I hardly know you. What I do know is that you have fucked my brains out almost from the minute I set eyes on you, and you are now going to take away my car and I'm coming to stay with you next weekend. Anything else?"

David shrugged. "I look forward to getting to know you. Come here. Off with that." He removed her flimsy dressing gown, picked her up and carried her, uncomplaining, to the bedroom. After they made love again, they slept.

Later, as they lay cuddled in each other arms, she said, "Cradle-snatching, that's what all my friends will say," she giggled.

David laughed too. "There's an obvious retort to that..."

She smiled happily. After a few more minutes she propped herself up on one elbow and said, "You said you wanted to get to know me a bit better."

"Yes, of course. At the moment though I'm rather distracted by the shape of your two very beautiful tits." He leant over and kissed them both in turn.

"Do you have any siblings? You've not mentioned your mother," David asked casually as he continued to fondle her very erect breasts.

She looked at him reflectively. "My mother died in a car accident with my twin brother twenty years ago now, so I was brought up by my father who was already in his late fifties by then. As one could expect, he was rather distant and almost wholly absorbed in his very successful engineering business."

David stopped what he was doing. "Sorry, painful memories. I didn't mean to…"

"That's okay. Long time ago now…"

***

David drove Lizzie's car back to base early Sunday morning. Once he completed the ten-day training assignment, he gingerly drove it back to Oxford arriving after midnight, just in time for his Thursday morning lecture. Before he left Hereford one of the sergeants, who saw him fiddling with something in the car's engine, asked him pointedly, "Doesn't that car belong to the gaffer's missus?"

"It did," said David, not displaying any of the nervousness he felt; he certainly didn't want it to be known that he was having an affair with the OC's wife. "I'm taking it to the knacker's yard, she'll never see it again. You might find her driving something a bit safer, within a week or so, perhaps more in keeping with her position."

The drive back to Oxford was slow due to David's caution in dealing with the poor condition of the car. He had plenty of time to reflect on the developments in his life now with the flourishing affair with Lizzie. *I've really bust a gut in getting into the SAS reserve,* he thought, *am I just chucking it all away on a girl? Surely the gaffer won't tolerate the situation once he gets to know. Maybe I should just let the whole thing go with Lizzie.*

But when he thought it through, he just couldn't bear not seeing Lizzie again.

***

The following Friday, David met the train at Oxford. Lizzie hopped off carrying a small overnight bag, which David picked up with an enquiring look on his face. "Just as well I didn't bring anything bigger," responded Lizzie with a smile after they had indulged in a long kiss on the platform with fellow passengers streaming around them. "I had to change trains twice, once at Newport and once at Didcot. Anyway I was hoping that, for what I have in mind, I wouldn't be needing much in the way of clothes..."

"Sounds good to me." He led her towards a nearby taxi rank. "Only, I've made an arrangement to see a car dealer – one this afternoon and two tomorrow."

Lizzie stopped. "This afternoon? Bollocks to that," she said much to David's surprise. "I've been looking forward to this for almost ten days, even now I can barely stand up, we're going straight back to your place. The car thing will have to wait."

David said nothing. Still carrying Lizzie's small bag and holding her hand, he hailed a taxi.

"Your place, not some horrid car yard?" enquired Lizzie.

David nodded. "I couldn't possibly ignore an invitation like that, we're going straight to my place."

"You're on your own, aren't you? You don't share with some other smelly student, I hope."

"No, no, it's a bit of a come down compared with your place of course, just a teeny bit smaller." David laughed. "I'm sure you'll like it."

David's small flat was on the top floor of a three-story building in a quiet street not far from the city centre. Lizzie took a quick look round. "It's very neat and tidy," she observed. "I expected a student shambles."

"SAS influence, it's much easier to keep it tidy," he said. They raced to the bedroom and, kissing passionately, tore each other's clothes off and leapt into bed.

Afterwards Lizzie said, "Nice clean sheets and a big double bed, perfect. I could do all that again, when you are ready."

"I've called the car dealer; he'll wait for us until six or so."

By then Lizzie was wandering naked around the flat curiously. "Well, you've certainly managed to hide all evidence of any other female presence," she said smiling.

"We've had that conversation," said David. "Actually, you're the first girl I've had back here in a long time. Come on back to bed."

They managed to make the car dealership on the outskirts of Oxford, just as the dealer was about to shut up shop for the day.

"I'd almost given up on you," David was told by the car dealer.

Lizzie was persuaded to test drive a BMW convertible. She unenthusiastically emerged from the car, then spotted her old car in the yard. She walked over to it amid curious glances from the salesman who quickly realised that Lizzie was the owner. "Careful ma'am," he said, "that vehicle should be approached with extreme caution."

Lizzie just laughed. "I was driving it until a few days ago."

"Well, ma'am, seriously, you're lucky to be alive. I've had the vehicle condemned. The wreckers are picking it up in the morning."

"How much will you give me as a trade in? You can't just take it away."

"If you buy a car from me, as a gesture of goodwill, I'll take one hundred pounds off the price. Otherwise nothing. As I said, the vehicle has been condemned."

David intervened. "Did you like the test vehicle?" he asked Lizzie.

"Yes, it was fine."

David said to the salesman. "We'll be back in a day or two. Thanks for the effort and thanks for dealing with the wreck."

"We're open all day tomorrow but are closed on Sunday. It takes a day or two to get a vehicle licensed and properly serviced."

Together they had a fun over the weekend, managing to see one more dealer on the Saturday morning. "Unless you're in a rush to get back to Hereford we can see the other dealer I lined up on Monday."

"You mean you're letting me stay another night?" Lizzie joked.

"Stay as long as you like, you'll have to do the cooking and cleaning of course, while I concentrate on more important things like lectures and rugby practice," he laughed.

She punched him playfully on the shoulder. "I'll stay, thank you. You won't like my domestic skills much, but then I don't suppose that's why I'm here in the first place."

David just laughed, "As I said, stay as long as you wish, I do have lectures and things though."

"Well, I'll definitely stay a day or two, but I do have to get back to my horses."

"I've never been passed over for a horse before."

Lizzie laughed. "Do you ride? You can ride one of my beauties at the next hunt meeting if you like."

"I certainly ride, and I actually would love to be at one of your hunt meetings. Are you sure about that?"

"Yes, I could arrange it, perhaps when Neville is away again."

During a meal at a local bistro, Lizzie said to David, "We've had conversations about me, I know nothing about you apart from your SAS activities."

He told her a little about his home life. "Dad is well-connected in the city. I'm hoping to get a job in a medium-sized financial advisory business when I finish up here at Oxford." He didn't mention his elder brother.

"Seems rather dull compared to the SAS. What made you join the SAS anyway?"

David explained the Gwyneth episode, giving as little detail as possible. He followed up with his need to make as much of his life as possible. "That is why I joined the SAS; it will certainly create another dimension to my life. I hope it will enable me to be something useful, apart from managing people's investments."

"What do you really want out of life?" Lizzie asked, more intently then.

"I'm obviously interested in the whole finance sector," David continued. "What I really want is to build something myself, without having to lick anyone's arse."

Lizzie laughed. "Well, the affair with me seems to be rather the opposite of licking anyone's arse, as you so delicately put it."

After a short silence David gave into his curiosity and asked, "Who looks after your investments?"

Lizzie mentioned a well-known merchant bank in the city.

"How long have you been involved with them?"

"Oh, years. They helped my father raise money for his business, more than once."

"You must be happy with them then?"

Lizzie looked at him and smiled. "I'm not sure. My father said I needed to keep them on their toes otherwise they would become complacent. I don't really know how to do that."

"What sort of return do you get on the funds invested?" David asked.

"About four percent."

"Are you happy with that?"

"It's more than adequate for my needs. I reinvest almost half the income every year. The house was purchased for cash, I have an interest in a racing stable and I have several hacks that I ride in the local hunt; my needs are not enormous. I pay all the costs relating to the house and I've continued to pay Neville a generous allowance, something my father started."

"Hmm, four percent is quite low. It must be a sizable trust."

Ignoring the obvious question Lizzie said, "You say four percent is low. What do you think is a reasonable figure?"

"Double that, say eight to ten. That's what I'd be aiming for if it were my money."

"Really?"

David nodded. "But sometimes, as with the SAS, you have to take risks to get results. One could say the same of relationships. Us, for example. It was some risk, getting involved with you. But then – what a result!"

She laughed and reached across the table to hold his hand.

They went to another dealer on the Saturday morning. On the Saturday afternoon, she watched David play rugby. The university won. He said to her before the match, "There's a party afterwards at the Randolph, would you like to come? We can either go or give it a miss, your choice. I'll introduce you around of course."

"Certainly, I'd love to come. I'd like that. I may have to buy some suitable clothes. I saw a place nearby where I can get something."

They spent a couple of hours at the party where David introduced her to all his fellow team members and many of the other guests. Lizzie was looking her stunning best. There were a few curious glances from some of his team members who, despite Lizzie's beauty, were curious about the obvious age difference between the pair. The team coach said to David as an aside, "I see that the SAS does deliver other attractions apart from running up and down mountains in Wales. The lady mentioned she lives in Hereford..."

David smiled but didn't rise to the bait. He was already playing with fire enough as it was.

Over the weekend, during one of their increasingly intimate conversations, David asked, "What made the gaffer think he would be in control of your inheritance?"

"Don't know. It was certainly never discussed with him. But you know the SAS, it's all men, it never occurs to them that women can be in charge of anything. He tried to pressure me to change the situation and make him a trustee, but there are a number of mechanisms in the trust deed that prevent that. He also came up with all sorts of wild schemes reinforcing Dad's assessment of what he would do if he ever got his hands on the money. He even wanted to buy a nearby castle that had some historical association with Henry the seventh, so I haven't and won't let him anywhere near the trust. He's totally frustrated by that. He didn't want to buy the place in Hereford, making comments like, 'it's just an ordinary suburban home' and 'can't we do better than that?' Against his wishes I bought that wonderful place."

On Monday morning David managed to get Lizzie to visit another dealer, but when he asked her which car she preferred, she said, "you choose, the difference in the prices doesn't bother me and I know nothing about cars anyway."

David then spent thirty minutes with the BMW dealer. "I got three grand off the price as well as the one hundred you negotiated."

"Three grand, that's ridiculous! You mean if I had walked in there by myself I would have had to pay that much more?"

David shrugged. "Just give him a cheque." He told her the amount. "We'll probably be able to pick the car up on Thursday."

"I'll have gone home by then, one of the horses is sick. Maybe, if you can spare the time, bring the car up to Hereford on Friday evening? There's a hunt meeting on Saturday."

"Spare the time?" He laughed. "Wild horses wouldn't to keep me away from an invitation like that, but I actually have to be in Hereford on Friday so can certainly bring the car up. The rest of the weekend is occupied with the SAS I'm afraid. I could spend Monday with you if you would like that? I have to be back here on Tuesday for lectures."

She hugged him once the cheque had been handed over. "Monday will be great. I'll look forward to that."

***

As David drove the new BMW into Lizzie's home in Hereford, he saw to his horror the commanding presence of Major Neville Powrie, Lizzie's husband, at six-feet-two and well-built standing in the driveway. He was dressed in uniform. It was nine o'clock in the evening. He was just closing his garage door. David parked the car, got out, stood to attention and saluted.

"Ah, Phillips, Daphne mentioned you'd helped buy her a new car." He gave the BMW a disinterested glance.

"Yes, sir, the old one was a wreck. It was dangerous and was condemned by the first dealer…"

"Hm, it was a bit old I suppose."

"If I may, sir, I'll just pop in to give ma'am the keys."

Powrie nodded.

Lizzie poked her head out of the upstairs entrance. Seeing the scenario, she said to David, "Thank you soldier, you've been a great help. I could drop you off at the base, if you like."

"Yes, thank you, ma'am." He looked at his watch. "Bit late for the bus…"

Powrie was waiting and watching. "I'll leave it to you then, Phillips. Thank you for your help."

David saluted, giving Lizzie the keys as Powrie went into his part of the house. David helped her adjust the seat. Nothing was said until they were well away from the house; then they both burst out laughing. Lizzie drove down a side road and parked. They spent five minutes kissing each other passionately. "Sorry, I have to be in barracks by nine thirty," said David interrupting, "but I look forward to seeing you on Monday."

There were others in the car park at the base, so David contented himself by squeezing Lizzie's leg as he hopped out, taking his kitbag.

During the weekend, David caught glimpses of Powrie, but there was no conversation. He thought he caught Powrie looking at him thoughtfully.

This is nuts, he thought. *Maybe I should just bugger off back home and forget all about Lizzie.*

He phoned Lizzie from a call box early on the Monday morning.

"He left last night," she reassured him. "I'll pick you up outside the base. The car is a beauty by the way. Neville took it for a spin yesterday; he said it was a good choice."

Back at Lizzie's mansion, they raced into the house. It was as if they had been separated for weeks. After an hour in bed, she looked at him. "Marvellous, that was lovely." They were silent for a few minutes while Lizzie cuddled up to him. "I'll take you to see the horses, if you like, maybe even go for a ride."

"Okay, great, I can catch the late train. I must be back in Oxford tonight."

"I'll take you, now I have a suitable car."

"No, absolutely not; that's crazy. But you can come to Oxford for the weekend if you like. Much the same as last time. Are you sure the gaffer doesn't concern himself with your whereabouts at weekends at all?" David added.

"I don't worry about his whereabouts much and I'm sure the same applies to him."

"Good. Because, after today, I won't have the excuse of helping you with your car anymore. It'll be obvious there's more to us than that. He could make life very difficult for me if he wanted." So difficult that David wondered again if he shouldn't just dump the whole business.

Is it really worth the risk? he thought. *I don't want to end up a casualty of some domestic war.*

He looked at her.

"I've never done this before, staying away for the weekend, I mean," she said, as if reading his thoughts. "I don't make a habit of this. I've had one lover since I found Neville in bed with the barmaid, and that didn't last. So if you're wondering if I care what happens to you if he finds out, then you have your answer: I care."

After that conversation there was no possibility that David could give up the affair with Lizzie. *I'll manage the risks.* He smiled to himself. *It is one of the things the SAS is supposed to teach people.*

The 'couple of hacks' turned out to be five very well-bred thoroughbreds in a well-kept stable. They went for a ride with Lizzie testing David's horsemanship to the limit, taking him over bigger and bigger jumps. "Pretty good," she said when they returned to the stables.

David realised it had been a deliberate test.

"You'll certainly do very well at the next hunt meeting," Lizzie exclaimed. "We just have time to go home for a bit of you know what, and I'll drop you at the station in time for your train."

It turned out that Lizzie owned and ran the stable, with two of the senior employees having small shares in the business. She explained, "Peter, the man that runs the place on a day-to-day basis has a five percent share and Stephanie, his sidekick, also owns five percent. It keeps them motivated."

From some of the conversations at the stables it was obvious that Lizzie knew all her employees very well. She seemed to know much about their daily lives. Lizzie explained further, "Peter's daughter had a major riding accident a year or two back and is partly paralysed. I'm helping with her rehabilitation."

David then realised there was a lot more to Lizzie than just being the OC's wife. The way she managed her people was admirable, and a clear lesson for him in the future, if he ever came to be responsible for managing people.

***

The next few months flew by, with Lizzie becoming a regular feature of the rugby fraternity and David going to Hereford for hunt meetings; he stayed with Lizzie when he could.

On one of Lizzie's early visits to Oxford she said to him, "You told me that a four percent return on the funds I have invested was low. How do I improve that?"

"Probably you need to change who looks after your investments! How big is the trust?"

"Oh, didn't I mention that? I inherited about fifty million. It's worth rather more than that now because of the reinvestment."

David was surprised but did not react. "It should still be making you more money."

"And I suppose you'd know how, if you were managing it?"

"Me? I'm not even qualified yet. But then again, if I'm being completely honest, yes if I had money to invest I'd certainly know how to make more than four percent off it. Even as an undergraduate! I think you're being taken for granted."

Lizzie was silent a moment, as if seriously contemplating what he'd said. David felt bad for her – four percent was pitifully low. Could he help her at all?

"You know, I wouldn't want to create a risk that would jeopardise your future, but I do think you could do better. If you wanted to give me a small portion to invest, I'd be happy to prove it to you?"

"How much is a small portion?"

He pretended to do a calculation. *Persist if you think you are right,* he told himself, remembering the Brecon Beacons. "A million?" It sounded a lot when he said it aloud. "If you want, I'll guarantee you the four percent, so you'll get that whatever happens. Then we could share any returns above four percent fifty-fifty – so if the investments make, say, ten percent, you will get another three percent and I will get three percent."

"What happens if the returns are below four percent in the first place?"

"They won't be, but I'll guarantee the four percent and make up any difference." It sounded like a great deal, even to David. Lizzie would get more money, and he could set himself up with a nest egg for the future and get real life experience of everything he'd been learning in theory. He found himself hoping she'd say 'yes'.

"I thought you were just a soldier," she said a moment later, smiling.

"I'm hoping to join an investment advisory firm when I leave university, Websters. They've already offered me a job, based on work experience I've done with them from time to time. For the sake of transparency, if I can join them with some sort of nest egg, which can be invested in the firm, it would really give me a leg up."

"Hm, I'll think about it. I have had plenty of financial fly-by-nighters come to me with idiotic schemes. How do I know you're not just going to rip me off and scarper with the money?"

David laughed. "How about, if you'd like to go ahead, I'll justify everything I do, and you sign it all off if before anything happens. If I run off with the loot, I am quite certain that the gaffer would get his mates in the SAS mafia to do me a great deal of damage. Anyway, I'm looking forward to a long career in the investment advisory business. Stealing your money would end that idea pretty damn quick. I'm quite sure the provisional job offer I have with Websters would be withdrawn if there was even the faintest whiff of any financial impropriety in my dealings with you or anyone else for that matter."

"Okay, I'll think about your million and let you know when we next meet."

David took her signal to drop the subject. But it made David think. "Following on from that, Lizzie, does Powrie know about our relationship? He sometimes looks at me in a strange, knowing kind of way."

"Yes. I decided to tell him before he asked any questions. As I have told you, he and I no longer have much of a relationship. He's almost like a tenant. He has his barmaids in from time to time. I don't worry about them. I don't suppose he worries about you. I told him I would have his balls for breakfast if he took it out on you. He's not an unfair man. It might be a bit different if our affair was more public."

"Not one person has said anything to me at the base."

Lizzie shrugged. "Good then."

It seemed good enough, so David let it go, along with his proposal to manage any of her fortune. He'd said all he needed to say to get her thinking.

It was Lizzie who then raised the subject, a few months later. "I've arranged with my advisors to let you have a million in cash. All you have to do is make contact with this man, here are the details." She handed him an unsealed envelope, which he opened, then scanned at the contents, which consisted of a typed sheet of paper on a formal letterhead using her Hereford address.

He kissed her, as he stuffed the envelope into his jacket pocket. "You are very sweet, thank you. I won't let you down." He made a promise to himself to ensure he didn't.

"No, I don't suppose you will."

Over the next few weeks, David committed himself to thoroughly researching every investment opportunity he could find, then ensuring Lizzie's money was invested safely and correctly.

In the meantime, they still couldn't get enough of each other, with both making every effort to meet as often as they were able. Sometimes David wondered if he was compromising his university results.

Could I be back to the situation I was in at the time of the Gwyneth business? he shuddered at the thought.

But no, he was dedicated to his new life – less and less student drinking, less and less sports ego; more and more study, more and more SAS. He was enjoying it too. On at least two occasions, he had even turned down invitations from Lizzie to fulfil an SAS request.

"Dammed SAS," she had griped. "I've given up half my life for that bloody organisation."

They'd laughed about it, but it had made David think. Where was their relationship going? Did it have any long-term potential? *I'm really not in a position to marry her... and the age difference...* he thought. *And if we were ever to take things further, would it put an end to my involvement with the SAS?*

He wasn't sure how he felt about that.

Lizzie must have been thinking about their future too, because after Powrie asked Lizzie to accompany him to a major British army function in London, she told David with a nostalgic tone, "I owe him, at least that much."

"Forgive me for asking," David responded, "but would you ever want to put your marriage back on track? You never mention divorce or anything like that."

She answered quicker than he was expecting. "Divorce is impossible for all sorts of reasons. But... since you ask, yes, I probably would like to put my marriage back together if I could." She allowed a tear to slip out, but continued, "You've given me so much, David, but I wouldn't want to be an old woman with a much younger husband, even if that was on the cards, which I don't think it is. If I'm going to have children it had better be soon too, and there's no way you're ready for that."

David held her hand. "I love you dearly. But, yes, I need to establish myself financially before I marry, and that might be years down the track. In the meantime, though, we can make the most of what you and I undoubtedly have. If you ever do want to go back to him, please just let me know. And if you want my advice, one way of repairing your marriage would be to settle a significant sum on the gaffer. He's probably mildly concerned about what he will live on when he retires in a few years' time."

"That's very kind of you, David, to think of that."

"I think of such things because I will always want you as a friend, Lizzie, no matter what happens. I would do almost anything to preserve that."

"What about the funds you're looking after for me – if I asked you to return them, would you do that?"

"Yes of course. Immediately."

Another tear slipped out. "Sorry," she said. "I know I can trust you, I just needed to check; but you're better than that. Come on, come to bed."

David followed her into the bedroom, determined to relish every moment he had with her. But, eventually, he saw that her analysis of the situation also reflected his views.

Thank God she is not some over-emotional teenager, he thought. *I suppose the way we're playing this out is a bit cold blooded.*

Slowly, the weeks between their meetings slowed; until a gap of three months had elapsed and they hadn't been able to meet. David was about to make what had become his twice weekly phone call when he was surprised to receive a letter. He recognised Lizzie's handwriting as he hastily tore the envelope open, revealing a three-page letter. He sat down to read it, knowing that it would change their relationship forever; she had never written to him before.

'Dear, dear darling David,' it started out. *'To say that I have enjoyed our affair would understate the situation by about a thousand times. I have loved every minute of it and I relive many of our little adventures from the time you rescued me in the shopping centre car park to the wonderful weekends in Oxford and so on. In many ways you have helped me put my life together again. You will remember your suggestion, that in order to rebuild my marriage I should settle a decent amount of money on Neville – so I gave him five million, telling him that that was all that was coming to him and that if he pissed that away that was it.'*

Five million! David thought. *Far too much, I would have given him two.* He read on.

'Under the circumstances, dear boy, I have agreed with Neville that my affair with you should end. I am so, so sorry about this, but I have sensed that the passion between us is waning. We haven't seen each other for a couple of months now...'

74

The letter continued, reliving much of the fun they had enjoyed.

'*I have just received your latest report on the investments you manage for me. All very satisfactory, as you know your results are a huge improvement on what I have been getting over the past few years. So I have instructed my advisors to transfer fifty percent of my remaining funds, about thirty million, for you to manage. You did well in going to cash, and then we repurchased many of the shares at lower costs. My advisors actually lost ground over the past two years or so. So thank you for that. I suppose we will meet from time to time to discuss progress on my investments. When you are established at Websters, I will be happy to recommend you to some of my friends and acquaintances, they should look to you for advice.*

If you wish to phone me, please do – you know when Neville is at the base. The other momentous news is that I am pregnant, something I am very happy about; I am certain Neville is the father.

Love, love, love, love. I will miss you but this is the best way for both of us. I am convinced that this break will be an investment in both our futures – sometimes you have to take risks to get results!

Lizzie.'

Pregnant? thought David. Maybe Powrie, but if she's already certain, then maybe not.

He phoned at the appropriate time.

"You got my letter?" asked a very thoughtful Lizzie.

"Yes, of course."

"It took me several attempts to get it right. Tell me what you think."

"It's a wonderful, wonderful letter. I can't believe that anyone would be able to write such a letter. I will treasure it always."

"Are you upset?"

"Lizzie, I will miss you desperately. I ask just one thing."

"What?"

"If things go haywire with Powrie in future, you'll let me know."

"I am not anticipating that, but yes, of course I will. We will have continuous contact with the investments so there is a channel of communication. Neville knows about your involvement in all that, in case you were wondering."

They chatted on for another few minutes before ringing off.

David then sat for staring into space for half an hour before jumping up and making his way to one of his lectures. He was down in the dumps for days after the phone call.

What have I done, what have I done? he kept saying to himself. *Why did you ever make that suggestion to Lizzie about sorting out her marriage?*

He picked up the phone several times, without actually making a call. The one time he did ring, it rang and rang, but luckily there was no answer.

After another month, he started to see sense in what had occurred.

The gaffer would surely not have tolerated the situation for much longer, he rationalised, *maybe he would have found a way to get rid of me...*

He shuddered at the thought of what the SAS mafia might have done to him if the situation persisted. Gradually he found he was able to distance himself from any thoughts of Lizzie.

I still have her as a friend, he thought, and he continued to do his level best to manage her investments as well as he possibly could.

His commitment to the SAS meant there was still contact with Powrie, but nothing was ever said, nor was there any hint of the role David had played in his and Lizzie's life.

In many ways, David simply found himself grateful that things hadn't gone worse for him, as they had with Gwyneth, or Powrie could have sent the SAS mafia after him.

Then he met Melinda in the university library and found himself grateful all over again that things had ended with Lizzie.

Chapter 5. Melinda

As soon as Melinda met David, she was deeply intrigued. Not only was he well-spoken and polite, but he was sexy as anything and charming with it. She knew they would soon become lovers.

The first time they made love, he even asked between kisses, "Mel, I would like to make love to you."

With her two previous boyfriends, she had just been treated to a bit of rough and tumble and then clumsy sex, nobody had actually asked if she wanted to make love.

"Yes, of course, undress me slowly," she had said.

She found he was the most considerate lover and always tried to ensure her pleasure first before worrying about his own.

But it was more than sex. Melinda just knew, somehow, that David was her match. Maybe even enough to marry one day. Everything she was lacking, he offered. Everything he lacked; she had in spades.

"You're so beautiful," David told her all the time. "I love your long dark locks, slim but well-endowed where it matters."

"David!"

"I mean your brains of course!" He laughed.

The only downside to being with David was that he went away every other weekend.

"Where do you go every other weekend?" she had asked early on.

"A while ago I was accepted as a member of the SAS Reserve. It's very difficult to get in, and even more difficult to be accepted as part of the team. But I've completed all the training now and will expect to be deployed on various operations soon."

"The SAS? That's something to do with the army isn't it?" she'd asked, confused.

"Yes." David had then explained why he had volunteered and what was involved. It sounded like the other reservists had an issue with David's privileged background, something he was determined to prove them wrong about. "I belong there, Mel. Sometimes I don't always know what I'm doing, but my instincts are good, my commitment is solid – all I need now is experience in the field. That will come, of course."

"Experience in the field? You mean you may have to fight in a war zone or something?"

"Yes. That is certainly part of the deal as far as I am concerned."

"Couldn't you have found something less dangerous and still achieved your objective of helping the country and developing yourself at the same time?"

"I couldn't think of anything. I still can't."

"What about Voluntary Service Overseas, VSO?"

"Hm, not quite the same thing. Mostly it's just a year. I'm not sure how valuable it is for untrained twenty-year olds to be sent to a country they know nothing about, to try to teach them something. I'm told they do some good." David had shrugged.

"Fine," Melinda had accepted his reasons, "but don't expect me to vacate your flat as early as you do on a Friday morning. I like my sleep-ins. And your place is so neat and quiet, especially compared to my own situation: on a busy road, shared with two other girls. It's... beautiful," she'd said generously, "unusual for a student."

"Parents insisted on it," he said. "I'm expected to get decent results of course."

"Parents?" She was instantly fascinated by David's relatively opulent background. She hesitated before saying, "You're very lucky. My scholarship only provides the basics. Mum and Dad can't spare much so I work during the holidays."

"If I get a reasonable degree, through family connections I'm more or less guaranteed a position at Websters," David said, barely registering what she was trying to tell him.

"What is 'Websters'?"

"A well respected medium sized investment advisory business."

"And what's a 'reasonable' degree?"

"Upper second, maybe even a first."

Melinda had laughed. "Anything less than a first would be a disaster as far as I'm concerned."

"What degree are you doing again?"

"Physics. But I'm considering adding another subject."

"That would be a huge commitment. What are you thinking of?"

"Commerce. I could possibly see myself being a part of something like Websters. I have a friend who graduated last year. She did physics, like me, and was snapped up by one of the leading merchant banks. She's told me that some knowledge of commerce would have been useful." In fact, Melinda wondered if she could inject a note of entrepreneurship into a business such as Websters.

"I thought physics usually led to research establishments?"

"Too boring. Opportunities in the commercial world are much more rewarding and immediate."

Two weekends after this conversation, Melinda was looking forward to having David to herself, David having spent the previous weekend on a training exercise; but he said to her, "Look, Mel, I'm sorry, I hope this doesn't spoil anything, but I've been asked by the university to play rugby for them this weekend. Their regular fly half is injured. The game is in town, I was hoping I could persuade you come and watch. I have a ticket for you in the very best place." He smiled his most charming smile.

She was disappointed but said, "Great, I would love to come. I've never been to a rugby game before; my family were all into 'the game'. You'll have to explain something of its rules to me."

David played well. He scored two tries, which he converted, and kicked two penalty goals. Oxford won easily. As considerate as ever, David had already told the team he wouldn't be able to attend the function after the game. And when she went to meet him, he was already freshly showered and changed. He was also talking with the team coach or manager, standing in the entrance to the football field, his kit bag at his feet. He had obviously taken trouble with his appearance, dressed in a pair of grey slacks and a light jacket. Melinda spent a few seconds, unseen, admiring her new love.

"You could be a regular member of this team," the manager was saying to David curtly, "but you'd need to be more involved for that to happen."

"I'd be happy to play for the team, whenever you want, but I'm committed to the SAS every other weekend, as you know. I also have my studies and other significant commitments," David glanced happily at Melinda as she approached.

The coach threw his hands up in frustration and walked away, clearly not used to playing second fiddle to anyone. He probably had people scrambling to get into the team, one of the most sought after in the university.

As they watched the coach disappear, David shrugged. "There is only one of me," he said to Melinda, "they may not ask me again."

"I don't know much about rugby, but if I were asked I would say you were the best player on the field."

He kissed her. "Thank you. Actually I don't care one way or the other; I suppose that's my strength in this matter. If they ask me and I'm available, I'll play. For the moment I'm all yours."

She glanced at him, thinking about those words: 'for the moment'. David was and would always be his own man, independent and forthright about it. Was that something she could live with, moving forward?

Whether it was or wasn't, they were together right now, and for tonight at least their path was clear…

"It's still early," she said, taking his arm. "So I suggest we retire to the bedroom for an hour or so, then that restaurant you asked me to book, and back to bed. It will be nice to have you to myself for a while." She hugged him, and he squeezed her back.

∗

It was clear to Melinda that David tried his best to manage his commitment to the SAS, while avoiding unnecessary clashes in his arrangements with her. Still, she was curious. On the first instance when he suddenly had to go away for the weekend on SAS business, she said to him, "Can't you tell me anything about where you are going and what you are doing?"

"I can't," he said. "I've signed something to that effect. It's to do with the Official Secrets Act."

"You mean running around with a pack and a rifle in the Brecon Beacons is secret?" Melinda had laughed. "Go on pull the other one."

An unfazed David had smiled. "That's all long gone. I do other things now."

"And you can't tell me anything about that."

"No."

"So this could all be a load of bullshit, just a cover for a secret girlfriend somewhere." She knew this wasn't true, but she enjoyed goading David.

"Ha, ha," David laughed. "You know bloody well that's not true. Our activities when I return would hardly be possible if that were the case."

"Is what you do dangerous?" she asked in a more serious tone.

"Ha, ha, again. If you think you can get me into any discussion on the subject, think again. You won't, sorry."

"What am I expected to do during these weekends when you're away?"

David shrugged. "Well, I don't suppose you actually need any advice on that subject. You do all that rowing. You're very smart. And your second degree sounds like it'll keep you out of mischief." He laughed.

Melinda knew that David always had to go to the SAS base in Hereford for all his assignments or for any training exercises, so the only uniform he kept in Oxford was the uniform he used for daily use. All his other equipment was kept in Hereford, so as far as Melinda was concerned there were few clues there.

"Not recently but in the past, I've seen you here and there in Oxford with a very attractive woman," said Melinda, curious to find out more about David.

"Yes," he said. "I thought I'd have to tell you about her at some point. Her name's Lizzie and we were together for a while. But it's been over for months now and we're just friends." He showed her a letter. "I've thought about this," David said, looking at her, "and I just don't want there to be any secrets between us. I realise dealing with the SAS is difficult for you, there is no need to add to that."

Melinda read the letter twice before handing it back to him. She said nothing for a few minutes. "Thank you. She looks a bit older than you?"

"She is."

"Promise you haven't been two-timing me?"

"I promise I haven't been two-timing you."

"You are most unusual. Rare as rocking horse shit as they say. Most people would have kept a letter like that to themselves."

"I'm not most people."

"Mnn, I think I'm beginning to realise that."

"As is obvious from the letter, I am still looking after some of Lizzie's investments, so I will have contact with her from time to time," said David. "I'm hoping the money make will set me up with a nest egg for the future. Is that okay with you?"

Melinda wasn't sure. She reminded herself that she was dating an independent and forthright man. Even as she nodded her head, it didn't make her feel any better.

***

University passed in a blur of assignments, exams, trying unsuccessfully to put all thought of Lizzie and the letter out of her mind, and seeing David whenever she could. He had arranged to spend a summer in South Africa between his second and final year, working on farms owned by some relatives. One of them was a mixed farm in the Natal Midlands, not far from Pietermaritzburg; and the other was a sugar farm near Eshowe in Zululand. As soon as he left, she already knew she would miss him terribly. They spoke and wrote as often as they could. His relatives were extremely hospitable, he said, and had lent him a vehicle so he could travel the country with Melinda when she joined him for a few weeks. As far as Melinda was concerned, being together with David, just the two of them, for those weeks would test their relationship and what it stood for.

Now almost ten years after Nelson Mandela's release from prison, and almost at the end of his five years as president, they discussed the changes that had been made to the country, with the advent of majority rule. The only black people David had had any real contact with, he said, were farm workers and, as far as he could see, nothing much had changed for them or indeed would change. His hosts were generally in favour of the changes but were apprehensive about the long-term developments and whether there was a cadre of Africans who had the skills to run the country; many of the younger generation of whites had emigrated, and continued to emigrate, to Australia, Canada and Great Britain in the main.

"The apartheid regime is an unworkable disaster," David told her as they drove to Cathedral Peak one day, one of the major peaks in the Drakensberg mountains. "Though I do appreciate the fact that the British Empire itself has been run on a racially discriminatory basis for centuries. Where hasn't, in fact? But no, though I've enjoyed my time in South Africa immensely, I'm ready to get on with my career now, happy to get home. Here we are." He parked in the car park. "It's a steep climb, with a couple of wire ladders at the end, as I understand it, to get to the top," David said to Melinda. "But we'll manage."

"Don't we need a guide or something? What happens if we get lost?" asked Melinda. "Or if the weather turns against us?"

"I am trained," said David smiling. "I can read a map and not get lost!"

They walked out of the car park and made their way to a footpath up the mountain. They both carried backpacks with warm clothing, rain gear and some food. Still, Melinda couldn't stop thinking about what David had said.

"A walk-up Cathedral is mere bagatelle," he told her, "compared to what we had to endure to be accepted as a member of the SAS reserve."

Melinda didn't reply. She, for one, admired the changes that had been made to the country's political spectrum over the past years, and David's apparent indifference to what had occurred was... irritating. "You don't seem particularly appreciative of the steep path these people have had to climb." She pointed to their own steep path as they puffed their way up it. "Can't you see the evil that has now been completely excised from the system here?"

"Well, of course, but I don't see it as having much to do with me personally. I won't win or lose anything by the changes here. It will have a profound effect on the lives of the people we have been staying with though, and of course on most of the black population." He further irritated her by adding, "Your remark seems to indicate naïvely that suddenly all is well under the new regime."

"And your remark seems to indicate you don't care what happens here. Your bloody relatives have lived high on the hog on the backs of the blacks and other races here."

"Sure, but all the colonies in the British Empire or Commonwealth were run on the same lines, exactly the same lines. And if you think attitudes are any different in Britain, think again; there's still massive discrimination at home. It's all very well to run around attacking the white population here in South Africa, when frankly we have nothing to write home about."

"I still think that you could be more positive about the changes that have occurred here."

David shrugged. "Maybe you should examine your own situation before you run around with this patronising attitude about what's going on here." Melinda was about to respond when David continued in his mild way, "How many black friends do you have, real friends? Have you ever invited them home? Have you got to know any of your black fellow classmates at university? Our society is as discriminatory as any I can think of, including the one here; if you want to do anything you should think of starting at home in England."

They stopped for a breather and to admire the view, with the majesty of the massive mountain range above them and the apparent benign beauty of the rolling hills of Natal extending eastwards to the horizon. They were able to make out the faint ribbon of the Tugela River flowing from the mountains to the sea. David attempted to distract Melinda by trying to identify the various peaks in the range, many of which were partially obscured by high cloud. He would have happily moved on to other subjects, but Melinda was determined to continue with the conversation.

As they moved on up the well-worn path she said: "At least we've never legislated for active discrimination," she muttered.

"We don't need to," said David, as he turned around again to admire the view, "the brown and black English people are in a minority. The society itself fuels the discrimination. What I have concluded is that, fundamentally, we are no different to the white people here in South Africa, many of whom have a similar background to us. The big difference is that our whole existence is not threatened by any changes that are made. Here, everything will change."

Melinda looked at him angrily without responding directly to his comments. "At least we have had black and brown representatives in our sports teams, people like Nasser Husain, the cricketer, and Basil D'Oliveira, he's a South African and should have played for South Africa; he played for England for God's sake."

David shrugged dismissively. "Sure. I still stand by what I have said. In the discrimination stakes we have nothing to crow about."

"Urgh, you do annoy me sometimes."

David laughed. "Sorry, that wasn't my purpose. Having spent time here I just started to think about our situation at home. Maybe we could talk about something else." He patted her on the arm as they continued their arduous walk up the mountain.

A gesture she regarded as patronising.

Will it always be like this? she wondered. *My point of view always so easily dismissed... I wonder.*

Indeed, she was beginning to wonder whether he would make the ideal partner for her after all. The dry way he analysed things often irritated her, especially as he was often right. He seemed to lack emotion. Now this.

They pushed on up the mountain, and by late morning they had arrived at what appeared to be a steep climb. "This is probably the climb to the top," said David. "I suggest we leave our back packs here under a bush, climb to the top, then come back and eat what we have for lunch. It's probably thirty minutes to the top and a bit less coming back. We should take the camera and binocs."

"Won't someone steal all our stuff if we leave it here?" asked Melinda.

"I've had a good look back at the path coming up. I don't see another soul. It's a weekday. Most people will be at work."

So they scrambled their way up the rest of the climb, negotiating a couple of steep wire ladders. It was breezy at the top and every few minutes they were enveloped in swirling cloud. They took several photographs, signed the book and replaced it in the tin that somehow managed to keep the weather out. They carefully edged their way down to where they had left their backpacks.

"We should get off the path a bit," suggested David, as he picked up both packs and walked fifty metres, finding a sunny little glade surrounded by bushes. "This should do."

Unaccountably Melinda still felt irritated with their political conversation; and unaccountably David seemed to sense it. He put his arms around her and leant in. "Come, kiss me, it's a beautiful day and there's nobody about."

She eventually relaxed and melted into his arms, and he slowly removed all her clothing piece by piece, as well as his own, and they made love lying on the discarded items in the soft grass.

"How far to the hotel?" asked Melinda as they ate the few sandwiches they had brought for lunch.

"Couple of hours, there's no hurry."

"We can stay here for a bit then?"

"Sure. Anything you like."

"I'm going to do a bit of sunbathing. Perhaps you could help me with the sun cream?"

"Certainly. I can't think of anything I would rather do, covering every inch of a beautiful naked you with sun cream. Gives me an additional opportunity to massage particular very attractive parts of you."

When he was in such a mood, all Melinda's doubts faded away completely.

"This one we'll call Cathedral Peak," he said massaging one of her now very erect breasts, "and this one the Injasuti."

"What are you talking about?"

"A couple of the peaks of this magnificent mountain range. I could make one of them Cathkin, if you prefer?"

"You are talking complete nonsense."

"And this down here, The Promised Land," he put his hand between her legs. "It can be the mighty Tugela, the source of all life, certainly as far as the Zulus go. This mountain range is the source of the river as you know."

She laughed delightedly. "You do talk utter nonsense. Come on, make love to me again…"

Late in the afternoon, they made their way back to the hotel. They struggled into dinner and slept the sleep of the dead once they had returned to their room.

***

A few days later, they found themselves in what was had been known as the Transkei. "Nelson Mandela land," David observed, then cringed as if wishing he hadn't.

"Along with all your other irritating observations regarding the situation here, how do you feel about Mr Mandela now?"

"Having been here a while," he smiled at Melinda, "for what it's worth, it's my opinion that he will be the man of the 20th century: he persuaded one of the most hard-line regimes in the world to release him from jail, without any conditions, he negotiated with that regime, over a number of years, to allow free and fair elections –

which they knew spelt the end for them and their regime, and would result in majority rule in this country. He almost certainly saved the country from a bloody civil war and the whole population supports him now: Black, White, Coloured, Indian. Somehow, he has persuaded the white population in particular to give up their power and, from all the conversations I've had over past months, almost every white I've met supports Mandela; quite amazing."

They drove on in silence for another half hour, thinking their own thoughts.

David then added, "All I can say is that the result is truly remarkable, right up there with Gandhi, King and possibly others I've forgotten. I just hope that some lunatic doesn't take it into his head to assassinate him."

Melinda looked at him with a surprised look on her face. Maybe he had listened to her after all?

"And you have to remember," David continued, "before he was released from prison, there was an on-going massive propaganda campaign vilifying Mandela and the ANC. The Nationalist Government had persuaded many western nations to brand him a terrorist. Coming back from all that, just one man, is truly remarkable. If there is a God, he certainly blessed South Africa by sending Mandela to rescue them."

Melinda looked at him. "At last, some emotion on one of the most significant events of the last half of the twentieth century."

"Mandela delivered the political solution. He won't last forever. Others will have to follow up and make sure it all sticks. I don't see many that are capable of that," David muttered, then quickly looked at her. "Please don't be angry with me for thinking that, Mel – many of our countrymen have run around crowing about what has happened here, as if they were personally responsible for the changes. The developments here are South African arrangements negotiated by South Africans on the ground, without interference from ignorant fools from outside. What pisses me off mightily is the fucking hypocrisy of it all from *our side*. We have a lot to do at home and that's where we should focus. Most of us British had no real idea what was going on here and accepted the dictum that Mandela was a terrorist as determined by most western governments." He hesitated before adding in a more conciliatory tone, "actually except the British Government, who I understand kept in the background, which really helped the process by talking to both parties – that is the Nats and the ANC – and providing safe houses away from prying eyes for constructive meetings to take place. Thankfully Mandela is now accepted as a statesman and a hero for what he has been through."

They drove on in silence for a few minutes, then Melinda leant over and kissed him on the cheek. "Sorry, I got carried away."

"Sorry I did too." David then explained that the area of the Transkei as it was known, was, during the apartheid years, a sort of independent country for the larger Xhosa tribe. "The whole bloody thing was ridiculous; the economy was propped up by the South African government and the president was just a puppet of the South African regime. The only country to recognise the independence of the Transkei was South Africa itself. The Thembu are a clan of the wider Xhosa hegemony; Mandela is a hereditary chief of the Thembu, based in Qunu." To Melinda's amusement David was even able to pronounce Qunu correctly, using the Xhosa click in the right place.

"The place looks like rather barren compared to the areas where your relatives live," Melinda observed as David carefully drove through a herd of goats moving from one side of the road to the other looking for a slightly greener tuft of grass. She glanced uneasily at the scrawny cattle being herded by what looked like ten-year-old boys dressed in loincloths or a ragged pair of shorts for the lucky ones; most had bare feet. To Melinda's surprise they all seemed to be remarkably cheerful, waving and grinning with their beautiful white teeth contrasting sharply with brown dusty faces. Melinda waved back, eliciting more friendly waves.

"Yup, it was set aside in the nineteenth century," David continued once they were past the goats, "for the then quite small Xhosa population. Now it is wholly inadequate, due to population growth. It's the same throughout Africa. As you can see it is thoroughly overgrazed. This population growth suited the Nationalist Government, because what they needed was labour to run the factories in the Witwatersrand and the other major cities, so many from the so-called reserve areas moved to the cities. Also, and despite the massive movement of people into the cities during the height of the hypocrisy of Apartheid, the government could claim that all the blacks were temporary workers from the various homelands and that they would all eventually return to those homelands, 'where they can run their own affairs as they like' was the quote. The white population with few exceptions bought all this crap, mainly because they were all doing very well economically. As you can see, the standard of living of the white population continues to be very high. There are of course an increasing number of blacks who are also doing very well. Maybe that will be the saving grace of the country in the end."

"Maybe," Melinda muttered, impressed with his knowledge. There was certainly a depth to David that she hadn't fully appreciated back in England. Or maybe South Africa had given him that?

I am certainly in love with him, she thought to herself. *And there certainly wouldn't be as much financial struggle as I was anticipating with him by my side, given he's already quite well off. I hate myself for thinking that of course – I should either continue our relationship because of love or bale out and go my own way.*

Still the thought remained. As did her reservations.

So it came as quite a shock when, a few days before she was due to go home, on a deserted beach near Jeffreys Bay an hour's drive from Port Elizabeth, David got down on one knee as Melinda was sunbathing topless and to her surprise said: "Mel, I truly, truly love you, will you marry me?"

In that moment, there was no hesitation. She simply reached up, put her arms round his neck and kissed him. "Yes, of course I will marry you, once I have completed both my degrees," she responded and kissed him again. She then added: "David, I hope you understand that I need to be able to do justice to my time at Oxford and all it stands for. I also need to be in a position to make a career for myself and see if I am able to really use the brains I've been gifted with."

David looked slightly surprised at her remarks, but said, "Of course you do, darling. Our degrees come first."

Melinda laughed at the pun, then kissed him some more.

It was hard to leave him a few days later, when he dropped her off at Johannesburg's recently named O.R. Tambo airport; but he'd already forewarned her that he was staying an extra three weeks. He'd been asked by the SAS to provide information on the strength and preparedness of the South African Military.

"Aren't you giving away state secrets by telling me that?" she'd enjoyed goading him.

"It's no big deal," he'd said, smiling. "It will be interesting, though, to see how they have integrated resistance fighters with the people they were fighting, mostly white South African soldiers."

"Interesting, but not dangerous?" Melinda clarified.

He merely kissed her and said, "I'll see you in three weeks."

PART 2: WEBSTERS

Chapter 6. Marriage and Websters

Not long after he returned from South Africa, David had a revelation. He was engaged to be married but wasn't spending nearly enough time with his fiancée. So he said to Melinda, "I would be very happy if you moved in with me here; we can get married as soon as both of us have graduated."

Melinda said she needed no second invitation, so they spent their last year at Oxford living together and beavering away at their studies. David converted his flat's small second bedroom into a study. "One of us can use the lounge area and the other the study," said David. "You choose."

"Well, if you are happy about that I would like the study," Melinda said, seemingly surprised by the opportunity.

But then David had been working from the sofa and table this whole time, so he really didn't care one way or the other.

They both worked very hard. David had his regular SAS commitments, together with his occasional game for the Oxford rugby side; and Melinda was almost totally consumed with doing enough work to do justice to her two degrees, as well as her rowing. Still, there was something he needed Melinda to do.

"I would like to introduce you to my parents," David told her one day. "A weekend at home maybe…?"

"Sure. If anything, I wish I'd suggested it myself!"

"They'll probably give us separate bedrooms. We'll have to put up with their old-fashioned views."

"Okay. Thanks for the warning. I expect I will be able to survive a couple of nights without being able to hug your nice warm body." She smiled.

The weekend seemed to go reasonably well, and Melinda managed to develop some sort of relationship with David's mother.

However, towards the end of the weekend, David's father Walter suggested father and son go for a walk. "I just want to talk to you on your own…"

Once they were away from the house and admiring the view across a sunny valley facing South, David's father said, "I really don't understand what you are doing with that girl Melinda. She comes from a poor working-class background. Frankly you could do much better than that. She's after your money, class and position…"

David looked at him aghast. "Dad, please. I love her, don't you understand that. I can't live without her and don't intend to. She is one of the brightest students at the university and will probably finish with two firsts in very difficult subjects, Physics and Commerce. Please don't think of interfering in any way."

"Your elder brother is a good example. He captained the England rugby side, has now got a position with a leading firm of lawyers in the city, and is engaged to marry the daughter of one of the leading aristocrats in England. I expect he will be nominated for a safe Conservative seat in the Commons shortly, and you are running around with this working-class tart."

David was deeply unhappy about his father's attitude, so much he briefly thought of just walking away from the situation, but instead said: "I'm disappointed in your attitude, Dad, which somehow seems to be steeped somewhere in the nineteenth century. If the SAS has taught me anything, it's that British class attitudes are holding us back as a country. Those attitudes are now quite out of date. I'm glad to say that more and more Oxford undergraduates are being admitted from State schools – at least the university authorities have woken up to the understanding that brains are not the exclusive privilege of the so-called upper classes."

"We should never have even started to educate the great unwashed…"

"Dad, stop. I hear what you're saying, but I can't reject it strongly enough. Could we go home now." He stalked off.

Somehow they struggled through the rest of the weekend and it was with some relief that on the Sunday afternoon David and Melinda were able to pack up and return to their neat little flat in Oxford.

"I got on reasonably well with your mother, Helen," said Melinda once they were on the road.

"Yes, she told me to try and not worry too much about Dad's attitude, so I won't. He had a go at me when we went out for a walk… he's obsessed with my elder brother's success and takes little notice of me."

"We should visit your brother and his fiancée; perhaps on one of the weekend's you play for the university rugby side."

"Smart idea. We'll do just that."

Soon after, they also had a weekend with Melinda's parents in Rochdale, which David saw as an outer suburb of Greater Manchester. He had taken the trouble to understand Melinda's father's interests. "He supports Bolton in one of the lower EPL leagues, heaven knows why. I'm sure he would he delighted to take you to one of the team's home games," Melinda had told him.

Predictably, Melinda's father Fred said to David on their arrival, "I've got you a ticket to the Bolton game tomorrow, Saturday. Should be a good game."

"Lovely," said David. They had a conversation about the prospects for the game and the team composition.

"You follow football?" asked Fred.

"A bit," answered David. "I actually play rugby for the university, but only occasionally now. My SAS duties come first."

"The SAS?" Fred sounded intrigued, so David told him what he could. Later, after the game, Fred took David to introduce him to his friends at the local pub and seemed proud to mention David's SAS membership.

David always parried any questions regarding his SAS activities by saying, "I'm sorry, I can't tell you anything much. I had to sign something to that effect when I joined." Still, he felt proud to be seen as part of such an esteemed group.

After their visit, Melinda told David, "Dad expected you to be a bit stuck-up, but he said you're alright. The effort you have made to get to know him is much appreciated."

"It wasn't a big effort. I enjoyed our outings to the football and the pub. The people are very welcoming and friendly. Also I don't feel that I have to be 'on show' all the time, I can just be myself..." He shrugged. "It felt natural."

Natural. That's how being in the SAS felt to David now – like it was a part of who he was and always had been.

Suddenly he felt very grateful to Gwyneth.

***

A month before they both took their final exams, over dinner one evening Melinda said to David: "I have some news for you."

"Oh, what's that?" asked David, disinterestedly thinking about what would probably be his last rugby game for the university on the coming Saturday.

"I'm pregnant. Two months, the doctor confirmed it today."

For a brief second David was stunned by the unexpected news, but then he quickly gathered himself, stood up and took Melinda in his arms saying, "Mel, that's wonderful, wonderful. How do you feel about that?"

"To my surprise I'm actually thrilled to bits. It's temporarily put paid to my ambitions of getting a job in the merchant banking business though..."

David picked her up, carried her to the bedroom, stripped off all her clothing whilst getting rid of his own, and they made the most gentle love that either of them had ever known.

Melinda giggled. "Well, that was a wonderful surprise. Just wonderful…"

"What do you want to do about your dinner?" asked David.

"Forget the bloody dinner. Just come here and let me hug you again."

They made love again a few minutes later.

David cleaned up the partly eaten dinner.

The next morning David said: "We'll have to get married a bit sooner than I thought, which is great. We need to think about that, as I'm due to join Websters in September, so there are a few practical issues we need to deal with. Exams first."

Over the next few weeks, they told each set of parents of Melinda's pregnancy. They all knew that David and Melinda lived together, and all seemed to be happy to be expecting their first grandchild, except for David's father who said nothing.

"Where are we going to live?" asked Melinda.

"Websters is in the Holborn Bloomsbury area, so it has to be London somewhere."

"Okay. Where?"

"Well, I've never mentioned this before but I now own this flat. My parents bought it for my brother when he was here. He passed it on to me and now, after his last visit, he has passed ownership on to me.

I have been doing a bit of research and I like the look of Barnes in Southwest London."

"Can we afford that with me not working, at least for a while?"

"I think so. If we sell the flat here we will have enough for a deposit on a house. I have also earned a fair bit from managing Lizzie's shareholdings, which will ease the burden a bit. We can look around after our exams…"

"And our wedding? I don't want a big hoo-haa by the way," said Melinda.

"Sounds good to me. So let's just concentrate on these final exams, then the fun can begin."

But a week or so later, David realised he'd already spoken too soon. Not everyone was on his and Melinda's exam schedule, and the kidnapping of Sergeant Jones almost put everything at risk.

He was still shaking with adrenalin when he sat his final paper – privately thanks to the rector. Afterwards, he said to Melinda, "I think I did it justice, despite the interruption. I'll just have to hope for the best."

"The real work was in the weeks, months, and years leading up to that exam," she tried to reassure him. "I'm sure you'll be fine."

After their exams, they were married in a registry office in Oxford. Both sets of parents attended as well as a number of their Oxford fraternity friends, including their rugby and rowing colleagues. Powrie and Lizzie were persuaded to attend. There was an informal celebration at The Randolph afterwards, paid for discretely by David's father, who had been persuaded by David's mother Helen to accept David's genuine love for Melinda. Their exam results helped.

David graduated with a first in history, which was somewhat overshadowed by Melinda being awarded two firsts, which she saw as a result of her hard work.

There was of course no mention made of David having to rescue Jones while he was right in the middle of his exam schedule.

***

After Milton Keynes, David regularly phoned the hospital where his fellow SAS team members were recuperating. He paid them several visits during their rehabilitation. Once James Templeton's good friend Alan Jenkins was out of hospital, David suggested they pay James' parents a visit. "Maybe Catherine Roberts should come as well?" suggested David.

David had been to James' funeral. His status was obvious as he was in uniform. He did briefly explain that he was James' OC during the rescue, but due to the large numbers of people attending there was no opportunity to have much of a conversation with either parent.

The three of them eventually made their way to James' parents' house in a well-to-do suburb of Chester. Catherine Roberts had already seen Mr and Mrs Templeton, together with Powrie, in order to tell them of James' demise.

They were greeted politely by Mrs Templeton, who had laid on tea and scones for her visitors. "I was not able to have much of a conversation with you at James' funeral, so I thought that now Alan is in recovery, we would just like to see if there was anything we could do to ease what is obviously a very painful situation for you both," said David. "You obviously know Catherine, but I would also like to introduce Alan Jenkins, who was also involved in the rescue and was injured in the explosion."

"Well, thank you for coming," answered James' father. "Death is so final, and there is nothing any of us can do to change that. James was very proud to have been selected to be a member of the SAS reserve, he was also in the process of setting up a plumbing business, here in Chester." Despite himself a tear dropped out.

"He was a very good soldier," said David, "that was one of the reasons he was chosen for the MOE role."

"He was thrilled to have been allocated that role," responded James' mother, "it meant so much to him to have had that extra recognition. Despite everything, I have to say he was thrilled to be serving under you Mr Phillips."

"David, please call me David."

Alan briefly explained what his and James' duty was, to force open the front door of the target house. "There was no advice regarding the booby trap, although the house had been under surveillance for several days by then, so we just walked into it."

"As I have explained, Lieutenant Phillips and I were also knocked over in the blast," said Catherine, but were uninjured and able to continue with the rescue."

"How many terrorists were there?"

"Eight men and three women," said David. "All are now either in custody or dead."

"Maybe we could go and see his gravesite," said James' father after a short awkward silence.

David and Alan followed the Templeton's and Catherine to the local Anglican Church and stood by James' fresh grave with a new headstone. James' father said a quiet prayer.

Afterwards they stood silently by the church. James' father said, "Thank you for coming, it is much appreciated. James always understood the risks, Catherine has been very supportive. She is going to stay with us for a few days. We were looking forward to having her as a daughter-in-law..." He allowed another tear to fall down his cheek.

David and Alan then shook hands with the Templeton's and made their way back home; Alan to Hereford and David back to Oxford.

***

After several weekends looking at properties in various locations in London, David and Melinda settled on a three-bedroom house on Barnes Common.

Michael was born five months after David joined Websters.

And Janice two years after Michael.

Chapter 7. Websters

Although David did briefly consider Powrie's offer of a full-time position in the regular SAS, he stuck to his initial plan of joining Websters. He immediately introduced Lizzie as his client to the business, which gave him a leg up on joining the company, as well as some financial benefit in recognition of the value that Lizzie's business accrued to the operation. His boss Harold Webster was very pleasantly surprised, since he did not expect junior staff to have such contacts. Lizzie had by now asked him to manage her complete portfolio.

"How do you know this person, Daphne Elizabeth Hall? I knew of her father but had no contact." From his tone of voice, Harold clearly felt Lizzie was way out of David's league.

"I need to explain something else about my activities in recent years."

"Yes," answered Harold, who had a reputation of not wanting to be involved in his employee's personal lives and affairs.

"While I was at university I was accepted as a member of the British SAS Reserve."

Harold was slightly taken aback. "I didn't know that."

"Jacqueline Briggs knows. It's included in all the information I supplied when I joined Websters. I don't often discuss it; the organisation prefers we generally keep a low profile, since we are sometimes required to deal with sensitive situations. I would be grateful if you would keep that particular piece of information to yourself please."

"Of course," said Harold with an impatient wave of his hand, "but what's that got to do with Ms Hall?"

"I have reasonable contacts at some of the more senior levels in the SAS. Mrs Hall is one of several contacts."

"Oh, I didn't realise that 'other ranks' had much to do with the wives and families of senior officers."

David shrugged. He wasn't about to tell Harold that he was a commissioned officer and that he had recently been promoted to Captain. Most of the senior officers were members of the permanent force.

Harold looked at David, asking him, "Are you still a member of the SAS?"

"Yes."

"What does that involve?"

"A few weekends a year and a three-week training camp, which I will take as annual leave."

"And if you are called up to go on active service?"

David shrugged. "If that happens, I'll have to come and have a chat with you. All my colleagues are paid in full while they are away." He looked at Harold to see if there was any reaction. There wasn't. "This is on the basis they're doing something out of the ordinary, for the country."

Harold wasn't totally comfortable with the way the conversation had developed but clearly saw himself as a patriot. "Hm, I did two years National Service, before it was abolished. I suppose it was useful," he said unenthusiastically. "Although I'm not very happy about one of my most promising new recruits dashing off to what are likely to be dangerous missions. I still don't understand how you've become the financial advisor for such a large client."

David was not about to reveal with his relationship with Lizzie and how his association came about so he said, "I've done very well for her. To start with, she let me run a small part of her inheritance, and subsequently, since the piece I ran consistently did better than her existing advisors, I gradually took it all over."

"Who were her advisors?"

David gave him the name of a well-known merchant bank.

"I don't suppose they were very pleased with your intrusion."

"I've not had anything to do with them. Mrs Hall dealt with them directly and gave them all the instructions."

When David returned to his office he phoned Lizzie, which he tended to do about once a month now. "How's the monster?" he asked.

Lizzie laughed. "Are you talking about the gaffer or my precocious two-year-old?"

"I see the gaffer fairly regularly, so I'm more interested in the junior member of the family."

"Bossy, is the best answer I can give you."

After they chatted for a while, David said, "I'll be sending you through some stuff on an investment I thought you might consider. I'll call in a day or two to see what you think. There is one other thing though – I was given the third degree this morning by Harold, my boss, on how I came to be your financial advisor."

"So?"

"My guess is that he'll phone you. He can't believe I have such an illustrious client."

She laughed. "Okay, what do you want me to tell him?"

"Nothing in particular. I just thought I would warn you."

"Okay." They rang off.

Harold did indeed phone Lizzie a few days later, making sure David was out of the office when he did so. Lizzie told him about it later.

After he had identified himself, Lizzie had said, "Oh yes, David said you might call. Is there anything on your mind?"

"You've spoken to David recently?" asked a surprised Harold.

"As he has done for three or four years now, he calls about once a month; more often than not the call is about an investment idea."

Harold was silent for a moment but then continued. "It is most unusual for such a junior employee to be advising a wealthy client such as yourself. I could give you a more senior person..."

"I'm not sure what that would achieve," answered Lizzie. "David has done very well for me since I took him on."

"He has very little experience..."

"Let me give you some advice, Mr Webster. Firstly, you should examine what he's done for me over the years. I would be surprised if any of your analysts could have done any better, with any client. Actually, I have a better idea. I happen to have here a summary of what he achieved with my investments since I took him on. I did this for my own purposes a few weeks ago; I'll send it to you. Secondly don't underestimate David Phillips – almost everyone I know who has made that mistake has come off second best, including many in the SAS. My husband has told me on more than one occasion that if he was in some sort of trouble, David would be the one person he would trust to extricate him. David is a very fine young man; I've persuaded him to be godfather to my two-year-old and I can't think of a better mentor for the boy in the long term. Just because David doesn't jump up and down about his achievements, doesn't mean he isn't competent. Frankly any employer would be lucky to have him."

Harold rapidly backed off. "Just treat this as a welcome courtesy call; I hope you continue to be satisfied with the advice we give you."

"I appreciate the call," was Lizzie's response before they rang off.

"Hm," David said when Lizzie finished her recount of the conversation. "Well, thanks to you, Lizzie; Harold and I are now having a genuine discussion about the long-term possibility of me purchasing shares in Websters, something he was not taking very seriously a few weeks ago."

David gradually cemented his position in Websters by introducing several more clients to the business over the next few months and years. To start with they were friends of Lizzie's, and then friends of those friends. Soon he realised that he was very well regarded by Harold, mainly because Harold involved him in more and more important issues, some of which were very sensitive. Also, he found he was liked and well accepted by the staff in general, having applied some of the lessons he had learnt from how Lizzie handled the people who worked for her. He was always very constructive and gave credit where it was due, which was unusual in an industry renowned for its cut-throat attitudes, where people tended to take credit for subordinate's ideas and pass them off as their own. He occasionally went out for drinks after work with a group of employees too. It helped them all get along and enjoy each other's company.

***

Periodically David had to go to Hereford to appear before the enquiry set up to examine the rescue of Sergeant Jones. David had provided a comprehensive report, which he had shared with Powrie before releasing it to the members of the enquiry. He and Powrie wrongly assumed that the enquiry would find he had operated within all the rules. He had, however, come prepared for some surprises.

The chairman of the enquiry, appointed by the Ministry of Defence, opened the enquiry by stating, "You Lieutenant Phillips, broke all the rules and, as a result, you put all the people under your command in danger leading to the death of James Templeton and causing serious injury to Alan Jenkins, among others. You acted without proper authority. Do you have anything to say to that?"

David was surprised by the approach, but outwardly remained quite calm. "Yes sir. I had full authority to engage in the rescue." He then referred to the transcript of the rescue and the appropriate paragraph. "You will see, sir, that the police said and I quote, 'We have all the exit roads blocked,' reported the senior police officer. 'We don't have the resources to take on a well-armed terrorist group, like the one present in the target house.' He then said, 'I formally authorise you, Lieutenant Phillips, to assume this responsibility and apprehend those who have illegally imprisoned Sergeant Jones and are a threat to his life.'"

The chairman looked disconcerted. He obviously thought David would be blindsided by his approach.

"I request that this enquiry be delayed by a week," said David. "I need to be able to prove that I broke no rules during the rescue of Sergeant Jones."

After a brief discussion with the other two members of the panel, the delay was granted.

A week later the enquiry reconvened. By this time David, with Powrie's help, had gathered all the support he thought he needed: Sergeant Jones, Catherine Roberts, Alan Jenkins, Sergeant Davis, the medical team from Milton Keynes Hospital, two members of the rescue team, James Templeton's parents, and Colonel Neville Powrie himself.

Each one of them was asked to describe what had occurred during the rescue, and what orders they had followed. None of them questioned the validity of any order.

Catherine Roberts also said, "Lieutenant Phillips operated by the book as far as I was concerned. He also always put himself in the most dangerous situations. To even suggest that he broke any rules is out of order."

Alan Jenkins reported, "The MOE intrusion was done by the book. There was no suggestion from the authorities – who had the place under full surveillance – that the target house was booby trapped, which was what caused the secondary explosion."

Sergeant Jones said, "Lieutenant Phillips, due to his quick action, eliminated the suicide bomber; the presence of whom had not been detected by those who had the place under surveillance."

James Templeton's mother said, tearfully, "My son had the greatest respect for Lieutenant Phillips, he would have followed him anywhere…"

The enquiry was shut down very quickly afterwards, with David being given accolades for his performance during the rescue. The last thing the Ministry of Defence wanted was for other questions to be asked, such as the possible failures of the surveillance of the target house.

The final report from the enquiry's chairman suggested that the MI5 contact be questioned about why he had not said anything about the booby trap and the suicide bomber in the cupboard. His report concluded, 'There is a suggestion that the rescue team were deliberately being led into a trap.'

***

One of the more sensitive financial issues Harold raised with David involved a company called Eclipse.

"It looks like a high-risk business to me," Harold told him. "Since it involves all this new technology, which I don't really understand. If you would just have a look at it and tell me what you think. My view is that we shouldn't touch it with a ten-foot pole."

David buried himself in the project and did an enormous amount of research after hours and at home.

"What's got you so excited," asked Melinda when she saw David hard at work on the dining room table night after night.

"Harold has asked me to look at a proposition that has been put to him. He's scared of it because he doesn't understand the new technology involved. I think it's likely to be an absolute gem. I just need to make sure I have all the bases covered so I can persuade Harold that it's likely to be a good investment."

"Do you want me to have a look at it?" asked Melinda.

"I'm nearly done," answered David, "if I get into trouble with Harold, I'll certainly involve you."

David could see that Melinda was slightly disappointed with his response.

"I won't waste your time now," he said. "If Harold has problems with what I have presented, I will involve you immediately. If he approves the proposition then there will be no problem. If not, we will then know precisely where he is coming from and take it from there."

"Makes sense," said a mollified Melinda.

Harold asked David on several occasions how his research was progressing. "I'm being hassled by the principals of this thing, maybe I should just tell them we aren't interested."

"No," David answered calmly. "There really is something in this, I'll be able to show you everything in a day or two."

David spent a whole morning presenting his findings to Harold who was sceptical from the outset.

At the conclusion of the meeting Harold said to David, "You want us to borrow all this money for an operation that has a limited track record. The whole thing is based on forecasts, which seem to me to be very optimistic. The answer is a big fat 'no'."

"Just give me a few days, I'll do some more work on the forecasts."

"Okay. By the end of the week then," was Harold's answer.

One of the things the SAS has taught me, David reminded himself, *is to persist if you think you are right.*

David returned early from the office, to sit at the dining room table and stare at his presentation. He was still there, feeling despondent, when Melinda and the children came home.

"It's that proposition for Eclipse," said Melinda. "Isn't it?"

David nodded. "Harold's not keen. He's worried about the forecasts."

"Let me have a look. How long have we got?"

David handed his whole presentation to Melinda, together with all the files. "End of the week. He wants to make a final decision by Friday."

Melinda looked at him. "I'll need a bit of time to read all this. If you do the dinner, or just order takeaways. I'll have some questions."

David did as he was asked, put the children to bed, and went to bed himself at midnight. Melinda crawled in beside him at what David could see was four am.

"You've done a fantastic job, David, I really like the proposal, but I do have some suggestions as to how you could convince Harold. But enough of that, make love to me now and we can talk in the morning."

David took the children to school and phoned the office to tell them he would be out for the day. He and Melinda worked for sixteen hours that day, and the next. By this time David was convinced he had all the bases covered.

On the Friday, Melinda said to him, "It's tempting to suggest that I should come with you this morning to see Harold but, thinking about it, I don't think that's a good idea. He doesn't know me that well and might be put off."

David was relieved, he was wondering how he should deal with Melinda's aspirations regarding her involvement. He nodded. "I'll phone you as soon as the meeting is over. You have made all the difference to my presentation, as I am sure you understand, so thank you for that."

He spent the morning with Harold, mainly dealing with Harold's reservations about the forecasts for the business. Due to Melinda's input, he had precise answers to Harold's misgivings.

"Okay," said Harold. "We're in. I'll phone the principals now. You will have to deal with the bank and we'll take seventy percent of the shares on offer."

Before David left the office, he said to Harold, "I involved Melinda after our meeting last week. Quite a lot of the additional detail in the forecast is as a result of her work."

Harold looked surprised. "I'm not very comfortable with people who are not actually employed here having access to such confidential information. Did you get her to sign a confidentiality agreement?"

"Of course."

Harold looked at him. "Make sure it's included in the file then."

David knew he had been caught out. The confidentiality agreement was the last thing on his mind. Once he returned to his own office, he phoned Melinda with the news. "He wants you to sign a confidentiality agreement, by the way."

Melinda laughed. "So you told him I helped?"

"I did. We should go out to dinner tonight to celebrate," suggested David.

"Lovely, I will arrange a babysitter."

David knew he had learned a lot with the whole episode; how he had handled the situation, how he had handled Harold, and in particular how he had handled Melinda. She was clearly a natural.

Down the track, when she is ready, I must somehow involve her in the business. She obviously has a lot to contribute.

Despite the fact that she was fully occupied with the children, she often did consulting work for various organisations where some of her Oxford colleagues now worked. She had told David of a job offer from time to time, "But I'm not really ready for that yet," she told David.

He was surprised that she was so fulfilled nurturing the children. From where David was standing, Melinda got as much of a thrill from offering financial advice as he got from the SAS.

Chapter 8. Africa

The Royal Navy frigate cut through the calm waters of the Indian Ocean on a moonlit night. David stood on the deck with Powrie, who had to yell to be heard over the whine of the Grey Merlin helicopter's engine and rotors.

"Captain Phillips, you do realise you tend to stir the pot with some of your demands, don't you?" said Powrie, who had recently been promoted to Lieutenant Colonel and had taken over as Commanding Officer of the SAS.

David, dressed in his 'black kit' – a one-piece flame-resistant flying suit, body armour, and chest rig – just smiled; he wore a khaki army shirt underneath. His face was painted black, and two of the soldiers he'd hand-picked for this mission – ruffling feathers as always – were Kenyan-born Britons, who both spoke Swahili. He'd had to tell the intelligence officer conducting the briefing for the mission that Kiswahili, not Arabic, was the most commonly spoke language in the part of East Africa they were heading for.

"One of my colleagues said something like this: 'Fucking Phillips, who the hell does he think he is?'" Powrie continued.

David had encountered a similar, though less profane reaction from his boss, Harold, when he'd asked for a month's leave, but had been unable to explain exactly why he needed time off.

"SAS stuff again?" Harold had asked with eyebrows raised. "A whole month? For God's sake don't get yourself killed. I need you here, not buggering about in some jungle."

David had just smiled at the backhanded compliment.

Now on the frigate's deck, fresh sea air filling his lungs, he couldn't think of anywhere he'd rather be.

"I tried to shut them up," Powrie continued, yelling over the noise of the helicopter, "I told them: 'With a bit of luck, he'll bring them all back safely, including the hostage'. I said I've watched this bastard for years now, he won't give a fuck what any of you idiots say. As always, he's totally focussed. Most people have completely underestimated him." He looked at David. "I'm hoping that sentiment will prevail."

"Thank you," was all David said.

Powrie waved a finger like a schoolteacher. "So you had better not let me down."

"You think this British businessman we're supposed to rescue is really called John Smith?" David asked over the noise as the Fleet Air Arm crew chief on board the Merlin gave a thumbs up, authorising David's team to board.

It was Powrie's turn to smile. "What parent would be so cruel? You know, and I know, he's most likely a spook, but ours is not to reason why. It's been two weeks since he was kidnapped from that holiday resort on Lamu Island. If he's still alive he'll be weak. Try and bring him back alive, old boy."

David had split his team in two – those who would accompany him on the Merlin and three who would travel by boat.

Earlier, David had advised the sergeant in command of the marine detachment, "Only travel at night," David reminded him, "so as not to attract attention." One of his Swahili speakers was on board. "If you get into trouble move on. The rendezvous, if we need you, is about one hundred miles up the Tana River, just south of a large village called Bura. We'll be going in from here in twenty-four hours when you're about halfway to your destination. Hopefully you won't be required and all you will need to do is to retrace your steps and come back here. Be careful, the river is full of hippos and crocs and possibly a few logs; and watch out for sandbanks. We'll be in radio contact as soon as the operation is over to tell you what to do."

"Yes, boss," the sergeant said.

The boat, a five metre 'Rigid Raider', was lowered into the water with the three men, then made off into the dark. David knew that in an emergency the craft was capable of thirty knots, even when fully laden, with its two one hundred and forty horsepower diesel outboards.

They were all heading for a village close to the border between Somalia and Kenya. It had been David's concept of operations to organise the combined air and sea mission. It was costing Her Majesty's government a fortune, but David had been adamant and Powrie had supported him.

David and his seven colleagues took off, precisely on time, an hour before dawn. Powrie waved them off.

They flew low, coming in under whatever radar was functioning in Somalia. The rotor downwash rippled the surface of the water. The silhouettes of palm trees loomed fast and large as David watched out through the cockpit. The chopper flew on for a few minutes; David knew that the target village was out in the desert away from the coast and actually just over the Kenyan border with Somalia.

"Ten minutes to target," the Navy pilot told David, who took off the headset the flight crew had given him and held up ten fingers to his men. They cocked their MP5 machine pistols and checked their gear. David, moved to the door of the chopper and removed the tie down strap from the coil of thick rope.

The helicopter crew chief, still in touch with the pilot held up crossed fingers. "Thirty seconds!" David yelled and flashed the same signal to his men.

The Merlin swept in over a village of shacks with palm thatch for roofs. David kicked the rope out of the chopper's door. Hardly had it fully unfurled when the first of his seven men was grabbing hold and smartly stepping out into space, to slide to the bottom.

Two ropes were in action and David counted his men out. He was the last to exit.

They landed in an open space in the middle of the village just as dawn broke. Three of the raiders accompanied David as they raced confidently towards the hut where they had been briefed Smith was being held. They had studied satellite photos and David had planned the raid using a scale model on a table back in Hereford, and in a full-size mock-up of the target hut and its neighbours.

As briefed by David, one of the team ran off to find and hotwire a truck or other vehicle they could commandeer as a getaway, should something happen to the chopper.

David pulled the pin on a stun grenade, tossed it through a window of the target hut, then barged inside. Smith was immediately visible, tied to a bed, but also in the hut were two women a man and five children, all sitting on the floor with their ankles hobbled by chains.

A jihadi dressed in camouflage and a headscarf came through the door of an adjoining room. He raised the AK47 he was carrying, but David was far quicker, putting two bullets into the man's face. David carried on, entering the room the dead man had just come from. A second man was pulling on his trousers, while trying to grab his rifle at the same time. David killed him. His men, who had encircled the hut then cleared the neighbouring dwellings, rejoined him.

"We all come with you!" shouted the manacled civilian man. "Otherwise they kill us."

"It's true," 'Smith' said in a weak voice, as one of David's men untied him. "The Al Shabab bastards have been beheading them, one at a time, to show the rest of the village what happens to unbelievers, and who's in charge here."

David hesitated for a moment and then said, "Get them all out of here and into the 'copter double quick." As had been pre-arranged, the 'copter had just landed in the middle of the village.

"We don't have room for all these as well as us," yelled a colleague.

David ignored him.

Due to the early hour and the very short time the soldiers had been in the village, there had not been any sign of resistance but as the ragged crew raced towards the helicopter several shots were fired, responded to by the soldiers guarding the machine. One of David's soldiers fell down badly wounded. David ran over, picked him up and carried him to the machine. His colleagues now maintained a murderous fire into all the surrounding area. The soldier appeared with a truck. They piled everyone into the 'copter, the hostage, the Somali man, his two wives and the five children.

"Too many," shouted the pilot, "three out."

David jumped out, "you and you, out." He picked the Kenyan, Sergeant Kariuki, and one other. "Swahili," he yelled, in an attempt to explain his choices, as they ran to the truck. The helicopter took off as David jumped into the front seat of the truck with his two colleagues in the back. David pointed. "That way, go like hell." The two in the back kept up a steady fire, for a few minutes as they left the village, making certain that there were no pursuers. "Looks like we've got away clean," said David as much to himself as anyone; he glanced at the image of the fast-disappearing helicopter. He made a call on his secure hand-held radio to the boat. "Barring accidents we should be with you in a couple of hours," he told them as the call was answered.

"How many…?"

"Four, I'll explain when we see you. Just confirm your exact location."

"East bank, we'll put a white flag in the tree above us." David was given the coordinates, which he had the presence of mind to write down.

They raced on as quickly as they were able on the very rough road, which was no more than a track. David looked about him: the undulating terrain was sandy desert like country scattered with thorn trees most of which were no taller than the average man. There was little sign of human habitation although they did see two collections of apparently unattended cattle. The cattle were small and appeared to be in poor condition. David was about to say something when they came tearing round a bend and had trouble in stopping at what appeared to be a Kenyan army roadblock.

"Oh, shit," said the driver, "now we are in real trouble."

"Hopefully not," said David.

"Kariuki, your show. If we get into any real trouble, I have a mobile number from a Kenyan Army general."

They were all made to get out of the truck and Kariuki had an animated conversation with the soldiers manning the roadblock. After a few minutes the tension eased and they all sensed that the conversation had taken a different turn perhaps in another language.

Kariuki said to David, "We need that number, so they can make the call." David wrote the number down on a piece of paper. Kariuki looked at him curiously, saying nothing. He gave the paper to the officer in charge. There was a lot of desperate dialling, to start with there was no result.

David and his colleagues were allowed to sit in the shade of a nearby thorn tree as the sun came up and the temperature rose uncomfortably. As they waited, David recalled the conversation he'd had with the man the Kenyan soldiers were now trying to contact.

***

David had arrived in Nairobi a week before the raid and made himself known to a senior General Kahinga in the Kenyan army, whose details had been given to him by Powrie. They arranged to meet at the Aero Club, on the outskirts of the city, right next to Wilson Airport, to the surprise of David's guest.

Once they had introduced themselves and each ordered a Tusker, the general asked: "Why this place; I'm expecting fucking Biggles to appear at any moment." He laughed.

David had quickly appraised the general as he sat down. David had quizzed his Kenyan colleague as to what he should expect. He was taller than David had assumed he would be, just short of six feet. The general was dressed smartly in a well-cut suit and his bright sparkling eyes similarly appraised David. His hair was short and as David had expected he was dark brown.

"Like you, sir, the people here, every one of them, waiters and so on, are all from up-country." David looked around. "I don't see anyone who could possibly be a Somali spy. The big hotels in the centre might not be so secure. Anyway, I'm flying from here tomorrow."

"How would you know what a Somali looks like? Presumably you are not familiar with this part of the world," asked the surprised general.

"One of the people with me was born here, I've had some long lessons from him."

"You have a Kenyan in your group?"

"Sure, he's a Kikuyu like you Sir."

"Why is he with the British army for God's sake? We need people like him here. We are short enough of people as it is. What makes you think I'm Kikuyu?"

"Your name, sir, gives it away. Although I did ask my colleague, Mr Kariuki, before leaving England. He's a civilian, as most of us are from the reserve battalion. He's almost qualified as a doctor. He's one of the toughest fuckers I've ever come across; that's the other reason he's with us. Unusually for a Kikuyu he is about six feet six and weighs a muscular two hundred and fifty pounds."

"You have reserve people doing this sort of thing?"

"Sure we do. We are as highly trained as the professionals; we are also more diverse with a wider range of skills."

The conversation continued easily. David declined another beer and the general soon left saying, "Here's a card; I broadly know what you are doing and don't want to know any of the details. If you get into trouble, I've written an emergency number on the back."

David spent a minute studying the card, then returned it.

"You don't want it?" responded the surprised general.

"I've memorised it all." David quoted all the details from the card. "If people rummage through my things in some hotel, finding the card would give the game away. I don't want to take that risk."

"Astonishing."

"Thank you, sir, for meeting me, I hope to be able to report back to you within a week or so." They shook hands.

He met two colleagues for a meal later on in the facility. "Food's good here," one of them offered, "the rest of the place is a bit old fashioned though."

"Sure, but it's safer here. You never know who is lurking in the shadows in other places in Nairobi. We don't want to create any suspicions. The people who are holding 'Smith' will be on the lookout for people like us. The good news is, I may not need you. It really depends if any of our other colleagues have been compromised; if they haven't, then I have a couple of tickets for a visit to the Maasai Mara, one of the best game reserves in the world. You'll also be pleased to hear that the hotel there, the Serena, is a bit of a step up from this place." David laughed.

"How do you get away with all this shit?" asked one of the colleagues.

David shrugged. "Detailed planning is the only answer I can offer."

***

David's detailed planning had paid off, even down to arranging the back-up vehicle.

After two hours of waiting at the roadblock the Kenyan Army sergeant came over and there was another animated conversation with Kariuki. "We can proceed but they want you, David, to go to Garissa, which is at least another two-hour drive from here, where you will be picked up in a military helicopter to take you to Nairobi."

"Mnn, okay," said David. "Just tell them we need a few minutes to sort ourselves out."

He called the boat on the secure radio, giving them the news, and handed the device to Kariuki. "Proceed as planned. Here, is where the boat is holed up," he handed Kariuki the scrap pf paper on which he had written the coordinates of the boats position. "As soon as you get there scarper back to the frigate as quick as possible. Sergeant Kariuki to take charge from now until you get back to the frigate. You will just have to tell Colonel Powrie what has occurred here. I hope to be able to update him when I get to Nairobi." David left his MP5 in the vehicle, he had his mobile phone, his passport, a credit card and some local currency with him, but other than that he had nothing but the clothes he stood up in.

"Aren't you concerned?" asked one of the men.

"No, not at all, I have an idea what all this is about; I met with the general in Nairobi. I'm sure I'm in no danger."

Kariuki smiled. "We're lucky, this group are all Kikuyu, like me, so I was able to talk to them in their home language. It helped."

They drove off leaving David. He was given a mug of very sweet milky tea, which he drank, but declined a portion of slightly burnt looking maize meal cake, which looked wholly indigestible. After another three hours and a lot of animated discussion David was directed to get into the nearby army Land Cruiser.

Sergeant Mwangi drove, indicating to David the importance of what he had been told to do. The sergeant spoke some English, so they had a desultory conversation about the threat of incursions from the Somali cattle herders coming across the border.

Kariuki had told David that the huge area bordering the Somali republic was largely populated by Somali tribesman who had never really recognised the colonial border with Kenya. Earlier Kariuki had added, "For the last hundred years or so they have always wandered across the colonial boundary at will, with their cattle, looking for grazing. With increasing populations on both sides of the border these incursions are becoming more and more threatening as far as the Kenyan's are concerned, especially now with Al Shabab egging them on. You can see from the terrain that the border is almost impossible to patrol and keep secure."

Chapter 9. Elephant Attack

Not long after leaving the patrol, with Sergeant Mwangi driving as carefully as possible along the rough track that passed as a road, to their absolute horror and surprise they were suddenly attacked by a very large and angry bull elephant, who smashed into the Land Cruiser hitting the driver's door and badly injuring the Sergeant. David had no time to think about what transgression had occurred to make the animal behave as it did. The vehicle, although still upright had been pushed off the track. David, sitting in the passenger seat and wearing a seat belt, was quite unhurt. The elephant was till trumpeting and behaving as if to make another charge. David grabbed the drivers old .303 service rifle, leapt out of the truck and fired two shots over the head of the animal, which backed off. David then found a box of matches in the truck cab and collecting a few handfuls of the wispy grass nearby he lit a small smoky fire which he let run for a minute or two in the grass. The wind was blowing towards the elephant, who immediately he caught a whiff of the smoke, dashed off into the bush. David then extinguished the fire.

David returned the rifle to the truck cab and went round the front of the vehicle. With difficulty he managed to open the driver's door. "Tembo," the barely conscious sergeant muttered. *Elephant*. David quickly examined the man. It looked as if he had two broken legs and he had a big gash on his head from which a copious amount of blood was pouring. It also looked as if he had some broken ribs. David tried his mobile phone: there was no signal.

Gently, amid groans of agony from the sergeant, David managed to pick him up and place him in the shade under a small tree. He looked round the vehicle for any kind of first aid equipment – there was nothing. So David removed his shirt he was wearing underneath his 'black kit' and with difficulty tore a few strips off it to bind up the gash on the drivers head, in an attempt to stop the bleeding. He then lay the driver down on a patch of leaves in the shade under the tree and returned to the vehicle. There was no water in the vehicle. The right-hand front tyre had been punctured. He found a jack and managed to replace the punctured wheel with the spare. Luckily there was a set of spanners and a wheel brace under the driver's seat. He unsuccessfully tried to start the vehicle. Opening the bonnet David could see that the electrics had all been dislodged, so, over about thirty minutes he checked everything carefully before trying to start the vehicle again. To his happy surprise it started first time he tried.

He went over to the now unconscious sergeant.

David, having engaged low ratio and four-wheel drive was able to coax the vehicle back on to the track. He opened the vehicle's passenger door and as gently as possible picked up the still unconscious sergeant and laid him down on the seat. He fastened the seat belt as best as he could. By this time, he had put on the remains of his, torn blood covered shirt, some of which had been used to try to patch up the driver. He then drove off down the rough track, every few minutes looking to see if there was any kind of signal for his mobile phone. After an hour there was a faint signal. He tried to phone the general, it went to voice mail. David left a short message explaining the situation. Half an hour later his mobile rang; it was the general's ADC. David quickly explained the situation asking that the helicopter that had been sent to Garissa be instructed to remain where it was until he appeared.

David continued to drive on, carefully, hoping not to further injure his passenger. His phone rang.

"The helicopter is in the process of returning to Nairobi, but he has now been instructed to go back to Garissa. How far are you from the airport there?" said a voice that David now recognised as that of the ADC.

"I don't really know, but it can't be all that far, since the mobile signal seems to be strengthening. I will do the best I can but my passenger is badly hurt. Will it be possible for the helicopter to go directly to hospital? The man needs urgent attention – he is not conscious, although he had a strong pulse when I put him in the vehicle. Does the helicopter carry water?"

"I will make sure the hospital is alerted. There is a helipad at the hospital. I will make sure it is ready," said the ADC. "Yes, the helicopters are instructed to carry water. They also have first aid kits, if that would be of any value."

"Okay," said David. "I will call you when we are airborne. Thank you for your help."

Within another hour they arrived at the small airport just northeast of Garissa, the administrative capital of the region. It was merely a tarred strip with the usual windsock in attendance, there was no sign of any sort of building at all. There was a new looking military helicopter in the parking area with a pilot standing next to it.

David stopped next to the chopper.

The pilot unloaded a stretcher and they both carefully placed the unconscious man on to the stretcher, and strapped him down, which they then secured in the helicopter.

"I will just get the Land Cruiser right out of the way," said David. "Phillips," David introduced himself, as he returned and seated himself in the chopper.

"Okongo, Flight Lieutenant Okongo," said the pilot smiling.

"The ADC said you had a first aid kit on board."

"Yes. I'll show you."

"Once we are airborne, I'll see if there is anything I can do for our colleague," announced David.

"It's only about a forty-five-minute trip, I'll alert the hospital that we have taken off. They are expecting us," said Okongo as the chopper took off.

David gingerly undid his seat belt and carefully moved to the where the patient was lying on the stretcher. He attached a saline drip. There was a phial of morphine in the first-aid kit, but David decided not to administer it since the driver was in any event unconscious. He cleaned him up as best as he could. He tested the man's pulse, which was racing.

"Is he going to be alright?" Okongo asked David, when he returned to his seat.

"I hope so," he smiled. "I have some first aid training, but I am not a doctor."

"Oh, I almost forgot," said Okongo. "I have a note from the general."

Dear Captain Phillips,

Since you had to make the emergency call, I thought I would take the opportunity to discuss a couple of things with you. There will be a car waiting for you at Wilson. I have booked you into the Norfolk, which you will find is a nice step up from that flea-pit you insisted on staying in when we first met. I will see you at lunch time tomorrow.

General Kahinga

"I have now been informed by the ADC that the car that was promised will be at the hospital," said Okongo.

The pilot spoke fluent English and they had a brief conversation during the forty-five-minute flight into the main hospital in Nairobi. David learnt the pilot had been brought up in Kisumu on Lake Victoria but had had the good fortune to have had a reasonable education at a mission school, and then been selected to train as a helicopter pilot in England for two years. He, wisely, showed no interest in what David, who still had a blackened face and was obviously wearing some sort of military uniform, now dirty, ragged and bloodstained, had been doing or what his mission was.

The pilot landed the chopper easily and safely on a helipad situated on the roof of one of the hospital buildings. They were met by a well-prepared group of doctors and nurses.

David shook the pilot's hand before he took off again. "Thank you" he said.

David accompanied the bevy of hospital personnel to the emergency ICU ward.

"I would like to know what happened," said the senior doctor, "and what treatment you have given the patient."

David explained the elephant attack and what treatment he had given to the patient.

"You weren't hurt in any way?"

"No, Sergeant Mwangi was driving and the elephant attacked that side of a very solid vehicle. I was lucky not to have been hurt in any way."

"You have some first aid training?"

"Yes." Anticipating further questions from the doctor he added, "I'm afraid I'm not at liberty to tell you anything about what I was doing. If you want any further information you will have to ask General Kahinga's ADC, who I understand was the original contact arranging for Sergeant Mwangi to be admitted here. However, if you any further information about what happened or the treatment I administered please call me on my mobile." David texted the doctor his mobile number.

"I will be around for a few days," said David. "If possible, I would like to pop-in to see how the sergeant is doing…"

"Please just call me, I'll let you know when you'll be able to come."

David found the car sent to fetch him easily enough at the hospital entrance.

The hospital was quite close to the centre of town so the trip to the Norfolk Hotel was fairly quick despite the always heavy Nairobi traffic. He knew the population of Nairobi had grown at least tenfold since independence in 1963. There was no conversation since David was firmly placed in the rear seat and there was a glass barrier between him and the driver, who leapt out once they had halted in front of the colonial façade of the Norfolk Hotel. The driver opened the car door, saluting and standing to attention.

David quickly glanced around, just noticing the red tiled roof of the establishment, the two muted columns gracing the entrance and the atmosphere of relaxed gentlemanly elegance, helped by the few trees along the short driveway. Conscious of his ragged appearance, David dashed to the front door which was quickly opened by the doorman. It seemed he was expected and David was treated as a VIP by the reception.

"I've left my luggage behind," he told the pretty receptionist, "so I need to be able to buy a few clothes and I have no toiletries, I also need a charger for my mobile."

She made no comment as if to indicate that his appearance was wholly within expectations. "I'll arrange for a car to take you in the morning," she told him. "Everything will be shut by now. I'll have a full set of toiletries placed into your room." She handed him a charger.

"I can go shopping looking like this?" David questioned, pointing to his blood-stained shirt and his ragged appearance.

"Please don't worry. I will explain the situation to the store." The receptionist smiled.

It seemed to David that more of the story of his escapade was known within the hotel, more than he was comfortable with.

Once he was in the elegant newly refurbished suite, he made a call to SAS headquarters in Hereford. Having identified himself, he was immediately put through to the duty officer. "I need to make contact with Colonel Powrie on the Navy frigate."

There was the sound of a muffled conversation.

"Where are you?" asked the duty officer.

David explained he was at the Norfolk Hotel in Nairobi.

There was a brief silence. "Are you alright then?"

"Yes. Probably the best thing would be to get Colonel Powrie to contact me here. He has my mobile phone number, but I'll give it to you as well." David gave the man the number.

"Okay. Willco." The call was disconnected.

An hour later, after David had managed to have a shower, his mobile phone rang. It was Powrie.

"Where the hell are you?" asked Powrie. "All your people have returned safely to the frigate. They all seem to be okay and 'Smith' is relieved to be safe again. What happened?"

David told him about the elephant charge and how he had managed to rescue Sergeant Mwangi, but that he was now ensconced in a suite in the Norfolk Hotel in Nairobi.

"Sir, there is now a bit more to the story than just saving 'Smith'. I have spoken to nobody but the hospital staff about the incident, but from the reaction of people at the hotel here, I'm guessing that it will be all over the papers and other media here tomorrow."

"Okay, thanks for telling me. There is probably nothing we can do about it. You did a good job, so thank you for that, and from what you say you handled the elephant business very well, but then you always were a lucky bastard. Anyway, what do they want from you?"

He went on to explain what had occurred and how he had the general's emergency number. "I have a fair idea, sir, but rather than going off half cock, I'll find out after the lunch with the general tomorrow. I expect to be on a flight in the next few days."

"Okay but let me know what transpires when you get back to England. By the way the UK press is full of how the brave SAS rescued 'Smith'."

"I hope no names were mentioned."

"No, no, you know our policy on that; but this episode will do the SAS a lot of good, again thanks to you."

Since Powrie was in such an ebullient mood, David told him that – apart from the bill for the Norfolk – to expect some bills relating to the two of his team he had sent to the Mara. He explained what he had done and why. "They were probably compromised; I had no choice. We took the hostage takers by surprise, so I think what I arranged put any spies right off the scent."

"Okay, as always you are a pain in the backside, but I expect we'll be able to cope with that." Powrie continued, "We didn't bargain on rescuing half the population of Kenya as a part of your efforts though..."

"Didn't have any option, sir," replied David. "They would have been slaughtered otherwise. 'Smith' urged us to help them too."

"So he told me. By the way," added Powrie, "we are steaming towards Cape Town, from where I expect to be able to catch a flight back home. I will need some help in understanding how we deal with the Somali's."

Shortly after the call to Powrie, David had a call from the general's ADC. "The general would like to talk to you, I'll put you through."

"Kahinga here. My ADC has given me some details of the elephant business you had to cope with. There have been recent reports of a rogue elephant in the vicinity. I may have to get the game department to deal with the situation. My people tell me that you are alright, not injured in any way."

"I'm fine thank you, sir. I just hope that Sergeant Mwangi is going to recover."

"Good. I'll get my ADC to check with the hospital. I have booked a table for lunch tomorrow at the Norfolk, so I hope to see you then."

"Thank you, sir. I look forward to that."

David decided that going down to dinner looking as he did would attract unwanted attention, so he ordered room service and phoned Melinda.

"Can you tell me where you are?" she asked, after they had talked about the last few days as far as she was concerned.

"Probably not."

"There has been a lot of stuff in the paper about the SAS rescuing a hostage in eastern Kenya or Somalia or something. That has to be something to do with you."

David said nothing, hoping that Melinda would put two and two together.

"Pain in the bum," she said. "You may need to think about reducing your commitment to the army. You've done your bit."

"Okay, fair enough." He enjoyed the SAS immensely, but he enjoyed being alive more. If risks brought results, one day soon his risks might bring an unwanted and decidedly fatal result. He said nothing about his conversation with Powrie, knowing that Melinda would resent being second cab off the rank as far as phone calls went, although he had never called her before from a live operation. "Mel, there is a bit more to the story than the media has so far revealed."

"Mnn, what more?"

He explained about the incident with the elephant and the sergeant.

"Jeepers, David. Bloody terrorists and now elephants. What next?" she muttered unsympathetically.

"I just thought I would tell you. I get the feeling that a bit more of the incident is known in the hotel than I am comfortable with. I just hope they haven't managed to get a photo of me. I just though you should know."

"Does Powrie know any of this," she asked shrewdly.

"He will," answered David.

"Please come home soon. We need you here," she now said more sympathetically.

The next day just after he had had his breakfast delivered to the suite, David phoned the hospital doctor who had been treating sergeant Mwangi.

"This is Phillips here," he said once the doctor had answered his phone. "I was just wondering how the sergeant was getting on."

"Oh Mr Phillips, yes, thanks for calling. The sergeant has now regained consciousness and in time he will probably fully recover, but it will take time."

"Is there any chance that I could see him sometime in the next few days?"

"I think he would appreciate that. If you call me tomorrow at about this time, I will see what I can arrange. He knows you saved his life.

If you hadn't got him here to the hospital when you did, he would not have survived."

"It was the least I could do."

Later, dressed in a fresh set of civilian clothes, David found his way to the dining room and was seated in a suitably private corner table when General Kahinga walked in, dressed in a well-cut dark suit and a tie. He shook David warmly by the hand saying, "Congratulations."

He handed David copies of the previous day's *Standard* and the *Daily Nation*, both of which featured headlines dealing with the hostage rescue, by the 'British SAS'. "But the story has now taken on a life of its own," the general continued, "these are today's papers."

To David's consternation, there was a picture of him on the front pages of both papers in a torn bloody battledress and shirt, entering the Norfolk the previous day. Fortunately, since he had run into the hotel it was only a picture of his back. The story was largely accurate about the elephant charge and the rescue.

I suppose the pilot couldn't resist the temptation, he thought.

"Could you tell me what happened?" asked the general.

David gave him a brief explanation of what had occurred.

"You mean, you somehow got rid of the elephant, then treated the sergeant, then got the vehicle operating again, and then somehow managed to call us?"

"The vehicle wasn't much of a problem, although I had to change the wheel with a punctured tyre. There was no water or first aid equipment in the vehicle, so I couldn't do much for the sergeant. I just did the best I could under the circumstances. It was fortunate that I was quite unhurt."

The general made extensive notes in his neat handwriting in a small notebook. "I would say that Sergeant Mwangi was very fortunate too."

"I phoned the hospital earlier. The sergeant has regained consciousness and will probably recover completely. I hope to pay him a visit tomorrow."

The general nodded. "My ADC told me the sergeant is expected to recover. Well done, Captain Phillips, well done."

"Well, sir, the critical issue was the number you gave me when we last met, and actually made sure we could finish the job, which we did. It was also critical in helping with the rescue of Sergeant Mwangi. So thank you again," said David wanting to get off the subject of the rescue.

When they had ordered, the general said, "There are a couple of things I would like to talk to you about, things you can help us with."

"The first one is to do with some training for our special services, such as your SAS."

"I don't know what the diplomatic protocols are, relating to that, sir," David answered, "but I will certainly speak to my Commanding Officer, Colonel Powrie, on the subject."

"I want you to be a part of anything we agree – to be a leader of any project."

"Well, thank you, sir, that's very flattering. The army has its own way of dealing with requests like that, so they may not think I was the most suitable candidate for such a venture. Can I suggest you send a note to Colonel Powrie, but as you probably know, you also need to go through the formal diplomatic channels… through the High Commission."

David gave the general the address of the SAS in Hereford, as well as Powrie's email address, which he wrote down in his pocketbook.

"Okay, I will write Colonel Powrie a note, which will be sent this afternoon. I will need his full name and so on, just so the letter is regarded as a formal request. I will also deal through the diplomatic channels; that may take a bit longer of course."

"Fine, it would be wonderful for me to come to this very interesting and beautiful country more often; I had not been here before this visit."

"Mnn, there is another more personal issue I would like to discuss. You told me you are an investment banker in civilian life."

Here we go, thought David. "Yes sir, indeed, I work for a firm called Websters."

"I looked them up; the wonders of Google," the general continued, "our family has substantial funds, but it's all rather disparate and the whole thing needs to be tidied up and more formally managed."

"Okay, well that's just the sort of thing we deal with; I will have to discuss everything with the Managing Director, Harold Webster, but once everything is agreed I can handle it all myself."

How the hell am I going to deal with this? thought David. *What happens if the family's fortune is the result of corruption, what do I do then? And in this country, corruption is a way of life.*

The general was somewhat disconcerted by David's apparent caution, but the conversation continued with David mentioning the sort of returns they would expect in a typical portfolio.

"We only get about half of that if we are lucky," the general said. He was obviously well on top of the issues and eventually pulled out a sheaf of papers from the briefcase he was carrying. "This will give you some idea of what's involved. My private email is in there and I look forward to your proposal. Most of our investments need to be in overseas operations; I have enough invested in Kenya, as it is, one way or another. We do not expect to pay a lot of tax." He added as he glanced sharply at David to see if there was any reaction.

David registered the comments but did not react in any way. "Right, unless there is anything else, sir, I will try to catch a BA flight tomorrow or the day after, and we'll get back to you as soon as possible on both issues; there will be a bit of catching up at Websters and some de-briefing with the SAS," David said, "and I must say thank you again for the help; it really saved our bacon." David hesitated for a moment, thinking about what he was about to say to the general. "Sir, I know you wondered why I chose to stay at the Aero Club when I first arrived. My room here has been turned over, more than once, by person's unknown, and I've only been here for less than a day. Someone is very curious about why I'm here. My caution was well justified, I think."

"How do you know that your room has been 'turned over' as you describe it?" asked an alert and very curious general.

"We have a way of leaving things, so we know if anything is disturbed, without alerting the person doing the disturbing. Something we may be able to teach your people if we indeed come to help your special forces people."

The general just nodded.

***

The next day, David paid a visit to the hospital to see Sergeant Mwangi. He had arranged to be admitted via a back entrance.

"I don't want any more publicity," he explained to the doctor.

David was taken to the ICU area where the sergeant was in a single bed ward.

The sergeant had been propped up and seemed to be sitting up comfortably.

When he saw David, tears trickled down his cheeks and he held out his arms. David embraced him.

The sergeant was quite incoherent and was obviously speaking in Swahili, which David didn't understand.

David looked at the doctor who translated, "He says thank you, thank you and thank you. Saved my life, saved my life."

At that moment a woman and three children all under twelve years old were ushered into the ward. The sergeant muttered something and the woman came over and hugged David as did the children.

"His wife and children," explained the doctor.

The wife went and hugged her husband.

David knelt down and hugged the children.

"Your father is a very brave man," he said to them, translated by the doctor.

After about fifteen minutes the doctor said, "We must let the sergeant rest now." He ushered them all out.

"How did the family get here?" asked David.

There was a quick conversation with the sergeant's wife.

"Bus."

"Are they staying here or going home?"

There was another brief conversation.

"Home. The kids have to go to school."

"Where do they live?"

"Langata Barracks. There are some married quarters there."

"Would they like a lift?"

They all nodded enthusiastically.

David called the car and arranged for them all to be picked up in a side entrance, since he thought that the media might have sussed that he was in the hospital.

They all piled excitedly into the car.

There was some desultory conversation during the thirty-minute journey, helped somewhat by the driver who was able to translate.

When they arrived, David was invited into the modest, spotlessly clean sergeant's quarters. He accepted a cup of tea. While Mrs Mwangi was busy, the kids all clustered round David showing him some of their school books. He read them two short stories in English, which they seemed to understand.

The driver then came to David's rescue, but not before Mrs Mwangi had insisted on taking several photos of David and the children on her mobile phone.

They returned to the hotel, where David arranged to buy Sergeant Mwangi's children two tee shirts each. He had some idea of their ages and sizes. He asked the hotel driver to deliver them.

Chapter 10. Africa Aftermath

David returned home the following day and went straight home to see Melinda and the children.

"It's such a relief you're home," she said, once they had hugged each other for a good five minutes. "I'll show you the papers and don't try to tell me you had nothing to do with it all. It had to be you. It looked dangerous."

The papers included the picture of David's back as he entered the Norfolk Hotel.

"It wasn't that dangerous until we were surprised by the elephant. It was well planned and well thought out; I think we had all the bases covered. I didn't plan on being attacked by an elephant though," he joked. "I'll be here for a few days, I then have to go to Hereford. After that everything will be back to normal."

"You really need these adrenalin rushes from time to time don't you?" she asked a day or so later.

"Yes and no. It's certainly a thrill. But what I enjoy more is planning everything well, minimising the risks, and bringing everyone back home safely, having done what we were asked to do. Sometimes that means making decisions those in charge might not like, but I'm the one operating in the field, so I try not to listen to too much crap. I try to do the same at Websters." He chuckled. "If you're the one taking the risk, it should be your call how you take it. Right?"

Melinda nodded like she knew all too well what he meant.

***

Harold was quite straightforward when it came to taking the general on as a client. "Under no circumstances should we break the law, not in any way. We can't be held responsible for clients breaking the law though. We will make recommendations regarding the gentleman's investments and, provided we have a sign-off on everything as we do, then Bob's your uncle; we do not have to understand the provenance of funds coming to us for investment. If we did, we probably wouldn't have many clients."

David was relieved, but still concerned about what had happened in Africa. After the frigate had dropped Powrie off in Cape Town, David phoned his crew to ask some follow-up questions while they journeyed back to England. He was told that the man who had been wounded was out of danger and would make a full recovery. One of the main issues was how they were going to deal with the Somalis they had rescued.

"I need to talk to Sergeant Kariuki about them," David decided.

But when David got Kariuki on the line, he didn't have good news. "They won't be able to return to anywhere in East Africa," Kariuki told him.

"I suspected as much. What are their names?" David asked.

"Asad, and the wives' names are Aamuun and Cawo; haven't really got to the kids yet. Why?"

"I don't want them dumped in some detention centre; they were as much part of the rescue as any of us. I will try to do something for them. How much English do they speak?"

"Asad, enough to get by; but none of the others speak any English at all. I speak to them in Swahili, which they understand."

"How old are the kids?"

"Boy is twelve, girl nine, girl six, boy four, girl two."

"Okay, I'll see what I can do. I will need the kid's names before arrival. Does Asad or any of the women have any skills we might be able to use?"

"Asad can drive. Both women were teachers in a local school. Anything else?"

"You could start by giving them English lessons, especially the kids. Asad may object to you having anything to do with the women though, as you well know. You could also all put your heads together for some ideas as to how we might be able to help them. I'm going to need some help from you in particular; you at least understand something of the culture."

"You haven't mentioned 'Smith'," said Kariuki.

"He's English, so I expect he will be well looked after. Probably get a book deal! Since you mention him, is he okay?"

"He's fine, and a total pain in the arse. He appears to think the sun shines out of that particular orifice."

"Is there anything you want me to do about him or for him?"

"No."

David then phoned Lizzie.

"An unexpected pleasure," she responded when she heard his voice.

Before she could say anything further, David said, "Has the gaffer mentioned the rescue business we were just involved in?"

"Yes, of course, it's been all over the papers. He's back here now and he told me you were involved."

"Yes. Did he happen to mention that we also rescued a family of Somalis – a man, his two wives, and five kids, mostly under ten?"

"No. I sense another curved ball coming up." She laughed.

"Well, I'm back home for all sorts of reasons, but the others – the person we rescued, and the Somalis – are all on a frigate on its way back here, they'll be in Portsmouth in a couple of weeks."

"Okay."

"The Somali man was our man on the ground, so to speak. He was an essential part of the team. I don't want him and his family to end up in a detention centre."

"So?"

"Is (b) occupied at the moment? I was hoping they might be able to stay there when they arrive. I am also hoping that I can get the gaffer to help them settle here in England without too much fuss."

"It's not really big enough for eight people."

"They've been living in a one roomed hut in the desert, up until now. How many bedrooms does (b) have?"

"Four, and a small study."

"Ideal," said David. "They won't know themselves." He laughed saying, "you can do it then?"

"You are a manipulative bastard, soldier. I'll pass it by Neville, but yes I can do it." She laughed.

"I need the gaffer on side, Lizzie, so you…"

"Need to break it to him gently, yes, yes. I wasn't born yesterday."

"Thanks Lizzie, I really appreciate it. You could easily have turned me down." David was silent for a moment. "How's Rupert by the way. I haven't seen him yet."

"Flourishing. And bossy – just like his dad," she said warmly.

"In that case, you'd better get his approval too!" David joked.

***

A few days later, an email arrived from Lizzie saying, "Neville has bought into the whole idea, so your refugees can come here when they arrive. Neville says he will sort out any visa or immigration issues. He's going to ask you to take on these people as a project: he made a comment that went something like: 'The bastard is full of ideas, mostly affecting everyone else.'"

***

A few days later still, Melinda brought in the daily paper. On the front page was a clear picture of David and three African children.

"Oh shit," said David. "I was ultra-careful no one knew my identity in Kenya. The sergeant's wife took me by surprise when she took that picture. I suppose she was persuaded to give it to the media in Kenya. So, my cover is completely blown."

"That's a shame," Melinda said. "Doesn't her husband have a decent position in the army?"

"They still need money. They live in quite poor circumstances. What would have happened to her if Mwangi did not survive, I hate to think. I had better tell Powrie."

David met the frigate when it docked at the naval base in Portsmouth. He made sure the families of the people in his patrol had been alerted so they were on the dock at disembarkation. He managed to spend an hour or so with Sergeant Kariuki, while making sure that 'his refugees' were correctly documented on arrival so there would be no difficulties down the track.

'Smith' – now fully recovered from his ordeal and benefitting from the expert medical facilities on the frigate – was whisked away by a senior government official, without a word of thanks to anyone.

"Who the fuck does he think he is?" David asked Kariuki, without really expecting an answer.

"There is a bit more to our friend than just being a businessman being held for ransom," answered Kariuki. "While we were on board, he had a whole lot of long animated conversations on some sort of secure phone."

"Mnn, well we can forget about him now. I need your help with these refugees."

An uncomfortable look appeared on Kariuki's face. "I've just spent more than a month on this caper; I need to get back to my studies and my other life."

"You've also had two weeks sunning your arse on that ship, you could have done some studying then." David smiled.

"Okay, what do you want?"

"Look, you are one of the few who understands the issues facing migrants from that part of the world, I just need some help putting all the pieces together."

"Where are they going to live?"

"For the time being, in part of the gaffer's compound in Hereford." David explained the set-up.

"Always full of surprises," answered Kariuki shaking his head.

"Perhaps the first thing we need to do is get them there?"

David had rented a small bus to take the eight refugees and Kariuki on the four-hour drive from Portsmouth to Hereford. Their guests were silent at first, but then started to chatter in wonderment at the pleasant green countryside they were travelling through; a vast contrast to the sandy, dry thorn scrub of their homeland.

They stopped on three occasions at motorway service stations and once at a high street café in a small town. Asad had spent time in Kenya and the Somali republic, having been recruited by the British on a visit to Mombasa some three years earlier. His two wives had been to school in Lamu on the northern Kenya coast. But none of the children had strayed very far from the small village where they lived.

Kariuki was able to chat to Asad and the children in Swahili, which put them at ease.

David phoned Lizzie a few minutes before they arrived, so she was waiting on the short driveway at the entrance to (b) when they arrived. The refugees piled uncertainly out of the bus and were introduced to a smiling Lizzie, who took them into (b) and showed them around. There were shrieks of excitement from the women and children, who ran around the house looking in all the rooms and the cupboards.

"I looked up various sources and have bought a few things I thought they might be able to eat – mainly lamb, rice and vegetables, but there is milk and cereal as well." She added, "Halal where possible. We'll have to go shopping later or tomorrow."

"Ma'am, it may be smart to show them how everything works," said Kariuki. "None of them will be very familiar with the toilet, the bath or shower, and you need to make sure that they know to switch everything off after they've used it, especially taps and the stove."

Lizzie spent an hour with the two women and the eldest child, while David and Kariuki talked to Asad about what he thought he might do, without much progress.

Powrie appeared half way through the process. To Asad's astonishment both David and Kariuki stood smartly to attention and waited for Powrie to say 'at ease' before they relaxed. "I have all their welfare papers, someone from barracks will take the man to the welfare office in the next few days. Daphne is going to have to help them with the shopping."

"Is there any way, sir, that Asad could be employed by the SAS?" asked Kariuki. "He can drive. They all need to learn English urgently."

"Okay, there is a lot to deal with," said Powrie.

Lizzie and the women appeared, giggling amongst themselves.

David raised his eyebrows.

"Secret women's business," smiled Lizzie. "Well, all that seems to be under control. We'll go shopping in the morning, I have a woman coming in to look after the kids, she speaks Arabic, so I hope will be able to communicate with them, even if that isn't their first language."

David said, "Thank you for this, sir and ma'am. Kariuki and I will be off to the barracks and we'll be back in the morning before returning to London."

"Not so fast," said Powrie smiling. "I will see you both in my office at nine am tomorrow morning, you are both going to help with this issue."

In the morning Powrie said to David and Kariuki, "So you two think you can just dump the problem onto me and scarper off to London leaving me to deal with these people, although I must say that Daphne seems to be enjoying herself."

"Having had to cope with coming here, I have some idea of the priorities," offered Kariuki. "Housing, language and jobs are a priority, then medical. You said you had dealt with the welfare issues, sir."

"I have arranged for all of them to have a full medical exam, here during the next week."

"One needs to be careful of the cultural issues with the women," said Kariuki.

"Sergeant, give me some credit," said Powrie, quietly. "Are you also from the David Phillips school of obvious ideas? I have an Arab-speaking female doctor coming in to deal with the women and girls. Okay?"

"Sorry sir, I was just thinking of my own arrival here…"

"I have been researching teachers of English as a second language in the vicinity," said David. "If you have the budget, sir, I suggest daily lessons for two women at home, for a month or so. I think two women would be ideal, one for the wives and one for the kids. I suggest that Asad comes here for lessons, if that's okay." He looked at Powrie before adding, "If that's alright I will leave the details with Mrs Hall later this morning."

Powrie looked mollified. "That leaves housing, which can be dealt with from here; based on one of your suggestions, sergeant, I have arranged for Asad to have driving lessons here at the base, so we can get him a driving licence; he will then work as a driver for us here. Anything else?" he asked. "You always seem to want the last word Phillips."

"Yes, sir, dependant on how Asad gets on, especially with his English lessons, he may be able to conduct sessions for our people on the cultural issues they should understand and may have to deal with when on operations in East Africa or the Middle East. I also have the address of a Sunni Mosque in Hereford, which I'll give to Mrs Hall."

"Okay, that's helpful. If we need you again, I'll let you know."

As they were being ushered out of the office, David asked his OC who the person was they rescued. "Seems to be rather more than a kidnapped businessman."

"Ask no questions, Captain Phillips…"

"He was also by all accounts rather aloof; not a word of thanks to anyone."

Powrie shrugged. "We were asked to rescue him, which we did. We didn't anticipate eight refugees as well. Anyway, what do you want, a fucking medal or something?"

David smiled. "Asad and his family would all be dead if we hadn't brought them back with us. Actually, there is one other small thing I would like to talk to you about though, if you have five minutes."

They trooped back in to his office and closed the door. David explained his meeting with the Kenyan Army general. "He wants help training the Kenyan special forces. I told him to put his request through the usual diplomatic channels, but I mentioned your name

– he may send you a private copy of his formal note. He also asked if I could be the person in charge of the training. I told him the army may have a better man in mind for the job other than me."

"I do have his note; I was wondering if you were going to mention it. I'll think about it when and if I get any instructions through the official channels. You obviously impressed him," he smiled, "with your luck it looks as if you might score a week every now and then in a Kenyan game reserve."

David shrugged. "He helped us out of a hole; it will all come out in the official debrief."

"In view of your photograph in the press, your identity has been compromised; we'll have to take that into account if you are sent to Kenya," said Powrie.

"Yes, sir."

David and Kariuki then spent an hour with Lizzie, six-year-old Rupert, and the refugees before returning to London.

"I'm enjoying this," Lizzie told David in a quiet moment. "I'll send you an update every few days, especially if we need anything."

He gave Lizzie a brief run-down on the discussion with Powrie, then took his leave.

On the way back to London, in the rented bus David and Kariuki chatted about inconsequential things. Eventually Kariuki's curiosity seemed to get the better of him. "You seem to know the gaffer and Mrs Hall quite well; you've got away with murder on this one, captain. I have never heard of a bunch of refugees being accommodated by a senior officer of our outfit before. How did you even know that they had that place?"

"I've had a bit to do with both of them, outside of the SAS. Mrs Hall is one of my major clients at the business I work in; we have an investment advisory business."

"Sweet little kid, that Rupert – maybe he'll learn something from having those people staying. He has a certain way with people." Kariuki raised his eyebrows as if implying more with the statement.

It hadn't escaped David's attention either – Rupert had an obvious likeness to David himself. But what was there to say on the matter? Instead, David moved the conversation along. "Actually, I have a delicate question for you, Kariuki. How well do you know the general I saw in Nairobi?"

"I know of him and his family. Why do you ask?"

"The fortune he seems to have – has it been earned legitimately?"

"How do you know he has a fortune?"

"I just do."

"Ah, he wants you to advise him on investments."

David shrugged, inviting him to talk.

"Well, I don't know the details, but very few Kenyan elites have fortunes garnered wholly from legitimate sources. Again, I know nothing of the details, but acquiring military hardware from western sources has generated quite a few fortunes throughout Africa."

"There are quite strict rules in place here in Britain preventing arms manufacturers from paying any sort of bribe or commission."

Kariuki laughed. "Most of them acquire their arms through third parties, which solves the problem altogether."

"Then the arms will cost the country more."

"Nobody gives a damn about that. A lot of the money comes from aid donations anyway."

"Okay, thank you Kariuki. It always helps to know more than less."

Chapter 11. Websters

Over the next few months, David turned his focus to becoming comfortably established in Websters, working directly for Harold as the founder and major shareholder of the firm. He wanted to become one of the boss's confidants, and eventually persuaded Harold to sell him shares in the business. He would buy more when he could too, often with the substantial bonuses he received, or with his commissioning fees from the major clients he introduced to the firm, including Lizzie.

David continued to be happily married to Melinda and delighted with their two young, very bright, increasingly rewarding children. His continuing SAS commitments made sure he kept fit, with regular gym workouts and the occasional rugby game.

David also ensured he maintained good relationships with most members of staff, though was so busy he was hardly aware of the arrival of the beautiful Samantha Wicks, a new junior analyst, until she introduced herself. As soon as she did, he knew she would be trouble.

It wasn't just the way she looked him up and down as she popped into his office saying, "David, if you aren't too busy, I wonder if you could point me in the right direction here…?"

It wasn't just the acute sound of his own voice when he answered, "Certainly. Anything to help."

It wasn't just the way she Samantha moved to David's side of the desk, indicating the information she required, lowering her cleavage until it was just a few inches from his face.

It was everything, and nothing.

After a few clicks on his laptop, David led her to a website providing the information she needed, which was over-easy to find.

She could have found that info herself, with a bit of research, he realised after she left. *No big deal, I suppose, always happy to help new employees.*

But within a few days, Samantha, wearing a short skirt showing off her long attractive legs, asked another question on another subject. As she left his office, she briefly glanced back at David, but – seeing her turn – he quickly buried himself in whatever he had been doing when she interrupted him.

Later on, she made a point of brushing past him in the passage when the opportunity arose.

"Whoops, sorry," he said, resisting giving her a backward glance.

After a few weeks of similar incidents, though, David started to get the message; and one lunchtime when he, as usual, popped out to get a sandwich, he found Samantha walking alongside him.

"I need to pick your brains on something," she said, smiling her most charming smile. As always she was dressed in a pretty, short skirt and an attractive blouse, with several buttons undone...

"Oh," said David, "we could just get a sandwich and go back to the office? I have a spare half-hour."

"It's such a lovely day," said Samantha. "If you like, we could find a bench, here in Bloomsbury Square. If you book the bench, I'll fetch the sandwiches."

David, mildly surprised at her forthrightness, handed over some money and told her what he wanted. In ten minutes Samantha was back. She laid the spread out on a paper tablecloth between them on the bench. David was charmed – he normally just took his sandwich and returned to the office to continue what he was doing and fetched a cup of instant coffee from the kitchen.

But it was a beautiful day, and the beautiful Samantha chatted away about how much she was enjoying working at Websters.

"I'm hoping to move into a flat nearby," she said casually. "Dad is working on something for me. It means I'll only be a few minutes from the office, and this is such a lovely part of London." David was beginning to wonder if she really had a serious issue to discuss when she said, smiling. "I'm sure you don't really want to know the intimate details of my domestic affairs. So, on a more serious note, I was wondering what you thought of an idea I had about the value of an investment in an internet start-up." She spelt out the details. "Isn't there a second board company that has just listed?"

"Yes," he answered, "the company is called Eclipse; Websters backed the float. We have a substantial shareholding in the business. Harold is on the board." In fact, so far, all David's forecasts regarding Eclipse had been exceeded.

He questioned Samantha about what she knew of the business and was pleasantly surprised by her knowledge of what made the business tick. There was very little knowledge in the public domain regarding how the business was tracking and both David and Harold were determined to keep it that way until the trends were clearly established. The conversation continued for more than an hour and, once they had finished their sandwiches, they retired to a nearby café for another cup of coffee.

After that, David started to involve her in his regular business operations. There was no further mention of Eclipse though.

He decided that if Samantha was to be brought more into the fold, so to speak, he'd better find out more about her and her background. So he went to see Jacqueline Briggs, Websters' painfully discreet human resources manager. "Coffee later?" he suggested. He often took some of the more senior people out for a coffee in the nearby shops, to maintain good relationships, as a result he often picked up snippets of information which he would not have known about otherwise; Jacqueline included when he needed to know about any new arrivals in the firm.

Jacqueline always jumped at the chance. David half-suspected she might like him in an unprofessional way, but if she did she was also very professional about keeping her feelings private. In her youth, Jacqueline might have been regarded as pretty but now, nearing forty, she was slightly overweight, smoked and was not wearing her years well. David merely regarded her as a very competent employee; he knew nothing of her personal life and indeed had no interest.

"I have someone coming in shortly," she responded brightly to his suggestion. "I'll pop by after."

Within the hour Jacqueline looked in on David. "Okay, I'm done."

Leaving the office, they walked across Bloomsbury Square and, as they often did, popped into a little cafe in Sicilian Avenue, a pedestrian walkway leading through to Southampton Row.

"So, what about Samantha?" he eventually asked. He noticed that Jacqueline was uncomfortable with the question and wondered why. David studied her. "Is there anything wrong? I haven't had much to do with her; I just wondered what her background was," he asked.

"Well, she's pretty smart, very good degree, a good reference from a similar operation to Websters, which seemed okay." She still looked uncomfortable.

"And?" David could see there was something troubling her.

Jacqueline took a deep breath. "I shouldn't be telling you this. She's Harold's daughter. No one else knows."

David paused to consider his reply. This was indeed a revelation as far as he was concerned. He wondered whether Harold had briefed Samantha in any way about Eclipse, to keep a check on him. He immediately dismissed the thought, as it simply wasn't Harold's style.

Still, he thought, *I had better watch my Ps and Qs. I don't want to blot my copybook in any way with Harold...*

He cleared his throat and spoke up. "If she's competent and has the right background that shouldn't be a problem," he said evenly.

Jacqueline shrugged. "I think she's probably a good recruit, but Harold made me rather rush things with her appointment, which I'm unhappy about. Anyway, enough said."

They finished their coffee and returned to the office.

As they went in the front door, David looked at Jacqueline saying, "Nothing you have said goes beyond me, but I guess you know that."

She nodded.

David decided to further involve Samantha in his own activities. He loved her quick mind and the way she dealt with issues. Once, when he gave her a set of accounts covering ten years for a company they were thinking of investing in, within a day she returned saying, "These accounts have been fiddled with; someone has tried to make the results look better than they could ever be." She produced a summary set of what she thought the accounts would have really looked like without the adjustments. "I've also done a bit of research from various sources on the internet. Frankly I wouldn't be investing in such a business."

David nodded. "My views exactly." He was astounded with the speed of her response.

On another occasion, when he invited her to a meeting with a prospective client she said afterwards. "The bloke is a crook and a liar, if you want my advice, leave him well alone."

David accepted the advice.

David and Samantha had on several occasions had to work late. David was always impressed with her commitment and the way she analysed situations; she went beyond just the figures but was able to understand the motivations of management and what they were trying to do. Once or twice Samantha suggested they should have dinner together after a particularly gruelling day.

"Not tonight," was his usual response. "I like to read to the kids before they go to bed. Anyway, Melinda will have kept something for me."

David had a feeling there was more on offer than just the job. Samantha was always well turned out and succeeded in turning many of the male heads at Websters. Their conversations became more and more personal. "What did you do at Oxford," asked Samantha innocently, one evening.

David laughed. "I played a lot of rugby, that was fun. Somehow, I managed to get a first, after having been kicked up the backside a few times by various tutors."

"Redbrick for me, none of the fancy Oxbridge stuff. I got a decent result."

"Yes, I know, I asked Jacqueline. She told me where you went to uni and that you had good results."

On another occasion Samantha said, "There's a rumour you are a member of the SAS."

"Reserve only."

"What does that involve?"

"Sorry. Can't discuss that. I didn't realise many people know about my involvement with the SAS."

"Most of us know."

Almost all these conversations were initiated by Samantha. David realised their relationship was developing but resisted taking it further.

"You've no idea," Samantha said to him one day, "how cute you are, do you?"

David couldn't help but grin at the compliment. "No cuter than men your own age, I expect."

"Oh, I don't know." She smiled back, and it was in that moment David admitted he was falling in love.

Don't be a damn fool, he said to himself, *talk about shitting on your own doorstep. Just don't be tempted.*

Nevertheless, he began to experience pangs of jealousy when she went out with a group of the younger people from Websters.

Soon he was unable to stop thinking of her, so buried himself in his work. He would never take the relationship further; he valued his marriage and the children it had produced.

One evening in mid-week, however, after eight in the evening, as was often the case, he thought he was last to leave. He closed down his computer and from habit packed a few things into his brief case; he occasionally wondered why he bothered since he knew it was unlikely he would do anything with it except plonk it by the door at home and pick it up in the morning on his way out of the house. Unusually the phone rang, just as he was about to shut his office door; it stopped ringing as he picked up the receiver, but a glance at the screen indicated that the call was from Harold.

I'll pop by on my way out, he thought. *I wonder what the old bugger wants; he's normally long gone by now.*

Closing his office door, he walked the few paces down the dimly lit passage, through an open plan area, now completely quiet, past the closed doors of two other senior people, and into the lit-up corner office. He knocked politely, opened the door and went into the boss's large well-furnished office.

Expecting to see Harold sitting behind the elegant wooden desk peering over his steel rimmed glasses, to his amazement all David could see was a pair of unshod female feet, with neatly painted toenails, resting on the top of the desk. He noticed a pile of what appeared to be women's clothes on one of the visitor's chairs. As he moved further in to the room he couldn't believe his eyes: there was a completely naked Samantha Wicks lying back in Harold's chair with her feet up on the desk. David was stunned. There was a cheeky confident smile on her classically pretty face, framed by her long blond locks. Her pale, big, well-formed breasts stood erect under his gaze and as his eyes feasted on her flat stomach, her slim athletic looking legs parted fractionally, almost driving him to distraction. He dropped the briefcase.

"What kept you?" chided Samantha playfully as she languidly got out of the chair. "You seem to be somewhat overdressed for what I have in mind." She started to undress him.

David needed no second invitation and within a minute he was completely naked apart from his socks.

Samantha took his impressive erection in her mouth briefly as David backed her up against the desk; he entered her and they made frantic love. "Harder," cried Samantha, "come on harder, harder, harder." She climaxed with a few cries as David flooded her with passion.

David gently lay down on the carpet with Samantha on top of him. "Stay, stay like that," he whispered. "Come again if you can."

Samantha looked pleasantly surprised and David became aware of two more faint mewling sounds of pleasure over the next half hour.

"I'm going to roll you over on your back now," whispered David, "wrap your legs around me."

Samantha's eyes flew open. "My god," she said, as he came again. "Twice off one stick, that's a bonus."

After a few minutes they clung to each other on the carpet.

"Recently laid," joked Samantha, "just like me."

Still lying on the carpet, David, sated and propped up on one elbow, could not get over the beauty that confronted him. "I had no idea..." he whispered.

Samantha glanced at him, stroking his slim strong body. "You wouldn't even look at me," she pouted, "so I took the only course I could think of." She kissed him. "Most rewarding, that was absolutely wonderful; I still can't believe it really." They kissed for a long minute. "We mustn't spoil it," she said, "there's plenty more where that came from; I think we should get dressed." She got up and went to Harold's private toilet, located discreetly in a door behind Harold's chair.

David, utterly bemused, dressed himself, leaving his jacket hanging on the back of one of the visitor's chairs, and watched while a fresh-looking Samantha now made a move to do the same. He also popped in to the toilet and was surprised to see a still completely naked Samantha had made no progress in dressing herself when he returned. She was also on the opposite side of the desk from her pile of clothes. He raised an eyebrow.

"There's no particular hurry," she explained.

"It's okay," joked David, "as far as I'm concerned you can prance about in the altogether as much as you like, provided I'm the only one in the audience." He hesitated a minute. "Has anyone ever told you, you are the most beautiful woman in the world?"

Samantha seemed very familiar with the office and, once she had dressed and carefully attended to her makeup, switched off all the lights. She tried to hide the fact that she locked the office door behind her, an act that surprised David. They kissed briefly in the passage.

"We should leave separately," suggested Samantha. "Cameras; there are cameras at the front door and in the garage, we don't want to be seen together. I will go out by the front door, maybe you should wait a few minutes before you leave?"

David nodded as she took the lift, which he could see stopped at the ground floor. What she said made sense, but by this time he was on full alert; he had thought the encounter was spontaneous, but now it

176

all seemed just a bit too organised. He wondered what Samantha was up to, his keys had an unusual feel to them, and they were in his left-hand jacket pocket; he always put them in the right-hand pocket.

He took the lift to the garage and drove home in a very thoughtful mood. On the one hand he was overwhelmed with guilt; on the other hand, he was mesmerised by the lovemaking with Samantha, there was no way on God's earth that anything or anyone could make him back away from that now.

He dropped his briefcase off at the door as usual and found Melinda watching TV in the lounge. "Sorry I'm late," he said as he pecked her on the cheek. "Boss needed something urgent for the morning."

"It's in the microwave," answered Melinda, referring to his dinner, "just switch it on." She waved vaguely in the direction of the kitchen.

"Quick shower," he said. "I'll be down in a minute."

He showered carefully and wandered down to the kitchen to heat up his now spoilt meal. In his dressing gown he sat on the couch next to Melinda as he ate. It was obvious the programme she was watching had at least forty minutes to run, so he said. "I'm bushed, I'll see you in bed."

She nodded.

David was happy to avoid any further conversation with his wife. His emotions varied from guilt to horror at what had occurred in Harold's office. *Remember Gwyneth*, he said to himself, but before he went to sleep he relived and savoured every moment of the episode with Samantha.

On the drive into the office the next morning he inevitably reflected on his encounter with Samantha the previous evening.

She's definitely up to something, he thought, *I will bloody well find out what. I suppose she, like everyone else, thinks I'm a soft touch. Don't be a mug, David.*

He genuinely valued his marriage to Melinda, their two children, and the stability that provided. Up until now there had never been any thought of straying outside the marriage boundaries.

During his early breakfast he happened to glance at some of the photographs of his SAS training group on the sideboard in the dining room. One photo in particular reminded him of his experiences when training for the SAS, particularly the final endurance test over the Brecon Beacons in Wales: the lesson was not to trust everybody, and to persist if he thought he was right. He reminded himself of the lesson learnt that day, now thinking of Samantha.

David was in the office as usual before seven, having also as he normally did, seen to the children's breakfasts. He dealt with his emails and, once people arrived, he spent a few minutes wandering around the office greeting them. He knocked on Harold's door and looked in to say hello. On his return to his own office, something made him examine his keys more closely: there was something odd about them. He sniffed at them.

Ah plasticine, he thought, *she's taken copies of my keys. Shit! Okay, now I get the picture.* He looked at the keys more closely. *Mnn, just the office keys. She may not have had time to copy the house keys. Smart.*

He thought for a minute; he was entranced by the encounter in Harold's office and, whatever the risks, he was going to continue with that.

Now I have an idea of what she's up to, I need to find out more about Samantha Wicks though, who she is and where she comes from.

So he reluctantly called an ex-school friend who was operating as a private detective, having blotted his copybook during a short stint with the police. After brief greetings he said, "I want everything you can get on a Samantha Wicks, very confidentially. She's an employee here."

"Pooed in her nest, has she?" asked Joe.

"Possibly, I don't know yet; not a bloody word to anyone though, you need to do all the investigation yourself and you are to bill me personally. Is that clear?"

"How soon?" asked Joe. "My own personal rates are higher than if I put one of my people on the job."

David didn't think Joe had any employees at all. He knew Joe was unable to resist a situation where he thought a fast buck was on the table. He shook his head saying nothing, then continued. "Two weeks max. Nothing in writing please, nothing at all, and don't keep any records relating to this investigation, none at all. Please call this special number when you have the info, but only after eight pm please. If there is no answer, don't leave a message of any sort, just call back later. Hang on a sec; I'll give you the number." He fumbled in one of his desk drawers finding a cheap mobile he had acquired for another purpose and not had to use. He read the number out to Joe. "And the bill is to be sent home," he gave him this home address. "Okay, all clear?" he asked.

"Yup, two weeks, thanks." The phone was put down.

David also made a phone call to a distant cousin, Des Murray: there was a grunt, which was Des's usual way of answering the phone. "Hello Des," said David, "how are you?"

"I'm busy, what do you want?" Des answered.

"Of course you are, someone as smart as you will always be busy," said David. As far as David was concerned, Des was a computer genius unparalleled in his experience. Des had been diagnosed with Asperger syndrome and was often difficult to deal with. David was fiercely protective of his distant cousin and had introduced him to colleagues and business associates saying, "He's a bloody genius, don't be put off by his manner, but if you get into real trouble phone me and I'll help you deal with him. However, if you underpay him I'll have your balls for breakfast and I'll make sure he never works for you again." David always explained Des's affliction. "He's always rude and has no people skills at all, he also tends to be less than interested in the financial side of his business, but I have a small firm of accountants looking after that to make sure people are properly billed and that they pay their accounts in full and on time."

"Des, this is urgent." David knew from experience that the only way of dealing with Des was to give him explicit instructions with no alternatives. "Come to my office at seven tonight. It's quite a big project, I'll explain it then."

"Okay," said Des and the connection was cut.

There was no sign of Samantha at work that day, which reminded him of another SAS reserve memory, a few weeks after his supposed reprieve with the endurance test. He had ambushed Jones as he entered his favourite pub. "What can I get you, sergeant," David offered to a very surprised looking Jones, just as he sat down at the bar.

Jones was about to get up to walk away, then stopped. "Two pints of bitter," David told the barmaid.

"I just want to know," David had asked, "why was I treated so differently to the other trainees in the endurance test?"

Jones looked sheepish but then appeared to pull himself together. "The standards in the service are important, we need to keep them up."

"By being dishonest? Bloody Hogarth," said David, "it's time he and you grew up." David took a long pull at his drink. "You're better than that, sergeant, much better."

Jones was quiet for a moment or two. "Don't push it, son. Another time you might not be so lucky." He then got up and retired to a corner.

David had left what remained of his drink and returned to barracks.

David reflected on the lesson he had learnt that day, *don't ever let the bastards think they have got away with something, especially if they haven't.*

The same was true of Samantha. If she thought she could avoid David by not showing up to work, she was wrong.

At seven that night, Des duly appeared in David's office as ordered. Despite his gruff manner, David was sure he was the only true friend Des had. As he often was Des was dressed in a scruffy pair of jeans and a tee shirt. His hair was unbrushed.

"I think someone here at work," David explained, "wants to steal information from me."

"Which you want to protect?"

"I do. I also want to provide that someone with information that will turn out to be wholly misleading. There may be more to it than that but that'll do for a start," he said.

Des grinned, fascinated, he loved anything with a little intrigue. "I'll be back in a week," he told David. "I'll have to buy some equipment."

"Right, just order it from the usual place and I'll arrange payment." For the time being, David would finance everything personally; if anything came of the situation he would ask Harold for a refund.

**

Samantha only appeared in the office two days after; telling everyone she'd been sick. A note was dropped on David's desk. "Tonight," was all it said.

David tried to think of a reason for not seeing her as requested but couldn't. He could keep his belongings in sight, which should be easy enough, then enjoy whatever Samantha was offering. There was no reason not to go; it might even help his investigations, now that he knew she was up to something. So he let himself daydream about their forthcoming encounter, until he was almost unable to do anything except anticipate.

However, late that afternoon, Melinda called. "You may have forgotten so I thought I'd remind you, but we are due at the school by seven. Parents' evening."

Surprisingly, David felt relief. *Saved by the bell,* he thought and phoned Samantha. "Sorry, can't make it tonight. Its parents' evening at the school."

"How disappointing! I've been looking forward to it all day," she said brightly. There was a momentary hesitation on the line. "Just to let you know I will be moving into the flat I once mentioned, over the weekend, it's nearby." She then added playfully. "So, soon we may even be able to have a little lunch-time recreation…"

David gulped. Soon he could indulge in encounters with Samantha whenever they wanted. The idea overwhelmed him.

PART 3: THE STING

Chapter 12. Charlie

Months before Samantha joined Websters, her stepfather Charlie Sandford had hatched a scheme.

Charlie had been brought up in what was docklands in the East End of London. His education had been at best desultory and often interrupted. He was very bright. What he knew was mostly self-taught and his attitude to the world, society in general, and his place in it was coloured by his own experiences:

"There is only one person in this world who has any interest in you at all," he used to tell Samantha, "and that's you."

Charlie never entirely lost his cockney accent, however hard he tried. Tall and good looking, he was able to charm the pants off anyone though, when he chose to do so. Somehow, he managed to avoid jail, although it was a close-run thing at times. He seemed determined to become wealthy by any means, and his lifestyle, which he was unable to afford, reflected this.

Samantha's mother Evelyn had fallen deeply under Charlie's spell when Samantha was ten years old. Back then, Samantha was already very clever, always achieved good grades at school, although she lacked confidence in her ability, and this only increased after Charlie joined their family. He was never satisfied with anything she achieved.

If she came second in class he asked why she hadn't come first; if she scored 90% in a test or exam he wondered why it wasn't higher. He decided to take her under his wing, telling her and her mother, "This child has fantastic potential but I'm clearly the only one who can develop that; I don't want that fusty old fart Harold interfering."

After that, Samantha rarely saw her real father, Harold Webster. Her mother never raised any objections, and Samantha felt too intimidated by Charlie to ask.

Meanwhile Charlie encouraged her to lie and cheat at just about anything she did. He started with card games. "I always take a couple of fresh packs of cards with me, just mark the high cards with small pen or pencil marks. Aces like this. Kings like this." He showed her. "An' always count the cards, jus' the high cards to start, but you'll get used to counting them all after a while."

He introduced her to shop lifting by saying: "The theivin' bastards, everything is overpriced. Take a few skirts into the change room put two on underneath what you have on. When you leave, jus' pay fer one. Hide pants in your bra or in your pants an' so on."

It all came to a head when Samantha was caught cheating in an exam and was rusticated from her exclusive private school for a term. Charlie blamed her for getting caught. She managed to get a scholarship to university on her own merits, however, suggesting a glimmer of what might be possible in future.

Once she completed university, Charlie taught her to falsify sets of accounts, and how to access other people's computers to steal information contained therein, without the targets knowing. If she knew it was wrong she didn't say anything, simply followed Charlie's lead.

Samantha was employed at Sandford's, a financial advisory a firm started by Charlie; he worked Samantha hard but made no attempt to interfere with her social life. She could see from the way that her mother behaved and from her visits to school friends' homes that Charlie's behaviour was unusual to say the least.

Samantha joined Websters shortly after her twenty-third birthday, seeing it as an opportunity to finally prove her own worth. None of the staff except Jacqueline Briggs knew of her relationship with Harold, and she started to do well.

But then, Charlie told her the truth – she wasn't there to work hard. She was there to steal information on a company controlled by Websters: "By whatever means," Charlie told her.

Even her mother seemed to be involved, which disappointed Samantha. Not that she was surprised. Her mother had apparently met Harold Webster when she was just a teenager, already pregnant. She'd been brought up in a middle-class household in North London, by a bookkeeper father who worked long hours for a firm of solicitors in Gray's Inn, and a mother who watched dull television programmes until bedtime at nine thirty. Saturdays was given over to bowls and Sundays to the local Anglican Church. They always spent their two-week holiday at a small hotel in Brighton. She had a brother, two years younger than she was, with whom she fought constantly; and a sister, Ida, five years older, married and living in Australia, who had over many years unsuccessfully tried to tame Evelyn's wilder instincts. But by the time Evelyn was thirteen, she was virtually crawling up the walls of their neat little house craving excitement. She lost her virginity at fifteen, and left school at eighteen having had half a dozen lovers.

Her parents had introduced her to Harold when she found she was pregnant and she married him hastily, much to everyone's relief. Naturally, she found marriage to Harold excessively dull. She had several – what she thought were – discreet affairs, then to everyone's horror and surprise she divorced Harold having fallen for the charms of Charlie Sandford, unable to resist or even criticise the excitement his activities presented. She went along with everything he did, even the highly immoral and possibly damaging plan that he had in placing Samantha at Websters.

Apparently, she had been persuaded to phone Harold and ask to meet him for lunch in a well-known restaurant in the vicinity of the Websters office, where she then convinced him to employ Samantha.

It hadn't taken much, Charlie told Samantha. "He feels guilty for not doing enough for you over the years. But this David fellow, he's the source of the info I is really after. 'Eclipse' is the name of the company."

Samantha already knew that. "But David takes no notice of me; I'm always popping into his office asking dumb questions, which he answers politely. I'm sure he knows perfectly well I could easily answer the questions myself with a little bit of application. I brush against him in the corridor whenever I have the chance; he doesn't take a blind bit of notice of me."

Charlie looked at her, frustrated. "He's a bloke for Christ's sake," he said, "you will have to be a bit more ruthless. Waggle a bit of tit an' bum at 'im and you will 'ave 'im eating out of your hand in no time. And get rid of that bloody stupid boyfriend of yours, he's a complete waste of space anyway. When this is all over, you can find someone else; if this all works out we'll be well off; puts us into another social stratum if you see what I mean."

So she put her bold plan into practice, hoping that once she was done Charlie would let her get on with her own life. She knew she was competent and had not disappointed all those with whom she worked at Websters, including David. Many of Charlie's lessons had helped her, much to her surprise; she could spot false information a mile off and she was able to deal with situations ruthlessly when the occasion demanded. She was soon involved with David's business issues. Frustratingly, although she had had one discussion on Eclipse with David, none of the business issues made any mention of Eclipse.

"I do have imprints of his office and desk keys, though," she told Charlie, leaving out how much she had enjoyed being with David and that she thought she was falling in love with him.

"Right, we've got 'im hooked," said Charlie, all business-like, "now we need to land 'im. If you give me those imprints, I'll have duplicates cut. Also, I've now lined up a flat from a mate near your office; together, tomorrow, we'll get it furnished properly and you'll have to set the computer up there to nick the info we want from those buggers."

"I have to be in the office tomorrow," said Samantha.

"Call in sick for Christ's sake, what we have here is much more important than any buggering around you may be doing at Websters."

I'll do what he wants. Hopefully I will be left alone to get on with my life after that, she thought unrealistically.

They spent the next two days and the weekend setting up the flat.

Chapter 13. The Set-Up

The next time they were getting dressed in Harold's office, Samantha handed David a key. "I told you about the flat I'm moving into? It's in nearby Lamb's Conduit Street. Maybe we can meet there at lunchtime sometimes, perhaps even tomorrow," she looked at him coyly.

David looked relieved. "Good, because I can't keep doing evenings. It's too difficult."

So at lunchtime the following day, a Friday, David let himself into the flat.

Samantha was laying out a light lunch on the dining room table. "Lunch or bit of you know what?" she asked smiling.

"You know the answer to that," said David as he took her by the hand in the direction of the main bedroom. "Bed, lunch and then more bed."

"Well, that was certainly up to expectations," said a laughing Samantha as they lay in bed, "much more comfortable than Harold's carpet I must say. Lunch?"

David nodded. "Stay as you are, I really am enjoying the view," he said, staying naked himself.

They nibbled at the salad Samantha had provided, but after she sat on his lap, they soon returned to bed.

Samantha found herself wondering if getting on with her life after all this did in fact involve David – things were just so easy between them.

***

David had a chance to wander about the small two-bedroom flat while Samantha was in the toilet. He picked out five discreetly installed cameras, well-hidden but visible if one knew what to look for. There was a newish PC set up in the second bedroom. The furniture looked as if it had been rented; there were no pictures or any other kind of decoration on the walls and no photos or anything personal in the establishment. The few drawers he looked in were empty and so was the wardrobe. There was very little food in the kitchen and all the fridge contained was a carton of milk. He dressed quickly and continued to peck at the lunch Samantha had provided. On the one hand he was infatuated with the relationship that was developing between them, he was certainly falling in love with her.

On the other hand, he was certain that Samantha was up to no good and the set up in the flat confirmed this; it was not a home that she would spend any time in, apart from the assignations with him. He guessed her real home was elsewhere.

Reminding him of the very serious risk he was taking with Samantha, Des was waiting when David returned to the office later. Risks to his marriage and his hard-fought position at Websters.

I wonder if I shouldn't just jack this whole business in, he thought, *most people would think I'm quite mad with where all this is going.*

An image of naked, beautiful Samantha interrupted. He shook his head. There was no possibility he could contemplate giving her up.

Des had the additional equipment and he and David spent a very long evening setting it all up.

He phoned Melinda, telling her he would be very late. "I have Des here. We are sorting out a whole new set-up for my PC and it's critical it's done tonight."

"Okay," said Melinda, though David could sense a frisson of excitement in her voice.

"Did you have a good day?" he asked, wondering what had excited her. "I'll be able to spend a bit of time with you and the kids over the weekend I hope."

"Yes, I had a very good day actually, I've been asked to speak at an investment conference in Edinburgh at the end of the month, as you know I have done a bit of consulting work, mainly on investment strategy, for various people over the years. This invitation came through one of those contacts. I'll be away two or three days."

"Wonderful," said David, "it sort-of gets you back into the game so to speak. Look I must go, Des is beginning to look impatient."

"Okay, see you later, grub will be in the microwave." The connection was cut.

"This machine here," Des explained, "fits neatly underneath your own laptop; unless you know about it, it's virtually invisible."

He explained that the top computer operated as normal and didn't have any effect on the operation of the lower computer. "If you want to use the underneath computer you need this device," he handed David a short pencil like object, "you then just press it into that very small aperture on the edge of the lower computer. This switches off the top computer and activates the underneath computer. You will have to use another password for the underneath computer, which we can establish now. This is the only weakness in the system, you must keep the device on you at all times, such as in a locked briefcase or something like that; if it gets into the wrong hands information in the lower computer becomes visible to anyone. The keyboard operates as normal on both machines, dependant on which one is switched on."

"Okay all that's pretty clear," said David, "but there is more to it now as I indicated before."

He told Des about the flat and gave him a key and the address. "We could walk over there now. Although she says she's living there I'm pretty sure she isn't, it's just a venue for our assignations and the real reason they've established it, is to collect info from me."

They walked over to the flat, which was in complete darkness as predicted. David pressed the bell; as expected there was no answer.

It was a block of four flats, recently constructed; there was no general security, each flat was accessed from the outside. Samantha's flat was at the back on the top of two floors.

"No cameras on the outside," announced Des as they went in and switched on the main light.

Des quickly walked round the flat. "Six cameras, very well hidden, all of which are sensitive to movement, they switch on when someone walks into the room and switch off after fifteen or twenty seconds of no movement. This is serious stuff."

"Six, I only counted five," said David.

"You may have missed the one above the bedroom door." He pointed.

David nodded. "Can we have a look at what's been recorded?" asked David. He soon wished he hadn't. Much to his embarrassment there were graphic images of him and Samantha running around the flat naked that afternoon and making love.

A very surprised Des looked at him.

"Just what I was worried about," said David. "Turn it all off please."

After a minute's contemplation David said to Des, "I want two things, firstly can we find a way of letting them believe that the cameras they have installed are working properly, but we must make sure any images that are taken disappear within a very short time, maybe to be replaced with some sort of porn movie. Secondly I need to know what info they steal from my PC at Websters."

"Finding out what info they have on the PC will be easy. I'll install a wireless device here, which they'll never find, and download everything they have here on a daily basis. I won't even have to come here; I'll have to install another PC somewhere in your offices or nearby, to pick up the signal though."

"And the stuff on the cameras?" asked David.

"I'll have to come in here to fix that," said Des, he looked embarrassed, "how often...?"

"Once or twice a week, I expect. This may go on for a couple of months. If I could just phone you and book you into a nearby hotel, when you need to be here to clean..." He was going to say, 'clean up' but rephrased it saying, "to deal with the problem."

"Okay, that would work," answered Des.

Des was looking contemplative and seemed to be about to say something but remained silent. David, used to his moods, looked at him saying, "Something else on your mind?"

Des nodded. "If we replace the film in here with porn movies as soon as they see the film they'll realise they've been rumbled. What I could do is to install film that automatically wipes itself clean after one viewing."

"Smart," said David, almost thinking aloud, "that means, after each assignation, all you need to do is to replace the new film that has been installed with doctored film. The people that have installed the cameras will then always go away with what looks like legitimate film. If they watch it the film will be blank next time they try to look at it. Could we test that once you are ready? Can we doctor or destroy the film in the cameras now; the doctored film will take care of anything after today."

Des nodded. "Just give me a day or two."

"We may need to think of your security," said David, changing the subject, "if somehow someone susses out what we are doing you may be at risk."

"Mnn, I'll install a movement sensor in the flat. It's a simple device. If someone is hiding in the flat I'll know, so won't go in, until he or she leaves. I'll make sure it's well hidden," Des was having fun and was intrigued with the clandestine nature of what he was being asked to do.

David also phoned Joe to remind him of his request to look into Samantha's background. "I thought we agreed that you would be back to me in two weeks," asked David. "It was a bit more complicated than I expected," responded Joe, "but I've now done all the investigation required. What do you want me to do with it?"

"Just tell me what you have found out please,"

"I've tried to contact you on the number you gave me," he grumbled, "a couple of times. Anyway, I now have chapter and verse on your friend Samantha."

He then proceeded to tell David about Samantha's paternity, about Evelyn's marriage to Charlie Sandford having previously been married to Harold Webster. "Samantha is supposed to be Harold's daughter, but frankly any of two or three men could easily be her real father."

He told David about Evelyn's affairs and Samantha's previous employment at Sandford's, as well as her education. He had even unearthed the fact that she had been rusticated from her school and the reason for that.

"There was a boyfriend," Joe added, "who seems to have disappeared, since she joined Websters." David was amazed at the fit of jealous rage he felt at the mention of a boyfriend in relation to Samantha; he was normally quite calm and was always quite controlled even in very threatening situations. He obviously knew Samantha was not a virgin before his entanglement with her, but he had never known such emotion in any previous relationships.

"Okay," he said to Joe, "anything else?"

"No that seems to be it, oh yes there's the new flat she seems to be using in Lamb's Conduit Street, but then you know about that..." He waited for David to respond.

"Thanks," said David, without acknowledging the last remark, "destroy all your notes and any reference to this investigation. As discussed, send me the bill. Nothing, absolutely nothing should be kept relating to this business; that is no information whatsoever should be kept anywhere relating to this investigation. Is that clear?"

"Yes, you made that clear from the beginning," said Joe, who was curious about the secrecy. They ran off.

***

Joe knew that what he had told David was valuable. He briefly considered how he could further profit from the information he had gleaned. Joe lived in the present, he very rarely thought beyond his current action. He phoned Sandford.

***

David now wondered what sort of trouble he might be getting himself into. He was horrified and a little apprehensive in fully understanding Samantha's relationship with Charlie Sandford. He knew Charlie Sandford's reputation, and he knew of Sandford's advisory business, although he had never met the man.

I would never touch anything involving Charlie Sandford with a ten-foot pole. He has never hesitated to get into the rough stuff if things aren't going his way, he thought.

When David had collected his thoughts, he said to himself, *this is all really dumb. You are risking everything, your career, your marriage, your whole existence. Maybe the best thing would be to go to Harold, tell him everything and get Samantha out of Websters and out of your life.*

He was, however, quite unable to even think of not seeing Samantha again. He idly wondered if he might 'rescue' her from the situation, but he knew if there was a hint that he knew what was going on, Samantha would disappear anyway.

His experiences in the SAS gave him another view of what was involved in taking risks. He really enjoyed understanding those risks and putting into place strategies and tactics to minimise the risks. Justifiably, he felt what he had put in place would minimise the risks involved in getting the better of Charlie Sandford and additionally, if he pulled off what he had in mind he thought Websters would be better off.

He made another call on the mobile he'd used for communicating with Joe, to an old friend: Jones from the SAS.

"Jones," the call was answered immediately.

"I expect you know who this is," said David.

"Yes, I can't say that I ever expected to hear from you again..."

"I need a favour."

There was a grunt at the other end, but the phone was not put down.

"I need your help," David told Jones. He then went on to explain the situation. "You may have to break a few bones; the people I'm dealing with can get very rough if they are thwarted."

"What makes you think I want to have anything to do with what you have in mind?"

David hesitated. "A few years ago now, I had the same dilemma. I had had a delightful evening in bed with my girlfriend and the next day I was well prepared to write the last paper of a university exam. Instead, I was told there was a certain sergeant who was in trouble, who had specifically asked for me to lead any rescue attempt... and the rest they say is history. How are your knees by the way, sergeant, the last time I saw them, they were not a pretty picture?"

"Okay, okay, just fill me in; of course I'll help you, as I said then 'I owe you one', I still do. My knees are actually fine. I need a cart to get about the golf course, but my limp isn't too bad."

"Mnn, I'll then expect a call from one of your colleagues within a week, on this number," he gave Jones the number he'd used with Joe. "No other form of communication please," David hesitated. "I'm pleased to find you sounding so well." The phone was put down as he finished.

David knew that Jones kept in touch with some of his ex-colleagues who were prepared to take on certain jobs involving their specialist skills, which he, David, thought of as the SAS mafia. Payment would be in the form of a donation to a pension fund set up by Jones, for colleagues who were not particularly well off.

Chapter 14. Melinda

Within eight years of David's marriage proposal, and two children later, Melinda realised just how very fortunate she had been to marry David; she also thought she was happy. She lived in a very nice house in Barnes, a well to do suburb in South West London. The children had either just gone to school or were about to go. She surprised herself how much she had adored having the children. She couldn't do enough for them; she ran from morning to night taking Michael to swimming or football or rugby and even to some music lessons. Janice was into ballet and learning the violin. It seemed to her that she was as fulfilled as she possibly could be; even though her aspirations in the business world had had to take a back seat.

At times Melinda felt there was something missing though. David consulted her occasionally on minor issues to do with the business, on some occasions he took her advice but on others that was not the case. In any event she felt she had no real influence on how Websters was managed, although she knew she had materially helped David in persuading Harold to invest in Eclipse. She had maintained some of her contacts in the wider business community with some consulting work on investment strategy and occasionally wrote well received articles in various business magazines. She still worried about David's SAS activities and thought he should focus more on his position at Websters. Both he and Melinda kept themselves very fit.

In past weeks it seemed to her that David was behaving peculiarly: he often arrived late from work using work pressure as an excuse, at times she thought she caught the faint whiff of another woman's scent, they hardly ever made love any more. Very reluctantly she concluded that David must be having an affair, he occasionally mentioned a Samantha Wicks, who had recently joined Websters. Whilst wondering what she should do about the situation she received a surprise call from an acquaintance asking her if she would be prepared to speak at an investment conference in Edinburgh in two weeks' time. "One of our speakers has withdrawn, so you would be filling in for him. Airfares and hotels will be paid for of course, but I'm afraid I can only offer you a small fee," she was told. She accepted with alacrity and found David was supportive, although he seemed to be more and more distracted.

David never again referred to his affair with Lizzie, but every now and then Melinda thought about the letter he had once shared with her. She knew he had kept the letter among a clutter of other mementoes, such as university Rugby photos.

One day after a brief visit to Websters offices in Bloomsbury, she was having a cup of coffee in a nearby café she noticed a pretty woman accompanied by her small son and another woman, at another table in the same café. She took no notice, but something made her look more closely at the woman; it was definitely the woman David had referred to as Lizzie, the one who had written the letter. When she finished her coffee, out of curiosity she deliberately walked out of the cafe past the woman's table and then wished she hadn't.

Lizzie, in an expensive skirt and jacket with a pretty pink shirt, was dressed more formally than had been the case when Melinda had seen her with David at Oxford. She'd lost none of her looks and seemed happy and content. Melinda sensed a personal surge of jealousy, something that almost never happened to her, but seeing Lizzie increased her already raised sense of insecurity. It was obvious Lizzie had also just had a meeting at Websters, almost certainly with David.

Her feeling of unease increased when she looked at the woman's son, three or four years older than her eldest child. She could not help noticing, to her consternation and horror, he looked just like David. On the way back to Barnes on South West trains she wondered what she should say to David, if anything, thinking, *I wonder if he really did tell me the truth when he showed me that letter from Lizzie...* She almost missed her stop.

She decided to mention to David that he had seen the woman and where.

"Yes. Lizzie." He had responded. "She's a client, as I have explained. She popped in today to sign some papers. She also brought along another possible client; that would have been the other woman you saw with her. I'm the godfather of her son, although I have done precious little for him. He spent an hour in the nearby British Museum during our meeting. Her husband is my CO in the SAS." He added unnecessarily, "They are very well off."

Melinda decided in view of the straightforward response from David not to pursue the issue any further. She took comfort in the fact that he had never been anything but totally honest with her about everything, including the time just after they had met when he had shown her the letter Lizzie had written to him. At that time, he had reassured her that he was not two-timing her.

Nevertheless, she still felt uncomfortable with what she had seen; there was no doubt in her mind that David could be and possibly was the natural father of the child.

Chapter 15. The Sting

David, understanding all the aspects of the game he was playing, felt he had protected himself and Websters as well as was possible.

Through Des he was now able to provide whatever information he felt like, false or otherwise, to the PC in Samantha's flat. Des had told him there was a wireless device installed on David's PC, which would not be visible to anyone but people who understood what they were doing. "It will only transmit the info on the 'top' computer; it must have been installed before we set up the 'underneath' computer."

David had Des switching the film in the flat, so once the images on the film were exposed all that would be visible thereafter would be blank screens.

He knew Jones would help if there was any rough stuff.

Despite the guilt pursuing him day and night David was intrigued and completely distracted by Samantha; they met in the flat two or three times a week. David was entranced and had the feeling that this was reciprocated by Samantha. He occasionally caught her glancing at him with a look of concern on her face. Part of him knew he was putting his marriage, his children and his future at Websters on the line.

This can't last much longer, he thought.

Once his computer set-up was fully established, David had ensured the folder keeping his sign in procedure was the only item in the narrow drawer in the front of his desk. All the drawers in the desk were always locked. David was quite sure Samantha had copies of all the keys to his office and desk.

Onto the top PC he loaded details, available in the public domain, of two companies that he might legitimately have an interest in but that he was certain they were way out of Charlie Sandford's league. To make the situation look authentic he allowed all his emails except those which were highly confidential to remain on the top PC, the one to which he was sure Samantha now had access to. All this involved him in very long hours and although he now spent no time with Samantha at night it was evident that Melinda was becoming more and more suspicious.

Almost since the beginning of the affair David had started to check the register of the out of hour's entry and departure to Websters offices. Whenever he found an entry for Samantha he checked on the PC that Des had installed in a locked office behind shelves in the stationery cupboard – only he knew of its existence. Sure enough, the info that he had placed on the top computer was always to be found there.

"Okay, that seems to be working," he said to himself. He regularly checked with Des after one of his assignations with Samantha in the flat. Mostly, the arrangements he had with Des, seemed to be working. On one occasion when Des was due to visit the flat to install the film that would wipe itself clean after one showing he received a call from Des in a panic who told him. "There's someone in the flat, only making small movements, but there's someone there. What should I do?"

"Don't go inside. If you can, Des, wait in the shadows until whoever is in there comes out and then see if you can get a picture of them, a clear picture. I'll deal with it after that. Just make sure you aren't seen though."

Des, obviously excited, but looking more dishevelled than usual, appeared in David's office at seven the next morning, knowing he would find David already there. He showed him the picture: it was Joe. There was a clear picture of Joe and the number of the flat. "Shit," said David, "double game, thanks Des; I can now fix the bastard permanently. Was he carrying anything?"

"No, that's the surprising thing," answered Des. "I went back into the place after he left. Someone had fiddled with a couple of the cameras, but it looks as if they didn't know what they were doing, all the films were still there. I've left them in place, of course, and once the film has been replaced with new film I'll change that for the stuff that wipes clean after one viewing."

"Okay," said David, "you've done really well Des, really well. I will certainly fix the bastard in this picture. I hope you won't have any more trouble but just keep doing what you've been doing and don't take any chances."

"You know this person?" asked Des after a moment's hesitation.

"I do, but don't you worry. He won't be around much longer."

"You're going to kill him?" asked Des. Des had difficulty in distinguishing between reality and fantasy.

"No, no," David laughed. Des had a penchant for watching violent whodunits on TV, "he'll be leaving the country for a few months, that's all. Nobody is going to be hurt."

***

Although David almost always treated people with thoughtfulness and consideration, he knew at times he would have to be ruthless.

A few days later David was waiting in Joe's office when Joe arrived whistling happily, shortly after ten am. Joe was dressed untidily, which was how he thought private detectives operated. He did a double take and the whistling stopped abruptly when he saw David. He tried to leave the office, but David was too quick for him. He grabbed Joe by the collar and pushed him into a chair; he pulled out the photo of Joe leaving the flat and shoved it aggressively at him, without saying a word.

"I can explain everything, David..."

"There's no need," said David, "you're a double-crossing little shit, and this is what's going to happen. I've taken over the lease of this grubby little shithole you occupy, by paying the rent you owe. A locksmith will appear shortly to change the locks. I've taken possession of the few files you have in that thing in the corner that passes for a filing cabinet and I've taken possession of the clapped-out piece of shit you call your computer."

"You, you can't do that... it's my whole life..."

"I had a quick look at a couple of the files I now have in my possession; if you want to play that game I'll call the police right now – there's enough evidence in those files to put you away for five years at least."

"But but..." Joe went as white as a sheet.

"No buts, this is what's going to happen. Here's a cheque for what I owe you, minus the unpaid rent. You'll leave the country today and not return." He threw Joe's passport on the desk. "With this money and what's in your bank account you'll be able to live in Greece or somewhere like that for six months at least... and remember if you set foot in this country before I say you can, those files will go to the cops."

Joe looked thoroughly intimidated.

"One other thing," said David. "Go anywhere near Sandford and this whole deal is off, exactly the same thing will happen. Oh, and give me the key to the flat Sandford gave you."

Joe handed it over without further comment.

David did indeed have the appropriate contacts in the police; one of his contacts had been in the SAS reserve battalion with him and he could easily have sent him Joe's files. Joe knew he had broken the law on several occasions and would certainly go to jail if any of that came to light. David obviously had no access to information on people arriving and leaving the country, but he was sure Joe didn't know that.

"Give me your mobile please, Joe." Joe now terrified and browbeaten handed it over without argument. David took out the sim-card, which he put in his pocket and handed the phone back to Joe. "You'll fax me a copy of your one-way ticket leaving the country and you'll send me your contact details when you've arrived at wherever you're going."

"What about my flat?"

"What about it?" asked David, thinking Joe would scarper to leave his unpaid rent to look after itself.

Joe was silent. There was a knock on the door.

"That'll be the locksmith," said David. "Out," he said to Joe, "time for you to leave."

Joe left.

David knew that Sandford would have other strings to his bow. He had assumed that, as far as Sandford was concerned, the fact that Joe had landed in his lap was wholly fortuitous and when he disappeared he would merely put other, temporarily shelved, plans into practice. David considered what Sandford might do about Joe's disappearance, *probably nothing*, he thought, *easy come easy go*. There was a small credit in Joe's bank account which could have come from Sandford.

***

A few weeks after Samantha joined Websters, Harold had invited David into his office to introduce Luke McLintock, a new arrival. Harold was unusually effusive in his introduction. "Luke has introduced his family here as clients," said Harold, "which will be a bit of a fillip to our business." David knew of the wealthy McLintock family.

Luke, however, would not look David in the eye, and ignored David's extended hand.

"It would be ideal for the business if you two could work together," offered Harold. After a short uncomfortable discussion Luke and David were ushered out.

"Drink later?" suggested David.

"Can't; busy tonight," was Luke's short answer.

David made several further attempts, over three months, at getting to know Luke better. Luke rebuffed all of them.

Luke's Cambridge background made their immediate rivalry all the more poignant. A slightly overweight five-foot-six, with mousy brown hair and spectacles, David realised that despite his benign appearance Luke was quite ruthless and unscrupulous. David had posted on the internal web, a well thought out analysis on the merits of a particular company. A week later Harold called him into his office saying, "I just want you to look at this marvellous analysis Luke has given me…"

David took one glance at the document and replied, "Harold, I personally wrote that analysis and posted it on our internal web a week ago. Ask anyone." He stormed out of the office. After that David made sure he emailed and also gave Harold copies of any analyses he had done, always a few days before he posted the analysis on Websters internal web.

David took no direct action against Luke. He always made sure his own collection of clients were well looked after based on comprehensive well thought through research.

David also noticed, when examining the after-hours register, that Luke often signed in soon after Samantha had signed out. He was obviously trying to find out what Samantha was up to. Danger signals loomed. On the way to his next assignation with Samantha he ducked into an alleyway and waited; sure enough, within less than half a minute there was Luke panting and half running trying to catch up, obviously following David.

Wondering what to do David eventually told Samantha what was going on. "Mnn," said Samantha. "I must say I've seen him flitting about. I haven't taken much notice though. He seems quite harmless."

"He's not harmless. That much I can tell you. He may try to do something stupid, if we aren't careful."

"Like what?"

"Well one possibility is he will tell Harold that we are having an affair..."

"I could pre-empt that, just by telling Harold myself. If he then went and sneaked on us, he would look like an idiot. Having told Harold, we could make sure Luke finds out..." she giggled, "what fun..."

"I need to think about that," said David, "can I ask you not to do anything for a few days."

David was now confident the system he had set up worked. He needed to find out what information Samantha really wanted. He though it probably had something to do with Eclipse and remembering now the conversation they had had some months earlier, he mentally revisited the conversation.

Samantha often talked about Twitter, Facebook and Google, which David largely ignored. After a few weeks prompted by an impatient Charlie she said to David, "A few months ago we had a discussion about Eclipse, you told me Websters backed the original float. Should we be recommending clients invest in such a company?"

"How is Eclipse doing?" she added.

"Results will be announced in a couple of months," he said. "We'll have to wait for that." The shares had risen substantially after the listing, but investors were waiting nervously for the current year's results. David and sometimes Harold kept in close touch with the company, but all the information they were given on potential results was closely guarded; the only people outside the company who knew anything about Eclipse were David and Harold.

David somehow avoided answering the question. He wanted no hint that he had a made any recommendation one way or another on the company.

A few more conversations over the next week or so convinced David that Charlie was after information on Eclipse. David could see that, if Charlie played his cards right, armed with secret correct prior information on the forthcoming results, he could legitimately make a fortune. If he stole the information through the system he, David, had set up, there would be no hint of any insider trading; Charlie had set the situation up to make it look as if he had merely made a lucky guess.

There was no information held electronically at Websters on Eclipse. All the information on Eclipse was on paper in a safe in Harold's office. David and Harold were the only two people who knew the combination.

David again considered taking Harold into his confidence, a route he decided not to go down. He knew that conservative Harold would veto the whole exercise and find a way of removing Samantha, regardless of filial associations.

David was sure he could foil the plot, and possibly help Websters make some money, but more importantly David wanted to continue the liaison with Samantha for as long as possible.

Surreptitiously from information contained in the safe, David obtained all the information he needed on Eclipse and copied it into the 'underneath' computer. Over some weeks he created another set of figures completely falsifying the information he had on the company. He gave the revised figures to a Chartered Accountant friend, asking him to do an exhaustive check to make sure there was no flaw in what he had done; mainly to make sure the figures looked authentic. The figures showed, falsely, that Eclipse was about to announce disastrous results for its latest financial year. He did nothing with the information, knowing that once he had exposed it, his affair with Samantha would be over, assuming that Charlie would act on it. He also hesitated because he knew that if Charlie acted as David thought he would, once he had the information, it would send Sandford bankrupt.

Not wanting to leave a stone unturned and being completely ruthless in unearthing everything involving the 'Eclipse affair' as David had termed it, he collected samples of both Samantha's and Harold's hair.

There is no way that Samantha is Harold's daughter, he said to himself, *for a start the bone structure in her face is all wrong.*

He found an agency and confidentially gave them the hair samples. When he was asked the reason for his enquiry he told them the truth. "We have someone in the office who is claiming a relationship with the boss, I just need to be able to verify the veracity of what is being said." They took on the assignment without asking any further questions.

Within two weeks the answer came back. "Female in her early twenties is not related in any way to the male in his early sixties."

Okay, thought David, *we're getting down to brass tacks now.*

The affair with Samantha continued, much to David's delight. In the meantime, David had up loaded more information on three other companies, which he didn't think Charlie would have any interest in. He also included substantial amounts of previously completed analytical information, which was all in the public domain.

Much to his surprise David had a call from Charlie:

"Mr Phillips, this is Charlie Sandford here..."

"Oh yes. Mr Sandford, this is a surprise," answered David. "What can I do for you?

"I have some rather confidential info that I would like to share with you."

"Oh yes, well why don't you come to the office here. We are very discreet..."

"Nah, it'll have to be outside. Meet me at The Swan, just off Queen Square. Tomorrow, ten in the morning, just after openin', just you and me. If you ain't there you will regret it, I promise."

David was about to respond to Charlie when the phone was put down. He thought for a minute. He immediately walked out of the office to the pub in question just to understand the lie of the land. The interior was all dark wood with a number of discreet booths. He could see why Charlie had chosen the place for a confidential meeting. It also suited David's plan. Returning to the office he made one telephone call, on his disposable mobile, to a number given to him by Jones, he was asked for a password.

"Doggerone," he answered. He gave them another number. "This number will be defunct after this call."

"Okay, what's the game," he was asked, when the return call came a few minutes later.

David gave them the name of the pub. "Please be there on the dot at ten in the morning, I will be there at about five past. My companion will probably play silly buggers and be a few minutes to half an hour late. You know what I look like, just take a good look at the man who comes and sits at my table, if you can get a picture of him without him knowing, please do that. There may be others in the pub, please get photos of them as well, again without them knowing. There is unlikely to be any rough stuff, but if there is, do nothing unless it looks as if I'm in real danger. Only two of you this time. The real rough stuff will come later I expect."

After the call he went back to the street; looking about making sure he was not being observed he removed the sim card from the disposable phone, dumping the phone in one street bin and the sim card in another.

The next day, as was his habit, he arrived in the office before seven and got on with the various jobs he had set himself. At nine he locked his office door and, underneath his shirt, attached the very small recorder Des had supplied him with. First, he made sure the device was working correctly and then he set it so that he was sure it was invisible to anyone, even someone who was looking for such a device. He was sure Charlie would also be carrying a wire. He then tested the on/off switch making sure he could activate the device without anyone noticing.

He left the office at nine thirty and sat in a cafe next to the pub and sipped the coffee he had ordered. He pretended to read the paper but kept a good lookout on the entrance to the pub. At ten on the dot, two casually dressed men, who he identified as ex-SAS, entered the pub, and a few minutes later two quite scruffy men having looked around, seeming to make sure they had the right place, also entered the pub. David followed them and seeing that coffee was available ordered one at the bar.

"I'll bring it over," the barmaid told him, smiling.

David's two protectors were sitting in one corner apparently chatting, but he could see they had a complete view of everything in the pub. The other two were sitting in a booth. David plonked himself at a table in the middle of the room. He continued to read the paper. The barmaid brought his coffee over. Just after ten thirty, David got up apparently abandoning what was left of his coffee and making as if to leave. One of the two that David had identified as Charlie's goons made a quick call on his mobile and a few seconds later Charlie came bustling in. He came and sat down at David's table and without any sort of greeting.

"This won't take long, I just 'ave some rather revealing pictures to show you and then I want some info; no fuss no bother. You are 'aving an affair with my daughter," Charlie continued. "These pictures will go to your wife if you don't cooperate." He pulled a small video player from his briefcase and switched it on. He fiddled for a few minutes and then turned the screen to face David.

After a minute or so David said, "Mr Sandford, have you got the correct film clip? All I can see is a blank screen." David turned the device round to face Charlie; the player was obviously working but all that was visible on the screen was some grainy film with no images showing.

"Just a minute," said Charlie. He quickly replaced the film in the camera and turned the machine on again with exactly the same result. Charlie had the grace to look embarrassed, he swore under his breath.

"Mr Sandford, you said you needed some information, what are you after?" asked David.

Without a word Charlie moved to another table and continued fiddling with the device. He returned. "Here, this is better," he said. An apparently bemused David looked at what he was being shown and then said, "It's the same, there doesn't seem to be anything on there. Look if you'll excuse me, Mr Sandford, I'll leave you to it. I've wasted enough time already today. When you genuinely have something to show me let me know." He got up and left.

Two hours later David received a call from what he assumed was one of the two SAS mafia that had been in the pub with him. "Your friend spent about forty minutes with those two scruffs in the pub. We managed to record most of the conversation, which I will send you, together with the photos you asked for. There is no doubt they are planning some rough stuff. From what we could hear they said something like 'switched the film' whatever that means. We'll keep in touch; this business is far from over."

David spent the next few days carefully planning what he would do next. He again considered taking Harold into his confidence, but again decided that Harold would veto any plans he might have, especially if there was likely to be any unpleasantness.

He decided that the first step was to ask Samantha to go ahead and tell Harold of their affair.

At their next assignation he said to her, "What was Harold's reaction when you told him?"

"Not much," was the answer, "he just said that it would come to nothing since you seemed to be happily married. He also said that he was disappointed and that you were his most trusted employee and he didn't want this business to mean you would leave."

David knew Sandford would probably have people watching the flat, so on the Wednesday he arranged to meet Samantha in the flat, as had become their habit, at lunch time. He said to Des, "Once you see us leave, go straight in, don't wait until the evening. But don't do anything; there will a ladder against the window of the main bedroom. Leave immediately by that ladder and scarper, away from the flat and come to the office."

Des looked scared.

"Do as I say, and you won't get hurt. Any buggering around..." David did not finish the sentence; he merely wagged his finger in Des's face.

Des did as he was asked and dashed through the flat and was out of the bedroom window and down the ladder within a minute of entering the premises. As instructed he ran into Guilford Street and then to Russell Square tube station, where he made a call to David. "Come to the office," David told him. Des saw nothing of the two men scrambling up the ladder into the flat.

Ten minutes after Des had escaped, two men emerged from the shadows and with a key supplied by Charlie went into the flat. "We'll catch him red 'anded," said the leader. To their utter amazement as they entered the darkened flat, they were both taken down by two masked men. They were gagged and tied to chairs. "Okay, we want some info and we want it quick," said one of the men. "Tell us what we want to know, and you won't get hurt. Who sent you here and what were you expecting to do?"

There was silence from both the men.

"This is going to be very painful unless you cooperate." The fingers of one of Charlie's goons was grasped and bent backwards. There was still no response. "Okay, have it your way." There was a sharp crack and a yell from the leading goon as one of his fingers was broken.

"Answer the question; unless you want more of that, you have two hands and two feet." Another finger was grasped and bent back.

"No, no please. We'll tell you everything."

"Our boss wants some very valuable info. from the bloke who comes here and shags our boss's daughter. Someone has been fiddlin' with the tapes. Our job was to stop him."

"Who's your boss?"

There was silence.

"I'm beginning to lose patience." Another finger was bent.

"Charlie, Charlie Sandford," was the quick answer.

One of the masked men went into the bedroom and shut the door, while the other kept his eye on the two captives.

The man in the bedroom phoned David who listened to what he had to say. "Okay," said David. "I know Charlie Sandford and I know what he wants. Tell those two to get the hell out of London; frighten the shit out of them. There is no need to hurt them anymore. I just don't want Sandford to have any access to them, at all, for a few months at least. Sandford just needs to know that his latest scheme has come to nought. Get them out of there and leave no trace of yourselves, nothing at all. No fingerprints."

"Okay, we're wearing gloves, but we'll clean up. Is there anything else you want us to do? What about the tapes?"

"Leave the tapes. I'll deal with them in the next few minutes. Just get those morons out of there. Tell me when you are done." David concluded the discussion.

He waited thirty minutes before he was able to tell Des. "It's all clear now. Go back in and do what you were going to do in the first place. That sensor, which will tell if there is anyone in the place, is still operating I presume?"

A very nervous Des nodded.

David smiled, trying to reassure Des. "Just be careful and phone me when you've finished."

***

Luke had initially told Jacqueline Briggs of his suspicions that David and Samantha were having an affair, "they go to a nearby flat at lunchtime at least twice a week," he told her.

"How do you know this?" Jacqueline had asked.

"I make it my business to know what's going on here," was the response.

Jacqueline looked at Luke, sitting complacently in front of her. She distrusted his motives. From the beginning she had thought that Harold was making a mistake with his appointment.

"He'll bring some wealthy clients with him," Harold had said.

"They will leave just as quickly if he decides to move on," she had responded.

"I'll bear that in mind and try to ensure his loyalty."

"My perception is that his only loyalty is to himself," Jacqueline had said in her usual mild way.

Jacqueline was upset and disappointed at Luke's revelation. Apart from her own feelings she knew such a relationship could only spell trouble. She did her own checks and it was noticeable that David and Samantha were both often out of the office at lunchtime. She concluded that Luke was right, so she went to see Harold and told him of her suspicions.

"Yes," he said. "Samantha has been quite open with me about the situation. I don't like it but I'm not sure what to do about it."

"The only thing to do is to try to persuade both of them that is a very bad idea and if it continues one of them will have to leave."

"I don't want either of them to leave," was Harold's response. "How widely known is this business?"

Jacqueline shrugged. "It's not something I discuss with people."

She was going to warn Luke not to say anything but had been busy and it was not until a few days later when Harold called her into the office. "Luke has also now told me what David and Samantha are up to. To his surprise I told him that Samantha had already told me. I also told him to mind his own business and that spying on other members of staff was not within his remit."

"Any reaction from him?"

"Surprise. I think he thought that he was providing me with a major revelation."

After the discussion with Harold, Jacqueline sought Luke out. "I just need to tell you that Harold has already been told by Samantha of her and David's affair, so I suggest you shouldn't take it any further."

Luke said nothing about his discussion with Harold. "Thanks, I'll bear that in mind," he said.

Jacqueline wondered if she should say anything to David. In the end she decided that during one of their usual coffee discussions she would tell him that she knew of the affair and what she thought about it. David's response surprised her, she expected denial.

"Harold has been told," David said. "I'm sure he doesn't approve. I can't tell you much but it's unlikely to last much longer. I'm also aware that Luke has been spying on us."

***

A few weeks went by. The affair with Samantha continued. David finally decided to bait the trap he had so carefully laid. He loaded up onto the top computer the doctored information he had on Eclipse, thinking that Sandford would probably act on it and knowing the action would rapidly bring his affair with Samantha to an end. He was sure she had no idea he knew what was actually going on. She had also made no mention of the shenanigans that had gone on in the flat and that Charlie's goons had been banished; he thought that she was unlikely to have any knowledge of Charlie's goons anyway.

Despite himself David knew he would desperately miss Samantha when it was all over.

Trying to persuade himself that it was the right thing to do, he said to himself guiltily, *Maybe it's just as well. Sooner or later Melinda would have sussed this out and I'm not ready for that.*

David was desperately trying to catch-up on some other work when unusually Harold walked in to his office with a concerned and very worried expression on his face; he normally asked David and anyone else into his own office. "Some bastard is short selling Eclipse on the market," he blurted out, "it makes..." He was going to add 'no sense'.

Harold looked at the expression on David's face and immediately stopped what he was saying.

David ushered him out of the office and went with Harold to his own office. David had a device given him by Des which allowed him to check for bugs. The device immediately lit up when they went into Harold's office; the bug was obviously in Harold's jacket, which was hanging over the back of a chair.

Without saying anything David indicated to Harold that they leave the office and the jacket. He took him to a nearby cafe where they were able to talk without being overheard.

"I understand from Samantha that you think she is your daughter." Without waiting for a response, David continued by giving Harold the DNA report on his and Samantha's filial relationship. Harold's mild but irritated response was a surprise. "I know that. I've always been sterile. I've known for years. For all I know, Charlie could be the father. However, I have always recognised her as my daughter and I wanted to make up to her for the little I've been able to do for her, mainly because Charlie wouldn't let me."

Harold looked at David with raised eyebrows, without saying anything, but begging the question: *Is that what this is all about?*

David shook his head and then gave him chapter and verse on his affair with Samantha.

Harold waved him away impatiently. "I know all that, Samantha told me weeks ago."

David continued on as if he wasn't aware of Harold's interruption. He went on to explain that he had sussed out that Samantha was a plant to try to extract information from Websters. "Having worked out how they were going to get the information I used it to test the system I had put together." He explained about the secret computer set up in the stationery cupboard monitoring everything that Charlie had downloaded from his, David's, PC.

"I also doctored some info on Eclipse, since that seemed to be the company they were interested in, which I loaded onto my computer a week or two ago knowing that Charlie would be able to access the info and would probably act on it."

"Stupidly, they seem to have acted on the bullshit information, without doing any checks; I have confirmation that it's Charlie who's short selling on the basis that the results of Eclipse are going to be terrible, which is the info that I've been feeding him through the process just described."

David looked at Harold to see an expression of horror gradually creeping over his face. He briefly reflected that his decision not to consult Harold in the first place on his plan of deception was the right one, before he continued, "I have six brokers quietly and carefully buying up all the shares Charlie's been selling. Shares of course that the stupid bugger does not have, and all at low prices. None of the brokers know anything about what the others are doing," he stopped for a breather. "All the dealings are through a series of nominee companies, so tracing any of this back to Websters is going to be impossible, although what we are doing is completely legitimate."

Harold's face had gone from an expression of terror to one of bemused apprehension, David thought Harold could now see where all this was going. David continued, knowing he had Harold's full attention. "We both know the results for Eclipse are going to be outstanding this year and the prospects for the company are still very good, so when the results are announced next week, I'm expecting the share price to double from its current low level. Websters will be in a position to make a fortune and possibly Charlie will go broke since he will have to cover his position on the thousands of shares he's sold short. We are completely in the clear, Charlie had no business filching the info in the first place and we've had no official contact with him, either now or indeed in the past."

Harold, silent for a moment, his expression moved rapidly from anger to horror, at the risks David had taken, but relieved in that it looked as if David's initiative would provide Websters with a very large windfall. He drew several deep breaths, with David adding, "There was never any risk to Websters, if he made no use of the data he stole, then our position would be unchanged, we could lose nothing, and I knew that if he behaved like I thought he would we would make a bomb, which is clearly now what's happening."

"I don't know whether to fire you or give you a fucking great bonus," Harold said eventually. "You know of course that if you had consulted me in the first place I would have vetoed the whole business."

David was quite calm, not adding anything to what he had already said, and knowing that whatever now occurred Websters and therefore Harold would be considerably better off as a result of his actions. "What needs to be done first up is to fire Samantha. You owe her nothing; her mother and that bloody Charlie obviously put her up to this." David knew there was no possibility that Samantha could stay with Websters.

Harold got up from his seat and went out of the cafe. He paced up and down on the pavement outside, furiously muttering to himself. After ten minutes he returned with a fierce look on his face. "We don't have any choice but to continue with your outrageous scheme, but never, never, put me in this position again." David could see that he was amazed at the developments and he seemed to have come to terms with what had been done and that Websters could come out of the situation well ahead in financial terms.

After two further hours they settled on a plan of action. On returning to the office Samantha was nowhere to be found and her desk had been cleared. Jacqueline had a note with Samantha's resignation letter.

David suggested that Harold should phone Evelyn, which he did with no success.

After several weeks with David keeping himself right on top of the issue, but now making sure that Harold was constantly kept in the loop, he finally reported to Harold, "Websters now owns most of Eclipse with a low book value; if we take the minorities out we'll own it all."

To start with David was unable to unearth anything about where Samantha had gone. When it was all over, knowing that Jacqueline could be relied on to be discreet he told her a modified version of the story. "Charlie Sandford somehow got Samantha employed here with the sole purpose of stealing info that he thought he could profit from. He got his just desserts."

"What about Samantha?" asked Jacqueline, once she had absorbed all that had occurred. "She's been the big loser in all this."

"What about her? She knew what she was doing. I've had no contact for a while now; she was as much a part of the conspiracy as Charlie." David did not reveal his on-going feelings for Samantha and was worried that he hadn't been able to make any contact at all with her. He tried to leave Jacqueline with the impression that he didn't care what happened to Samantha. "You should also know that Samantha is not Harold's natural daughter. He's well aware of this."

Jacqueline looked surprised. "How do you know that?"

"DNA test, I found some hair samples around the place and had them tested. It's conclusive. Harold knows, he told me he's sterile so has always known of the situation."

Jacqueline nodded cautiously, as if realising that David – despite the fact that he had always treated her and all the other employees at Websters with kindness and consideration – was ruthless when he needed to be.

David did manage to raise Evelyn on the phone once, but she put the phone down when she realised who it was. She wouldn't answer any of his other calls.

Once all the dust had settled, David had a long discussion with Harold about what he had done and why; particularly why he had not brought Harold into the picture early on. Harold eventually agreed to refund all David's expenses relating to the affair and also agreed, after a long tussle, to grant additional shares in Websters to David up to the value of half of the additional value that had accrued to the business resulting from David's initiative.

"The business still has that very substantial holding in Eclipse at virtually no cost, which was not the case before this episode," David had the last word.

Chapter 16. The Sting (continued.)

Charlie had been delighted with the information on the first two companies David had loaded onto his computer to test the system. He could see that the system he and Samantha had set up worked. He was, as always, impatient for the main game. "Go fer it girl," he said to Samantha, "we're very close now; jus' remember, it's Eclipse we're after. This stuff jus' tells us the system works."

Charlie was mildly concerned – having received Joe's message – that he had been rumbled. *'E was always a lightweight. Pity, I'll now have to bring in the heavies*, he thought.

But then David had up loaded more information on three other companies, including substantial amounts of previously completed analytical information, though it was all in the public domain. It drove Charlie to distraction, saying to himself, *What's the stupid fucker doin' with all this nonsense. I may have to use the other stuff we have on him just to force the info out.*

Charlie had to look at other options, most notably the idea of blackmailing David with images of him and Samantha in the flat. He had not properly examined the tapes he had recovered from the flat, but now thought he would have a look.

I'll just choose the bes' ones and then pay Mr David fuckin' Phillips a little visit. We'll get the info I want then, he thought to himself.

He started to look at the film. "Got 'im, got 'im," he muttered as he looked at the first three films. Charlie had no interest in the content except that the films showed graphic images of David and Samantha in very compromising positions.

Without further delay, he phoned David and met him in the pub in Queen square. He was furious with the result and realised he had somehow been duped.

Charlie then carefully briefed his two goons, giving them a key to Samantha's flat. "Somehow, they is swichin' the film in them cameras. Keep a real good look on who goes in after Samantha and that stupid bugger Phillips leaves the place. If someone goes in, follow 'em in. Ruff him, or her for that matter, up a bit, but make fuckin' sure you get all the film. Weak as piss that Phillips; he'll gimme all I need as soon as he sees the film, with him and Samantha screwin' all over the flat."

Once Charlie had the information David had uploaded on Eclipse, Samantha's flat had been vacated and all the equipment removed, Charlie, supremely confident that he had the correct information on Eclipse, was ready to make a fortune when the share price collapsed – as soon as the results were made public. He took Evelyn and Samantha away to Portofino in Italy for a week.

On his return he was idly looking through the images from the cameras installed in the flat, expecting to see Samantha and David locked in various embraces; all he got was more blank screens; he had not heard from his two goons after their visit to the flat, but had mistakenly assumed they had done what he asked. He had no reason to think otherwise.

He then realised that something was drastically wrong, and the next day when Eclipse announced outstanding results, he went into a complete panic knowing he would have to cover his short selling spree, which would continue to help to the share price increase in value. He was furious. Samantha was clearly to blame for the fiasco.

There was a flurry of telephone calls to his lawyers, who told him they were powerless. "You obtained the info from a source that you should not have had access to. The fact that it was bullshit, and you acted on it, is nobody's fault but yours."

***

It would have come as a complete surprise to Charlie that Samantha had fallen deeply in love with David and she loved every minute of the affair as she thought of it. Charlie had never considered Samantha's feelings in this or any of his other schemes; as far as he was concerned she was there to do his bidding. Knowing her time at Websters was likely to be short-lived, she decided that whatever happened she would allow David to get her pregnant. *At least then I'll have a little piece of him forever,* she thought.

Knowing the game was up, she then resigned from Websters, and – once Charlie had told her ecstatically that he now had all the information he needed on Eclipse – went home.

Charlie had not shared any the content of any of the downloads he had received due to Samantha's subterfuge, actions which told her that she was mere pawn in the whole process. She confided in her mother that she was pregnant. Evelyn was phlegmatic, assuming that they would be well off as a result of the scheme that Charlie and Samantha had concocted. During the week in Portofino Samantha said to herself, *now I've done what Charlie asked, maybe I can get on with my own life for a change.*

She had no idea of the whirlwind that would engulf her when they returned back home.

Chapter 17. Melinda Again

Melinda couldn't wait to get to the conference she was to address in Edinburgh. She had been unable to pin any of her suspicions on David – when she phoned the office on his landline there, he was where he said he would be. When she had popped into the office on two occasions to see David, he appeared to be overwhelmed in whatever he was busy doing.

"Mel, I know the past few weeks have been difficult for you," he explained," but it won't be long before everything returns to normal; I have just been buried in the past few weeks."

"Is there anything I can do to help?"

"No, not really," he said in his usual calm manner. "I'm about eighty percent through it all now; I'll get through it all in the next couple of weeks, I know how to pull it all together."

She had tried getting David to look through her meticulously prepared presentation, but after a glance through it he said. "I can't fault this, it looks great."

So Melinda went to the conference, trying to put her concerns about David's behaviour out of her mind. She was determined to make the most of her opportunity. With the conference due to start on Monday, she arrived in good time on Sunday afternoon. She had arranged for a housekeeper to come in and attend to the children and David's meals. "I expect to be back on Wednesday," she told Johanna.

"Okay, whenever..."

Melinda spent the time she had on Sunday reviewing her presentation and making sure she had everything at her fingertips. She checked out the meeting room, familiarising herself with the set-up, checking the equipment. Together with the conference organiser she loaded her presentation on to the equipment in the room and flipped through it, making sure it all worked.

She had dinner in her room and had an early night. First in the gym when it opened at six thirty the next morning, knowing she looked stunning in her new skin-tight gym outfit, she tried to ignore the admiring glances of the few men also taking advantage of an early start to the day.

Following her normal routine of a few minutes stretching, fifteen minutes weights, fifteen minutes flat out on the stationary bike, and finishing off with a very fast thirty minutes on one of the treadmills, she was standing by the treadmill, out of breath and sweating profusely, towelling herself off when a man with a strong Australian accent asked her. "Are you part of this investment conference today?"

She smiled at the very good-looking man in front of her, also out of breath and sweating. "Yes, second up, bit nervous actually."

"Do you know where the conference room is? I only got in late."

"I'll take you there."

They took the lift from the basement to the second floor. "I'm Andrew, by the way. Pretty solid workout you had there," he observed.

"Melinda. Yes, I try to keep myself in shape." She thought she had successfully hidden her excitement at the obvious interest he was taking in her. They shook hands briefly. She left him in the hands of the organiser, showered, had breakfast and was in place on the podium of the rapidly filling up conference room a few minutes before nine.

She glanced through the very full programme, noticing an Andrew Economos was due to speak later in the day; she presumed he was her earlier acquaintance from the gym. Melinda had acquired a completely new wardrobe for the event and was dressed conservatively in a dark pant suit to which she had added a bit of colour with a bright pink shirt. She knew she looked stunning, being tall at nearly six feet with her shoulder length brown hair and pretty face.

Her presentation went down very well with the bright fresh audience. She managed to make the subject interesting which was the result of her own personal research on investment trends and which sectors she thought would do well in coming months bearing in mind the slowly growing world economy. Questions lasted half an hour.

"One last question," announced the organiser.

Someone in the audience asked her opinion of a particular company, which she knew had invested in two quite unrelated businesses.

She was tempted to say that she didn't have enough knowledge to comment but then she decided that a little levity was in order, she laughed saying, "Investing like that is like mixing horseshit and ice cream, the ice cream does nothing for the horseshit and the horseshit certainly doesn't do much for the ice cream."

There was a stunned silence for a second or two, then the whole audience burst out laughing uproariously.

The organisers briefly looked embarrassed, but then relaxed as Melinda lead a feisty discussion on the merits of conglomerates.

Eventually the organisers brought the gathering under control and the meeting progressed.

Melinda was mobbed during the break with most people wanting to talk to what they now saw as the amusing, beautiful, smart presenter.

Andrew emerged from the throng saying, "Congratulations. As I'm sure you don't need me to tell you it was a very good presentation. Stirring the pot at the end made everyone's day. You are most unusual, rare as hen's teeth, as they say," he laughed easily.

Not wanting Andrew to move away, Melinda said to him, pointing at the programme, "This is you, isn't it? Sometime this afternoon. I look forward to that."

"Yes, it is. I have a few clients here, so I need to impress them." He added, "You've set the standard for the next few days; I expect we'll hear a lot of really dumb jokes added at the last minute to people's presentations, people trying to compete with you," he laughed again. "Hopefully I won't be tempted to fall into that trap. I'd better go and look after my clients, I'll see you later."

Melinda nodded, feeling a frisson of excitement go through her as he walked confidently away. She had lunch with the organisers who despite their initial reaction to the final remarks of her presentation were delighted with her contribution. A number of people asked her for her business card; one woman in particular said, "When this is all over maybe we can have lunch in London, we can certainly use a person with your obvious talent, I will phone you next week."

Melinda spent the rest of the day listening to various presentations, some of which were useful. From time to time, especially during elements of certain presentations which failed to engage her attention she allowed her mind to wander back to David, wondering what he was up to.

Two calls she made to his mobile went to voicemail. and the only answer from a text message sent to him was, "Busy, sorry."

Bugger it, she thought, *I'm going to enjoy myself here, make the best of the opportunity and put all thought of what is going on at home right to the back of my mind.*

She thought Andrew made a good presentation on client relations. There was a formal conference dinner in the evening, which thoughtfully started early and was therefore all over by eight thirty. Melinda was wondering what to do, she was too excited to go to bed; disappointingly she was unable to see Andrew anywhere. She went to her room and tried to phone David, but the call again went to message. Earlier she had phoned home and spoken to Johanna and her children.

She turned on the television, more or less resigned to a dull evening watching CNN or the BBC, when the phone rang.

It was Andrew. "I meant to call earlier," he said, "would you like to go out for a drink somewhere? My clients have just left. They don't need me for what they are going to do."

"Yes, great, I would like that," said Melinda.

"I have one thing I must finish, but rather than hanging about why don't you pop up here, rather than waiting. I have a small suite, which I needed for a meeting." He gave her the room number.

"Okay, I'll be up in a minute."

Melinda quickly changed into a fashionable pair of slacks and a pretty red shirt; she had a new light leather jacket. In view of her height she rarely felt the need for anything but flat shoes. She looked at herself in the mirror. "You'll do," she muttered.

The door of the suite was on the latch which she took as an invitation to go in. She knocked and saw Andrew furiously typing away on his laptop. "Come in, come in. I won't be much longer. Please help yourself to something from the fridge." Melinda found a mineral water and a glass in the fridge and sat down looking around. There were a few plates and glasses scattered though the room. "Find somewhere comfortable," offered Andrew, "the hotel people will be up here in a minute to clear up. Just a few drinks before dinner," he explained. He went on bashing away at his computer, he then spent a few minutes in silence; Melinda assumed he was reading what he had written. "Done," he announced in triumph as he pressed the send button. Andrew then disappeared for a few minutes into the bedroom and emerged more casually dressed in a pair of slacks and an open necked shirt.

"You look great, really great," he said as he pecked her on the cheek.

"You don't do so badly yourself." Melinda observed as she took more than a good look at the tall, dark, handsome man in front of her.

"Okay, do you want a big noisy place with a band, or would you prefer a something a bit classier where we can talk," he asked.

Melinda smiled. "The latter, I've grown out of big noisy places."

They walked for ten minutes. Melinda was pleased when he took her hand to cross a street and then didn't let it go as they walked down a narrow laneway, "it's hard to find a really good pub in this place, we'll go somewhere small and quieter where one can at least have a conversation. Hopefully none of the others at the conference will have found this place, yet. They settled on a corner table in a crowded small but tastefully decorated pub.

"What would you like?" asked Andrew. "I'm having a twelve-year-old scotch."

She laughed. "Ugh, cough mixture, I'll have a glass of white wine, thanks, not chardonnay if you can help it."

They briefly reflected on the value of the conference. "Some of the presentations were excellent, yours particularly," offered Melinda. "As with all these conferences, it's the contacts that are more important. I've made several new contacts, one woman in particular, who I think I'll be able to do some business with."

"You made a big splash," said Andrew. "Oxford and Websters, people were impressed."

Melinda looked surprised for a minute. "Ah the wonders of Google," she said laughing, "the kids are growing up, I'm trying to re-establish myself, before it's too late."

"What about Websters?"

"I'm involved there to some extent, but David tends to want to row his own boat. I need to establish myself a bit more independently." She looked at Andrew. "What do you know of Websters?" she asked.

"A little, Harold seems to run it on very conservative lines though."

"My thoughts exactly," confirmed Melinda.

The conversation flowed easily, with Andrew's upbringing in Melbourne. "the largest Greek community in the world outside Greece itself. Most of us arrived after the Second World War and the boat stopped in Melbourne," Andrew told her. "We're very much part of the Australian community now of course. And you, are you part of the so called upper classes here, with your Oxford background and so on?"

"Far from it, I was lucky enough to get a scholarship to Oxford and then I worked my arse off and somehow got a double first. Would you like another drink? My 'shout' – isn't that the Aussie expression," she laughed. Melinda had only finished less than half of her drink.

"I was thinking of a grappa or another scotch."

"Grappa," Melinda pulled a face and laughed, "one step-up from weasel piss," she laughed again. "Still if one is used to drinking cough mixture I suppose it's okay."

Andrew looked amused. "Another twelve-year-old," he said.

"You're not big on the grog then," observed Andrew when she returned with his drink.

"No, mum and dad spent far too much time in the pub down the road. It caused problems."

Andrew could see she was uncomfortable with the turn the conversation had taken and changed the subject.

"Why two degrees?" he asked.

"I originally went to study physics; I decided that there was more opportunity in the commercial world, so I added a commerce degree to the agenda." The conversation meandered along easily; they found they were sitting closer and closer together. They were oblivious of any of the other pub patrons. He obviously knew she was married to David; there was no mention of marriage or even a girlfriend from his side. She assumed from the conversation that Andrew was much the same age as she was.

During a brief lull in the conversation, Andrew looked at Melinda and said, "Melinda, you are so beautiful, can I kiss you?"

She leant over and kissed him full on the mouth. "I was hoping you would somehow get around to that. Thank you."

He kissed her again. "It's almost closing time," he said.

They looked at each other in anticipation and she whispered, "Your place or mine? To coin a phrase."

"The suite will have been cleared up by now, we can go back there."

Melinda nodded, and they made their way quickly out of the pub and almost ran back to the hotel. A woman she had made contact with earlier in the day was sitting near the entrance talking to one of the other conference attendees, she glanced curiously at Melinda.

"Ah, good," said Andrew, as he opened the door of the suite, "it's all been cleared away." They fell into each other's arms as the door closed and kissed passionately.

Melinda pulled away briefly. "Sit down, please don't do anything, I just need a couple of minutes. I would like to take it slowly; I'm really going to enjoy this." She disappeared but was back after a short while. "Let me do this," she said, "all you have to do is to sit back and enjoy it." She started to undress him item by item; she removed one piece of his clothing and then one of hers, she sat on his lap and they kissed and kissed, she then did the same again, nearly driving him to distraction. After twenty minutes their clothing was scattered around the suite and they were both standing quite naked admiring each other's bodies. Andrew couldn't wait any longer; he picked her up and carried her to the bed, which she had already stripped back. He laid her down gently and lay down next to her.

"You on me to start," he said.

She needed no second invitation and took his large erect penis inside her. Within minutes she had climaxed. Then he rolled her onto her back and thrust into her until she came again. Afterwards, he rolled off and cuddled Melinda, pulling the bedclothes over them both. "Wonderful, beautiful," he said, "just wonderful."

"Same for me," whispered Melinda as they fell asleep.

In the darkest part of the night, Melinda could feel Andrew was stirring and they made love again. It was almost three am.

Later Melinda woke with a start, briefly wondering where she was. There was no sign of Andrew, she then found a post-it note on his pillow. "Please, please don't go anywhere, I have had to deal with a problem, I'll be back as soon as I can." Melinda relaxed, reliving and savouring every minute of their lovemaking. Half an hour later Andrew reappeared, he kissed her longingly. "Sorry, one of my clients got into trouble, I had to bail him out."

"Bail him out – literally?"

"Yes. I've spent the last couple of hours with the police. I got a message about four thirty, you were dead to the world."

"Is everything okay now? What did he or she do?"

"Yes, everything's fine, although the silly bastard will get a very heavy fine, I think. You don't want to know what he did."

"Come back to bed then, you obviously need some essential therapy that only I can provide; you had better make sure the 'do not disturb' sign is on the door though."

"What about the conference?" asked Andrew as he undressed and returned to bed.

"First things first," responded Melinda. They made love again.

Later, Melinda got up and drew the curtains, allowing a shaft of bright sunlight to flood in. She sat on the edge of the bed allowing Andrew to feast his eyes on her large breasts and slim trim body. "So what's the programme? I could go on with this for another day or two, what about you?"

"I've already arranged to stay on until Friday, assuming you would want to do the same. There are a couple of presentations I would like to attend, otherwise as far as I am concerned I'm here in bed with you."

"Mmm, I'm relieved you added the last part," she giggled. "I was due to leave tomorrow morning, so I need change a few arrangements and make a few calls. I'm assuming we'll be staying in this suite. What time is it?"

"Creeping up to ten am."

"Jesus, I'd better get on then."

"Oh, by the way, there's been a bit of a reaction to your ice cream and horseshit comment yesterday." He handed her the business pages of a national daily, which she read avidly, sitting up in bed.

"Mnn, interesting, it says here that Ms Melinda Phillips was unavailable for comment; they didn't try very hard, I was here all bloody day. We'll see what happens. I don't suppose Harold will be thrilled; apparently, he denied that what I had said was Websters official position. I don't give a shit for Websters official position."

They had a shower together, then Melinda put away all her clothes from the previous night, borrowed one of the bathrobes in the suite, and within half an hour she had packed up her own room and moved everything to Andrew's suite. She left David a text message and phoned Johanna. "Can you hold the fort until Friday, about mid-afternoon?" she asked.

"Of course, no problem, David has been working late every night, so it's been very quiet round here," Johanna responded.

Melinda then changed her flights and spent much of the day listening to various conference speakers. Many people approached her, some to ask her opinion on particular investments, others for a business card. "It seems that I have struck a chord here," she told Andrew later. "I can see the potential exists to expand my business activities almost as much as I like; we'll see. Anyway, I'm jack of the conference for the time being."

Andrew smiled. "Do you have any suggestions?"

"Sure, maybe we could go for a run together, then I expect we'll be ready to make love again, then maybe we could find a decent place to have dinner together."

"Okay, wonderful, we can run from here to Holyrood Park; it's not far. I'll get the hotel to book somewhere for something like eight." Andrew looked at Melinda admiringly as the lift took them down to the foyer. "You look absolutely delectable," he said to her as he kissed her on the cheek.

"Later, later," she said, "plenty of time for that."

They stretched and then ran up Princes Street and soon found themselves in Canongate; they passed the Scottish Parliament and ran into Holyrood Park. "We'll run around the park," suggested Andrew, "then back. Should be about ten k's."

More than an hour later, pouring sweat, they found themselves back in front of the hotel. Melinda insisted on a few minutes stretching. Back in the suite they helped to remove each other's sopping wet clothes and drank some water. "I must cool down for a few minutes, before I jump into the shower," said Melinda as she sat, comfortably naked, on a towel on one of the chairs.

Andrew picked up all the discarded running gear and dressed in a bathrobe. "I'll see if I can get this laundered for tomorrow."

When he returned they hugged each other and kissed.

"Shower first," said Melinda. They washed each other carefully and thoroughly in the shower, then dried each other. "I'm ready for a bit more action," said Melinda, as she stripped back the bedclothes. They made love and slept for nearly an hour. "We'd better get a move on if we're going to that restaurant you booked," she said. "Frankly though I could happily stay here. What do you want to do?"

"I cancelled the restaurant when I went downstairs. There's a room service meal on its way, I ordered a selection."

"What are you getting? If you are going to keep up this performance you'll need at least a kilo of raw steak," she joked.

The pattern was set for the next two days: some attendance at the conference, a daily run, the occasional meal in a nearby restaurant, and as much sex as they could manage. Melinda just lived for the moment, making certain that she enjoyed all of it and making the most of her time with Andrew. She brushed aside any thoughts of David, home, the children and what she was going to do next week.

On the Friday after a long morning in bed, they both packed. Andrew said to Melinda, "I have had a marvellous week; I just couldn't imagine anything better or more exciting. Thank you, I will be in touch of course."

"Same for me," she said, "same for me."

They clutched each other happily before they left the suite, then checked out and made their individual ways to the airport. There had been some curious glances for Melinda at reception, but nothing was said, she supposed that Andrew had smoothed everything over.

For Melinda, reality set in halfway through the flight back to London. The last few days had been a dream; reality was David, the children, the house in Barnes, her life, even Websters. She suddenly felt a ton of guilt drop down on her. She gazed out the window, glancing down at the benign pretty English countryside, and allowed a tear to slip out, which she wiped away impatiently.

"Is everything okay?" asked the woman sitting next to her.

"Yes, yes, fine, tears of happiness," she explained lamely.

She had arranged for a car to pick her up at Heathrow and she was back home by tea time. The children leapt all over her, giving her pictures they had drawn; she gave them each a book that she had belatedly picked up at Edinburgh airport, waiting for her flight.

Johanna looked on happily. "They've been great. I'll do this anytime, it was a real pleasure. Dinner is all done; all you have to do is switch on the oven. David said he would be back by about six; he's been working like a dog, barely getting home before ten most nights."

Melinda glanced at her, wondering if indeed it was all work. "Can I take you home?" asked Melinda.

"No, no, I have the car here, thanks." She left.

Melinda unpacked, making sure there was no trace of Andrew anywhere to be seen. She hung up all her clothes and laundered everything that needed it. She played with the children. When David arrived home a little after six, she went out to greet him, put her arms around him and kissed him. It felt awkward, but she made herself behave as naturally as possible.

"Drink?" she asked as he plonked his briefcase down next to the front door, as he always did, "dinner will be at about seven."

"Shower and change first, then a glass of red please."

Melinda poured him a glass of red wine and waited. Eventually he appeared, dressed casually. She handed him the wine. "You look tired," she said.

"It's been a fairly rough week, a few weeks actually, but I think we're through it all now. We're going to come out of it very well financially from what I can see. How was the conference?"

"It was great, my presentation went down well, and I have made a number of very good contacts."

David laughed. "Oh yes, the ice cream and horseshit remark, I had a quick look at that companies' last report. You are quite right, of course. Harold was not very pleased since somehow the comment was sheeted back to Websters. I told him you were one hundred percent on the money and that if any of those media pollukers phoned again he should tell them that Websters now endorse the observation. I don't think he will, but we won't hear any more of it."

Melinda could sense a feeling of relief, almost triumph on the one hand, tinged with a deep sense of regret on the other. "What's all the drama been about? What are you coming through, to use your expression?"

"I'll tell you when it's all over and done with," David replied, looking as if he wanted run away. "I'm going to be really busy for the next couple of weeks, with late nights and Saturdays, after that it should all return to normal."

"Hm, that's what you said a few weeks ago."

David nodded.

During dinner it was all David could do to stay awake. He nearly fell asleep in his dinner; the kids giggled.

Melinda put her hand on his arm. "Go to bed, David," she said affectionately. "I'll put the kids to bed and clear up here, you've obviously been working much too hard." He stumbled off to bed. In a way Melinda was relieved, after the past week with Andrew the last thing she was ready for was sex with her husband.

The next morning, she got up early. Being Saturday, she left David asleep.

Having played with the children for an hour or so. David excused himself. "I still have a lot to do in the office, I'll be back later," he told Melinda.

Despite herself, Melinda's survival instinct allied to her own sense of guilt got the better of her and mid-afternoon she phoned him at the office, on his direct line. To her relief he answered the phone immediately. "Making sure you're alright, David."

"Yes, I'm fine," he said abruptly, as if defensive.

In all the years, Melinda had almost never phoned him in the office. "Why don't you bring home a takeaway for dinner," she added quickly. "You know what the kids like."

"Okay, done, I'll see you about six." He put the phone down.

Chapter 18. David and Melinda

David still had a great deal of work to catch up with and, as he had told Melinda, he was spending much more time than usual in his office even at weekends. He was actually beginning to feel that he had 'got away' with something that might have turned sour. The arrangements he had with Harold now gave him some twenty percent of the company. But he was worried Melinda had become a little distant, particularly after her sojourn in Edinburgh – they hadn't once made love since her return. He wondered if she had come to the conclusion that he was behaving suspiciously, and what that meant for her and their marriage. He hadn't altogether worked out what he would tell her about the drama he had been through, though he knew he would have to tell her something, as close to the truth as was possible.

The Saturday a week after Melinda's return, he was beavering away alone in the office at about noon when he became aware of someone standing in the doorway of his office. He looked up surprised to see Melinda herself: "Hello, love, is everything okay? I'm surprised to see you here."

Melinda had always had her own key to the office. "Are you alone?" she asked.

"Yes, there is seldom anyone else here on a Saturday. As I told you it's been rather hectic here recently. I'm just catching up on a few things.

Another week or so..." He hesitated; there was something about her manner that made him think this was no ordinary visit.

"I want you to fuck me, now, here in the office."

David was taken aback; it wasn't the sort of language Melinda usually used. He realised Melinda must have had her suspicions about his activities over past weeks and this was some sort of a test; he thanked his lucky stars that he had not seen or heard from Samantha for more than a month now.

He got up and took her in his arms.

"Now," she said, "here in the office."

"I have a better idea," he said and took her by the hand to Harold's office, which he unlocked and relocked once they were inside.

Melinda kicked off her shoes and undid the straps of her dress, which fell to the floor. She was stark naked.

Wordlessly she stripped David's clothes off him. They kissed urgently. David pushed her up against the desk and entered her.

"Harder," she said, "harder, harder, come on harder." She came with a few little yelps of pleasure.

David lay down of the plush carpet...

Afterwards they lay there for a few more minutes; David looked at her but said nothing. There was a look of mild satisfaction in her expression. After a little while she said to him: "I was happy to actually find you here today." She hesitated. "There is obviously a lot more going on than you've told me. You've hinted at some major developments; can you tell me more?"

David thought, *maybe this is as good an opportunity to tell her what has transpired over the past weeks as any. I've kinda sorted out in my mind what I need to say.* So, feeling somewhat apprehensive he said:

"Mnn, yes," he hesitated, as much as anything to get full control of his thoughts. "I can now tell you a little about the business that has had me mired in all this work. I knew someone was trying to steal some very confidential information on a company we control, Eclipse, actually, which you know something about. I realised how and what he was doing so I arranged to feed him a lot of crap. He actually stole the crap, in a way that nothing could be sheeted back to us. He acted on the crap info; he short sold thousands of shares in Eclipse, which as you know we have a substantial interest in, thinking the results would be a disaster. They never were going to be a disaster and as it turned out the results were brilliant, better than we ever expected. In the name of Websters, I bought all the shares he sold, at very low prices. When the results were announced the shares soared and our thief had to buy shares at high prices to cover his position, which has sent him close to bankruptcy. There were some minority shareholders who have profited handsomely from the situation and Websters now owns one hundred percent of the company through a whole string of dummy companies; the person who tried to do the dirty on us has no idea we are back in control and he'll probably never be able to find out. I did it all without telling Harold; he was furious to start with but somehow, he didn't fire me.

"The minority shareholders in Eclipse," he continued, "are of course thrilled and have now heaped praise on Harold; in the end he paid me half of what Websters gained from the whole messy business. I used the money to buy more shares in Websters from Harold, and this is the important bit, I now have an agreement with Harold that I have first option on all the remaining shares he owns in Websters, if and when he wants to sell. There are a few minority shareholders, about ten percent, mainly old pals of Harold's who funded him when he started out, which we can mop up over time. If you are happy with such an arrangement, any shares I acquire from such people will be registered in your name."

"Okay," said Melinda. "It's important for me to be on Websters share register, that makes sense, but why couldn't you have put me in the picture earlier? I obviously know a lot about Eclipse. From what you have said you obviously took very serious risks. Harold may have fired you, for example, putting us all in jeopardy, me the kids, the house. Unknowingly we all shared the risk with you…"

David was surprised by her very forthright statement. He had naively expected her to be pleased with the revelations.

"I couldn't; I'm really sorry about that. There were so many balls in the air I don't think I could have coped with another one."

"I could have helped, David. Two heads instead of one should have made all the difference. Now and in the future." It sounded like she had some particular kind of future in mind.

"Okay, point taken; hopefully it's water under the bridge now." After a short silence he added, "Oh, and by the way I am now deputy managing director, not that that means much, I was fulfilling that role as things stood anyway."

Melinda looked at him, then laughed out loud. "We're having the most serious discussion materially affecting our futures, lying stark bollock naked on the MD's carpet," she said, "having just had one of the most satisfying fucks of my life," she giggled, "unusual, to say the least."

David laughed with her and again thanked his lucky stars that the affair with Samantha was over; in fact, he didn't even know where she was.

They made love again.

∗∗∗

With David's explanation fresh in her mind, Melinda felt more at peace lying on Harold's office carpet than she had in years. She also didn't.

I'm bloody sure I've not been told the full story of what has been going on over past months, the story just came out much too pat; maybe I never will be told. Anyway, with today's performance he's certainly not fucking anyone else at the moment, so I suppose that's one worry out of the way.

Two weeks later, Melinda felt slightly nauseous when she got up in the morning. She looked at herself in the mirror and cupped her breasts, which looked a bit larger than usual.

Oh shit, pregnant, that puts a bit of a spoke in any plans I might have had, she thought.

The doctor confirmed her condition a month or so later.

"That little episode in Harold's office has had an unintended consequence," she told David later in bed, their sexual relations having now returned to normal.

"You mean the day you came to the office and seduced me."

"Yes, not that you needed much seducing. Anyway, to cut to the chase, I'm pregnant."

David immediately cuddled her saying, "How wonderful, that's wonderful."

"You mean you aren't unhappy about having another child running about," Melinda was happy at his reaction.

"Far from it. The two we have are great; if the new one is anything like they are I couldn't be happier."

She was relieved that there was no question of an abortion, which she would, in any event, have resisted to the bitter end.

Andrew had, in the days and weeks following the Edinburgh conference, unsuccessfully tried to get Melinda to attend various 'investment conferences' as he described them. In view of David's reaction to her pregnancy, there was now no question that Melinda would have the child. All the tests were positive, and she was still only twenty-seven. Whatever the temptation, she finally decided to cut her ties with Andrew.

However, two months after Edinburgh he invited her to attend a genuine conference in Switzerland, where she was asked to speak. She fought with her conscience for almost a week. She knew she should not go, with the new baby and David's reaction to her pregnancy. In the end after a very persuasive phone call from Andrew she accepted.

Almost like a last fling, I really have to see him just one more time and I'll take the consequences, whatever they are, she said to herself, justifying the adventure.

She excitedly flew to Lugarno, in the Italian speaking part of Switzerland, where Andrew met her and drove her to a luxury resort situated on nearby Lake Lugarno. As she had expected she was booked to share a suite with him. They didn't even start to unpack; as the door of the suite closed they leapt on each other kissing wildly, clothes were scattered in all directions and they made frantic love, something that was repeated within an hour.

"You look really well," observed Andrew as they both paraded around the room naked, quietly unpacking and picking up discarded clothing,

Melinda glanced at Andrew's dark lithe well-kept body. "You don't do too badly yourself. It's wonderful to be with you again."

For three days they participated fully in the conference, they went for long runs through the beautiful Swiss countryside, they had wonderful sex and they even managed a decent meal in a very good nearby restaurant. Melinda lost herself completely in the situation and managed to put her pregnancy right out of her mind, she found she was able to focus entirely on her own pleasure and fun.

On the final morning, having packed ready to go to the airport Melinda said to Andrew, "These few days and the week we had in

Edinburgh have been absolutely marvellous, some of the best days of my life..."

He looked at her in trepidation, knowing what was coming. "You're going to bail out on me, aren't you?"

"Hear me out please. I repeat, I want you to understand the days and not forgetting the nights I have spent with you have been some of the best in my life. Despite that, there is much in my present situation that is worth preserving, so I won't be seeing you again. I am so, so sorry; I hope that you can respect my position. I will treasure the days we had together all my life and I hope you can too." She realised that what she had said came out stiff and uncaring.

Can't be helped, she thought, *it had to be said, I really have no other option.*

They clung to each other for a good five minutes, both teary. Andrew said nothing as Melinda picked up her luggage, she kissed him quickly on the cheek and left. She had arranged for a hotel car to take her to the airport.

Melinda cried silently for most of the flight back to London; she knew that if she had met Andrew when she was at university seven or so years earlier, the outcome may have been very different. She thought she would be able to put him out of her mind and time would heal the hurt; she reflected she did have much to look forward to, the new baby, her already wonderful children, having David to herself, the prospects for building up an independent advisory operation, her lifestyle with the elegant house they had in Barnes. Although, perhaps for the first time in her life, she had fallen deeply, deeply in love, with

Andrew, she realised she knew little about him, his background, his family and how he had come to where he was in life; she knew now she would never find out any of those things and she was determined to leave any association with him well alone.

She had the strength of mind not to even open the two emails he sent her after the meeting in Switzerland.

***

When Melinda got home, David noticed she was unusually silent and withdrawn for almost two weeks, and assumed it was a reaction to her pregnancy. He didn't worry about it too much, as far as he was concerned life had returned to normal, except that he had substantially improved his position at Websters.

Baby Rory was born nine months later...

PART 4: SAMANTHA

Chapter 19. Samantha

"You stupid bloody bitch, 'e must have deliberately set you up and you fell for it." Was Charlie's immediate reaction to the fiasco that now unfolded.

"All I did was to do what you asked; it's just as much your fault as mine," Samantha responded. "You didn't have to act like you did in such a hurry, why didn't you do some more checking. You never asked me to help in any way; you never showed me any of the figures and there's no way I would have acted like you did."

The argument went on endlessly for a few days.

Charlie eventually appeared with an air ticket. "Australia, you are goin' to Oz, and don't think of ever darkening these doors again. I've managed to rescue us from bankruptcy, but only just. Evelyn has arranged for you stay with 'er sister in Sydney. I never want to see or hear from you ever again."

After a day or two reflecting, reinforced by an angry phone conversation she had with Jacqueline Briggs, Samantha thought that putting twelve thousand miles between her and Charlie would be the best for all parties.

"You have to understand Ms. Wicks," said Jacqueline, "you are virtually unemployable here in the UK. We would be obliged to tell any future employer making contact with us how you behaved while you were here. There is no possibility we would give you any kind of reference."

Her mother Evelyn kept out of the way; just looked on helplessly as the argument thundered on around her. She did manage to say to Samantha as she was bundled into a taxi to the airport. "Ida is a good person, she'll look after you." She stood there wringing her hands as the taxi drove off.

The flight to Sydney on China Southern Airlines was not particularly comfortable. Samantha thought it was probably the cheapest flight available, involving a long stopover in Guangzhou. She picked at the food she was offered and gradually pulled her emotions together. Charlie, a year or more earlier, had had some idea they should all emigrate to Australia, so she had the requisite visas and would be able to work. On the negative side she regretted having to leave England, her job at Websters and what she had decided was the love of her life, David. In view of what she had done, the job at Websters would have been terminated anyway and despite her own feelings, it seemed that it was unlikely that David had anything but contempt for her; if Charlie's plan had succeeded it would have severely jeopardised David's position at Websters.

David must have known from the very beginning what I was after. He used the situation to get back at us. I feel such a fool, she thought. Despite everything she was still in love with him and tried to put what he had done to her out of her mind.

On the positive side she said to herself, *I am at last completely rid of Charlie as an influence in my life, I am smart, I have very good experience, so I will find a way of coming out of all this with my head held high. Maybe, perversely, Oz is a good idea, where Charlie will have no influence on anything I do. Also, with all that's gone on, I wonder if I would ever be able to rescue my reputation in England.*

Deep in thought for a while longer she added, again to herself, *Somehow, sometime, I will get myself back to England, and I certainly will have the baby, David's baby.*

She had transferred the twenty thousand pounds she had in a savings account to a bank in Australia, money she had saved by living at home.

She was met at Sydney Airport by Evelyn's disapproving elder sister, Ida.

Ida took one look at Samantha as she emerged after a lengthy delay in customs saying, "I know you're pregnant, like mother like daughter. You mother was unable to keep her pants up and it looks as if you have the same problem. Come on then, we'll take you home. Tom will not be pleased, being a strict Catholic – I've told him you're pregnant."

Tom, aged fifty-five, was the headmaster of a local Catholic secondary school; Ida taught in a local state primary school. They had no children. From the start, both Tom and Ida made it very clear that they thoroughly disapproved of Samantha and her condition. The one thing they were able to agree on as staunch Catholics (Ida had converted to Catholicism when she married Tom) was that Samantha was going to have the baby and that termination was most definitely not on the agenda.

"It God's will," Tom had pronounced.

After a week or so staying in the modest three-bedroom house in the suburb of Epping, owned by Tom and Ida, Samantha decided that, while she needed their support until she had given birth, she would have to find a way out of the situation. She saw Epping as a solid middle-class suburb and found it was some twenty or so kilometres north west of the city; the central area was easily accessible by public transport, which in her case meant the train.

She approached several merchant banks, none of whom were prepared to give her the time of day. She scoured the city and soon came up with a small financial advisory firm, which from her research Samantha could see had on some occasions sailed very close to the wind in terms of the law and in terms of general ethical behaviour. To start with during one of her several perambulations around the city making certain she understood the geography, she found her way to the address of 'Berkshire'. She had already established where the big banks and other reputable firms in the finance industry were located. Momentarily her shoulders slumped, just the sight of the decrepit looking building made her shudder.

Looks like the hideout of a con artist, she thought briefly, *I suppose with my training and background, it could be ideal.*

Bracing herself, she made a call and after a long conversation on the phone went in for an interview. Samantha assumed the name 'Berkshire', part of the name of Berkshire Hathaway, a major brilliant and well-known American investment company, was a naive attempt to create a positive image. In most cases it had exactly the opposite effect. The premises were in an old seedy looking building close to Sydney's Central railway station, well out of the way of the usual location of reputable financial institutions.

She was met by a man in his mid-thirties, of medium build and height, who introduced himself as Reg Holdsworth, the managing director. He was dressed fashionably in casual, well-tailored clothes with an open neck shirt; his hair was short but gelled up into a sort of quiff. At a glance she could see exactly the type of person she was dealing with.

Could be a clone of Charlie, she said to herself.

There were a few others in the untidy looking main office, who all kept their heads down, when Reg led Samantha through to an even messier corner office. "You are pregnant," said Reg without any kind of formality, as he sat down. He had had the grace to clear some files off a chair in his office, so there was somewhere for Samantha to sit. Reg was proud of his apparent ability to observe people and their condition and capabilities.

"Yes, I had noticed that too," responded Samantha, "it's a perfectly normal condition."

Reg looked nonplussed at the response and then laughed. He then proceeded to interview her about her experience, an exercise that lasted more than an hour. Apparently satisfied with Samantha's responses he dumped three sets of accounts in front of her saying, "Assess these please."

"Okay, how long do I have?" answered Samantha.

Reg looked surprised before saying, "ten minutes."

In the stipulated time Samantha flipped through the accounts and then said, "Someone has fiddled with these accounts, if the oldest set is kosher then the two following sets have been manipulated; the earnings appear to be overstated and the borrowings understated."

Reg looked amazed; he blinked a few times and said, "You're on."

They spent thirty minutes arguing about the modest salary Samantha was to be paid. She said she would start the next working day, which was a Monday.

"How disruptive is that thing going to be?" asked Reg, pointing at Samantha's stomach.

Being quite used to this sort of attitude as a result of Charlie Sandford's ministrations, Samantha laughed saying, "Well, the actual birthing process takes up to twenty-four hours, or so I'm told." She didn't actually know, but she thought she needed to put Reg off with what she thought was a robust conversation on the subject. "This means I won't be able to concentrate much on anything else while that is in train..." Reg looked uncomfortable. "And then," she continued, "I may need a couple of weeks to settle the child down, but I'll employ a nanny, so I'll be able to work full time after that. I could probably work from home on some of the stuff."

"There won't be any of this crap of twelve months maternity leave; I won't take you on if you think that's going to happen."

Samantha shrugged. "I have five months to prove my worth, so that's what I will focus on for the moment. I don't know anything about maternity leave regulations here and whatever. If you like, I'll draw up a contract we can sign on Monday."

Reg nodded and showed her out.

Reg had not asked her one question about her personal circumstances, how long she had lived in Sydney, where she was living and so on. He didn't even ask her if she was allowed to work in Australia, although she had come prepared to show him all the requisite paperwork.

Suits me, Samantha said to herself, *he's only interested in cheap labour; the less he knows about me the better, frankly.*

She said to herself on the way home back to Epping, *You got yourself into this bloody mess; it's entirely up to you to get yourself out of it.*

She knew she would be utterly ruthless in the way she dealt with everything, including Reg. Her dealings with Reg reminded her uncomfortably of Charlie.

At least I know where he's coming from, she thought, *which gives me a half decent chance of being able to deal with him, and the interesting thing is he just sees me as a naive little girl who got herself knocked up; for him easy meat. If he gives me half a chance, he won't know what's hit him.*

Ten days after her arrival in Sydney, Samantha was able to explain, to her bemused hosts, over dinner one evening, that she had taken a job and who with. "So I'll be happy to pay you some sort of board, if you like. We also need to discuss how I'll cope with the baby once it arrives, if you're happy to keep me here that is."

Tom and Ida were somewhat mollified with her attitude and were pleasantly surprised by her approach. Over the weekend they said that, being family, she could stay with them as long as she liked.

"We wondered what you were doing with all your visits to the city, we now know," said Tom. "We hardly ever go down there anymore; for us it's a ghastly noisy money-grubbing sort of place." He then added, "We were thinking of extending this place a bit, anyway, I'll show you the plans. Your arrival here gives us an excuse to go ahead."

After some discussion and with input from Samantha they adjusted the plans to suit the new situation. They settled on two bedrooms, a bathroom and a modest lounge. There was plenty of room for the extension on the half acre block.

"I'll see if all this can be done before the baby arrives," announced Tom, looking happy. "I've already lined up a builder and I'll have to get council to agree to the amended plans, but I don't think that'll be a problem. The builder will have to get a move on though. Your contribution will pay for the interest on the additional mortgage, and it makes this place larger, which suits us."

Samantha made certain that her relationship with Tom and Ida was maintained and improved. She occasionally bought them small useful gifts which she knew they would value; soon she had them eating out of her hand.

Samantha settled in to her new routine. It took her time to get used to the weather; in the early days she found the summer temperatures sometimes at nearly forty degrees very uncomfortable, especially as there was no air conditioning either in Berkshire's offices or at home. As the season changed, she revelled in the mild winter. She always rose early and was in the office before seven each day; she caught the train from Epping to Chatswood, and then from Chatswood it was an easy ride into Central. Due to the early hour she always managed to get a seat on the train; often though on the return journey she found the trains uncomfortably crowded; although, due to her condition someone usually gave up their seat for her.

After the first day she was given a key to the office. A desk was cleared for her in the main office; curiously, although she introduced herself around to the four others in the office, none of them were in the slightest bit forthcoming. They merely kept their heads down and did whatever they did, always arriving on time just on the dot of nine am and they all left promptly at five. She dropped two signed copies of the contract she had prepared on Reg's desk on the first morning and found a fully signed copy on her desk late the same afternoon; he obviously had not read it properly or at all.

That, my friend, is your first mistake, she said to herself. His action indicated to Samantha that he didn't care what the contract said.

Reg was embroiled in a potential acquisition for a client and was having trouble with the arrangements, judging from the swearing emanating from the corner office. Eventually he asked Samantha to look at it; she spent a day reviewing the details and was horrified at the amateurish way the deal had been constructed, with what she concluded to be very expensive financing arrangements. The next day she went to see Reg and together they restructured the deal in a way that made sense to Samantha. She carefully made it look as if Reg had decided to make most of the changes that she, Samantha, thought were needed. They had had one furious argument regarding a particular aspect of the deal. "Look Reg, what you are suggesting is illegal where I come from, and I for one have no interest in ending up in jail. The way around it is what I've suggested." He reluctantly accepted her suggestions. After that Reg involved her in anything that appeared to be half- serious. Samantha made certain that she understood the relevant parts of the tax code, after having consulted Berkshire's auditors.

After the first day she said to Reg, "I'm quite happy to be sitting there in the main office but I need somewhere to be able to lock up some of my papers at night. Much of this stuff is quite sensitive and should be kept confidential."

He asked one of the staff to clear a small cupboard in the main office and she was given a key. Instinctively, all Samantha ever kept in there were papers from her job at Berkshire. She used her own laptop, which she always took home with her and whenever she was out she made sure the laptop was shut down. The access codes were in her head, nowhere else.

She always had the office to herself in the mornings. Within two weeks, remembering all she had learnt from Charlie and at Websters, she had downloaded every piece of information contained in the computers at Berkshire, onto memory devices. She secretly stored that information on another machine, which she always left at home. Most evenings she also downloaded all the Berkshire information from her own laptop onto the home machine.

Within a month Samantha had a comprehensive view of all of Berkshire's business, which she examined in detail at home at night. Once she had read all the stuff on the files she realised that Reg was a crook and that he had been involved in all sorts of dodgy deals. It was obvious the reason he had not read the contract she had given him was that he had no intention of honouring it; there were a number of documents relating to the mistreatment of staff, which helped confirm her thoughts.

One morning when she went to unlock her office cupboard, it was obvious someone had had a good look through all the contents. Some attempt had been made to shuffle the papers into roughly how Samantha had left them. *Reg*, she thought. The other staff had left the office as usual at five and when Samantha had packed up her things to go home, Reg was still at his desk.

On a day when Reg was out, she managed to get one of the women in the office to go out with her for a coffee.

Linda was obviously terrified saying, "We mustn't let Reg see you out here with me; we've been warned off you anyway." She wasn't able to get much more than that out of the poor terrified girl.

Reg told Samantha later, "I don't want you fraternising with the people here." He had obviously been told about going out for coffee with Linda.

"Why ever not?" asked Samantha. "I just took Linda out for a coffee; she had done a few things for me over past weeks."

"I know. Just leave it at that. Okay."

Samantha spent many sleepless nights wondering what to do. Finally, with her heart in her mouth, she emailed David, profusely apologising for her behaviour while she was at Websters but emphasising that she had been forced to do what she had done by Charlie:

'In the end he paid heavily for his dishonesty,' she said in her note. *'Please understand that despite my subterfuge I fell deeply in love with you, a situation that still persists, despite efforts to put you out of my mind.'*

She then told him that she was pregnant with his child.

'There is no doubt that you are the father and I am carrying your baby. I have convinced my aunt and uncle that I am not all evil and mercifully they have taken it upon themselves that it is their Christian duty to nurture me.'

She told him about her job and what she had found out about Reg and the business.

'I know that unless I do something I am going to get screwed. I can see that with what I have learnt at Websters, and to give him some credit, from Charlie, I'm sure I can make a success of an advisory business here, I need help though. What I really need is finance to set the place up.'

She finished by telling him she would phone in a few days, which she did. It took a two-hour call to convince David to do as she asked. David's natural caution made him want to question every aspect of Samantha's submission, but from the outset he was going to agree with her proposal. There was no possibility that a child of his would be allowed to grow up in penury.

"How much do you need to finance the operation?" David had asked.

"One hundred thousand pounds," she answered.

All Samantha heard was David taking a deep breath, answering, "Okay, I can manage that."

Although David had never said anything to her about his feelings, from the sound of his voice, he clearly still missed her. Samantha knew she was taking a risk of being rebuffed by David, but she thought that he would be unable to resist her request when she told him she was expecting his child.

To his surprise David was overwhelmed with happiness that she had at last contacted him and he now knew what had happened to her. He felt he had no option but to trust her and felt her requests for assistance were manageable.

***

From the moment he spoke to Samantha on the phone in Australia, David knew that he would always have to be part of Samantha's life. *Another son or daughter,* he said to himself; he wasn't really sure how he felt about that.

David for his part was bemused with the developments as far as Samantha was concerned. He was obviously unable to share anything of the arrangements he had made for Samantha, with Melinda; he was racked with guilt whenever he thought of both Melinda and Samantha expecting children fathered by him.

He tried to persuade Harold that it was appropriate for Websters to make the investment in Wicks Financial, but he got short shrift from him who said, "What you are telling me sounds completely barmy, despite the fact she is my daughter, this girl could have destroyed your career, your marriage and God knows what else. Websters is not going on the line for this." In the end he did manage to persuade a grumbling Harold that the investment was made in the name of Websters but that he, David, fully guaranteed and underwrote it. This meant that the investment was hidden from Melinda. David paid all the interest on the investment.

David for his part, as was the case with Melinda, felt there was much to be valued in his present life: his position at Websters, which he had risked all to be where he was in the business, and his involvement with the SAS, which he felt gave him a further stake in the community, his beautiful wife Melinda, now pregnant with their third child, his two wonderful children, the house in Barnes. He also loved England and everything it stood for. He knew that again he was risking everything with the renewal of his relationship with Samantha, but there was nothing on earth that would allow him to back away from that now.

David was often in a reflective mood after one of his phone conversations with Samantha. Sometimes over a weekend, he took the children on to Barnes Common, which their house overlooked. He had kicked a football with his six-year-old son, Michael, and he had gone and sat on a bench while Michael and Janice fed the ducks in the nearby pond. It was a bright sunny day. He spent the time reflecting on how things had turned out with Samantha and that it wouldn't be long before he would be the father of her child, albeit some twelve thousand miles away. He was brought back to reality when heavily pregnant Melinda, sat down next to him. She'd been to the local grocery store and vegetable shop and was carrying some shopping bags. "Are you alright David?" she asked. "I spotted you from over in Church Road just as I popped in to Two Peas in a Pod and you don't seem to have moved a muscle in twenty minutes."

"I'm absolutely fine, just reflecting on some of the things that have happened in past months, all now thankfully over." He kissed her and patted her stomach. "How's the third party?"

"He couldn't be better and I'm sure it's a he, the way he's throwing his weight around."

David smiled. He was delighted with the way Melinda was dealing with her pregnancy, which he knew would delay her plans for her own development. They watched the children for a few minutes.

Melinda added, "We'll cope for a year or two after the baby is born, but we're going to be short of space in the longer term. We may need to think of getting a bigger place."

"Yeah, I've been thinking about that and thinking about schools and such like. Wimbledon may be a better bet in the longer term."

"Wimbledon?' Okay, I hadn't got that far. I'll miss Barnes and its village atmosphere and being right on the river. What I won't miss is the bloody aeroplanes coming over at five am though. I presume that Wimbledon is out of the flight path."

"Yes, I think it is, now that you mention it."

***

Occasionally Melinda couldn't help but reflect on David's behaviour. At times he seemed distracted. She always persuaded herself that there was nothing to worry about. He was at home at weekends when not on duty with the SAS and he spent time with Michael, teaching him the finer points of rugby. He was persuaded to help the coach of the local junior rugby side. He took the children out to movies and to the numerous museums in London.

Essentially, they were happy; and wasn't that all that really mattered?

The arrangement with David allowed Samantha to put into place a plan that would rescue her from Reg's clutches. She emailed David every month or six weeks with progress and on rare occasions asked his advice. David phoned her from Websters office occasionally.

By the time the baby was due Samantha had dealt with another three major acquisition prospects for Berkshire. A few days before she left Berkshire to attend to the birth of her first child, addressing Reg, she said. "I won't be in for a while, for obvious reasons," she said patting her now very large stomach, "you can call me almost any time though. I have left the issues relating to the latest acquisition on your computer. I hope to be back in about three weeks."

"Three weeks unpaid," responded Reg, "none of this crap about maternity leave and all that bullshit."

Samantha just nodded, looking at him directly. *You will get your come-uppance very shortly, you ugly little shit, just watch me*, she said to herself.

Samantha had, with strictly confidential agreements, the week before, using all her powers of persuasion, managed to get three of Berkshire's major clients to agree to move their business to a new set-up, owned by her. They had recognised that Samantha was the brains behind their own acquisitions and dealings and that Reg was actually a liability.

Chapter 20. Samantha's Independence

Jane Evelyn Wicks was born a week after Samantha's last day at 'Berkshire'. With Ida's help, Samantha had engaged Marcia, a middle-aged lady living nearby, who was only too pleased to be looking after Jane. The additions to the house had been completed and Samantha had bought suitable furniture, which was delivered just before Samantha returned from hospital with her precious bundle.

She emailed David, 'You are now the proud father of a beautiful daughter, Jane Evelyn Wicks.'

From his reply, Samantha could tell David wasn't really sure what to feel about the situation. On the one hand he said he was wildly happy, though his feelings were sprinkled with concern about the baby and the risks Samantha was taking with her own life, and his own position in what had become a hugely complicated business. He also spoke about his wife's pregnancy, his own duplicity and the need to make absolutely certain Melinda got no whiff of Samantha's new baby.

Once all was in order, however, Samantha returned to 'Berkshire'.

"I tried to 'phone you," Reg complained, "but only got your bloody voicemail." He asked nothing at all about the baby.

Samantha nodded. "Reg, you and I need to have a little chat, before I get embroiled into anything new." Her attitude was intentionally more aggressive than it had been in the past.

Reg looked at her showing a slight flutter of anxiety. "Yes," he said, "but we need to get on, there's a lot to do."

"It's about my bonus," said Samantha as they walked into his office.

"Bonus, what fucking bonus? Have you gone dilly or something?"

"Here's a copy of my contract, which you signed a few months ago. It's quite clear." She pointed out the relevant paragraph. "This is what you owe me." Samantha gave him a sheet of paper.

Reg glanced at the bottom of the page and went white. "This is complete bullshit, I have no intention of paying you any kind of fucking bonus and you're dreaming if you think you can pull this one on me."

"Okay," said Samantha. "This is my resignation letter. As my contract states, I am obliged to give you a week's notice. I have taken legal advice and will certainly be suing you for every cent you owe me." She mentioned the name of a reputable leading firm of lawyers in the city.

"Get the fuck out of here, now, out, out, you are not getting another bloody cent from me," he yelled and opened the door of his office allowing all the other employees to hear.

Samantha picked up her briefcase and laptop and walked out. She had effectively been dismissed, so the weeks' notice was now irrelevant.

The short taxi ride to a small but smart new premises in Hunter Street, in the heart of Sydney's financial district, was filled with the taxi driver's complaints on the subject of short rides and small fares. Samantha took no notice, she was wholly engaged in the next step in her quest to resurrect herself. She had engaged one new employee, Susan, who had started the week before as a secretary; Susan had some legal experience and was in the final stages of obtaining a law degree. Samantha had said she could expect to be engaged in all or most of the deals she expected to come their way. "I will teach you everything I know," Samantha told her. She spent a moment or two admiring the sign on the door, 'WICKS FINANCIAL'. The requisite licences had been obtained in the months she had worked for 'Berkshire'. She briefly admired the small suite of tastefully furnished offices. "All neat and clean," she said to Susan. "Thank you. We'll see if we can keep it that way."

"You have a two o'clock and then a couple of meetings tomorrow," Susan told her.

Samantha arranged with the law firm she had engaged to send Reg the package they had agreed on the previous week.

She knew from a couple of emails she had received from Reg that he was relying in her to help resolve a particular issue that had arisen with a new client.

Samantha spent the morning organising the office with Susan's help; she made one telephone call to Josie, the finance director of the active account where Reg was hoping she could help resolve the difficulty that had arisen. There was a short greeting from Josie, which included a discussion about Samantha's baby. Josie then said, "We really need you on board now, Reg does not understand the issues."

"Mnn, Josie, I just wanted you to know that as of this morning I no longer work for 'Berkshire', I can't discuss it, but that's the situation."

There was a sharp intake of breath from the other end of the line.

"If you want to go on with 'Berkshire', that's your business, but I have already set up my own advisory firm," continued Samantha. She gave Josie the appropriate address, phone numbers and email address. "I already have a couple of clients. If you want assistance in this matter I would of course be only too happy to help, and you can phone me at any time of the day or night."

"Phew, that's a relief," was the answer on the other end of the line. "I'll speak to the boss; hopefully we'll be able to come back to you later in the day."

Two days later she had another client.

She wouldn't take any of the mountain of calls from Reg.

A distraught Reg kept phoning the offices of Wicks Financial mostly when Samantha was out. He tried to bully Susan into telling him where he could find Samantha. After several conversations Samantha told Susan she would meet Reg in a café, neighbouring the office, later that day. "Susan, you need to be in the cafe, but out of sight, and warn the owner there might be trouble, he should be prepared to call the police."

"Scary," said Susan.

"Not really, he's all bluster, but if I have to I will take an AVO out against him."

Samantha appeared at the cafe, deliberately ten minutes later than the time she had indicated. She was able to watch an increasingly distraught looking Reg, sitting down, standing up, walking around before she went up to the counter and ordered herself a coffee. She acknowledged Susan, who was one of several customers and who was sitting a little way away and then went and sat down in front of Reg. Reg had never met Susan.

"What do you want?" she asked Reg. "I don't have much time, so tell me your business."

"Mistake, I have made a mistake, I want you to come back."

"Too late, it's much too late for that. You burnt your bridges with me, not just the other day, but all the time I was with 'Berkshire'; respectfully all you really wanted were my brains, without having to pay for them. Frankly you can stew in your own juice."

"You set your own operation up while you were working for me and you stole my clients."

"You chucked me out of your offices, which is how you behave all the time. If I had done nothing I would have ended up as another of your bloody victims. If you feel wronged, then sue me. I hope you do, and I can assure you that if you do sue me, I will have your guts for garters." She had decided that some robust Charlie-like language was what Reg would understand.

"I'll pay all the money I owe you, you can have a share in the business," he offered desperately.

Behind her back Samantha waved at Susan. A prearranged signal to tell the café owner to expect trouble.

"You are going to pay me the money you owe me whether you like it or not. I now own all of my own business, so your suggestion is not interesting. And one other thing Mr Holdsworth, I'm just going to mention one word..." and she whispered, "Druitt."

Reg went a deathly pale; he stood up, picked his empty cup up and would have thrown it at Samantha, but for the intervention of the café owner who, unbeknown to Reg was standing immediately behind him. He grabbed Reg's extended arm and quietly removed the cup from his grasp.

"Out," he said to Reg, "or I call the police." Reg was then marched out of the cafe and pushed into the street.

"Bitch," he yelled at Samantha. "I'll get you one day."

Susan joined Samantha and they had another cup of coffee. "I don't think we'll hear from him again," said Samantha quietly. "I have something on him, something very big, if it gets out he'll spend twenty years in Silverwater jail. I found it a few weeks after I started at 'Berkshire', which is what prompted me to set the new place up; I knew the situation there would never work for me. Mr Holdsworth is a very nasty piece of work indeed, and no it's better you know nothing," she said to Susan's raised eyebrows. "I have the information stored in a bank vault in London, with copies in two other banks here in Sydney."

They sat in companionable silence for a few minutes. Samantha went up to the cafe owner, a dark handsome man in his thirties sporting a three-day growth; she kissed him lightly on the cheek. "Thank you, Theo," she said smiling, "he's stupid enough to have thrown that cup, so you saved a lot of nonsense. Anyway, you now have a customer for life. We've just set up shop nearby."

The man smiled. "More than a pleasure to save a damsel in distress. I can organise lunches, breakfasts and all that in your offices, if you want. Tell your boss."

Samantha smiled. "I am the boss, although there are only two of us at the moment."

Theo looked slightly embarrassed as she and Susan returned to the office.

Samantha always woke early, to spend time with her daughter Jane. She was able to express sufficient of her own milk into bottles, so the baby was fed breast milk for the first six months of her life. Ida taught in a school within walking distance so was willing to look after Jane until Marcia, the nanny, arrived, before eight. Samantha made sure she was home by six, she always spent as much time as the baby would allow before she put her to bed. She made a point, when possible, of having dinner with Tom and Ida, who were now supportive, especially Ida, who doted on the baby.

Samantha often spent an hour or two after dinner working. The first months were hard, since she had to tend the baby at night. Once the child was sleeping through the night things became easier.

Wicks Financial grew rapidly and within another year they had five people in the office, including Samantha and Susan. Samantha tried not to travel much but it was unavoidable from time to time. If any travel was required, Marcia was persuaded to move in to look after the baby.

Samantha found she had to keep her wits about her. Especially in the first couple of years before she had established a reputation for integrity a number of proposals were put to her, which she rejected after trying to understand what was on offer. She was paranoid about her staff and for the first year of employment with Wicks, unbeknown to them she monitored all their emails.

She had engaged Jake, a tall handsome man in his mid-thirties. Perhaps because she was in a hurry she was less thorough with some of the details of his recruitment than she was with others in her employ. She actually liked his charming ways. Three months after he joined he asked Samantha out on a date, just dinner, which she enjoyed. He asked her to 'come back to my place for coffee'. As far as Samantha was concerned this was just an invitation to sleep with Jake. She thought of her affair with David and then briefly compared Jake to David – after which she just couldn't bear the idea of sleeping with Jake. She certainly wasn't in love with him. She pretended to receive a text about Jane. "Sorry Jake, thanks for the evening, perhaps another time. There's a problem with the baby, I'll have to go home."

She went out with Jake once more, when he repeated his invitation to 'come home for coffee'. She made another excuse.

After working for Samantha for six months, Jake approached her with a proposal for a company whose major asset was vegetable oil stored in two hundred tanks in Brisbane. From the very start of his employment with Wicks, Samantha felt there was an underlying agenda as far as Jake was concerned. Instinct more than anything told her to make one hundred percent sure all was in order before she proceeded with Jake's proposal. As far as Samantha was concerned how this panned out was as much a test of Jake's integrity as to whether the proposal was viable or not. "Jake, the critical thing here is the value of the oil in those tanks, so we must be one hundred percent certain that the oil is all there, and we need to be certain of its quality and therefore its value."

"These people are completely straightforward," Jake had responded, a bit too forcefully for Samantha's liking. "I doubt if there will be any problem with that."

"Okay, but this what you will do; we need to establish beyond doubt that the oil is actually there so firstly we need to measure the quantity of oil in each tank taken at the same time, so when you arrive there you will get the electricity supply to each tank switched off so oil can't be pumped from one tank to another, and then you and the twenty or so people supplied by the company's auditors will measure contents of each tank with the dipsticks the auditors have had made, you will also take a sample from each tank for analysis."

Jake tried to argue but Samantha waved him away. "Unless we can establish that the oil they say is in stock is actually there I won't touch this thing with a ten-foot pole," she said to a surprised and nervous looking Jake.

Two days before Jake was due in Brisbane for the exercise, Samantha noticed what she considered to be irregular emails from Jake to the Managing Director of the Brisbane Company saying, "It's all under control. She thinks I've set up a proper control process…"

There was also another email between the pair referring to the dates she and Jake had enjoyed, which put her on full alert.

Why would he be discussing that sort of thing with a client? she asked herself

She immediately phoned Jake saying in a friendly kind voice, "Jake, just give me a brief run-down of the process for checking the stock of oil." Which he did.

"It's all set up," Jake said defensively.

"Okay, if you and the MD there just formally sign it all off when you are done, then fax me the documents. I'm excited about this; we need to get a move on."

"Okay," said Jake warily. "Why do we need to sign it off?"

"Just a formality, if you aren't able to sign it off I will have to come up and conduct the exercise myself."

"No, no that won't be necessary, we'll sign it off."

Samantha then also re-examined the paperwork relating to Jake's employment. The company that provided Jake with a glowing reference, after several phone calls, denied all knowledge of him. She checked with the recruitment company who had introduced Jake. After many denials they admitted no checks had been made on his references.

She kicked herself for being so careless. *Jeepers you nearly got caught. You silly bitch. I'll be much more careful in future,* she muttered to herself.

Samantha went to the police. With the emails between Jake and the Managing Director and the fraudulent references in hand she argued her case; it took her half a day to convince them that a very significant fraud was in the pipeline.

***

In Brisbane, on the day immediately after the stock take had been completed and duly signed off, Samantha, helped by the police and twenty people from an independent firm of auditors arrived at the company's premises at dawn and insisted on entry.

Earlier, she had persuaded Jake to take a week's leave.

They had a professional electrician with them who made sure that the pumps servicing the oil tanks were unable to function. Halfway through the process a very agitated MD appeared, threatening to call the police. The senior policeman showed him the warrant enabling them to search the premises. "We are the police," he said, "you will sit in your office and are instructed to not to communicate with anybody." Notwithstanding that he managed a text to Jake who appeared at about midday. He was immediately arrested.

By three pm they had a full picture, one hundred and fifty of the two hundred tanks were empty; of the remaining fifty tanks most contained genuine quantities of oil although three had only a half tank of water. "We have samples from all the tanks that contained anything; we'll test them and see," Samantha was told by the police. They spent the rest of the afternoon and night comparing the signed off stock sheet Samantha had been given with the actual facts; there was no doubt that a scam of massive proportions was planned. The police had also unearthed emails on the MD's laptop that indicated that he and Jake had planned to escape to one of several possible locations where Australian jurisdiction had no authority. They also discovered that Jake would have been paid thirty percent of the potential profits from the scam, if it succeeded. Jake and the MD were arrested and charged.

"It will take months to put all this together, for a trial," Samantha was told by the police. "We'll need you to give evidence, of course. Thank you for the quick action you took."

Samantha nodded and made her weary way back to Sydney. The MD posted bail for a million dollars; Jake would languish in jail until the trial. When the facts became known within the financial community in Sydney, Samantha's reputation grew and grew; many more potential clients approached Wicks Financial. Samantha wanted to be able to service her clients personally, so she was able to pick and choose. The security surrounding Wicks Financial was upgraded.

She spent an hour on the phone to David explaining what had transpired. She did not mention her dates with Jake.

"How did you suss it all out?" asked David.

"Charlie again – being a crook himself he was a past master at identifying his fellow travellers, he taught me how to smell them out." She laughed.

Chapter 21. Samantha (continued.)

Samantha continued sending monthly emails to David, always including a picture or two of the growing baby. At the end of the second year of her company's operations, Samantha had sent David a set of accounts for Wicks, which showed a modest profit.

"We have most definitely kept our heads above water," Samantha told David on one of what she perceived to be their increasingly intimate and personal telephone calls, "next year will be quite a bit better, with all the new clients that are walking through the door." She then took a deep breath. She desperately wanted to see David again, mainly to confirm her own feelings for him as well as trying to understand his feelings for her. "I think you should pay us a visit, soon, if that's possible."

David hesitated. No doubt he was thinking that helping her set up her business and acting as a sort of consultant to that business was one thing; whereas a visit to Australia was injudicious at best and would further compromise his marriage to Melinda. "I'll see what I can do," he finally responded.

Tom and Ida were disappointed not to be able to persuade Samantha to go anywhere near the church they attended, although they did manage to persuade her to have Jane baptised there.

Samantha tried to spend as much time as possible with the baby at weekends, taking her for walks and playing with her. She always brought work home with her though. Not long after the birth she started going for long runs right across Epping and neighbouring suburbs on both Saturday and Sunday; she tried to go to a local gym at least twice a week.

Reg never found any of the hidden programmes Samantha had embedded in his computers, so Samantha was always aware of what he was up to. On one occasion she found he had dredged up a scheme directly aimed at destroying Wicks Financial; he was amazed when Samantha didn't fall for it.

Two years after Jane's birth, David eventually added an Australian leg onto one of his usual trips to New York. He didn't often discuss the detail of his trips with Melinda and in this case, he altogether failed to mention to her the added leg to Sydney. He spent a short day in the office with Samantha; he was well up to date with all her activities and in any event rarely interfered with what she was doing and only occasionally offered a suggestion.

"I have booked a week on Hayman Island," Samantha told him when she picked him up at the airport.

David was booked into a hotel in central Sydney and his visit was not mentioned to Ida and Tom; Samantha knew they would disapprove. Samantha merely told them she had booked a week's holiday on Hayman Island.

"Maybe you'll meet a nice young man there," observed Ida wistfully.

They flew from Sydney to the Great Barrier Reef Airport on Hamilton Island and they all enjoyed the fifty-minute ride in a high-speed boat to the Hayman Island resort over the tranquil azure blue waters of the Pacific Ocean.

They spent a glorious week eating, sunbathing and making love.

***

David was mesmerised by his pretty beautiful two-year-old daughter. To him, Samantha was just as beautiful as she had always been, having matured and was more self-assured without the cancerous shadow of Charlie following her. Samantha was now a confident young woman, still in her mid-twenties. David knew he was still in love with her, which created all sorts of dilemmas, especially after Samantha made her feelings clear to David.

"There is nobody else in my life," she told him. "I spend all my time on the business or with Jane. I do understand your own situation," she told him. "Still I can't help but hope that in the future things may change."

David said nothing, but he looked at her and nodded.

David had one minor concern, in that he thought he recognised a banker colleague at the resort who looked at him speculatively.

Once he was home, Melinda looked him up and down suspiciously saying, "Sunbathing in New York, in winter? You're as brown as a berry."

"I had a couple of days at a clients' place in Florida," David responded lamely.

Melinda said nothing, but the information was clearly stored away in her prodigious memory.

***

In the months following his trip to Australia, there was a rumour within the parts of the finance industry that Melinda had contact with, that a man matching David's appearance had been seen on Hamilton Island with an attractive young woman and a small child.

She wasn't sure what to make of that.

***

After her holiday on Hayman Island, Ida said to Samantha, "What are your real objectives? We thought we were going to be responsible for a welfare case when you arrived. We couldn't have been more wrong. All you do is work and look after the baby. You've shown no interest in any man at all, you do need to try to have a bit of fun you know. You don't mention the father of your child at all. Are you in touch with him and has he helped you at all?"

"I couldn't have done any of what I have managed to do without the solid base of support you and Tom provide, but to answer your question I am in touch with Jane's father, he has been helpful." Noticing Ida's questioning glance, Samantha added, "No, I won't be joining him. He lives in England. I'm having a lot of fun at work and have built a very good business here. Regarding men, I got burnt; I'm not ready for any of that again. I'm determined to give Jane the best start in life that I can manage; living here with you has made all the difference as far as that is concerned. We have agreed that Jane will go to a local play group as soon as it makes sense and then to Holy Spirit School in North Ryde", she added trying to deflect the line of questioning, "anyway I may repeat the Hayman Island experience again next year with Jane."

A few days later, Ida then said to Samantha, "Jane seems to have enjoyed her holiday, she keeps pointing up in the sky saying 'Daddy'. What do you suppose that's all about?"

Samantha felt a jolt of embarrassment; Tom and Ida had done everything for her, although initially they had felt very uncomfortable about her condition, so after a few days' introspection she said, "Ida, I haven't been as straightforward as I might have been about the holiday." Without waiting for any kind of response from Ida she continued, "Jane's father, David, spent the time with us on Hayman Island hence the reference to Daddy, I suppose David told her he had arrived by plane or something like that." She then explained more about how David had helped her set the business up and their on-going communication.

"Mnn," responded Ida smiling. "I'm not supposed to approve of such liaisons, but I could see more of a sparkle in your eyes after the holiday, more than just a week with Jane on some beach would have generated. It's alright, I don't want to intrude any further; but you are more like the daughter we never had, so if you need to talk anything over I'll always listen." She hugged Samantha.

On a few occasions one or another of the young men employed by Wicks Financial made a play for Samantha, which she always parried. Those who had any sense backed off. She had to deal with one rather persistent young man rather brutally; a lesson which gradually reverberated though the company, putting off any further incursions into her life.

Within three years, through a third party, Samantha bought one hundred percent of the shares in 'Berkshire'; she knew there was some unexploited value in some of 'Berkshires' clients. Reg never knew who the real purchaser was. Reg packed himself off to the Gold Coast, where he became involved in fixing horse races and building shoddy blocks of flats.

Chapter 22. Charlie Again

Samantha thought she had everything under control until she had a panicky phone call one morning from Marcia. "Tom and Ida are out at work, but there are a couple here who claim to be your mother and father. They say they have come to stay…"

Samantha was struck dumb for a moment.

"Hello, did you hear that?" whispered Marcia.

Samantha eventually pulled herself together saying, "Put the person who calls herself Evelyn on please."

There was some mumbled discussion and a shuffling noise on the line.

"Hello…" said an uncertain voice.

Samantha was furious. "Mum, what the hell are you doing here, just pitching up without any notice and not having heard a word from you for all this time? This is not a pleasant surprise. Charlie up to his usual tricks. What do you want?"

"Darling, we just wanted to come and see you all… Ida told me about the baby."

"For God's sake, you knew I was pregnant when I left England. You knew where I went. I've heard nothing from you at all, wondering how or where I was, nothing. Jane's almost five years old now."

Evelyn tried to interrupt, "No Mum, forget it, I don't want to hear it. You and that bloody Charlie put me up to all that nonsense at Websters, to my great shame, and then you thought you had abandoned me to my fate, when due to Charlie's ineptitude it all went haywire. Frankly both of you can go to hell, just don't be there when I get home later. Put me back to Marcia please."

The phone was put down.

Samantha phoned Ida and then Tom, who were both busy. Wondering what she should do she emailed David. Tom and then Ida phoned back. Ida said, "I have just had a word with Marcia. I have sort of kept in touch with Evelyn in a desultory way over the years, so she knew about the baby; she also knows that you have set up your own business."

By this time Samantha had calmed down and had time to think about what she might do. "Ida, as I have told you many times none of what I have achieved could have been done without your support. I haven't told you the full story of the shenanigans that Charlie got up to and what he forced me to do. I never heard a word from either of them after I was dumped on a plane to come here. I really cannot contemplate having anything whatsoever to do with either of them. Mum is so weak, and Charlie will just be a leach; I am certainly not letting him anywhere near my business."

"As a Christian, maybe you should find it in your heart to forgive them?"

"It's not a question of forgiving them," said Samantha. "Led by Charlie all they will do is to take advantage of the situation. He will take everything you let him take and then want more. I am never going to let him or Mum get anywhere near me again. In particular, they must have nothing to do with Jane."

"I'm going to have to let them stay."

"Ida, I'm really sorry about this, but I simply cannot contemplate being in the same house as either of them. Could I ask you to get Marcia to bring Jane to me here in a taxi together with all her clobber; if you have to, make it two taxis." Thinking quickly, she added, "Get it all sent to the Four Seasons, where I'll book a room. People from here will come and collect my computer and personal possessions; I will stay at the hotel until the situation is resolved."

"Is this necessary?" said a very worried Ida.

"One day I'll tell you what those two made me do, so yes I'm afraid it is necessary. Please, please do not tell them where I'm staying. Anyway, when Charlie finds out there is nothing doing as far as I'm concerned, knowing him he will scarper back to old Blighty. Hopefully then everything will be go back to normal."

"Don't you even want to see them?"

"No, for me they ceased to exist when I was exiled from London. When I tell you the full story you'll understand the reason."

Tom then came on the line and Samantha had a very similar conversation with him.

"Ida and I have a lot of respect with the way you behaved since you first came here so we will see to it that what you have asked us to do is done," he said. "I can't say I understand it though."

"Okay, thanks Tom, there really is no choice as far as I am concerned. I hope it all resolves itself quickly."

Samantha phoned the Four Seasons and booked a suite for a month. Marcia, Jane and all the related paraphernalia, including her computers were delivered to the hotel.

There is no way that I will allow Charlie anywhere near any of my computers, she said to herself.

During the evening Samantha got a call from David on her mobile. She had earlier emailed him to explain the developments. Samantha explained the situation.

"I think Charlie may try something stupid," said David. "He's obviously desperate. Samantha, you need to look after yourself and Jane. I have some contacts in Australia who will be able to substantially improve your security. I have to make some calls and will call you back."

"That seems to be going a bit far. What do you think they might do?" asked Samantha.

"I don't know, but it's better to be safe than sorry."

***

It was clearly time for David to call Jones again, who, this time, was more receptive to his call, "Thank you for your on-going donations to the fund," he said. "What can we do for you this time? Hopefully it's more than just breaking a few fingers."

"Maybe, maybe not, it's in Australia. The idiot I am dealing with is the same. All I need is for you to help an associate who needs a bit of security protection. You may have to scare Charlie a bit."

David spelt out the details.

"Okay," said Jones, "tell her to phone this number and the password is 'barrier two'," he gave David a number, "the people concerned are in Sydney or nearby, so contact should be easy enough. I'll make a call now, but your contact should phone as soon as she can." David phoned Samantha again and gave her all the details.

"I don't want any rough stuff," said Samantha. As soon as they see they'll get nothing from me, they'll just return home. I'll leave it a day or two I think."

David said, "As I have told you, Charlie is probably desperate, so you never know what he might get up to. My advice is to make that call right now, hopefully just as an insurance."

David sat and thought for a few minutes. He then made the call to Sydney, knowing that Samantha was reluctant to do so.

"Hello," answered a gruff voice.

"Barrier two," said David.

There was a momentary hesitation on the line. "Jones has just called, I was expecting a local call from a woman," said the voice.

David then explained the situation. "The lady concerned is not taking the whole thing seriously enough. I know the people in question. They are desperate and will certainly resort to violence if they think they are being thwarted in any way. The lady is holed up in the Four Seasons. Her name is Samantha Wicks. She has a five-year-old daughter with her, who will probably be taken out into the botanical gardens for some fresh air by a nanny in the morning. You also need to be sure that her offices are not tampered with." David gave the man the address of Wicks Financial in Hunter Street. "Someone also needs to keep an eye on Samantha herself, she just doesn't see the need for any further security on her part. I'll send you a photo of her."

"Mnn, that's quite a big job…"

"Phone Jones if you are worried about cost," said David. "I'm sure it's not a problem."

✱✱✱

The next morning, Samantha ordered breakfast in her room for herself Jane and Marcia.

"I hope this nonsense doesn't last too long," she said to Marcia. "How long will you be able to stay?"

"Let's see how we go," said Marcia. "I'll stick with you until it's all sorted out."

Samantha didn't notice the large, fit looking middle-aged man dressed in a security personnel uniform in the corridor as she hurried down the hotel passage to walk to her office. Neither did she notice another man following her, at a safe distance, to the office.

A very nervous and worried Samantha was trying to concentrate on the details of a takeover deal when her mobile rang.

A hysterical Marcia was on the line. Initially Samantha was unable to make any sense of the conversation. "Jane!" she yelled. "They... tried... take... Jane."

An icy cold fury overtook Samantha.

"Marcia, for heaven's sake, listen to me," she yelled down the phone. There was a brief silence from Marcia. "Is Jane alright?"

"Yes, she is now."

"Where are you?"

"In the Botanical Gardens."

"You'd better tell me what happened."

A very shaken Marcia said, "A woman... the one you called Evelyn, tried to take Jane... away from me, but there was someone nearby, who had said a few pleasant words to me earlier, came to my rescue... the woman has been taken away by the police. The man I spoke about has been very helpful. We're now walking back to the hotel."

"Can I speak to the man please?"

"Barrier two?" asked Samantha before anything could be said.

"Yes, we've been keeping an eye out. I was in the hotel earlier. Instructions from a London source."

Samantha thought for a moment, *David, thank God for David.*

"Ma'am, you need to be very careful. I'll stay with Marcia and the child, but I got the impression that there is a bit more to all this than just trying to snatch Jane. You need to watch yourself at the office."

"Could you put me back to Marcia please?"

"Marcia, just go back to the hotel…"

She was halfway through the conversation when Charlie walked into her office followed by a panicked, red faced and very flustered PA. "He just walked in."

"It's okay," answered Samantha, "not your fault, let me deal with this."

The secretary fled.

Before she put the phone down, she managed to yell to Marcia, "It's Charlie, tell…" Charlie had overpowered her and tried to snatch the phone from her grasp. There was a violent struggle, which Charlie eventually won. The phone fell to the floor.

"Charlie, get the hell out of here," yelled Samantha. "I want nothing whatsoever to do with you. Get out."

Charlie produced a gun. "I'm gonna get what is due, you double crossin' cow. We've got the kid…"

Samantha remained silent; she knew that Charlie might do something stupid if he was provoked. She sat down and looked at him, she was shaking uncontrollably. "Sit down Charlie…"

"As I said, we 'ave the kid, an' you are gonna play ball…"

In her panic, Samantha managed a few coherent thoughts, *David must have alerted the rescuers. I just need to keep the bastard, talking…* She couldn't help shaking. *I'm not ready to die, especially from anything*

Charlie might deliver. She knew Jane was safe, something Charlie was obviously not aware of.

"Okay, okay, Charlie, put that bloody thing away. What do you want?"

"Your bloody incompetence almost cost me the business; I taught you everything you know. I want you to hand over the whole of this operation, now." He was still waving the gun about.

"Don't be ridiculous. With your antics you would screw this place up in five minutes…"

"Don't forget we've got your little Jane. You'll get 'er back when I get what I want."

Samantha thought for a moment, *I need to put some doubt in his mind about Jane. He'll panic when Evelyn doesn't answer the phone.*

"Charlie you're bluffing when it comes to Jane. Can I talk to her? Just get Evelyn on the mobile."

"'Of course we got 'er," he said. "I had a call from Evelyn sayin' it was all go."

"I don't believe you. Marcia was told not to leave the hotel. You're just bluffing." Charlie shifted uneasily in his chair. "Go on, call Evelyn on the mobile."

Charlie looked at her, laughed and then said, "Silly cow, that's one of the lessons I taught you." He laughed again. "I'm no' gonna fall for that one."

"Charlie, put that gun away, then we can talk. I'm quite sure that Jane is actually safe and that Evelyn has been taken away by the police."

Charlie momentarily looked uncertain and then there was the sound of a terrible crash in the outside office making Charlie turn away for a second. Samantha took the opportunity to pick up a heavy paperweight on her desk and fling it at Charlie. By sheer luck the paperweight hit him on the side of the head stunning him for a moment, which gave Samantha the opportunity to make a dash through her closed office door to safety. Three large men rushed past her, then minutes later dragged Charlie, bleeding from a head wound, out of the office. The staff fussed around Samantha making sure she was unhurt.

"Somehow your mobile had not been turned off and we could hear everything that was said," Samantha was told. The police had already been called. "I'll get you one day you stupid bitch," he yelled at Samantha as the police dragged Charlie away.

"Could we find Marcia and Jane, I just need to see that they are safe," asked Samantha in a weak voice. She was sitting down and shaking uncontrollably.

Thank god for David, she thought to herself again, *we would have been in a real pickle otherwise.*

The police eventually pieced together what had happened and Charlie and Evelyn were remanded in custody and charged. The police tried to understand the role of the 'SAS mafia' but gave up when the only response they were able to elicit was that they were a group of 'concerned citizens'.

Samantha returned to live at Ida and Tom's. "With all the fuss I now feel that I have to give you an explanation of why Charlie and Evelyn behaved as they did. I'm going to tell you absolutely everything," she said. "You won't like much of it. I behaved very badly and probably don't deserve to be where I am now."

She left nothing out. "The worst and best part was that I fell in love with David; a condition that still persists," she reflected for a moment. "I did everything Charlie asked me to do, he received the information I stole. Fortunately, or unfortunately, dependant on your point of view, David had sussed out what was going on and he made sure that the information was misleading. Unfortunately, Charlie acted on that information, without showing it to me and without doing any of his own checking so he fell right into the trap that David had laid. It almost sent him down the drain; he hasn't really recovered from the debacle. It seems they thought that once they realised I had set up a successful operation here that they could rescue their own situation by doing what they did."

There was silence for a few minutes when she had finished. What she had told them was way beyond any of their own experiences; they really had no idea how to respond.

Samantha continued, "I can absolutely assure you that the business I now own and run is one hundred percent legitimate. Reg Holdsworth is a crook, something I had worked out within a few days of being there and there have been a few attempts by some of the local fly-by-nights to get me to deal with underhand and illegitimate operations. I have never touched any of them – once I had to get the police involved. I could well understand that you may want to see the back of me with everything I've told you. I did behave appallingly but I have made every effort to reform…"

"No, we won't have any of that nonsense about leaving us," said Tom firmly, "thank you for telling us what happened in the past. There is nothing more to be said. The police will deal with your mother and father. They will both go to jail I expect, and then be deported back to England," he drew a deep breath, "you may have to think about what you will be prepared to do for them when they eventually emerge from jail; this experience will completely destroy them I'm sure."

Samantha sensibly kept her mouth shut. She looked at Tom admiringly, *here is a genuinely good man, rare as… as they say*. She smiled inwardly.

"You haven't told us who the men are who rescued you," said a relieved Ida, changing the subject.

"David was, maybe still is, a member of the British SAS Reserve, I have no idea what he gets up to in that situation, but they do have to deal with potentially life-threatening situations. The men who came to my rescue are ex-members of the SAS, and that includes the Australian Special Forces, who sometimes help to look after other ex-members. David must have done something very special to be able to call on their services. I asked him for help but told him that I thought I could deal with the situation myself. He must have taken another view, thank heaven he did." A tear slipped out.

"You see something of this David?" asked Tom.

"Yes, I've told Ida about that. He helped me set up the business by providing finance. Jane and I now spend a week a year together with him on holiday somewhere. He's married with three children."

Ida cautiously put a hand on Tom's arm. He understood the message and stopped asking questions. Finally, he stood up and clumsily hugged Samantha. "You're like the daughter we never had. Whatever you've done we'll look after you, don't worry. Just bear in mind what I said about those two when they eventually emerge from jail. I will visit them there, so we'll know what sort of shape they're in."

Chapter 23. Back to Kenya

After the rescue of 'Smith' in Kenya, David had been asked by the SAS to review the training programme for the Kenyan special forces. Mostly he was able to provide advice on the training regimes by correspondence, and he had support from Powrie to arrange for individuals, including Sergeant Kariuki, and other small groups to visit Kenya for specific training purposes. It also involved him in paying an annual two week visit to the country during major training exercises.

David had explained his commitment to Samantha saying, "You and Jane could meet me there, once the exercises are complete; there are some wonderful places to visit such as the various game parks and reserves in Kenya, Tanzania and Uganda; some of the places in Zimbabwe, Botswana, Namibia and South Africa itself are also worth a visit."

For the next few years, David's commitment to the SAS was fulfilled in Kenya, and was sometimes followed by a week or so, with Jane and Samantha, in one of the game parks or one of the resorts on the Kenya coast.

When such a trip was mentioned to Melinda she said, "Africa, forget it. To me all it represents is flies, mosquitoes, AIDS and corruption. As you know it's increasingly dangerous. Our little trips to Italy and the South of France will do me just fine thanks." She occasionally asked why some of the trips were so long but didn't persist with her questions. Instead, every now and then she attended an 'investment' conference of her own, mainly in the United States, and she didn't answer too many questions regarding those trips herself.

***

Along with the new baby, Melinda enjoyed the occasional job, mainly involving assessing the value of particular investments, her conference trips with Andrew, and spending time as a family. From time to time, she heard rumours that a person fitting David's description had been seen at some resort on the Australian coast with a pretty young woman and a small child. But, in view of David's apparently loving approach to her personally, she chose to ignore the rumours...

***

David found out about Andrew when, one weekend while Melinda was out, he had to use her computer to access some research he was conducting on a particular company. Quite by accident, just as he was about to close the machine down, an email was highlighted which started, 'My darling Melinda.' He was unable to resist opening the said email.

To his great surprise it was a very affectionate and intimate note from someone called Andrew about an invitation to an 'investment conference'. He didn't register when or where. He thought about it briefly and mentioned nothing to Melinda on the subject.

Makes me feel a little less guilty about my own behaviour, he thought.

To David, Samantha and Jane, a visit to the Maasai Mara, in Kenya, was a wonder. David was going to rent a vehicle and after a long conversation persuaded one of the Kenyan Special Forces officers to accompany them.

"Why the fuck do you want to go there," Captain Otieno Boniface had asked David over the usual Tusker beer, one evening in the officer's mess.

David, rather taken aback by the response said, "Well, it's one of the premier game reserves in the world. I have a visitor and her child arriving from Australia within a few days and have made some bookings there. I was hoping to get one of you locals to come with us; it seems that most tourists take these trips with other tourists and learn nothing of the country. Most of the time they hardly know where they've been. You would be welcome to bring your wife or girlfriend, if you wish; it's all booked. You would have to take some time off but otherwise it's all on the house so to speak."

"Those places are just for you *Wazungu* tourists. Us locals, the *watu*, which means people in Swahili, as the *Wazungu* (white people) describe us, thought we had escaped all that stuff with the advent of your so-called civilisation," he laughed. "I would jump at it if you were offering a week in a five-star hotel on the coast…"

"If you've never been, you might even find it interesting."

Boniface looked doubtful.

"Okay, we'll come, thank you," Boniface said to David after a few days. "I will bring my girlfriend Zipporah, but my colleagues tell me

312

the roads are terrible and it's a very long drive, and as you'll have a young child with you, it's probably unfair on her. Maybe you can arrange for us to fly; you can rent a Land Cruiser from the hotel I expect." He smiled. David could see Boniface was mainly concerned to avoid the bad roads, but what he said made sense.

They flew in a single engine Cessna from Wilson and were met by hotel staff an hour later at the rough airstrip a short distance from the Serena Hotel in the area of the Mara known as The Conservancy. Both Zipporah and Jane were sick during the bumpy ride.

The beautiful Serena Hotel, nestled among some rocks near the top of a hill fitted in perfectly with the unspoilt surroundings of the Maasai Mara game reserve. Game was visible from the hotel rooms but they found that one had to be careful to keep doors and windows closed, otherwise there might be an unexpected visit from a small vervet monkey or a baboon.

During dinner the first evening David said, "As you suggested, Otieno, I have rented a Land Cruiser for the next few days. We were thinking of going out just before six tomorrow morning to catch the game before it gets too hot and the game go and hide in the shade."

Zipporah looked uncomfortable, but Boniface said after some thought, "Okay, I'll meet you out at the front at five forty-five."

Boniface arrived promptly at the stipulated time. Samantha and Jane had parked themselves in the rear seat, which enabled Samantha to stand and look out through the now open roof.

Boniface almost always spotted any game before anyone else; David supposed it was part of his historic DNA when his antecedents shared the land with the wild animals. To David's amazement though Boniface had almost no knowledge of any of the game animals at all. All the antelope were just that, antelope, or *'nyama'* (meaning meat) as he described them, and David had to go into an elaborate explanation about the annual migration of the herds of mainly wildebeest and zebra from the Serengeti which lies to the south of Mara, in Tanzania, to the Mara and then the return to the Serengeti as the seasons changed.

Samantha and Jane just revelled in the experience, with Samantha taking hundreds of photographs. Of the 'big five' they saw Elephant, Lion, Buffalo, Leopard – in a tree, but no rhino. "In this part of the world they have all been poached out," David told them. Even young Jane was able to distinguish most of the major animals after few days in the Mara.

They all wondered about the large herds of Maasai cattle in what was supposed to be an area reserved for game.

"The Maasai seem to be out of control," David observed. "Is nobody able to keep their cattle out of the reserve? In the long run one wonders whether they will destroy the place altogether. It seems that they think they have a right to graze their cattle in the Reserve; it's almost as if they thought they owned the place."

"That's what all the *Wazungu* say," said Boniface in a dismissive way. "In the past the Maasai did own it," he continued, "they occupied everything here in the Mara and indeed in the Serengeti, south of here in Tanzania. They also occupied all the land from here right through Laikipia, beyond Nyaharuru. They were persuaded to abandon their claims to the northern, Laikipia, areas, partly with the aid of *Wazungu* guns, in the early part of the twentieth century. It's also interesting that there has never been any conflict between the Maasai and the game, they live off their cattle and don't hunt the wildlife, their main diet is a mixture of milk and blood from the cattle-bit of a contrast to this I suppose". He waved his arm around the elaborate display in the restaurant where they were eating, "so they have lived in harmony with the wildlife for ever."

He looked speculatively at David, before adding, "Of course Kenyatta made sure, once the *Wazungu* had left at independence, that the whole Laikipia area was occupied by the bloody Kikuyu. All the names in the area are Maasai – Ol'Kalou, Ol'Joro Orok, Ol'Bolossat, Oleolondo and so on; that could cause trouble as populations grow in future. Before the *Wazungu* came the Maasai kept the Kikuyu hiding in the forests. If they got too uppity they raided them, took all their cattle and their women and killed the men and boys. The Kikuyu have benefitted more than any other tribe from the advent of the *Wazungu*. They now steal the place blind at every opportunity. I could go on." Boniface, unusually, showed some emotion at the end of his dissertation.

"Please do, most interesting," David answered. "All the Governments in Kenya have had a reputation for corruption."

"Yes, it's bloody nightmare. The Kikuyu are the worst, they started it all, but that Moi, he wasn't any better." Referring to President Daniel Arap Moi, who succeeded Jomo Kenyatta as president.

"Excuse my ignorance," said Samantha, "most visitors think you are all one people, obviously that's not the case. Anyway, surely it's in everyone's interest that it gets sorted out."

Boniface looked at her kindly. "Just because we are all black it doesn't mean that we are one race. It's like saying that all Europeans are one race, say the Anglo-Saxons – the English – are the same as the Slavs in the east. There are maybe 70 tribes in Kenya from different ethnic groups. The Kikuyu are Bantu like the Kamba and a couple of others. We Luo are Nilotic same as the Kalenjin tribes in western Kenya, and the Maasai, then we have what is known as the Cushitic, the best known of whom are Somali. There is also a small Arab community who mainly live at the coast. All have quite different roots and origins. Even you British have problems with the differences between English, Welsh, Scottish and dare I say it Irish. Many of our people make the same mistake assuming that the *Wazungu* are all the same."

The conversations continued and David got just what he wanted, namely an authentic view of the country.

"Since Moi, the WaKikuyu, are back in charge. There is no end to the corruption though; it's just as bad as it always was," said Boniface looking despondent.

Zipporah, was quite unused to the luxury the hotel provided, the luxury rooms, the elaborate meals, the spa, and the swimming pool were her idea of what a few days away from the bustle of Nairobi should be like. She was persuaded to go on one of the game drives in the afternoon but was unable to show any enthusiasm at all. "This is what we all left behind us when we became civilised." She pulled a face. "I have no desire at all to be reminded of what our grandparents, and in some case even our parents, put up with," she confided in them, "sitting in a smoky grass hut and worrying about snakes and lions and things."

During David's first visit after his escapade with the elephant and Sergeant Mwangi, David arranged with Captain Boniface to pay a short visit to Sergeant Mwangi at Langata barracks. He was greeted rapturously by Mwangi and the family and had a meal with them. David was rather overwhelmed with the reception he received. He again read the children a story and Mwangi and his wife were effusive in their praise for having saved Mwangi's life.

During another one of these visits at a resort near Diani on the coast south of Mombasa David noticed that Samantha was more than usually quiet and thoughtful.

He asked her what the matter was.

"It's Mum," she said. "Tom and Ida over many months persuaded me to go and visit her in jail. Ida goes once a month and has done since Mum was incarcerated. She's in a place called Silverwater, which is in Sydney, so it's easy enough to get to… a prison for women." A tear escaped.

"She's only got a couple of years left in there; indications are that she will only serve about half her sentence, and then she'll be deported back to England, with Charlie stuck in prison there for another five years at least," continued Samantha. "She's completely broken... She couldn't stop crying while I was with her. She kept saying sorry, but in reality, as always, the only person she's thinking of is herself. She's been involved in two escapades involving me, either of which could have done me a great deal of damage and she was no help when I really needed her... but she is my mother, I just don't know what to do."

"What do you want to do?"

"She deserves nothing, but I somehow, after much urging from Ida and Tom, feel obliged to do something." Samantha repeated. "She is my mother after all."

"What about Charlie?"

"I really don't have any obligations towards Charlie. He's never behaved like I would expect a father to behave. From the beginning, when Mum married him he always set out to exploit me for his own purposes. He even restricted my real father Harold's access so as 'not to spoil me'. Harold tried to help, not very successfully I'm afraid. He's kept in touch with me in Sydney, with occasional letters from time to time, bless him, despite my behaviour at Websters."

David bit his tongue. He suddenly realised that Harold had never mentioned anything to Samantha regarding her paternity; he meant to keep it that way.

"I told Harold you were forced by Charlie to do what you did; he must have forgiven you."

Samantha looked at him gratefully. "You have been one of the few people in my life to help me in any way," she then added guiltily, "as well as Tom and Ida of course."

"What do you want to do?" David repeated the question.

"I can afford to buy a small cottage or flat somewhere, which she could live in. Reluctantly I think I will have to remain as the owner; when Charlie comes out heaven knows what he might persuade her to do if she actually owns the place."

"Smart," said David, "why don't you do that then. The only suggestion I have to make is to ask her where she would like this place to be."

"Mnn, at some stage when I can afford it I am hoping to return to London to live. If possible, I would like Jane to have the final years of her education in England. I'm not sure I want Mum to be too close."

David swallowed uneasily, thinking, *that would really complicate my life, almost unbearably.*

"What about Wicks Financial?" he asked.

"I could get someone else to run it and maybe buy me out over time, or just sell it. That's a long way off anyway. Buying a place for Mum adds a year or two to the agenda, I suppose. It's all going to be cash, whatever I do; I think I'll have had enough of the financial advisory business by then, so I will need enough to live on. I may try some community work or something like that."

David failed to conceal his relief at this remark. "Where would you want to live?"

"My imagination hasn't gone beyond South Kensington or Hampstead."

"Expensive," said David.

"I will have to come over if I'm to sort something out for Mum, I can have a look around then."

"I can probably help, even if it's just with the right contacts both for Evelyn and yourself."

Samantha looked at him. "I know me moving back to London will complicate both your life and mine. It may not be something you wish to face, but I can't help it. England is my home and I want to return to live there, before it's too late," she hesitated for a few moments. "You have to know you are the only man I have ever really loved and I mean that; even Ida is surprised that I don't have some young man in tow, by now."

David just leant over and kissed her. He was perfectly happy in his marriage and the three children were a delight. Despite this, he was still in love with Samantha and he knew that when she returned to London he would be torn in two.

"I perfectly well understand. We'll work something out," he said not looking at her.

She put a hand on his arm, patting it. "It's okay," she said with a sad tone in her voice, "you've done more than I could possibly have expected under the circumstances." And the gaze in her eyes told David the truth: she was clearly still in love with him.

Chapter 24. Complications at Websters

Although David had regular contact with Lizzie, their phone discussions usually centred on her investment portfolio. They only met irregularly for a cup of coffee at a local café near Websters offices, when she happened to be on a visit to London. Both steered well clear of any situation that might have compromised their existing relationships.

They had had some discussions regarding Asad and his large family. The Asad's had moved to Council accommodation after a few weeks staying in Lizzie's flat in Hereford. Lizzie mentored the family for two years but had now relinquished those responsibilities having judged the family to be well settled. Asad had worked for the SAS for two years as a driver, but he was now the owner of a small tobacconist/convenience store in Hereford, which David had helped to finance from his own personal sources, thinking that such a venture was outside the scope of Websters usual activities. Asad's two wives had managed to secure teaching positions in the local primary school, to start with as teacher's aids with the hope they could become fully fledged teachers in time once their English language skills had been judged to be up to standard. They also helped him in the shop, in view of the long hours it stayed open.

Lizzie and David met in a little Italian restaurant in Sicilian Avenue. David knew Lizzie would be bringing her son Rupert with her, now aged twelve. David had not seen the boy since he was six; he was curious to know what he looked like and was reminded of Kariuki's curious looks at the time of the Asad family rescue.

David was already seated when Lizzie and Rupert walked in; somehow David managed to keep his composure. The child being introduced to him was his spitting image.

Almost a clone of me, he thought. He chastely kissed Lizzie on the cheek. They spent five minutes dealing with an investment prospect, which David had unearthed for Lizzie to consider. David then spent most of the rest of the meal getting to know Rupert, a task he did not find difficult.

They talked about his school, what sports he played and what he was interested in. Rupert was tall and appeared more mature than his age.

"Mum says you are in the SAS, like Dad," said Rupert.

"I'm in the Reserve. Your dad is my commanding officer. It means that I only work part time for the army."

"Only part time. What do you do the rest of the time?"

"I work for a business providing advice on investments to people like your mum. I have an investment proposal for her at the moment, which we just discussed."

"I think I would rather be in the army. Sitting in an office all day seems rather dull."

Lizzie smiled and was about to say something but David quickly responded, "I joined the SAS while I was still at university. Many of the things I learnt from the army, especially when dealing with people and dealing with the risks involved in any assignment, have been very useful in my business life."

"Mr Asad told me that you rescued him and his family."

"I was the leader of a small group of men, but yes I helped to rescue him and his family." As with all his missions, David never went into any detail.

"We often buy stuff from his store," interspersed Lizzie.

The conversation continued. Rupert had just started playing rugby, so they discussed the position he might play.

"I played fly half," said David.

"I wish he wasn't so keen," interrupted Lizzie. "I'm afraid he might get a bang on the head."

"Mum!" protested Rupert, "anyway I'm playing as a centre three quarter for the time being. I'm practising my kicking and catching so maybe I will be good enough to play fly half next year."

Towards the end of what had become a very relaxed meal Rupert went out to the toilet leaving Lizzie and David alone for a few minutes.

"We don't discuss it," said Lizzie, glancing at David before he was able to say anything, "as far as we are all concerned Neville is his father, end of story."

"Neville is obviously aware of the situation," David observed.

"It's been mentioned once; as I said we don't discuss it."

"He's never taken it out on me. Most men would have retaliated in some way, especially in the position he finds himself vis-a-vis me."

"He credits you with saving our marriage... he also credits you with many other things, mainly to do with the SAS."

"Extraordinary and admirable," said David.

"Yes, anyway here comes Rupert."

"Well, down the track if I can do anything..."

They spent another ten minutes chatting. Once he had paid, David hailed Lizzie a taxi. He pecked her on the cheek again and shook Rupert by the hand, as he and Lizzie clambered into the vehicle. "Three fifteen train from Paddington, all the way home," she said cheerfully as the cab moved off.

David walked slowly back to his office. Although he had seen Rupert at the time he rescued Asad, he had put the matter of Rupert's paternity out of his mind altogether; it was now front and centre of his consciousness. He really had no idea how to react.

He was sitting in his office quite unable to do much when Jacqueline Briggs popped in. "You look as if you've seen a ghost," Jacqueline joked.

"Mnn, well yes in a way I have."

"Do you need to talk about it? I saw you with a lady and a young boy in Sicilian Avenue."

"Yes, she's an important client. I took her to lunch. She brought her young son with her."

"Is she about to walk? We've lost a couple of clients recently according to Harold."

"None of mine, if anything my list has grown. I've dealt with her for years," he said referring to Lizzie. "I'm quite sure she's happy with the service we're providing. We're way ahead of the pack – they're all rather jealous of our record," said David.

"We've lost a few clients recently. Why?"

"Whose clients are they?" asked David, knowing the answer full well.

"All Luke McLintock's. He managed to poach a couple from other account managers and now they've also gone elsewhere."

David thought he would find out how much Jacqueline knew. "Do you know where they've gone? Is it all to the same place?" He also wanted to steer Jacqueline away from any discussion relating to Lizzie.

"I'll confirm that, but I think the answer is yes. You'd better be careful; he'll be after some of yours next just to prop up his position at Websters. Anyway, what about this ghost?" Jacqueline was always curious about David and his activities; she was sure she had not been told the full story about his relationship with Samantha, and his escapades with the SAS were also a mystery. Harold wouldn't tell her anything, but there had been rumours throughout the building about David's role in the rescue of a British hostage in Somalia or Kenya.

"Don't worry about that. What you have just reminded me of is more important than any of my personal issues."

"Who was the client, by the way?" asked Jacqueline innocently.

"Daphne Hall, she's my SAS commanding officer's wife. She inherited quite a large sum and we manage her investments."

"Your SAS involvement has brought in some very wealthy clients; isn't there a Kenyan general or something now?"

David thought he had said too much already. David could see that Jacqueline sensed there was more to his relationship with Lizzie, so he brought the discussion to an abrupt halt to avoid any further questions.

David phoned Joe. Despite the fact that David had forced Joe into exile, he thought he'd managed to rescue his relationship with him and had used him to investigate some sensitive matters once Joe had returned to live in England. David had spent half a day with him and thought he had him under control; in some ways he felt sorry for Joe and was a bit uncomfortable with the way he had treated him.

David briefed Joe fully on the phone. "Luke McLintock is the employee's name," he explained to Joe. "I want to know what he's up to. He's lost some clients to another business and the reasons for that are not clear. You must also find out the ownership of that business, and I mean the real ownership; you must find out who is behind any front names. In this case, as before, you are to keep no records of your investigation and you are to phone me the information on a mobile phone number I will give you. Also bill me personally. Is all that clear?" David gave Joe the name of the company to which they had lost clients.

"Yes, it is, anything else?" asked Joe.

"Joe, just be careful, this person is well connected and I don't want him to get wind of your investigation. And no funny business, you remember what happened last time."

***

Joe needed no reminding of what David had done to him. He shuddered as he put the phone down.

To his astonishment, a week or so later Joe got a call from Jacqueline Briggs. She had wondered what she should do about her suspicions regarding David's relationship with Daphne Hall. She didn't have much idea how to go about researching the situation but days earlier she had seen, in a payment schedule she had had to sign, for an invoice from a private investigator, which happened to be Joe for a job recently done for David. She went to accounts and after a few minutes they found the invoice to which the cheque related. She phoned Joe.

"All I want is a clear photograph of Mrs Hall and her son, who I suppose is about twelve years old. That's all." She gave him Lizzie's address. "It's important that she doesn't know what you are doing; I don't want her to be aware of anyone taking photos of her and her son. If anyone sees you the SAS will be all over you, so be careful."

"What should I do with the photos and the bill when I've done what you ask?"

"Just send it all to me here."

Joe was intrigued. He was immediately aware that Jacqueline was quite unused to any sort of clandestine activity; there were no instructions about not keeping any records and he was to send it all to her address in the office. He wondered how he could profit from the situation. He was still looking for an opportunity to get back at David.

Within days he had the required pictures and had posted them to Jacqueline as requested.

When he had taken a careful look at them, he whistled through his teeth, *That kid looks exactly like David*. He thought to himself, *Intriguing. I'll get the bastard now.*

He thought long and hard about how he might exploit the situation, firstly how to profit from his discovery, and secondly how he might be able to hurt David.

While he was contemplating what he might do with what he thought was explosive information he completed his research on Luke McLintock. Despite his other failings Joe was a good investigator and he quickly established the business Luke had 'lost' clients to was actually owned by Luke himself. Luke had been careless and there were only two nominee companies in the ownership chain between Luke, the real owner, and the new company. Joe delayed telling David anything, while he was trying to find an angle to exploit. He put David off by telling him that the investigation had a little way to go, which was partially true since he was trying to establish what sort of relationship existed between David and McLintock. Eventually he discovered, by taking one of Websters more junior employees for a drink in a local pub, that the relationship was poisonous; he found that Luke had discovered David owned a substantial chunk of Websters stock and that he, Luke, was never going to be allowed to own any part of the company. The employee, in an unguarded moment, told Joe that Luke had lost some of his clients to another business; he didn't understand why, as far as he could see Websters was doing as well or better than most of its competitors. He had high praise for David.

"Many of the really good ideas come from David; he seems to have some sort of instinct for the business. It's a pleasure to work with him, I always learn something and he's always patient and gives credit where it due. Luke on the other hand is a bastard to work for; he does nothing for the business and uses about ninety percent of David's recommendations anyway."

Joe didn't want to hear any of this, but it made him delay the action he had in mind.

***

A week or so later, David was authorising payments to various creditors, which he always did thoroughly – not because he was expecting to turn up any kind of fraud, but just to see who the business was dealing with. If he didn't know why a certain payment was authorised, he always asked the person who originally generated the payment request what it was for. Unintentionally this kept people on their toes. He was whipping through the items when to his surprise he found a request for a payment to Joe. After some thought he decided to take Jacqueline Briggs for one of their usual coffee breaks out of the office. The conversation concerned a new very promising employee and Jacqueline was seen to relax. David then pulled Joe's invoice from his jacket pocket and said to Jacqueline,

"You have to be fairly careful with this gentleman, unless the job is straightforward he sometimes becomes tempted to play silly buggers."

He suddenly became aware that Jacqueline had gone deathly pale; as she put her coffee cup down it rattled noisily on the saucer. "Anyway what was it for?"

She hesitated, clearly debating whether to tell him something. Eventually, she was able to look him straight in the eye. "You're not going to like this."

"Go, on," he answered quietly.

"I got him to take pictures of Mrs Hall and her son; I'm sure you know why."

David was quite calm. "Where are the pictures now?"

"I have them, they're in my office." Jacqueline sighed as if relieved to be telling him.

"Did you give Joe any instructions about not keeping any details of his investigation?"

"No."

"Then we can expect he kept copies of the photos."

Jacqueline bit her lip. She was way out of her depth.

"Okay, say nothing to anyone. One other thing," he looked at her.

"What?"

"Destroy the fucking things." His look scared her a bit.

On returning to the office, he phoned Jones again.

"Not you again," said Jones in a not unfriendly tone. "What's it this time?"

"It's not all about me this time; as much as anything it's about the gaffer."

"You have my undivided attention."

David explained about the photos of Lizzie and her son and then about the search Joe was conducting on McLintock.

"Let me get this right: you want any trace of the photos removed from the premises altogether and you then want a brief verbal summary of what this joker has turned up on your friend McLintock. The files on McLintock are to be left as we find them." Jones grunted. "It's as much about you as the gaffer, but we'll do it."

"Any communication is to be on a phone number I will give you. This one will be dumped within the next few minutes. And a couple of other things."

"What?"

"It's urgent and Joe must have no inkling that anyone has been near his place."

"For fuck's sake, you always were one with just a few too many instructions; you really do think we're just a bunch of stumble bums."

Jones put the phone down before David could say anything. David smiled to himself and waited for a call, which he knew would arrive within minutes. Which it did.

He carefully briefed the anonymous caller, giving him Joe's address. He repeated his instructions. "I will be on a number which I will give you now. As soon as you have the info, no matter what time it is, please call. The info must be complete. This phone will be destroyed after the next call; you won't be able to reach me again on this number."

The call came through at three am, much to Melinda's annoyance. David went downstairs.

"The file with the photos has been removed and burnt; there is no trace of anything left."

"Okay, good. And the other issue."

David was given a thorough briefing. "He has had the info on McLintock for a while," the caller informed David, "at least a fortnight. We left the file as instructed."

The little shit is playing games again, thought David. "Anything else?"

"We had a trawl through all his emails. There are a few surprising ones, especially with McLintock."

"Directly with McLintock?"

"Yes."

"That's very useful. Thanks. Anything else. As I told you, this phone becomes defunct after this call."

"I think that's all. McLintock is going to meet your friend at his office tomorrow or the next day. Joe told him he had something special to show him."

"Hopefully you have removed whatever was so special."

"Yes."

The connection was cut.

"What was all that about?" Melinda muttered when he crawled back to bed an hour later.

"Just sorting out a little problem. Two double crossing little shits are going to get a very nasty surprise, before the end of the week."

"Forget about all that, just come here. I need a cuddle."

Before he went to the office though, David explained the situation to Melinda.

"What are you going to do?" she asked. "Shouldn't you just go to the police?"

"As a last resort, maybe. I think there are better ways of dealing with this. If we go to the police we'll be bogged down for months." He explained to Melinda what he intended to do.

"Keep me in the loop, if you need any help…"

"Okay." As always he kissed her as he went out of the door.

***

David went to see Harold as soon as he could in the morning.

"You know the clients that McLintock has lost…?" David started to explain.

"I don't want to hear any more about the feud between you and Luke. If that's what this is about you can leave now."

David smiled, much to Harold's obvious discomfort. "All the clients have been lost to a single business. Would you like to know who owns that business?"

Harold looked as though a cold hard knot was developing in his stomach. "You are going to tell me whether I like it or not, so go ahead."

"Luke owns it, through a series of nominee companies. He's keeping his position here so he has access to our superior research. All he does is to make sure his clients are invested as they would be here. He can then run around crowing about what a wonderful investor he is. He's certainly set himself up to make a fortune, mainly as a result of our efforts." David gave him a sketch of how Luke's operation was set up.

"This is not proof," Harold protested. He clearly had his position in the wider investment community to consider, and recently he had become acquainted with Luke's influential family. He didn't want this to be true.

"Come on Harold, you know what I am telling you is kosher. We're being taken for a ride and, in the not too distant future, we'll be the laughing stock of the whole investment community."

Harold remained silent but looked balefully at David.

"If you have an hour or so, come with me. I am sure by the end of the day you'll have all the proof you need."

"I have an important meeting this afternoon," said a reluctant Harold.

"This may be all over by then, but if you want to be cautious I suggest you postpone the meeting."

Harold told his personal assistant to try to postpone the meeting, and he and David left the building together.

"My contact can't afford fancy offices, so we are going to a place in Finsbury Park. We'll take the Piccadilly line." David confidently led the way to Joe's office as they got off the train.

"Didn't know you had such up-market connections," observed Harold looking around with an expression of distaste.

David said nothing as they entered a grubby looking building and climbed up two flights of stairs. He walked into Joe's single office without knocking.

"Hey, I'm expecting visitors," said a shaken-looking Joe.

"Well, you've got them," said David as he introduced Harold, who sat down on the only visitor's chair.

"You can't do this…" Joe protested.

"We just did. Joe, I want the file you have kept on McLintock. I need to show it to Mr Webster here. He is most interested in what you've found out."

"You told me not to keep any files on the investigation. Anyway, I haven't finished it."

"We'll look at what you have." Said David.

Joe hesitated for a moment.

"Just get the bloody file Joe, or do I have to get it for you?" said David.

Harold looked on, shocked at David's aggressive tone.

After a minute Joe got up and scratched around in a drawer for a moment and soon produced the file. "I was going to phone you and then destroy the file… it's been a very complicated investigation and I didn't want to miss anything.

"Okay, let's have a look," said David.

Joe had left them to it and was frantically looking through all his filing cabinet drawers. "It was here," he muttered to himself. "I saw it yesterday."

Meanwhile, David assessed the few pages in the very thin file.

"Look here, Harold," David said, "it's quite clear Luke is the owner of the operation, called Enterprise Limited, to whom we have lost clients. Isn't that right, Joe?"

"What?" answered a very distracted Joe.

"Concentrate on this for a minute," said David, "please confirm to Mr Webster here that the owner of this business," he jabbed his finger at the name on the schedule, "is Luke McLintock."

"Yes, yes," said Joe, "it's quite clear, he tried to disguise it through a couple of nominee companies, but it was easy enough to unravel. If he really wanted to hide the ownership, he should have tried a bit harder."

Harold looked stunned. He said nothing for a minute and then whispered, "Fraud, common or garden fraud and from such a respectable family."

Joe continued to hunt ever more frantically through his filing cabinets, all his desk drawers and everywhere else he could think of. David glanced at him with a mildly amused look on his face and then he started to talk to Harold. "How do you want to deal with this, Harold? It's blatant fraud, as you say. Perhaps a job for the police?" He knew Harold would panic at the very idea of the police being involved in any way but he knew that any delays in dealing with the issue would give Luke time to find a way out of the situation.

"No, no police," said Harold, "we just need to get all those clients back."

"McLintock has to go as well."

"Yes, yes, I suppose so."

"I have a suggestion."

"Go on."

"Luke hands over the company to us with all the clients intact. He also leaves Websters. All this to be done within the next twenty-four hours. We need to get the lawyers involved of course. He undertakes never to approach any client currently on our books; maybe there should be a threat to go to the police anyway."

"Yes, I suppose so…" answered Harold in a distracted tone.

David was about say something further when there was a knock on the door and Luke McLintock walked in.

Joe peed in his pants and sat down heavily.

Luke looked very surprised; he was clearly not expecting to see his nemesis, David, there and he was horrified to see Harold. He tried to leave but David anticipated the move and blocked the door by standing in front of it.

"Ah, Luke, as it happens we need to have a quiet chat with you about some of the things that our mutual friend Joe has unearthed. While I won't say that it's a pleasant surprise to see you here, it is at least useful."

Luke looked desperate.

"I want you to just take a look at this…" David showed him Joe's file. He explained in detail what Joe had uncovered. "So you thieving little shit, you 'lost' all those clients to a business you own."

Luke had gone deathly pale. "I can explain, I can explain."

"I bet you can. Any more crap from you and you will be explaining it all to the police and various regulatory authorities," said David, who had now taken over the discussion with Harold looking helpless and wringing his hands.

"It's Phillips here, Mr Webster, he has always had it in for me and he's now dredged up this bullshit to discredit me."

Harold then pulled himself together and surprised them all saying, "I'll speak to the family just to tell them what we have unearthed here and then perhaps, David would you call the police and the regulatory authorities? If Luke here doesn't spend tonight in jail, then it will be tomorrow night and a few more nights after that I expect."

Luke then tried to distract everyone by turning on Joe. "This is a trap, you grub, set by you and Phillips. I'll get you for this one. You made the phone call suggesting you had some compromising photographs. Now I can see that's all bullshit. It's just a conspiracy by you and Mr Famous Fucking Phillips here to discredit me."

Joe just sat there with his mouth open not able to say anything.

David took over again. "Mr McLintock, I will phone the police as well as the regulatory authorities if you are going to go on like that. There is a better way though, which might keep you out of jail. You choose."

Luke knew he was in trouble and that everything Joe had uncovered was true. He cursed inwardly; he hated being put into such a position. Normally it was he that had the upper hand in such situations.

"What better way?" he almost shouted.

"You hand this company over to Websters with all its clients intact and give an undertaking never ever to approach any Websters clients again and we might then be able to forget this whole dirty business. There will be a number of guarantees you will also have to give, so all the arrangements are watertight, but that will be for the lawyers to work out. This will all have to be completed, signed sealed and delivered within the next twenty-four hours."

"I have other arrangements for tonight," said Luke. "I…"

"I take that as a no then," said David. "I'd better get hold of the police." He started to flick through the phone numbers on his mobile, "you have ten seconds to make up your mind, Mr McLintock. Once I make the call everything will be out of my hands…" David had no such number on his phone but thought Luke wouldn't take the chance of calling his bluff.

"No, no, no," gabbled Luke, "we need to talk."

"Not here," said David. "You, Mr McLintock have two hours to appear with your legal representative at this address." David had scribbled the address of Websters solicitors on a piece of paper, "if you aren't there I will most certainly be phoning the police and the regulatory authorities."

Luke grabbed the paper and dashed off.

Joe tried to leave. "Stay," said David as if he was talking to a disobedient dog, "you're going to be with us every step of the way. At this stage it's about this business with Luke. It seems from some of the conversation you had with Luke that we may have other issues that we need to explore as well."

Joe started, "I can…"

"Joe, save it. Whatever it was, we will deal with it later."

David then made another call. "Mr Gibson please."

"He's in a meeting."

"Emily, its David Phillips here," said David in his most charming voice. "I really must speak to him. It's a matter of life and death. I must ask you to interrupt him whatever he's doing."

There was hesitation at the other end of the line. "He said not to interrupt him."

"I'm sure he did, but this is desperate, trust me, I really do need to speak to him. I'll take all the blame."

He had always treated Emily with kindness and respect on the many occasions he had visited Websters lawyers, so she relented. "I'll see what I can do?" she said eventually.

There was silence on the line for what seemed like an eternity.

"Frank Gibson here," came the lawyer's voice. "David, this had better be important."

"It's critical," said David, "this is going to be an all-nighter. Harold and I will be with you in forty minutes or so. We'll need a secretary and someone to do some research, and probably sandwiches or something to eat for six or seven of us. Luke McLintock and his legal representative will be joining us in less than two hours."

"Can you give me an inkling what this is about?" asked an irritated Gibson.

"Fraud, major fraud, you will be properly briefed when we get there," answered David.

"Is that all? If Harold is there I would like to talk to him."

David handed the phone over to Harold without another word.

"Harold," he announced.

"Is this really that important?" asked a still livid Gibson.

Harold looked at the expression on David's face and answered. "Most certainly it is. We'll be there in thirty minutes or so."

"Okay, it had better be worth it," said a mollified Gibson.

"Are you sure this is needed?" Harold asked David as they left the office with Joe, having changed his trousers, in tow.

"I am quite certain; you never know what that little toe rag Luke will get up to if we left him alone for a couple of days."

"And if he doesn't pitch-up,"

"I'm pretty sure he will, but if he doesn't I'll get the police, etc, involved."

"You have the right numbers for that?"

"No, but I will have by the time we get to Gibson's place." David smiled.

"You are a real bastard," said Harold, glaring at him.

Ignoring Harold, David made another call. "Text the numbers through, when you have them," he said to the person on the other end, "but hang around until I call you, there may be a number of questions." He closed the phone and he hailed a taxi as they emerged on to the street.

David phoned Melinda and explained what had occurred.

"I will meet you at Gibson's office," she said. "I'll leave Rory with a neighbour. The others have gone to school."

They were in Gibson's well-appointed offices on the tenth floor of a new building in London Wall located in the city, within the stipulated forty minutes. To Harold's surprise, Melinda joined them shortly after.

"I've cancelled all my appointments for today and tomorrow," said a still furious Gibson, glaring at David. "As I said this had better be good and it's going to cost you."

David smiled. "So what's new Frank, and yes I think you will find it really is necessary."

Joe had been left downstairs near the building entrance. "Just phone me when you see them, hang around in a coffee shop or something, where you can observe the entrance to this building," David told him.

He and Harold then briefed Gibson, with Melinda listening in, who was by now fully engaged in what had been unearthed. They spent an hour discussing tactics. Gibson briefed his assistant to do some research.

"It's more than two hours since Luke left the office in Finsbury Park," observed Harold.

David nodded. Thirty minutes later he received a call from Joe. "McLintock and two other men have just walked into the coffee shop, I scarpered before they saw me."

"Okay, do you have a mobile phone number for Luke?"

Joe gave him the number.

"Just hang around for a few minutes, if you would," said David. "When they come into the building follow them up."

David phoned Luke. "McLintock, if you want to rescue this shambles, I suggest you and your two side-kicks get your arses up here and stop deliberately wasting time. If you don't want to deal you know what the other option is." He put the phone down without waiting for an answer.

Harold looked at him. "They were always going to play silly buggers," explained David "It's just in their nature. They think it's clever. They now know it looks stupid."

Luke and his lawyer friends appeared shortly afterwards with Joe arriving a few minutes later.

David allowed Frank Gibson to run through the issues to the visitors. He told them what the process was and the nature of the agreements to be prepared and signed before they left the office.

"That's not acceptable," one of Luke's lawyers said to Gibson.

"What is not acceptable?" asked David.

"We don't accept that Mr McLintock has done any of what you allege?"

"Okay, then this meeting is over. I'll refer the matter to the police and regulatory authorities," responded David.

Luke and his cohorts looked blankly at David.

"Out," he said, "you can leave right now. You know where the door is. Go on, go. I've had enough of this. The financial press is going to have a field day with the story when it gets out, which it will." David glared at them as the three of them picked up their files and made for the door.

"Is that the smartest thing to have done?" asked Harold, looking at Melinda for support.

"Give it thirty minutes. They'll be back. We can spend the time making sure that the agreements we want them to sign are all in order."

"I thought you were going to make some phone calls," said Harold.

"Not yet. I don't expect to be making them at all, as it happens."

Ten minutes later Luke and the two lawyers returned. "We need to talk," he said.

David made them wait in a spare room. "I'm waiting for a call to be returned from the police," he said, "you'll have to wait until I've dealt with that."

Harold shook his head, looking at David, once they were alone again with Gibson. "You really are a bastard," he said.

David and Melinda continued working through the documents prepared by Gibson. Melinda came up with several points that, after discussion, were included in the documents.

An hour later David said to Joe, who was waiting outside in the reception area. "Go and fetch those creeps, from now on I expect the process to be more straightforward."

"Are you okay to continue with this?" David asked Melinda.

"Yes," she said. "You said it would be an all-nighter, so I've got Johanna to come in and look after the kids."

"Ah, I see, you've now got the first team on board…" said McLintock, looking at Melinda.

He was ignored.

By dawn the next morning, all the agreements transferring the ownership of Enterprise Limited and its nominee shareholder companies to Websters, had been signed. Websters, as well as Harold and David had all the guarantees they needed. David had insisted that signatories on any bank accounts were nullified, so that no cash could be transferred, he also obtained a written guarantee that there had been no cash movements in any of the accounts in the past twenty-four hours. Also, that all dividends and management fees paid out by Enterprise since its inception would be immediately refunded to Websters. Harold was asleep on a couch in Gibson's office. Joe was wandering around the office looking worried and wringing his hands.

Melinda had played a leading role right through the process, reviewing every document making certain that all the i's had been dotted and all the t's crossed.

David let Gibson usher the exhausted visitors out of the office. David gently woke Harold up. "It's all done," he said. "I even have a resignation letter from Luke acknowledging his misdemeanours and that Websters owes him nothing. He has waived his right to any termination pay on the understanding that there is no publicity regarding this issue."

"Don't I have to sign something?"

"No, as you know I have all the authorities needed. We can all go home now."

Joe tried to talk to him.

David merely ignored him but said, "You can find your own way home, I expect." He hailed a taxi, which first took Harold home. "I'll leave copies of everything on your desk," David said.

"I don't like any of what we've had to do," said Harold as the taxi sped through the early morning London traffic. "If this sort of thing is needed in a business such as Websters I don't want to have anything more to do with it. I don't like dealing with gangsters. We need to talk."

"Yes," said David. "I'll have to spend time with the clients we've rescued, but yes, we need to talk. When I've put some thought into it."

David and Melinda returned home in time for breakfast. "I need some sleep, but I will have to go into the office this afternoon. You were brilliant by the way, your input made all the difference," he said to a very tired Melinda, who was busy talking to Joanna.

"You both go and get some sleep," said Johanna. "I'll deal with the kids."

He phoned Jacqueline Briggs. "McLintock has resigned. Under no circumstances is he to be allowed back into the office. Clear his desk and send all his stuff to his personal address. Don't even think of looking at any of it. I will be in after lunch and will explain it all to you then. Harold may not be in today. Could you please make sure that these three," he named them, "are available for a lengthy meeting this afternoon."

"There is no need for me to come to the office, is there?" Melinda said after he'd finished the call. He shook his head. "What you have achieved is a very David Phillips sort of arrangement, and we are all better off as a result. That even applies to that horror McLintock, who won't spend any time in jail thanks to you – I don't suppose he will give you any credit for that though."

"I don't suppose he will," David said, and kissed her forehead.

***

When he eventually made it to the office that afternoon, David told Jacqueline all the gory details. "McLintock somehow persuaded some of our clients to go with him and abandon us. For my money this is lesson number one; we can't have been looking after them well enough, so quite a few things need to change in that regard, but first things first. We must make sure that these six clients he stole, for want of a better expression, are overwhelmed by the reception we'll give them, so they are not tempted to run off again."

Jacqueline behaved like a rabbit in the headlights of a car. She was quite unable to focus on what she was being told, probably wondering whether her days were numbered as far as Websters was concerned. At the end of the briefing she asked unsteadily, "What about me. Where do I stand with all this?"

"Where do you want to be?" asked David.

Jacqueline was again taken aback. "Well, I haven't exactly behaved like I would have expected me to behave," she said, "do you still want me in Websters?"

"None of us have behaved impeccably over the years. You made a mistake. I've made many mistakes. Only you and I know about this. I think it should remain that way."

When she tried to say something, David held up his hand. "I have nothing further to add." As far as he was concerned, she had only once stepped away from the straight and narrow and had already gotten bitten. There was no way she'd attempt anything similar again. *I've no doubt she will always remain firmly committed to Websters.* "Is everyone here who needs to be?"

"Yes," she said, and after giving him a peculiar look, she ushered in the three people that David had nominated to attend the meeting.

"You've probably got other things to do," he said to her. "I'll manage from here." He again registered a peculiar look. *Mnn, there is something going on here,* he thought, *I'd better follow-up.*

He briefed the three people fully, giving each of them the details of two of the clients that had been 'rescued'. "We are going to have to tread very carefully with all this. These people left under McLintock's guidance in good faith. For each one we will have to really do our homework in understanding the relationship that had been developed between the client and McLintock and why they thought they were going to get a better deal with him. We also need to understand who the client is and what their needs are. We then need to give each one the royal treatment. I will be involved in the initial meetings with every one of the clients, after that I hope to be able to leave them to you but perhaps there should be a twice-yearly review meeting to include me. Also, they will be told they can phone me at any time if they feel the need. What we do here will form a basis for dealing with all our other clients; we seem to have fallen down a bit on all this and for that I take full responsibility."

Dealing with five of the clients turned out to be straightforward. "We were told that the new company we were dealing with was just another subsidiary of Websters and that nothing would change. We were also told that we would continue to have access to all the research conducted by Websters," each of the clients said to David and his associates.

"Well," said David smiling, "that is indeed the situation we now have. You do have to understand though that Luke McLintock was the one hundred percent owner of the new company. That situation has been rectified."

"Isn't that blatant fraud?" David was asked.

"Yes, of course."

"Won't there be consequences? For Mr McLintock I mean."

"There have already been consequences," answered David. "There will be no consequences as far as you are concerned though."

"What do we say to Luke if he calls us?"

"He will be breaking the terms of our agreement if he does that. If you feel able to, you should let us know and I will deal with the situation. Please don't get into any kind of discussion with him on any issue involving the arrangements we have with you, it will just lead to further complications."

The sixth client turned out to be very different. "It's really a can of worms," said Pru, the investment manager now involved in this account. "I have dug and dug and the real owners of this set of investments are all members of Luke's family."

The meeting with the representative of the client was very hostile and kept questioning why he was being 'buggered around'.

"All I want is for some decent advice," the client said, "which Luke was providing. I'm not sure that you can match his efforts."

"Respectfully, Luke was wholly reliant on our research," David responded, "one hundred percent of his recommendations were based on Websters research."

"That's what he said you would say."

"We can do one of two things," said David mildly, after a moment's hesitation, "we can continue to provide you with investment advice and review the situation in say twelve months' time. If you are still unhappy then we will assume that you will take your business elsewhere. Alternatively, maybe in view of the fact that you are uncomfortable with the situation I won't try to prevent you from taking your business somewhere else from today."

"What have the other clients involved in this issue done?"

"What makes you think any other clients were involved? There has been no mention to you of anyone else as far as I know."

The man looked absolutely furious but to his credit remained silent.

There was an uncomfortable silence for a few minutes. Eventually the man picked up his papers and as he left the room he said threateningly. "You'll be hearing from us."

David nodded and said politely, "Thank you for coming."

Pru looked uncomfortable, then said, "Couldn't we have been a bit more forthcoming in trying to keep them on board."

"Don't worry, Luke will have told them they have to hang in there because he knows he needs our research. Without us he's floundering." He added, "I'll bet you a month's salary that they will be back with us within the week. All that was bluster, perhaps to try to get a better deal from us in terms of fees etc."

Pru smiled saying, "I can't afford a month's salary, but I'll put a tenner on the table."

David fished out a ten-pound note from his wallet and gave it to her. "You hold the bet; I'm quite sure they'll be back. If they raise the issue of fees just tell them what our standard terms are. No compromise. I also have a little plan that will flush our friend Luke down the pan forever. I'll let you know what to do and when."

"What do you have in mind?"

"Let them come back to us first."

Within a few days Harold received a rude letter demanding a reduction in fees. There was no mention whether they were going to leave Websters or not. David and Pru drafted a suitable reply restating Websters policy on fees. It was signed by Pru.

Harold was then subjected to an unpleasant phone call. "Thank you for drawing this my attention, but I am well out of the loop on this one. I'll transfer you to the appropriate person."

Pru was then subjected to a barrage of abuse but she had now begun to understand the name of the game and stood her ground. "I want to speak to someone in authority," demanded the man.

"I have all the authorities required," said Pru. "Am I to understand that you don't wish to continue doing business with us? If that is the case, please let me know and I will make arrangements to hand your portfolio over to the outfit you nominate."

"I want to speak to that stuck-up little prick David Phillips."

"He's not in."

The phone was slammed down.

When David returned, Pru said to him, "I've prepared this short email saying that since they are so uncomfortable with our service that I have suspended all our dealings with them and we merely await their instructions as to whom we should transfer their portfolio. I have also mentioned that we are about to send out some interesting updates on our investment recommendations, which they will not receive due to the suspension."

"Have you sent it?"

"Not yet."

"Send it."

An hour later Pru received another vitriolic phone call. She waited until the man on the other end of the phone had run out of steam when she said, "In view of the tone of recent phone calls, I'll shortly be sending you a new contract stipulating the terms and conditions of our service. As soon as I get it back, signed and unaltered, we'll continue to provide you with appropriate investment advice. In the meanwhile, as I have already discussed with you the service is suspended."

There was silence on the other end of the phone, Pru waited, knowing that David would back her up whatever action she took.

There were several more attempts on the client's part to recover some lost ground by phoning Harold and David.

Two weeks later Websters eventually received a complete and fully signed contract. Pru then set up a meeting with the client and went through all Websters recommendations in detail.

"There are very few changes?" was the observation from the client.

"Mr McLintock has always relied on Websters research. We don't know specifically what recommendations he made to you, though."

The man was about to respond, but just sat there looking angry. "You had better make sure that we get the benefit of all your advice and not just some of it…"

"Of course."

Afterwards, with Jacqueline in the office, Pru repeated the conversation to David.

"Our strength," he told them both, "was that it made little difference to us whether we had their account or not. We were then able to stick to our guns."

Jacqueline looked surprised.

After she had left the office, David said to Pru, "I have prepared this little piece of investment advice, which I would like you to assess. Don't do anything with it until you have spoken to me."

David then spent much of the next three weeks negotiating to buy the shares he did not own in Websters from Harold. Harold had hated every minute of the episode with Luke and his family and all he really wanted was to retire from the business. He knew that whatever deal he made with David he would be comfortably off, so once the deal was sealed Harold gracefully retired from the business allowing David to take over. David would buy the fifty percent of the business still owned by Harold over five years. Harold would remain on the board for the period as Chairman of Websters.

Once David had settled himself into Harold's old office, one of the first updates he had was from Pru. She had completed a very satisfactory review before she looked at David and hesitated. "Go on," said David, "you have something else on you mind."

"Two things actually," she handed over twenty pounds.

David laughed. "Thank you."

Pru then waived the investment advice David had given her now some weeks earlier. "This is crap," she said.

David laughed again. "Got it in one, my thoughts exactly."

"What should I do with it then?"

"In a few weeks, maybe months when all is running smoothly with your problem client just leave it lying about on your desk. We'll see what happens."

"Nothing will happen. It obviously won't be included in any of our recommendations for investment."

"No it won't, just let me know when you have done what I suggest."

As suggested Pru, having advised David, left the advice document casually lying on her desk, together with another document detailing some of Websters other investment appraisals.

A few days later she received a phone call from the belligerent man running the affairs of what she thought of as her problem client. "I knew it, I knew it," he said, "you are deliberately short-changing us on the advice you give. You're telling all your other clients to buy a certain share and are leaving us out of the loop."

"What company are you talking about?"

The man gave her the name of the company discussed on the advice sheet that David had agreed with her was not a good investment proposition.

"I have never and would never recommend that you or anyone else buy shares in that operation."

"But I know that you have made recommendations to other clients regarding that company," the man spluttered.

"The only recommendation that I would give anyone with regard to that company would be not to touch it with a ten-foot pole."

"You are just trying to prevent us from making a good investment; something that your other clients are taking full advantage of."

"Look, I've told you my position. However, if you wish us to acquire shares in that operation on your behalf please send us the instructions."

"I will."

Pru then received an email instructing Websters to make a substantial investment in the said company. She took the instruction to David.

"I will deal with the situation by telling them not to invest in this company," he said. "I will give them some reasons. Having said that we will have to act on their instructions."

There was a flurry of abusive emails over the next day or so. Websters then made the investment as instructed.

David then wrote to the client advising that they had made the investment but that Websters view was that the value of that investment would probably reduce by forty percent or so within the next six months. His advice was to sell the investment immediately. No notice was taken of the advice.

Pru gave the client weekly advice regarding the value of the investment, which gradually declined in value. The advice was eventually accepted and the client suffered a loss of almost fifty percent on the investment. All their other stocks had either remained stable or increased slightly over the period.

When it was all over Pru came to see David. "You are a bastard," she said smiling, "just a common or garden fucking bastard. You set them up."

"There is someone here passing on information to Luke McLintock they think is valuable, which is not acceptable under any circumstances, stealing our research. If he has any other clients, they will probably have also suffered bad losses. So I don't think you'll have any more trouble from this lot, at least for a while. It would be useful to know who the mole is though, although I don't think any advice they proffer will be taken seriously in future."

A few days later he had one of his regular morning coffee breaks with Jacqueline Briggs. They dealt with some routine matters but there wasn't the usual sharp exchange of ideas.

"Is anything wrong?" asked David.

Jacqueline looked at him. "You really are a bastard, you know. A real fucking bastard," she said as she walked out and left him to his coffee.

There seems to be considerable consensus on my parentage, he said to himself, *at least I know the mole won't be active anymore.*

Sometime later Pru asked him if he had identified the mole. "Yes, they will not be troubling us again and I have no intention of identifying anyone."

A few weeks later Jacqueline resigned by leaving a note on his desk. "Any particular reason," he asked, once he had managed to corner the increasingly evasive Jacqueline.

"I just need a change."

"There is no need to resign; I obviously understand the reason. Whatever you decide to do you will get a good reference from me and indeed Harold if you ask him."

She just looked at him and shook her head. A tear slipped out. "The resignation stands," she said as she stalked out of his office.

He and Melinda had long discussions about what had been achieved.

"Many people would have just gone to the police," she observed. "I think Luke McLintock is very lucky you behaved like you did. He is lucky not to be in jail. And I would have fired Jacqueline Briggs. What you did is admirable. Also, we now own the business, something that might not have been the case otherwise. Admirable in every sense of the word. I don't think I could have done what you did."

David smiled, and thoroughly enjoyed the moment.

PART 5: FINALE

Chapter 25. Hussein

Some six years after the Kenyan rescue operation, and not long after the episode with Luke McLintock that had enabled David to take control of Websters, he had a panic phone call from Asad. He'd had very little contact with Asad or the family for more than two years so was surprised by the call.

Asad was incoherent. "Captain David, Sir Philips," he yelled down the phone. "Bloody jihadis. Hussein." David remembered Hussein was Asad's eldest son. "I kill that bloody Imam."

David managed over about a thirty-minute period to calm Asad down. It turned out that Hussein had left home and was intent on joining Al Shabab, the group that had captured 'Smith' in Somaliland. "When did he leave home?" asked David.

"Today, yesterday – not really sure?"

"Where was he going?"

"Bradford, Birmingham, the Imam not say."

"Did he have any money?"

"Yes, he took everything from till, maybe one thousand."

"Jesus, a thousand pounds."

"He want buy gun," Asad continued.

Oh shit, thought David, *there is some sort of domestic agenda here. Not only Al Shabab.*

"Mr Asad, just listen to me for a moment. If you see Hussein, try to stop him and call me again, but don't go looking for him, it will only make matters worse. I will find him and bring him home, I promise." It took David another ten minutes to convince Asad that he had everything under control.

I'll bring him home alright, even if it's only in a body bag, he thought.

He phoned Jones and explained the situation to him.

"Why don't you get the gaffer involved?" asked Jones.

"We don't want the hint of any publicity. We got a lot of goodwill about how we handled the original rescue and its aftermath. Any hint of things going wrong and the media will eat us alive."

"What do you want me to do?"

"Pick-up the gaffer's wife and son and my wife and three children and take them to a safe house as soon as you can, then I want two of yours at each of our addresses. They are to apprehend this Hussein and any accomplices, if indeed those are the targets they have chosen; they may of course have another target altogether. When they have done that I will tell you what to do. Take him alive if possible and any others that may be with him."

"Where will you be?"

"At my own house, tell your people to text me when they are near the house. I'll phone the gaffer. He'll probably be at his home so…"

"Okay. Okay, we'll text him as well. Just give me your number."

He phoned Lizzie, then Melinda and then Powrie explaining to them what the problem was.

To Lizzie and Melinda, he said, "Do not open the door to anyone unless they have given you the password, which is 'Bristol three'."

He phoned Powrie and explained what was going on. Powrie was about to interrupt but something made him stop and listen. "Two of Jones' colleagues will have picked up Mrs Hall and Rupert within the last thirty minutes and taken them to a safe house. There are another two waiting at your home for Hussein and any others, which I have assumed is the plan. If I may, sir, can I suggest that you go home and see if you can make contact with the two waiting near your home." He gave Powrie the password. "I will be at my own address."

"I asked Jones to try to deal with this issue rather…"

"As always Phillips, you make the obvious fucking point. I understand perfectly why you've done what you've done. I have your number and will keep in touch." The connection was cut.

David went home. By this time it was close to midnight. He parked two hundred metres away and walked through various neighbours' gardens until he had sight of the front door of his home. He watched while two heavily armed men arrived in a four-wheel drive, knocked on the front door and after what seemed like an interminable delay saw Melinda and their three children being bundled into the vehicle with two small suitcases. The vehicle drove away.

David waited. An hour later he had a text that enabled him to meet up with two other of Jones' colleagues, one of whom he knew. They waited, hidden in the front garden in some large bushes. Another hour passed. He received a text from Powrie saying that Lizzie and Rupert were safely ensconced in a safe house in a farmhouse in Gloucestershire and that they had apprehended three people who attempted to knock down the front door of (a). "No sign of Hussein though, I'll leave him to you."

David was almost ready to call it a day when they saw movement in the short driveway. Three people were creeping slowly towards the front door of his home. They were obviously armed.

Fortunately, the outside light had been left on so when they arrived at the front door and knocked they were clearly visible. They knocked for two or three minutes.

"Take them in the legs," said David, "and stay hidden, they may have some back-up."

Five shots were fired leaving the three writhing on the ground.

"Wait," said David.

All they heard was the sound of a high-powered car driving away at speed.

"Okay, we need to keep these idiots alive." The three soldiers rushed up and kicked weapons out the attacker's hands, one of whom was indeed Hussein. Within minutes all were subdued and tied up. David phoned the ambulance service and the police. One of the other soldiers applied tourniquets to wounds.

The police asked, "Is that the disturbance in Wimbledon?"

"Yes."

David then phoned a number he had for internal security. When the phone was answered he gave a brief outline of the situation saying, "Yes, the danger is over, but you need to get here as quickly as you can. This is a major security issue, so you need to get here as quickly as you are able," he repeated himself.

By the morning the three wounded attackers were firmly in the hands of the security services together with the three that had been apprehended at the Powrie house. David had spent most of the rest of the night explaining the situation to the security people, making sure there was no hint of any kind of media interest. He looked in on Hussein and then phoned Asad. Having told Asad what went on, he reassured him that although Hussein was wounded his life was not in danger.

"You say Hussein attack your house, the house of man who rescue us, the man who got out of helicopter so we could get in... This is insult to family..."

"Mr Asad, you need to phone this man." David gave him a number of the man in charge of the captives. "Also, we need to talk. I know it's very difficult but I will try to help you handle this. You have four other children, we must look after them as well." After a further half hour's conversation, Asad calmed down and agreed that he would continue to talk to David to see what suggestions he might make.

David then dashed off to the safe house in Gloucestershire where he arrived just after nine in the morning. Powrie was already there talking to Lizzie and Melinda, who, much to David's relief, seemed to have at least come to some sort of accommodation with each other. He spent ten minutes trying to reassure everyone, then David gave Powrie a detailed briefing. "Nobody in the media got anywhere near this story and all the perps are safely in the hands of the security people. I suppose it will all come out if there is ever a trial though. One of the very surprising things though is that two of the six people involved are English people who have converted to Islam. The others have a similar background to Hussein, although two of them were born here. I do have some suggestions as to how we may be able to handle the situation though."

Powrie looked at him. "I bet you do," he said with a look of resignation on his face. "Again, thank you, Phillips, for acting as you did. You obviously saved us a packet of trouble. I think, now, I had better get Daphne and Rupert home. Both of us need to think about future security issues; if these bastards know our addresses I wonder who else does."

David shook Rupert by the hand and Lizzie chastely pecked him on the cheek as she left the safe house. "Thanks David," she said, "as always one step ahead of the sheriff."

Powrie looked on, saying nothing.

David returned to the safe house. He hugged Melinda for a good five minutes, then each one of the children.

"Were we in any real danger?" asked Michael.

"I'm afraid the answer to that is yes," answered David. "If we hadn't acted as we did, we would all have been in trouble."

"Rupert said he sometimes played with that boy Hussein, but not for some time."

"Yes, somehow Hussein has gone bad. I don't really know the reasons."

"Rupert was nice, we played some exciting games. His dad is in the SAS."

David nodded. "Maybe we should go home. It's quite safe for now, all the people who wished us harm are in jail."

During the interaction Melinda said very little but David could see she was watchful and worried. He knew there would be serious discussions on a number of subjects once they were home.

They said goodbye and thanked the two people looking after the safe house. "Be careful," they were told.

The children chattered and played little games during the two-hour drive home. Melinda was quiet but was quite cheerful when they stopped at a café for coffee and ice cream for the kids.

There was a policeman standing at the door of their house in Wimbledon. The only sign of the fracas the night before was two bullet holes in the brickwork and concrete surrounding the door.

Melinda and Janice dashed into the house trying not to look at the evidence of the close call they'd had. Michael and Rory examined the bullet holes saying, 'cool,' every now and then. They had no sense of the danger they had been in.

The policeman said, "There will be someone here for another week. After that I don't know."

David spent the evening trying to make sure that his precious family had settled down. He and Melinda prepared the evening meal; the boys chattered on in their fantasy world. Janice shed a few tears. Melinda was silent except for dealing with issues surrounding the meal. David poured her a glass of wine.

When the children were safely in bed, they were both sitting in their comfortable sitting room Melinda, still drinking her wine, said, "I got on quite well with your friend Daphne, she seems a nice person."

"Lizzie, I call her Lizzie, can't stand the name Daphne."

"Yes, she told me. She also said that you were responsible for rescuing her marriage."

"Well not really, I merely suggested one thing she could do to put it together again. She and the gaffer made up once I had removed myself from the scene. I showed you the letter she wrote me. As you know she is still a client."

"I can see you are very fond of her."

"I suppose so; I speak to her about once every six weeks or so. Only about her investments. I am godfather to Rupert, I feel completely inadequate as far as that is concerned, I don't really know what to do for the best. Despite my affair with her, Powrie has never taken it out on me, although he has had many opportunities to do that." He then looked at her. "You've always known about Lizzie, having met her how do you feel about her?" David was tempted to add some other observations but kept his thoughts to himself.

"Fine. I should feel threatened, but don't really. I have been aware of Rupert's paternity for a while now. I bumped into them outside your offices once; she was quite unaware of me, but I recognised her from our Oxford days. I had seen her with you before I actually met you, if you remember." She smiled at the memory. "What you did for her was wonderful, but it's a very David Phillips type of arrangement, almost denying any emotion, it's just practical. With most people there would have some sort of a bust-up, shouting, throwing things maybe. Even Neville seems to behave in the same way. He must know that you are actually Rupert's father." She stopped and looked at him. "The boys may not have noticed but Janice certainly understands that you are Rupert's natural father; so by now he, Rupert, would certainly understand the situation."

David was astounded. How could he have been so lucky to actually marry a woman like this? It took him a moment to respond. "Powrie has always regarded Rupert as his own and I only saw him for the first time when we rescued Asad. I have done nothing, hopefully, to make you or anyone else feel threatened by what happened. At some stage we may have to talk to the kids. I'm a bit surprised you didn't mention it when you first had doubts about Rupert's paternity."

Melinda laughed. "Doubts. Once I set eyes on him there was never any doubt. Just one question: have you fucked her even once since we met?"

David looked surprised. "No absolutely not. The affair with Lizzie was all over by the time I met you."

Melinda regarded him, unsure. "At times I feel I know everything there is to know about you; other times I hardly know you at all." She got up sat on his lap and kissed him. "Come on, bed, at least we are all alive and unhurt, mostly due to your quick actions." They made love then and twice more in the night.

David told the office he would be away for a few days. He phoned Powrie. "Sir, I just phoned to see that you and the family got home alright."

"Yes, of course we did," was the impatient response, "why wouldn't we be alright?"

"I was just wondering what I was going to do about security and thought I would see what you were going to do before I acted on anything. Somehow someone knows our current addresses, for reasons best known to themselves they wish us harm."

"Don't know. I have a couple of troopers on duty day and night, but that's not a long-term solution. What are you going to do?"

"Not sure. I am having a meeting with a half dozen neighbours this afternoon. My guess is that they would like us to move away, but I don't know that. If we could get Hussein to talk he could be persuaded to spill the beans I think. I also have another idea regarding Hussein."

"Ah, oh, another crazy David Phillips idea I expect, go on tell me. I'm sitting down."

"Well, you probably remember the US President Lyndon Johnston's joke about, 'it's better to have people inside the tent pissing out rather than outside the tent pissing in'."

"Oh no, I don't think I am going to like this."

"He's just a kid looking for some direction. That bloody Imam gave him that. The SAS would give him much more direction. We should take him on and prove that we can turn these people around."

"For Christ's sake, David, the stupid bastard is going to spend the next twenty years in jail. Don't go there just don't go there."

David reflected, *He has never ever called me David before.*

"Sir, just think about it. I must go to this meeting."

Earlier he had discussed the situation with Melinda wondering what they should say to the neighbours.

"Can't you just tell them the truth?" asked Melinda.

"Probably not. I will be in breach of the Official Secrets Act if I do. I think."

"Why don't we just ask the police to deal with it then?"

"Smart. Really gets us off the hook," said David, looking relieved, "the local force doesn't know much anyway."

He phoned the local commander and delayed the meeting with the neighbours by two days.

David, in confidence, briefed the local police commander. He gave him the full background, including the rescue of the Asad family and Hussein's role in the attack. He also told him of the planned attack on his CO's house which was also foiled.

"Unfortunately, you can't use any of that information in the briefing to neighbours. The security people don't want any of the details to be made public yet; there may be some more arrests. They especially don't want any connection to be made between the two planned attacks."

"Who the hell are you?" asked the commander.

In response David gave him two phone numbers: Powrie's and the head of the security detail who now had responsibility for understanding who was behind the attacks.

Before the meeting the commander said to David, "I don't have much to go on. I've been told that nothing that you or Colonel Powrie or the security people have told me is ready for public consumption."

David merely shrugged. "I'm obviously in the same bind. At least you have an official position."

The dozen or so neighbouring households met in the well-kept back garden of David and Melinda's property. Melinda and David concentrated on serving the people tea and cake. Fortunately, there were no members of the media present. The policeman told them that three attackers had been apprehended and were now being held in police custody answering questions. "We are not sure whether it was merely a robbery gone wrong or what. It was fortunate that Mrs Phillips and the family were away for the night."

"Who apprehended them?"

"There was a tip-off and they are in the custody of the police."

"Yes, but who apprehended them?"

"At the moment I can't answer that; as I told you they are in the hands of the police answering questions."

The questioners were stonewalled for an hour. Eventually one of them said to David. "You work for some sort of bank, don't you? Can you tell us if the attack was the result of a deal that had gone sour or something like that?"

"I work for Websters. One of the things we do is to advise people on investments. I am quite certain that the attack had nothing whatsoever to do with Websters."

The policeman intervened. "We have gone down that line of questioning. There is no shred of evidence that links the attack to Websters."

"It's clear that you either don't know or are not prepared to tell us who the attackers are or who they represent. What we do know is that here in a quiet, suburban street there was an attack on your house Mr Phillips. There were bullets flying around. It obviously has something to do with you personally. Frankly the sooner you sell up and go somewhere else the better."

The policeman said as the people were leaving, "Mr and Mrs Phillips had absolutely no obligation to hold this meeting. I think you should recognise that. Any questions should be referred to me in future." He handed everyone a business card.

Afterwards Melinda said to David, "Well if anything that made things worse. One of the women who sends their kids to the same school that Michael and Janice attend asked me if it was a drug deal gone wrong."

David put his head in his hands. "Maybe we should move."

"We've now got the place looking just as we want it. There must be other options. Maybe you should reconsider your commitment to the SAS; that is the direct link to where we are now," said Melinda firmly.

David thought about the situation for a few days and then he paid a visit to the security people in their monolithic building on the South Bank of the Thames, almost opposite Parliament House.

He was treated with respect due to his record and the knowledge that he personally had probably saved the lives of several people due to his quick action. They were a bit suspicious of the people who had helped him.

He spent most of the day trying to persuade them to at least consider his proposal. "Look, you have a very small window of opportunity. Soon this issue will be all over the media; at the moment nobody knows who you have in custody. Just release Hussein to my custody and I will take full responsibility. Maybe, just maybe, I can turn him into a decent citizen. He's just a misguided teenager looking for direction and excitement. I helped to rescue him for God's sake; he would have been killed otherwise."

"But he wanted to kill you and your family."

"He didn't come close to succeeding in that; something he knows. When I turn him, which I will," David said confidently, much more confidently than he felt, "he will spill the beans on the rest of the set-up, such as it is, which makes everyone much safer."

David was eventually allowed to see Hussein on his own. Hussein was still recovering from a bullet wound in his right thigh.

"You wanted to kill me," he said to Hussein quietly. "Why? And my wife and children and Mrs Hall and her husband and child."

There was no response from Hussein, although David did sense a wariness in him.

"I helped rescue you and your family. You would have been killed otherwise."

"My father is a traitor to Islam."

"You would have died if we had left you all in that village. You would not be talking to me now. Your body would have been thrown out into the bush and left for the hyenas to eat. Hyena shit that is what you would have ended up as. Instead you were brought to this country, you went to school, you have earned a place at university, your whole family has been well looked after, but you want to run around killing people."

Hussein remained silent.

"You are eighteen years old. If you want to spend the rest of your miserable life locked up in some jail, probably being regularly raped by the bunch of thugs in the jail with you, you can. You might as well have ended up as hyena shit for all the good you've done. Don't you understand the situation you're in? There's no escape from where you are."

Hussein impatiently wiped away a tear. "I want to see my father."

"Your father!" shouted David, "he wishes you were dead. He wishes he had left you in that village to become a piece of hyena shit. He says you are a disgrace to the family and have destroyed their lives. Your mother, your brother and sisters, you've made their lives worthless in their eyes."

Hussein then broke down completely. "The Imam, he told me all the infidels were evil and they all must die…" Hussein was not able to articulate his feelings, despite all the help he had received from David and the general community. He told David he felt alienated from the community and was often discriminated against, which caused on-going and deep resentment in him.

"And you believed them? Smart educated Hussein, believed that nonsense." David just walked out, slamming the door behind him. "I'll be back later," he told Hussein's captors, "keep him isolated. At worst it will create suspicion among his colleagues."

David returned at eight in the evening. He insisted on seeing Hussein in another room. "Hussein, did I rescue you?"

A tearful Hussein nodded.

"Did I and Mrs Hall look after you?"

Another nod.

"Who provided money for your father to set up his business?"

There was a hesitant response from Hussein, "you, Mr David."

"And you want to kill me?"

Hussein just looked down.

"Do you want to spend the rest of your life locked up in jail?"

There was no answer from Hussein.

David left again. "Let him join his colleagues," he told the security detail. "They will almost certainly beat him up. Don't let it go on too long. I will be back at six am and will want to talk to him again."

David returned at six the next morning as promised. Hussein was brought to him. He had two black eyes a cut lip and a puffy face.

"Who did that?" asked David pointing at the damage.

No answer.

"Your friends?"

"No. Guards."

"Crap."

He left and returned with a small camera projector. He turned it on and showed a ten-minute clip to Hussein. It showed the other five captives attacking Hussein in the cell they shared. They showed him being rescued by several guards.

"In prison, it will be worse. More prisoners, fewer guards. They already think you've talked too much."

Hussein just sat there shivering.

"Now Hussein, you know me. I can help you if you want. Hard work but no prison."

Hussein looked up hopefully.

A day later Hussein was released to David's custody.

He had had a furious argument with Powrie in the intervening period. "I told you not to go there, I don't want anything to do with it," Powrie had shouted. Eventually Powrie had quietened down having spoken to the security people. Hussein was to be held in the SAS detention barracks in Hereford under a sergeant Ackerman. "Your job, sergeant," David told him, "is to get this fellow fit enough to join the regular SAS, that's all. No mistreatment. I will be here every couple of weeks probably with a member of his family."

"Who is he?"

"I will tell you later, once the programme is complete."

David did indeed visit Hussein every two weeks, to start with on his own then with his mother and sisters then with his brother. His father was even persuaded to pay him a visit. He eventually took Melinda and the children to see him, then Lizzie and Rupert.

During Hussein's time in Hereford, David showed him a clipping from a national newspaper stating that five people had been jailed for life under terrorism laws. Three of the individual's names were listed, two other names had been suppressed due to their ages. "That is what would have happened to you, Hussein, and still could if you don't behave," David told him.

After nine months, Hussein easily passed the endurance test to be admitted to one of the SAS regular battalions. Before he was admitted David had another interview with Hussein. "I want all the details of the scheme you were in and the people involved. All of them. If anything gets out, we will say it was one of your jailed colleagues that gave us the information."

Hussein then provided another ten names, all of whom were arrested and jailed.

During one of his visits, David said, "Look Hussein, we have almost rescued you again but if we find there is even a small detail that you have missed out telling me you will be back in that prison so quick you won't know what hit you; and I will make sure that all those ex-colleagues of yours know it was you that spilt the beans, if you see what I mean."

By this time Hussein trusted David and knew he meant what he said, so he said in a terrified voice, "No, no, there are no more people, but that Imam I told you about he collects money from everyone and sends it away, to support jihadis. I don't know where he sends it and he is clever so it may be well hidden."

"How do you know about this?"

"He left some papers lying about once. He did not know I was well educated and probably thought I would not understand what was included in the papers…"

"Okay, anything else?"

"No, I have told you all I know."

At the end of the discussion David concluded by saying, "I am authorised to tell you that, as you may know, you have passed all the tests and will be admitted to one of the regular SAS battalions within a few days. Congratulations. Not everyone manages to get in."

Hussein grasped David by the hand. "Thank you, Mr David," he still used his father's terminology when addressing David, "you have saved my life, twice now. I will never forget."

"Just make the most of it. For my sake do your very best. I expect to see you as an officer some time in the future."

A few days later, after the children had been sent to bed, he explained to Melinda, over a glass of wine what he had achieved with Hussein over the past year. Nothing more had been said about moving to a new house.

"Mnn, I wondered what was going on. At one stage I even thought you might have a mistress somewhere," she smiled.

"The SAS detention barracks is not the most romantic place, I know…"

"Just pulling your leg…"

"Anyway, there is absolutely no reason to move. We're settled here and I am quite sure the danger has passed. There is one other thing though to complete Hussein's rehabilitation."

"What?"

"Once he has settled into his new battalion, I want to invite him here for a few days."

Melinda looked at him and shook her head. "This bastard wanted to shoot us a few months ago and now you want to invite him here. I don't know David, sometimes I don't think I know you at all. What's this, some sort of ego trip on your part?"

"Just to show him what he could have destroyed. Also, maybe give him some idea of what life might be like. I've spoken to Lizzie about this as well. She knows him as well as any of us, since he stayed there for a few months. The gaffer put up a bit of a fuss, but he seems to have been reconciled to the idea. Phone Lizzie if you like."

"I'll certainly phone your Lizzie. Seeing him in those detention barracks was one thing, but I am really not sure that I want someone who bore us extreme ill-will anywhere near me or indeed the children. Couldn't we do it at a neutral venue, if you are so keen?"

David just smiled at the barb but did not rise to the bait.

Later on, Melinda told David, "I've discussed this whole business with Lizzie. She seems to understand what you're trying to achieve. This is what we have agreed: Hussein is well aware of what Lizzie's place is like so there is no purpose in returning there, so she will bring herself, Rupert and Hussein's mother here for lunch, the weekend after next. We will all be here, obviously including you. I seem to remember that Hussein's mother is one of Asad's two wives?"

"Yes, Aamuun is her name."

Melinda looked at David, smiled and said, "With Lizzie here, you'll have what amounts to at least two of your wives and presumably all your children, all under one roof. Maybe we should all convert…"

David laughed. "Under those circumstances I'm entitled to four wives. Going down that track, I still have to identify another couple of potential wives; maybe I should work on it…"

He kissed her thinking, *Samantha, she knows nothing of Samantha.*

***

It took Melinda some time to work out the look she'd seen on David's face, when she'd joked about having all his wives and children under one roof. There was clearly something he wasn't telling her. Surely not another child? Another woman?

She reflected briefly on her suspicions about David having an affair immediately before her Edinburgh sojourn, and the reports she'd received about him seeing a woman and child in Australia.

I wonder if I've been told everything about other women.

But thinking about Edinburgh just made her think about her affair with Andrew, which she still felt guilty about. Although in idle moments she relived the fun they had had together, and indeed continued to have, discreetly from time to time.

David clearly wasn't the only one with secrets, so she couldn't blame him for that.

Still, it made her think. Was this how a marriage was supposed to be – couples believing themselves happy, yet keeping such big secrets from each other? Things were easy between her and David, convenient, she was mostly happy – they'd been together so long, had such gorgeous children and a lovely home.

And yet she couldn't help but think now that there was something deeply wrong with their marriage.

***

On the appointed day, David fetched Hussein from Wimbledon station.

Hussein, tall and handsome in his SAS uniform appeared somewhat nervous. "Mr David, I don't know how to thank you," he said as he got into David's car.

"Please either call me David or Mr Phillips, calling me Mr David sounds subservient and it's not necessary." He hesitated before continuing, "While you are much better off in your present position what we have done together will benefit the country as much as either you or me. There is little or no understanding of how people like you got into the mess you got yourself into. Locking everyone up may not always be the best solution."

"Your wife is very gracious, inviting me into your home."

"She's a bit nervous, of course, but Mrs Hall will be there as well as all our children."

The introductions were stilted and hesitant until David got Hussein, Michael and Rory involved in a game of backyard cricket. Even Janice was persuaded to participate. There was a muted but joyful reunion when Lizzie, Rupert and Aamuun arrived.

Lizzie was quite straightforward. "Mnn, Hussein, you look very smart in your uniform, handsome too if I might say so."

Hussein said he remembered her well from the time he had spent under her roof and instead of being embarrassed he just smiled.

Aamuun was given the space to spend ten minutes alone with her son; she had seen little of him in the past year, just once or twice in the SAS detention barracks with David. Afterwards she came to David and held his hands between hers and said to him, "Mr David, you have saved the honour of the family. I don't know what else to say. Maybe one day we can repay. You have great understanding."

"I am sure that Hussein will do us all great credit. That is the only repayment I need."

Melinda made certain that everyone knew that the roast lamb she had laid on was from a halal butcher and that everything in the meal was acceptable to followers of Islam.

"What's halal?" asked Rory.

"It's just a way of slaughtering an animal," answered Hussein, "it ensures that the animal bleeds out completely. In hot climates that is very important. Interestingly the Jews use the same process, for the same reasons."

Janice seemed quite bashful around the somewhat older and handsome Hussein. "What happens with meat in the army?" she asked him coyly.

"The food is not halal; I will work on that when I have been there a little while. There is a growing sensitivity to religions other than

Christianity. I have learnt from Mr D..." he stopped himself from saying 'Mr David'. "I have learnt from David that tolerance is the only way forward."

The day finished happily; even Melinda was able to spend a few minutes with Hussein and his mother; she seemed to be a bit more comfortable with what they had done after that.

David spent an hour talking to Lizzie on her own, more time than he had spent alone with her, face to face, since the end of their affair. "Well, what do you think," he asked her.

"Think, what about? You do have a delightful place here, and I have got to know Melinda a bit now."

"Come on. You know what I am talking about."

"I would like to say that all in the garden is rosy as far as Hussein and his mother are concerned. Just be bloody careful is my advice; I think this story has a little way to play out... I hope I am wrong but..."

David looked at her and the cold hard lump of fear quietly gripped his bowels. "Thanks, I hear you. I'll be very careful. How is the gaffer in his retirement, by the way?"

"He's really good. Getting himself involved in local affairs, which keeps him out of mischief, most of the time. He's now got time to do all sorts of things with Rupert, like taking him on long walks in Scotland and Wales; he's taught him to read maps. I also have Rupert on horseback at least once a week."

"What do you think he might want to do, after university; I presume he has aspirations in that direction."

"Neville and I were going to talk to you about that. Can you take him on as an intern at Websters? Just to see if has any inclinations in that direction."

"Of course. Give me a few months' notice so I can set him up properly."

David returned Hussein to the station. Lizzie had left by the time he returned. "Oh, I would have liked just to say goodbye," observed David, "doesn't really matter, I'll call her in a day or two."

"I saw you had a long chat with her," said Melinda once the children had gone to bed.

"Yes, I think that was the longest I've spent with her, on her own, since before I met you. She wants Rupert to spend a few months at Websters. I said I'd see what I could do. Do you have any idea how bright he is?"

"Of course he is – same as all your children!"

David laughed. "Come to bed, you smart clever wife of mine!"

Chapter 26. Return to Kenya

On his last trip to spend time with Kenya's Special Forces before he finally resigned from the SAS, David took Samantha and the now thirteen-year-old Jane on a trip to Tanzania. Despite the passport stop at Namanga, the bus trip from Nairobi to Arusha was easy on a good road and quite uneventful. The early morning start from Nairobi meant that, once they were in Arusha, they were met by the driver David had arranged to take them to see the wonders of the Ngorongoro crater about one hundred miles west of Arusha. The view from the hotel situated on the rim of the crater was truly spectacular with the pink tinge of the flamingos in Lake Magadi adding a touch of colour to the already mind stopping view. The steep drive down into the crater increased the sense of anticipation, spoilt somewhat in David's view by the sight of herds of Maasai cattle charging down the steep inclines of the crater wall, until he remembered the conversation with Boniface.

Maybe they've always had cattle grazing down here, he thought.

There was plenty of game and they even saw one of the twenty-five black rhino left in the park, now heavily protected from poachers. Jane and Samantha, as before, were completely entranced by the experience. David said, "It's all a bit contrived, with mainly white tourists, from the developed world, staying in luxury hotels being driven about in fancy four-wheel drive vehicles. Maybe our experience in the Selous, where we are going next, will be a bit more like the real wild Africa."

The chaos of the small Arusha airport saw them board a single engine Cessna, which did not have a seat to spare. On the left-hand side of the aircraft they admired the spectacular view of Mount Kilimanjaro, with its snow-covered summit, reminding David of a Christmas pudding, with icing on the top. Kilimanjaro, the highest mountain in Africa, at some nineteen thousand feet. They stopped briefly in Zanzibar, the small island off the Tanzanian coast, taken over by the Tanzanian army in 1964. A short hop over to Dar-es-Salaam, the Tanzanian capital, where they changed planes; forty-five minutes later landing at the airstrip at Mtemere, one of the gateways to the Selous, reputed to be the largest game park in the world. Their host from Selous Great Water Lodge met them and took them for the thirty-minute drive to the primitive bush camp on the banks of the wide, fast flowing Rufiji River. The dining/bar area was a thatched shack open to the river and the accommodation a series of thatched huts a bit further away. The whole area was unfenced, and game animals wandered through the camp at will.

"Just the sort of wild Africa I imagined," mused David as they sat enjoying a Kilimanjaro beer looking out over the wide expanse of the river sweeping majestically on the curve below them.

Having been given some idea of the serious tribal rivalries in Kenya by Captain Boniface, David innocently asked what tribe occupied the three villages they had passed through on their way to their camp.

"That's one of the curious things about Tanzania," he was told by his host. "Julius Nyerere, Tanzania's first President after independence, insisted on a programme where all the rural villagers were herded together into collectives. The programme was an economic disaster and caused great hardship, even starvation, among the people it was supposed to help. However, one of the unexpected benefits is that it reduced the tribal rivalries to almost nothing with intermarriage and so on. The villages we passed through have their roots in three different tribes, but nobody has much awareness of which tribe they came from and they speak a common language as well as Swahili. Many people speak English as well, although that facility is not as well developed as it is in Kenya."

"What about corruption?"

Their host shrugged. "Bad as it is in most of Africa, although it's possible that might change a bit; there is a Mr Magufuli in the wings here, who I think might get elected as President sometime in the near future – he has very different attitudes to many in power in Africa. Another exception I know of is Botswana, whose first President, Sir Seretse Khama, made a non-corrupt regime part of his original mantra, something that has prevailed, although the insidious influence of the Chinese may be changing that."

One of the very pleasant surprises of the visit to the Selous was Patrick, the African guide provided by the lodge, who lived in one of the nearby villages. Patrick had an encyclopaedic knowledge of the game in the area, all self-taught, which made their visits to the reserve all the more interesting and exciting; he knew a great deal about each animal species and their habits, he also knew where to find the game. Patrick also turned out to be a herbalist, so his conducted walks around the area of the camp were rich with interest. Although there were other lodges in the area because of the size of the park, they only saw one or two other vehicles on their daily game drives into the Selous.

"That vehicle there," Patrick pointed out, saying, "always tries to follow me; he thinks I know where the game is."

David smiled, thinking, *He's probably right.* He said nothing though.

They had all been told that, because the camp was open and unfenced, not to wander too far from the settlement without an escort. But it was no surprise to David to hear a commotion that evening of elephants and Jane screaming. She was nowhere in sight, but had mentioned seeing a small waterhole earlier, just outside the boundaries of the camp.

David ran down.

Jane had tripped and fallen into some bushes, just as a small herd of elephants were emerging from the other side of the waterhole. Both parties were clearly unhappy with the situation, with the female elephant bellowing to protect her young calf.

David quickly helped Jane up, her arms and legs covered in scratches from the thorns, then they backed slowly away, and scampered back to the bar area, where their host was talking to Samantha.

Their host, with a handy first aid kit, calmly cleaned up and disinfected the several self-inflicted scratches Jane had sustained. He then took them all to a recently completed hut built on stilts which over-looked the waterhole, and there were the elephants, quite undisturbed now and looking benign.

Jane just shivered. "She chased me," she said pointing.

Later, in bed, Samantha said quietly to David, "That was about as close to the 'real Africa' as I ever wish to get."

He merely hugged her.

Chapter 27. Melinda

Melinda still spent much of her time with the children, but they were becoming increasingly independent, so she started working on a part time basis at Websters, firstly two days a week, then three. Being a significant shareholder, she had been on the board for several years, so was familiar with the operation of the business. She admired what David had done to grow the operation, but felt, as she always had, that he could have been more adventurous in some of the policies he pursued.

Over two years, it became clear to her that David wanted to continue on the path he had set and that some of her 'wilder' ideas were unacceptable. Rather than have a confrontation at board level she thought that the best way forward was to discuss any proposals she had directly with David, before they were put to the board. He approved one of two major proposals, she had worked on and said to her in a kindly way, "let's see how this one goes. If we could put the other one on hold …" He had also supported a few minor initiatives, which did not need board approval.

However, almost immediately after the finance had been approved for the venture that had been approved, the person leading the project – which required a great deal of energy and effort – became very ill and the project limped along.

She reported the issue to David as soon as she became aware of it. "Also, the other project that we put 'on hold' has decided to engage with another finance operation. The problem I have with my position here," she continued, "is that everything has to go through you. I have no real authority. The market is now becoming aware of this situation, so my reputation is suffering. People are becoming wary of dealing with me."

David listened intently. "What do you think we should do about that? The way that we have managed Websters for a while now has created a very good and sound reputation for us in the industry. I wouldn't want to disturb that in any way."

"You have to understand, David," she said in her own quiet way, "how frustrating I have found the situation, with you calling all the shots and me being relegated to some sort of assistant. Do you really understand what I am saying? I need more than I have now." When she reflected on that statement, she realised it applied to more than just her career. She valued her marriage and everything it had given her, so she didn't pursue the matter much further. Yet her frustration remained. As did her doubts about where their relationship was heading.

The business with Hussein also worried her, with David seemingly putting not only his personal safety on the line but hers and the children's as well. He had finally resigned from the SAS but something told her it was too little too late.

Andrew had also told her of an investment conference in San Francisco a few weeks hence. "In view of your responsibilities for uncovering new investment opportunities, I have taken the liberty of booking you in. I have attached the information brochure related to the conference."

She accepted the invitation and mentioned it to David after dinner one evening. She needed a break. Some distance. A new perspective.

David looked surprised but raised no objection, simply made a note of the dates. "I may be able to take a week or so off at that time, which I will try to spend with the kids," he said. "They will all be on holiday then. We could have a ball running around London, but I'll see what they want to do."

Melinda was relieved at the response, so said nothing further.

She arranged to meet Andrew at a five-star hotel at Fisherman's Wharf, which he had booked. The conference was being held in a nearby hotel, but they agreed to preserve their privacy, hence the arrangements for different accommodation.

They went two days before the conference started. "To get over the jet-lag," Melinda joked.

As was always the case with Andrew, they spent the first twenty-four hours in bed, making do with desultory room service offerings when the mood took them. As far as Melinda was concerned the magic never wavered, it was the same as it had been in Edinburgh and Switzerland and various other places they had met briefly over the years. They spent three days at the conference, attending some of the talks and making contacts.

After two days Andrew asked, "How much time do you have?"

"Why do you ask?"

"I wondered if you would like to extend the visit a bit. I would like to see more of you. Frankly I've never gotten over you and now you are here…"

"What do you have in mind?"

"Have you ever been to the Canadian Rockies, Lake Louise, Jasper and the Athabasca Glacier? That's one option at least."

"Sounds like a plan. I don't care where we go. Being with you for a few days will be very special though."

She phoned David – the first time she had made contact with him since she'd been away. Andrew had gone to do some shopping, realising she needed to be alone for a little while.

"How's the conference?" David asked.

"Fine, I've learnt a lot and made some good contacts. How've you got on with the kids?"

"Terrific, we've been all over the place, some of the museums, the Tower, Madame Tussaud's. Even the Proms, which they all liked. We even took Rupert to the Proms. Would you like to speak to them all?"

"Yes, in a minute though. I just needed to tell you I'll be away for a further week." She knew she just had to tell David what her plans were, rather than asking any sort of permission.

David was unusually enthusiastic. "Great, I will certainly enjoy mucking around with the kids for another week. What's up?"

"A group of us are going to Canada for a few days, you know Lake Louise and the Rockies. It seems like a good opportunity." She felt no guilt about the little lie about there being a 'group'.

"Lovely. I'll put you onto the kids."

She had a half hour on the phone with all the children, who excitedly told her what they had been up to with David.

Afterwards she reflected on how fortunate she was with her three delightful children and even David, though when Andrew returned she was able to put her thoughts of home right to the back of her mind. She focussed on enjoying their time together. When she was with Andrew, she felt so free and at ease. She could be Melinda, rather than David's wife, the mother of their children, and an assistant in David's firm.

She and Andrew took an early morning flight from San Francisco to Vancouver International and rented a car, which took them over the Rockies to the famous Fairmont Chateau Resort with its spectacular views over Lake Louise itself. Andrew insisted on completing the eight-hour drive in one hit. Melinda was happy and relieved to be at the hotel.

The area close to the hotel was crowded especially during the day, with visitors from nearby resorts coming to admire the views.

"Don't worry," advised Andrew, laughing, "if we go for decent walk all we'll find will be a few bears. I understand the scenery is truly spectacular."

On one of the walks they were warned that another walker had seen a bear. "We'd better be careful then," Andrew observed without taking much notice. They found a little café high up in the mountains, with a surprising number of other walkers, enjoying the rest and a beverage of one sort or another.

Melinda was entirely consumed with her on-going relationship with Andrew; it was like a dream. They drove on to Jasper further north, they walked on the Athabasca Glacier. "It seems to have shrunk over the past fifty years-global warming," muttered Andrew. They enjoyed some long walks in the Jasper area. Melinda surprised herself, she didn't care where they went and what they did, she was completely consumed with Andrew. And then it was all over. Andrew dropped her off at Calgary Airport and within a day she was back home in Wimbledon.

During the few days she was with Andrew, one of the conversations they had stuck in the back of her mind. Andrew had asked, "Are you looking at Australia, as part of Websters expansion plans?"

"Yes, certainly that's on the list."

"Well, there is a medium sized investment advisory business, which seems to me to be a good match for Websters."

"Okay."

"I hear very discreetly on the grapevine, that the business is for sale. Name of Wicks Financial."

Melinda said no more, but she made a note to research the matter, when the opportunity arose.

Chapter 28. Wicks

Melinda knew that David had gradually and cautiously built Websters into a considerably bigger operation than the one he had bought from Harold. Due to his caution, he was never burnt by any of the 'fast buck brigade', as he often explained to Melinda. Melinda had joined him in the business once Rory managed to gain entry to Sutton Grammar at the age of eleven; Rory was able to get himself to and from school by train from Wimbledon.

Melinda had charged herself with sussing out opportunities to expand Websters and continued enthusiastically searching out opportunities despite having had some of her recommendations turned down by David – she hoped her discussion, with him, on the subject had changed his views a bit.

When she started to look for opportunities in Australia, she remembered the conversation with Andrew regarding Wicks Financial. "I am led to believe that in a very discreet way the business is for sale," she told David, "it was started some fifteen years ago and has a very good reputation in the market there."

The very thought of Australia and meeting Andrew on his home ground created a further sense of excitement in Melinda. She had revelled in the memories of their week in Canada.

"Who owns it?" David asked with a strange quiver in his voice. "I don't think it sounds very good."

She hadn't even told him anything substantial about the place yet.

"I'll tell you what, I'll look into it and let you know."

But Melinda wasn't about to leave it to David, given his lack of interest. So she researched the place thoroughly and, a few weeks later, tackled David again on the subject. Despite all indications pointing to it being an excellent match, he wasn't even interested. "I don't get it," she told him. "You somehow seem to be opposed to any arrangement regarding Wicks, yet you've given me no coherent reason why. Can you tell me what the issue is? I know we deal with them from time to time."

He looked at her, hesitating. "Some time ago," he said eventually, "Samantha Wicks worked here at Websters for a few months. She's the daughter of Charlie and Evelyn Sandford, well, Charlie is actually her stepfather. She was born when Evelyn was married to Harold. Charlie short-sold a very large quantity of shares in Eclipse, which we still control, based on incorrect information, an episode you may remember? Charlie blames me for all this. Frankly I don't want to have anything to do with any of them."

There was more to it than that, Melinda was sure. David was hiding something. But she said nothing further, and instead continued her research, concluding that Wicks was a gem and would fit in very well with Websters modus operandi. She decided there was only one way to handle the matter. "I think I should go and have a look at Australia on the ground," she told David. "My guess is that I'll need a couple of weeks. There are several opportunities to suss out." Really she was only proposing to seriously look at the one opportunity and that was

Wicks Financial. In the end David agreed, though seemed very nervous about the situation.

The British Airways flight took Melinda to Sydney with a short stop through Singapore. Despite the comfort of a business class ticket, she found the journey long and tedious. She stayed in a modest hotel not far from the Wicks office.

Although her main objective was to seriously look at the opportunity Australia represented, she was of course excited at the prospect of spending more time with Andrew during her Sydney visit. During her almost three week stay in Sydney, she managed a couple of weekends with him, staying in a borrowed house in Palm Beach, the northern most beach of Sydney's spectacular Northern beaches. It was wonderful. *Is this real life though*, she wondered, *or just a fling*? She couldn't be sure.

In the end, after several meetings with Samantha, Melinda at least made the conclusive decision that Wicks was an ideal partner for Websters and they signed a 'heads of agreement' for the sale of Wicks to Websters. "I'll have to get David to agree," she warned Samantha, "for some reason he was a quite reluctant before I left, and even on the phone since. Do you know of any reason why that might be so?"

"Not really, but years ago now, my stepfather Charlie Sandford, short-sold some shares in a company Websters control based on wrong information," said Samantha with a straight face. "It almost broke him. Maybe David thinks he still holds a grudge against Websters, and that may contaminate the relationship; you should ask him."

"I have. He said the exact same thing." Which made Melinda suspicious. They had said the same thing almost word-for-word.

Once Melinda returned from Australia, David, somewhat reluctantly, agreed to the purchase of Wicks Financial.

"Samantha has told me that once all this is done and dusted she will return to England."

"Is she?" David responded, a little too enthusiastically.

"Yes. She mentioned owning a flat in South Ken. Therefore, we'll need to find someone to run Wicks," Melinda reported.

"Maybe one of us should run the place for, say, three months," David offered, "a month for the handover and another two while we look for a Managing Director?"

"Maybe," Melinda said, though for some reason she didn't want David hovering around Samantha, even for a few days. It had been fifteen years since Samantha had worked in London, but she was certain now that she hadn't been told the full story, so she said, "I suppose that has to be me, I did the deal and am already moderately familiar with the operation." Plus, it would give her the time she needed to work out what she really wanted. Especially with Andrew. How would their relationship stand up when given three months together?

"Okay," David agreed, "it makes sense if you're comfortable."

"Michael and Janice are at university much of the time," she told him, "and don't need day-to-day attention. Rory is doing so well and is becoming increasingly independent. I will arrange for Johanna to come in and housekeep for both of you and cook an evening meal."

So they agreed and Melinda left for Australia within a week, staying at the same modest hotel near the office.

She spent every hour possible at Wicks and Samantha was very helpful in making introductions and helping where she could.

Melinda also spent time with Andrew, and time by herself – giving herself every chance to think about her life and what she was going to do with it. She was frustrated by the minor role she played at Websters, and knew David was unlikely to contemplate any change as far as the management of Websters was concerned, since that was how he had built Websters into the successful business that it was and continued to be. She would have encouraged the business to move on in a very different direction, if she was given a real say in how it was managed; but a clash was inevitable unless she did something about the situation. Was Australia the answer?

***

Ida and Tom had been the rocks that Samantha had been able to rely on while she built Wicks Financial. She and Jane still lived with them, and they all got along very well. She would miss them, and she wanted to do something for them before she left.

"Ida, you have to understand I have made an obscene amount of money doing what I've done. I couldn't have done it without your support. I don't want to embarrass you in any way but if there is anything I can do to make your retirement more comfortable, I would like to do it."

"We are actually already quite comfortable, thank you; we have our pensions and want for nothing; the house is paid off. Tom would probably ask that you make a donation to the church instead? I'll ask him."

"Please do so and let me know."

Meanwhile, Samantha made sure that Melinda understood what there was to understand about the business and answered as many questions as she could while she was still around.

When Melinda asked how the business was started, however, and where the funding had come from, Samantha knew her responses had been too vague to satisfy a woman as intelligent as Melinda and got the impression that she knew something was being hidden from her.

After she thought she had told Melinda everything she needed to know, Samantha left for her new home in London. *She needs to row her own boat now. The last thing she needs is for me to keep putting my oar in*, she thought.

Chapter 29. Samantha and David

While Melinda was still away, David had an unexpected call from Samantha, who had arrived back in London and was living in her flat in South Kensington. Jane had been enrolled in The City of London School for Girls, something Samantha had arranged over the past two years. With Melinda away and all the children either at school or university, David was unable to resist her invitation for lunch at her flat.

The flat turned out to be a three-bedroom mews house, off a quiet street.

"Very fancy," said David as he was shown around. "I like the tasteful way it's been furnished. Not something you learnt from Charlie I presume," he said laughing.

"Much of this is courtesy of Websters," Samantha responded. "I got some professional advice about the furnishings. Harold has been very helpful. He recommended the agent I dealt with. Now he has time on his hands, he has taken a very grandfatherly interest in Jane's welfare. He helped me select the school and pulled a few strings so she could jump the very long waitlist."

"Harold is still Chairman of Websters, so I see him at least once a month. Strangely he's never mentioned seeing or talking to you at all."

"You've told me about your son Rory," Samantha said, as they sat down to lunch, quite formally at the dining room table.

"Yes," said David wondering what was coming.

"He leads the debating team for his school, Sutton Grammar. That's right, isn't it?"

"Certainly, he seems to be very good at it."

"They were at Jane's school last week. Jane is also very good at public speaking and took part in the debate. She seems very taken with your Rory. I would say she has a real crush on him."

"Oh my God," said David, sensing that all his chickens were now coming home to roost. "They obviously have no idea they are brother and sister. Under the circumstances, any sort of relationship between the pair is completely inappropriate."

"My thoughts exactly. I've tried to discourage her, but whenever I raise the question I get a flea in my ear."

"What do you think we should do about it?" asked David.

"Does Melinda know about us, and about Jane?"

"Not officially, I think she has her suspicions though."

"Some of the questions she asked during the handover were very intrusive, in a way. I agree she has her suspicions."

"I need to think my way through all this," said David. "Before I do, I need to understand what you want from our own relationship, moving forward."

Samantha looked at him thoughtfully. "I know I behaved appallingly all those years ago at Websters and I am sorry for that. I fell in love with you then and Jane was the result, my pride and joy. I still love and want you."

David needed no further hint, so took her immediately to bed.

"Do you think," asked Samantha, later, as they were lying in bed, "Melinda will come back to England?"

David looked at her. "You obviously know something I don't."

"Well, she's made no effort to even define what is needed for a new MD, or at least she hadn't when I left. I also saw a whole lot of brochures on her desk, for schools suitable for a sixteen-year-old boy, and," she hesitated, "there was a fellow hovering around. I found him in the office a couple of times, after hours. I was never introduced, but Melinda made no effort to hide her affection for him." She hesitated. "Although I invited her to dinner several times she never accepted; she either stayed late at the office or went off with the fellow I mentioned."

"Mnn," said David, "I have spent much of the last sixteen years thinking of you and also trying to deny you. Melinda and I have a very good marriage, but maybe I've been deluding myself. We will both have to be patient, and you have certainly been the epitome of patience over all those years. First, we need to make sure that our precious children don't get into any sort of trouble because of their parentage."

David hoped that nothing would come of the growing relationship between Jane and Rory. Rory had spent an afternoon, and then a night after a visit to the theatre, in Samantha's flat, with Samantha clucking about making sure they got into no trouble. David then knew he would have to take action.

During one of their weekly phone calls about the business, David said to Melinda, "I have something very important to tell you and it can't be done over the phone. Either I fly down there, or you come home for a few days; it's very important, it will have big impact on Rory in particular."

Melinda hesitated before answering. "Maybe we could meet halfway, in Dubai or somewhere like that?"

"Okay, Dubai it is." They agreed a date.

Just before they rang off, he asked, "Any progress on recruiting the new MD, by the way?"

"Not yet," was her abrupt answer. "I may have something to tell you about that when we meet."

Melinda had arranged a suite in a luxury hotel in Dubai, which David was relieved to see had two bedrooms. She responded unenthusiastically to David's peck on her cheek, somewhat to his surprise and consternation. He knew it would not make what he had so say to Melinda any easier.

"I'm in there," Melinda pointed.

David had left his small suitcase in the lounge area.

"I've booked two nights," she said, "hopefully that's all that's necessary."

They ordered a light meal from room service.

"This is quite a long story," said David. "But please know my priority is to protect Rory. Other issues will arise from what I have to tell you, but I would be grateful if you would leave any questions until the end."

David told her the whole story, the seduction in the Websters office with the objective of stealing information. How he had managed to provide false information, which Charlie had acted on. He even told her of the flat. "I presumed they were going to try to blackmail me with what they hoped they had on tape there. All they got was a lot of blank tapes, courtesy of Des." Melinda shuddered. She couldn't stand Des. "Samantha then disappeared, and I was unable to find any trace of her, so I tried to put it all out of my mind. I then got an email and 'phone call from her about a month after she had arrived in Sydney, and a few months after I had last seen her. She told me she was pregnant with my child and that she needed my help. I lent her the money to start Wicks Financial, all of which has now been repaid, on time and as we had agreed." He then explained the growing relationship between Rory and Jane Wicks. "I don't want either of them to get hurt, any more than can be helped. As a matter of urgency both Rory and Jane need to be told they are brother and sister and so any sort of romantic relationship between the two is therefore impossible."

Melinda sat opposite him stony faced, but as the story unfolded David got the impression that she was relieved at the revelations, although she said nothing.

There was silence for a few minutes while they both gathered their thoughts.

"How much have you seen of Samantha during the past fifteen years?" asked Melinda.

"Not much, we met for a week every now and then. I wanted to see something of Jane."

"And now, with me being away in Sydney?"

"We've met here and there," said a squirming David, "we are concerned about the children who met at some sort of school debate."

"Do you want a divorce?" asked Melinda.

David saw an opening. "Do you? Samantha mentioned she had seen school brochures in the office, which would suit Rory. You haven't done much about finding an MD to run the place when you return."

"I'm not sure about a divorce," said Melinda coolly. "But maybe a separation? If we can work out a financial settlement? I haven't put any thought into this. But, now that we're here and talking, you've known for a while that I've been wanting more authority in my career. And I've known for a while that there might be someone else in your life."

David looked at her, surprised that her reaction was not stronger. He briefly thought of Samantha's revelation that there was another man hovering around Melinda in Sydney. And he remembered the email he'd seen, from 'Andrew'. "Just tell me this for now: do you want to stay in Australia? If there is trouble with Rory, it might suit everybody if he goes to live with you there."

"Maybe, I don't know yet," answered Melinda, frowning.

"Do you have any suggestions about what we say to Rory?"

"You'll have to take the lead in that; if I have to return to London after you have said your piece then so be it."

David noted that she made no reference to 'home' in the conversation. Maybe she had already moved on from her marriage to him, regardless of his revelations.

When David returned from a session in the gym later, where he was able to think calmly about his next steps, he was relieved to find a note telling him that Melinda had already left for the airport.

'I managed to get an early flight,' the note said. 'I've told the hotel you'll settle the bill.'

Chapter 30. Kariuki in Kenya

David still had some loose ends to tied up in Africa. He was to hand over his SAS duties for the training in Kenya to Kariuki, who was now a Captain in the Reserve.

"I see that Hussein is included in the people you are taking to Kenya," David observed during the handover.

"Yes," Kariuki looked at David speculatively.

"I was instrumental in rescuing him from twenty years in jail."

"I know."

"I still have some concerns about him. You need to watch him..."

"Okay, the reason he's in the group is, along with me, he comes from that part of the world and is thought to be able to contribute something…"

"Please be careful. If you want my advice keep a very close eye on him." David repeated his warning.

Kariuki looked surprised and concerned. "Okay. If he fucks me around he will regret it for the rest of what will be the remains of his very short life."

On arrival in Kenya, Kariuki and his ten SAS colleagues were all accommodated at Langata Barracks pending deployment to the Northern Frontier District (NFD) where the exercises were to take place. Kariuki had made contact before arrival with his extended family, who put him in touch with a member of Kenya's internal security services.

Kariuki, dressed in civilian clothes and trying to look inconspicuous, which was difficult due to his build, met Isiah, a small wiry little man dressed in rags as suited the atmosphere of a shebeen in Kibera, one of the many slum areas in the bustling burgeoning city of Nairobi. Isiah had contacts throughout the Moslem community. Kariuki ordered a Tusker beer, Isiah a Coke.

"You have a problem?" asked Isiah.

Kariuki noted that Isiah was a N'derobo, in the past a forest dwelling tribe, who had probably gravitated from being a tracker, the traditional N'derobo role in the military, to his present position, where he was part of the local secret service, reporting to the military. He could see that Isiah would be able to unobtrusively slip in and out of situations and places without attracting any sort of unwelcome attention.

Kariuki decided that honesty was the best way forward, so he said, in the lingua franca, Swahili. "I am with the British Military on a train…"

"I know who you are and what you are doing here. What do you think I can do for you?" replied Isiah in Kikuyu somewhat to Kariuki's surprise.

Continuing in the same language Kariuki responded, "One of the members of my group, a man named Hussein…" He then went on to explain Hussein's background, the rescue and how the family was settled in England plus the attempted attack on the people who had helped him and the rest of his family. "Instead of a twenty-year jail term the man in charge of the rescue had him enrolled in the SAS. We have some concerns that he was never fully rehabilitated and that he might use the opportunity of a visit to Kenya to reconnect with some of his fellow travellers, with heaven knows what unpleasant consequences."

"You want to find out what, if anything, he gets up to on his time off in this city."

"Yes, and who he talks to, most of all." He handed over several photographs of Hussein in uniform and also dressed in civilian clothes.

"What are your movements?" asked Isiah.

"We have five days here, mostly concerned with me briefing the senior people. We then go to the NFD for ten days and then another couple of days back here in Nairobi. The lads will have time off in Nairobi from now; a few, including Hussein, are staying over on holiday. After the exercises are complete the rest of us will probably go straight back to the UK. I can change my plans if I need to…"

A day before the group was due leave for the NFD, Kariuki had a text from Isiah saying that it was urgent that they meet again. He was given the address of a shebeen in another one of Nairobi's recently built shanty areas. With difficulty Kariuki managed to find the place.

"Sorry about the venue," Isiah apologised, as before in Kikuyu, "this city grows and grows, mostly in shanty areas like this. The population is something like five million now, which is at least ten times what it was at independence fifty years ago. I try to keep tabs on what is going on…"

"Okay, okay, what do you have for me? You must have asked me to come here for a reason."

"Mnn, your fiend Hussein is far from rehabilitated, which is the expression I think you used. I have an agent who is Moslem and therefore has access to the various mosques in Nairobi. He followed your friend Hussein into one of the mosques…"

"Nothing wrong with going to a mosque,"

"No, but this mosque is the meeting place for an extreme group of Somalis, who are based in the south of that lawless country. We think they're planning all sorts of mayhem in Kenya, probably in Mombasa and Nairobi. Hussein is planning on deserting your operation once you return from the NFD. I seem to remember you said he'd applied for leave after you've completed your programme here."

"Yes, he's applied for a week's leave."

"Despite the fact that he was born in this country he has no status here. He's intending just to disappear."

Kariuki looked uncomfortable.

"So, unless you deal with him, he will certainly just disappear, if you see what I mean. The last thing we need here is someone who has been trained by the British SAS to get himself involved in an organisation that is planning all sorts of mayhem in this country. He's something of a hero within that organisation, because of his training and because the claims he has fooled all the infidels. He apparently says he's even been to the house of the person who led the original rescue attempt and had a conversation with his wife."

Kariuki tried to hide his discomfort. "We will deal with him..."

They didn't even finish their drinks but shook hands as they left the shebeen.

The exercises in the NFD went off as planned. Kariuki was something of a celebrity because he was Kenya born and had returned to help the fledgling country. He had kept his eyes on Hussein during the exercises but did nothing to alert him to the fact that he had been rumbled.

The troop had returned to the Langata Barracks, settling down to organise everyone's next move. Kariuki had kept an eye on Hussein and in a military Land Rover, followed him as he left the barracks. Hussein, dressed in civilian clothes and carrying a small back pack was walking down the road towards the city. Kariuki stopped the vehicle next to him, pushed the passenger door open saying, "Oh Hussein, it looks as if you are going into town, I'll drop you off anywhere you like, probably in the centre somewhere."

As Hussein stepped into the vehicle and was busy doing up his seat-belt, Kariuki hit him as hard as he could on the head with a small club he'd bought in a local market. He then drove into a side street, stopped the vehicle, parked and tied his unconscious captive up as tightly as was possible and gagged him. He wondered what to do with the backpack.

"Now Mr Hussein, we are going on a little journey," he muttered conversationally to himself.

He drove back towards the NFD, travelling the two hundred and twelve miles to Garissa and arriving as planned by three am. He parked just short of the bridge across the Tana River waiting for a few minutes, making quite certain he was alone.

By this time Hussein had recovered consciousness and was struggling weakly against his bonds. Kariuki partially removed the gag.

"Just listen to me you little toe-rag. You were rescued from being hyena shit all those years ago. You really should be in jail. What you are now going to end up as here is crocodile shit. You planned just to disappear; well that's just fine with us, since it's exactly what's going to happen." He replaced the gag and dragged Hussein out of the vehicle onto the bridge. He checked again to ensure the bridge was deserted. Several pieces of meat he'd brought with him were tossed over the side of the bridge. There was a flurry of splashing. "Just the appetiser," he said to the struggling and terrified Hussein, who had voided his bowels. Using his great strength, Kariuki, one handed, picked the still bound and gagged Hussein up and tossed him into the murky water. There was some further splashing for a few minutes and then silence. Kariuki spent five minutes looking over the side of the bridge; he could see nothing in the very dark night. Returning to the vehicle he retrieved Hussein's back pack which followed Hussein into the fast-flowing river.

Kariuki arrived back in barracks just as the dawn broke. The vehicle was scheduled for a complete wash and clean; the keys were left in the ignition.

Later in the day as the troop packed up to return home one of the sergeants reported to Kariuki that all Hussein's equipment and uniform had been left behind.

"Maybe he was in a hurry and forgot it; bring it all with us, we can return it to him after his holiday," Kariuki told him.

"Are you sure he's coming back?"

"Well, sergeant, do you know something I don't? He has a week's leave…"

"Not sure Sir. Just a few little hints. Maybe it was nothing."

"Right at this moment he is not under any kind of suspicion. If he fails to return, we'll deal with it then."

The troop returned to England and Kariuki to his civilian duties in a hospital in London.

A week or so after Hussein was supposed to have returned from leave Kariuki was informed that Hussein had not returned from leave and that he was now officially AWOL. He did nothing. The Kenyan Military were delighted with the help they had received and Kariuki was given fulsome praise, he was even offered a permanent position with the Kenyan Special Forces, which he declined.

After a few months, obviously with no sign of Hussein returning, Kariuki paid a visit to Asad, thriving in his now enlarged convenience store in Hereford.

Asad looked nervous as the bulk of Kariuki darkened the doorway of his store. "I've come to ask you if you know anything of Hussein's whereabouts," said Kariuki after some perfunctory greetings, briefly recollecting the original rescue in Kenya.

"No, we have not heard from him for some time," answered Asad looking away.

"He was on an expedition with me to help train Kenyan Special Forces. He was then scheduled to go on leave for a week, so he stayed in the country. We haven't heard from him since. How much communication have you had with him in recent months?"

"We didn't even know he was supposed to go to Kenya," answered Asad in a weak voice.

"Was he involved any extremist groups, as far as you know?"

Asad shook his head without answering.

"Have you paid money under pressure to one of these mosques who are talking jihad type violence?"

Asad didn't answer.

"Well?"

"Hussein, he ask us to pay some money to a mosque in Bradford."

"Did you pay anything?"

Asad failed to answer.

"Well?"

Asad nodded.

"How much?"

"Five hundred pounds…"

"Five hundred – how many five hundreds?"

"For last six months. Hussein say they were good people."

"And you believed him. Did you check?"

Asad looked down

"I want the name and address of the mosque," Kariuki asked quietly.

Asad looked terrified.

"I can report this to the police and then you will go to jail maybe."

"No. no." He gave Kariuki the name and address of the mosque.

"What is the name of the Imam there?"

Asad gave him the name of the Imam.

"Okay," said Kariuki. "No more money to that mosque. If you hear from Hussein, or any other extremists, you will let me know." He gave Asad a phone number. He left. Kariuki knew he would never hear from Asad again, but he had the critical information he wanted.

Kariuki then paid David a visit. He just walked into David's office unannounced and plonked himself down in a chair.

"Hello Captain, this is a pleasant…"

"This is not a social visit, David. Two things: Hussein was not rehabilitated. The matter has been dealt with." As David opened his mouth to say something Kariuki waved him away to silence and continued, "Ask no questions…" "Secondly stop interfering with things you only partially understand. The little bastard would still be safely locked up in Dartmoor if you hadn't interfered."

David looked at him blankly.

"Your interference has put a lot of SAS personnel at risk, not to mention your own family, the gaffer's family and many others besides." David tried to say something. "I don't want to hear it David…."

"One final thing," said Kariuki. He handed him a piece of paper with a name and an address on it. "There will be some compensation if this gentleman is dealt with; I know you have the capacity to do that. Use it."

He got up and left, without saying another word.

David just sat there for ten minutes. On the one hand he was furious. Everything he had done as far as Hussein was concerned was with the best possible intentions. He knew he had prevented further attacks from some of Hussein's colleagues. After going for a walk and having calmed down he made one phone call. "This number will be defunct after this call, he told the person who had answered the call. There should be no further communications on this subject under any circumstances." Afterwards he went out and dropped the mobile he had used in one public rubbish bin and the sim-card in another.

Two weeks later there was a small entry in one of the national dailies. "The Imam from one of the better-known mosques in Bradford was killed in a car accident yesterday. No other vehicle was involved." The article mentioned the name of the Imam.

Weeks later, David was told by one of his contacts in the SAS reserve that Kariuki had resigned. All his efforts at contacting Kariuki came to nothing; it was as if he had disappeared off the planet.

Some months later David had a call from Powrie. "David, I've arranged to meet with Kariuki in a pub in Bloomsbury. I've told him you'd be there."

They met at The Lamb in Lambs Conduit Street, not far from David's office. David saw Kariuki huddled in a corner of the old pub, which didn't look as if anything had changed in half a century. He bought David a pint of Young's bitter. He shook David warily by the hand. Powrie joined them a few minutes later. Kariuki insisted on buying him a pint of Peroni. There was a desultory conversation for a few minutes after which Powrie said firmly, "David, many of the things you did for me and the SAS have benefitted all of us and I want you to know we are all very grateful for the personal risks you took and generally the good outcomes that have resulted."

"But you both think I took a step too far with Hussein," David interrupted contritely. "All I can say is that I'm sorry."

"You may have thought you acted in the best interests of the community, David, but none of us really understand how these extremists are motivated," Kariuki added. "I was probably very harsh with you when I came to see you in your office, but in the end what I said, was correct."

"Okay, as I have said, I am sorry, truly."

"Well, there is nothing more to be said," Powrie added. "One more drink to show there's no ill will between us."

They all had another drink on Powrie, but the atmosphere was still uneasy and they all left the pub going their own ways. Kariuki hung back for a few seconds, letting Powrie go on ahead. "I saw the piece in the paper about the Imam, thank you. It's all over now."

They walked out of the pub. David knew he would see nothing of Kariuki again. *At least there is no longer any overt hostility,* he thought.

He would still have an on-going relationship with Powrie though, since Rupert had just joined Websters on a permanent basis having completed a good degree and a six-month internship.

PART 6: THE SPLIT

Chapter 31. DNA

David was barely listening to the conversation when suddenly his ears pricked up. "Sorry, my boy, what was that you just said?" He and Rory were having dinner together, cooked by David, just the two of them; the other children were away at university, with Melinda still away in Australia, and David having just returned from Dubai.

Rory looked at his father saying, "During recent biology lessons at school we were taught all about the work that has gone into identifying people's individual DNA, it's most interesting." He then went on to explain the research that had been done over many years and the value of what had been established. David made an innocuous comment saying that he had had occasion to use the technology in his business. He noticed that during the conversation Rory was becoming more and more nervous; he wouldn't look at his father.

"I discussed it all with Jane," said Rory, "and we decided it would be interesting and fun to see if we could test it on all of us, plus her and her mother." He looked at his father. "You aren't going to like this," he looked very unhappy and almost tearful.

David interrupted, "It's one of the things that I went to Dubai to speak to your mother about." He then went on to tell Rory that Jane was his half-sister; he clumsily tried to explain why.

Rory looked at him through his tears, then almost smiled said, "Oh we have known about that almost since the first time we met. We understand that brother and sister should not be involved romantically. We were just wondering what to do about it." He continued to look at David tearfully, "Jane is the best friend that I have ever had; we thought it was maybe because she is my sister." David tried to interrupt but Rory ploughed on, "Dad, the DNA test says that you are not my real father." He then burst into tears and ran out of the room, leaving his half-eaten dinner.

David was too shocked to say anything; in a half-dazed state he cleared up and then made his way to Rory's locked room.

"Rory, my boy, we need to talk about this, please open." Which he did a few minutes later.

They spent an hour discussing Rory's findings, agreeing to get a professional agency to re-do all the tests. "There may be a mistake somewhere, we'll see," said David, he hesitated for a minute before he added, "Whatever we find, you will always be my son, I have loved you since the day you were born and that will always be the case, always, always." He hugged Rory.

They sat on Rory's bed for another ten minutes, each engulfed in their own tumultuous thoughts, Rory then added, "We were very careful with all the samples we used, the results were just as we expected except for mine. It is clear that Michael and Janice are your and Mum's children, and Jane is your and her mum's child. The results suggest that my real father had genes that are normally associated with someone of Greek ancestry." He hesitated for another minute. "I wonder what Mum will say to all this."

"We should get the fresh tests done before we worry Mum."

Before David went to bed he spent an hour reflecting on what he had been told. Was it really possible that Melinda had had an affair? He remembered the very intimate email to Melinda he had inadvertently opened and the episode in Harold's office where he thought Rory had been conceived.

Somehow, he managed some sleep. He could see a watershed in all his relationships emerging.

The next day, he and Rory collected another batch of samples and sent them off to be tested. During this exercise Rory said to David, "We asked Rupert, now that he is working full time at Websters if he wanted to participate. He quite firmly said no. Anyway, we all agreed that understanding his paternity did not really require a DNA test. It's obvious that you are his real father; he looks just like you."

David was speechless for a minute before he said, "How have Michael and Janice reacted to this information?"

"Oh, we have all understood for some time what the situation is. When we were all taken to that safe house, after the raid by Hussein and his friends, it was quite obvious that you are his real father. Then afterwards when Hussein and his family came for the day, we had a discussion about it afterwards."

"Mnn, are they upset about the situation?"

"No, just curious. You obviously know Mrs Hall very well. Anyone can see that."

* * *

Ten days later, David was in a meeting in the office at Websters; he wasn't really concentrating thinking about the report that he had just received where all Rory's conclusions regarding the DNA tests he had conducted were confirmed. He was wondering how to communicate all that to Melinda when his personal assistant put a note on his desk. "Melinda is here, sitting in your office."

He apologised to the people attending the meeting and almost ran to his office. There was Melinda, looking elegant as she always did.

She appeared to be in a very agitated state. "I want an explanation for this," she shoved an email in front of David, he recognised the handwritten papers from Rory's original research. "I feel ambushed, you are a disgrace, using your own son to ambush me, sending me stuff like this..."

David, as fast as he was able, read the email that detailed the research that Rory and Jane had conducted, it concluded with a sentence which said, "It seems that Dad is not my real father..."

"Melinda, please sit down and listen for a moment. You will see from the date that this email was sent while we were still in Dubai, this is the first I have seen of it," said David. "I had no idea he sent it to you. I would have dealt with all this quite differently if I knew. Please listen to me." She looked slightly mollified but still angry. He then went on to explain a day or so after he had returned from Dubai that he and

Rory had had the conversation about their experimentation with DNA testing. "We agreed, in view of the nature of his findings, we should get all the tests done again. I have this morning received a full report." He handed her a copy of the report. "The conclusions are precisely the same as those that Rory and Jane came to. I'll get you a cup of coffee while you read it." He went out leaving Melinda alone for ten minutes.

He returned to a very thoughtful but composed Melinda. She had calmed right down and was even looking slightly guilty.

"In the whole process," said David, "I have tried to think of just Rory and that needs to be where our focus is. He's a wonderful, wonderful child and I'm proud to be thought of as his father; I have made my feelings known to him on several occasions in past days. There are obviously other issues, but we need to make sure he's okay before we deal with any of those. Jane spends every spare minute with Rory; I suppose our concerns regarding their relationship are no longer pertinent, they had in any event sussed out Jane's parentage."

Melinda took a deep breath, David's calm non-judgemental demeanour clearly helping her to contain her emotions. "You have to understand," she said eventually, "until I saw the results of the DNA tests, I had absolutely no idea that you were not Rory's father. But now that we know, I suppose I should apologise, for my behaviour today and possibly all those years ago."

David inclined his head, encouraging Melinda to continue.

"You were obviously up to something at that time yourself, which you have now explained. You will remember I was a speaker at a conference in Edinburgh; I was pissed off and lonely and I fell for this Aussie and we spent a large part of the conference in bed together, I even stayed on a couple of days, something that did not even register with you. When I got home, I was wracked with guilt. Part of the reason that I came to you in the office that Saturday was to try to assuage that guilt; I also wondered what I would find you doing," she smiled for the first time that morning. "I was relieved to find you genuinely working."

There was almost complete silence for a minute or two.

"Forgive me for asking, but have you seen anything of this Aussie, since Edinburgh?" David asked.

"I kept in touch in a desultory way. I have spent a week or so here and there with him. I have now made contact again with my various trips to Australia. Much the same as you and Samantha I suppose. He does have a Greek background."

"Thanks for telling me that. Can we now make sure we do what we can for Rory? You'll come home now, won't you?"

Melinda nodded. "I have a suitcase in a nearby hotel, I need to check out and then we can go home together; you have the car here?"

David nodded.

When they got home later, David quickly went and found Rory in his room. "Here are the results, what you worked out is one hundred percent confirmed. You should actually be proud of what you did, firstly you did a wonderful job and secondly it will help to resolve some issues. Mum is here by the way."

Rory looked surprised. "Mum, here? I thought she was still in Australia."

"Your email brought her back. She now knows it's all true. You'll find her in the spare bedroom." Rory looked downcast. "Nothing to do with your emails; she will explain some of it to you I expect."

***

Melinda was unpacking a few things in the spare bedroom when Rory tore down the stairs and flew into her arms. They clung to each other for a few minutes, both crying. Melinda then spent a half hour explaining to Rory what the situation was. "I will be returning to Sydney soon. David and I have to sort out a few things before I go. You must understand I don't hate him in any way, but we have both got to a certain point in our lives and we will both move on. I am in touch with your actual father; you will meet him soon, his name is Andrew, and yes he does have some Greek blood in him."

Rory spent a minute working out what he wanted to say. "Jane and I understood that being brother and sister meant that nothing could ever come of our friendship; we're so happy that, as it turns out, we are not brother and sister, she is the best friend I've ever had." He was reluctant to end the conversation, so he asked, "Will you and Dad get divorced now?"

"I don't know."

Rory cried a little. Melinda hugged him. "He has always been a wonderful Dad; he's made it clear that nothing changes as far as that goes," said Rory through his tears.

"We'll stay in touch, of course, apart from you three we will continue to have common business interests."

David and Melinda spent a fruitful two weeks sorting out their business interests, both somehow managed to keep any emotions in check despite the ticklish situation. If anything became even the slightest bit emotional, one or the other of the pair merely said, "Let's leave it until tomorrow, when we've both calmed down."

Melinda already held a twenty percent share of Websters which she kept, and David agreed that she should have a fifty-five percent share of Wicks Financial, and a pathway for her to buy up to eighty percent.

"You will have to agree to take some of the debt that I needed to make the Wicks acquisition in the first place," he told her.

Melinda conceded the point after a short discussion. They both agreed that there was no need to involve lawyers except to merely document their final agreement.

Michael and Janice became aware of the developments and were told the whole story, most of which they already knew, except Rory's parentage.

A few days before she was due to return to Sydney permanently, David asked Melinda, "I've asked you this before, but do you really want a divorce?"

"I may do, but not yet. Can we leave things as they are for a while? It will only make a difference as far as our personal relationship goes; we have sorted out any possible claims that either of us have on any of our assets. I have no idea whether I will want to marry again."

"Yes. Same for me."

***

Melinda had spent the entire two weeks in the spare bedroom; she had played no role in any of the housekeeping arrangements during that period. She had packed many of her own personal things from the house that had been her home for thirteen years and sent them on separately to Sydney.

Her elder two children returned to their respective universities. Rory was happily ensconced at school; and he spent every spare minute with Jane.

David, Melinda and Rory spent a companionable evening together, and after Rory had gone to bed David pecked Melinda on the cheek and went up to his room, the room they had shared for so many years.

He was about to turn off the lights, when she opened the door quietly, stark naked. She didn't know what exactly she was thinking, but clearly David was thinking the same because he whisked the bedclothes back so Melinda could creep in beside him. They made love then, and again during the night. "I couldn't just leave you," Melinda said, by way of explanation.

The next morning there were a few tears when David popped her suitcase into the boot of the car. She had one last look at the elegant house she had brought her family up in and indeed where she had considered herself to be happy.

***

On the way to the airport, David glanced at the strong, elegant, sophisticated, beautiful woman sitting in the passenger seat next to him. She briefly put her hand on his arm. "I hope that you understand what I am doing with everything we have agreed."

"I think so; I hope it makes you more fulfilled than you are now."

"That remark makes me think that you do understand, at least some of where I'm coming from. I could have stayed here, always playing second fiddle to you in the business and to a lesser extent at home. Now Samantha is back in England, I would be forever wondering about your relationship with her, always looking over my shoulder, so to speak. The kids have largely grown up; Rory will be out with me in Sydney at Christmas, and Michael is looking for a job there as you know. This feels right. As for Andrew, I am most unlikely to be sharing a house with him, or anyone else for that matter, at least for a while. I want to just be me for a while."

David nodded. "Putting it that way, I think I would have made the same choice. We will in any event be in touch, and if you need advice please ask. I will certainly be asking your advice on many issues. Do you think the children are unhappy about Rupert's parentage?"

"It seems not." Melinda responded. "Michael has said he wants nothing to do with the merchant banking business anyway. He likes what he sees of his half-brother, and will probably stay in Australia for a while; luckily, I'll be able to provide a home for him there if he wants one. Janice is really smart, as you know she is in the process of becoming a lawyer, but I think she will go into politics eventually, she's just wondering which of the ghastly alternatives she thinks she might choose. In view of the fact that Jane is also going to stay in England, I think there is no chance that we'll be able to persuade Rory to stay in Australia for very long."

She shrugged and continued. "All of them have plenty of good options. I don't think we have any major worries with any of them; hopefully they will all come to us for advice from time to time."

At Heathrow Airport, David retrieved her luggage from the car boot.

She pecked him on the cheek. "Don't come in," she said. "I'll be fine." And with that she was gone.

David sat there for a full five minutes with a hollow feeling in his stomach; it all seemed so final. He looked up when a policeman tapped on the car window saying, "Are you alright, sir?"

He nodded and drove back to the office in a daze.

He phoned Samantha, something he had only done once during Melinda's visit. He explained much of what had transpired over past days.

Samantha was silent.

"If I may," David told her, "I'll come and spend the weekend with you, completely guilt free. I just need a couple of days to sort myself out. This may be the end of a long and actually happy and rewarding road."

To his surprise Samantha said, "Not this weekend. I have to go and sort Mum out. I'll call when I've dealt with that."

"Oh, okay," David muttered, wondering what the hell was going on.

Chapter 32. Reconciliation

Melinda rented a three-bedroom luxury apartment in Potts Point in a newly constructed block. She got on reasonably well with the competent well-trained staff at Wicks. Susan in particular, who had been with Samantha from the very beginning, was now a very competent analyst and financier and was always a great help. There was however no one who could really challenge her on issues relating to proposals that were put to her.

She always shared everything with David, so they had constant contact. Occasionally they had very long Zoom meetings on some of the larger and more serious proposals. However David always allowed Melinda to 'call the shots' as she saw fit. The business certainly progressed and in the first year it grew substantially.

Rory spent the first Christmas with her. They managed a quick trip to Uluru during his visit, but he had to return to England for his final year at school.

Michael originally had a job in the music industry in Sydney, but had been asked to move to Melbourne, which he did.

"The experience here has been valuable," said Michael, "but in this industry all the action is really in London or New York, so in time I will probably head over there. Australia is a bit of a backwater as far as all that is concerned."

Melinda understood. "Australia hasn't been everything I hoped it would be either." Indeed, while the business side of things had gone very well, other aspects of her life had been… disappointing.

Although the first few weeks with Andrew had been amazing, as time had passed she'd seen less and less of him. His everyday life wasn't as thrilling as their clandestine meetings had been. He also seemed to have friends with very doubtful backgrounds, who as far as Melinda was concerned seemed often to sail very close to the wind. *Part of the 'fast buck brigade' by the look of things,* she thought.

Then, to finish things off, Andrew hadn't reacted well at all to the news that he was Rory's natural father. "I don't believe it," he said. "It's better to leave things as they are – as far as I am concerned, David Phillips is his father. Now, about my idea…"

Andrew had an idea of a hi-tech launch, which he presented to Melinda, which she didn't really think would go anywhere.

She discussed the proposal with David, without disclosing the origin of the proposal. David in his own gentle way pointed out the many flaws in the proposal. "I'm not sure why you are even considering this idea, it really has been very badly thought through… It's up to you though."

In the end she decided to tell Andrew that it was a 'no go' and the reasons for it.

Andrew tried to get her to change her mind....

"No Andrew," she told him, "I'm not going to go with this. It's big and if it goes haywire it will put the whole of the future of Wicks Financial in jeopardy. Try one of the big boys."

She had done her research though, and already knew that Andrew's proposal had been rejected by at least one of the other major players in the market.

After that their relationship deteriorated further, and although there was no major break-up, she found herself no longer interested seeing anything of Andrew. It had been a fling after all, one that needed a jolt of reality to be realised.

So Melinda focussed on work, and, eighteen months after she moved to Sydney, she found a major proposal that she was very excited about. She sent it to David and the phoned him a day later, "this needs your brains as well as mine. I think it needs a bit of work."

"I agree with you," he told her. "But it needs some planning. Maybe we could meet somewhere for a few days. How about Singapore? I can spare the time if you can," he said.

And there was something in his voice that made Melinda excited to see him.

***

A week later they met at the newly refurbished Raffles Hotel in Singapore. David had booked a suite for a week, with two bedrooms.

"Where are your things?" she asked.

David pointed.

She looked him up and down, assessing his demeanour, then promptly moved her suitcase into the same room and started to unpack a few things.

He followed her in. "I thought you'd want your own room?" he said quizzically.

Melinda raised an eyebrow. From what she understood from Rory's emails over the last eighteen months, David hadn't progressed much in his relationship with Samantha. Rory was still spending as much time as possible with Jane, although he had gained admission to Oxford and was about to follow in David's footsteps and major in history. Still, Rory would surely have known if the two of them were spending time together.

Now, from the way David leant against the doorway, watching her unpack, she knew there was an opening.

"First things first," she said, walking over. "There was no real reason to meet in person to talk about this proposal, and you know it. You clearly wanted to see me, correct?"

"Correct," he said.

So they looked at each other a moment, then Melinda gently started to undress him, and he undressed her in turn.

Afterwards, lying in bed together, Melinda told David the truth. "Regardless of everything, I've actually really missed you – the kids, our home and England. Australia is okay, but I've found it has its limitations, and I have no friends there… What about you?"

"I think," said David, "that the best thing in the world would be for you to come home."

"No Samantha?"

"I've hardly seen her."

"Okay then. Let's see where this goes."

Apart from intervals in bed together, Melinda and David spent a great deal of their time together working on the proposal.

"It's got legs," said David. "We'll trial the proposal in Australia, mainly to iron out any problems that may arise; but after that we can take this worldwide very quickly, with you running it, so having you back in London makes sense from that point of view. But I have also missed you very much... I think we've made a mistake."

"I think I might agree with you." She hesitated to continue. "Forgive me David, but I need to say this... these last eighteen months have made me realise what I almost threw away in terms of our own relationship, and having the kids around, so... I'm sorry."

David looked at her. "Mel, it's not all your fault. I am as much to blame as you are. Perhaps what the last eighteen months has done, though, is to help establish our own *working* relationship. With this current proposal, and it's all yours as far as I am concerned, it will probably occupy you full time for years I expect. Again forgive me for asking this, but what about Andrew?'

"I didn't like much of what I found when I got to see him on his home ground. I haven't had anything to do with him for almost a year now. But Samantha – you might not have seen her, but she's still the mother of your child. What if she comes back on the scene?"

David smiled. "Well, that's the best bit. Although I haven't seen her, we've naturally had contact over the phone and email because of Jane.

We've never had that before – a shared parenting relationship. So, and I haven't told her this, but I simply don't see her in the same way anymore. Whatever there was between us… I'm over it. Apparently she's running a charity supporting refugees, and wants nothing to do with what she describes as that 'ghastly, money-grubbing merchant banking business', or so Harold's told me. She still looks after her mother and of course Jane, who I see from time to time, mostly with Rory. Jane is friendly with all our kids, who know that I'm her natural father. So I think that's all that now. Satisfied?"

"Potentially."

They hugged each other for a good five minutes, then David picked up some of the proposal's paperwork. "What about this, how do we now proceed?"

"We need to get hold of the principal who put this proposal to us," said Melinda. "As we agreed we'll take eighty percent of the equity. You will have to come up with the finance for that. I have kept the principal involved during our discussions, he may need persuading with one or two of the changes we have asked for, but I don't see a problem with that. Whatever happens he will make a fortune."

"When do you think you'll be able to return home?"

"Six months. I will appoint Susan as MD of Wicks, but we'll need to keep an eye on things, so a visit every three months is probably in order. Visits to OZ are not a big hardship – you could even come on the occasional trip? There are plenty of unusual and attractive places to visit. We could do them together?"

"We could indeed. I can also think of some other attractive places I'd like to visit." And with that David took her hand, and led her again into the bedroom.

**

David's flight back to England was due to leave half a day before Melinda's flight to Australia. It was still early when his alarm went off and woke them both.

"Sorry," he told her, slipping into the clothes he'd left out ready for his airport transfer, "you sleep in some more if you like."

She groaned and rolled over in bed. She looked so beautiful in the dawn light flooding through the curtains, her skin soft and warm. He stopped fastening the buttons on his shirt, instinctively drawn to her. As always. Tempted to join her in bed once more. But there was much to sort out before his wife returned to him in England – she'd need a new office at Websters of course, with her own assistant. He'd need to draw up some documents allocating them both joint control of the business – she hadn't asked but he was ready now to share everything with her, including the company. And he probably needed to tidy up their room a bit.

Their room. He could hardly believe it. It had been such an empty space since she'd left, one that he'd soon realised would be impossible to fill – not with Samantha or anyone else. There was only one Melinda, and now she was his again.

So he dressed in his travelling clothes, and leant over to kiss her instead. A long lingering kiss that would see him through the weeks to follow. Who would have thought they'd be back here again, about to restart life after living such a tangled web of deceit and life and love. He was at least certain now of one thing: when it came to navigating the messy road that no doubt still lay ahead in life, there was only one woman he'd even attempt it with, and he was looking right at her.

The End

Lightning Source UK Ltd.
Milton Keynes UK
UKHW020728161222
414034UK00017B/1166